Also by June Faver

Dark Horse Cowboys

Do or Die Cowboy

Hot Target Cowboy

When to Call a Cowboy

Cowboy Christmas Homecoming

The Best Cowboy Christmas Ever

JUNE FAVER

Published by Sourcebooks Casablanca, an imprint of Sourcebooks
P.O. Box 4410, Naperville, Illinois 60567-4410
(630) 961-3900
sourcebooks.com

Printed and bound in the United States of America.
OPM 10 9 8 7 6 5 4 3 2 1

Chapter 1

Angelique Guillory let out a gasp when her car started to skid. She tried to compensate, her heart racing as she struggled to guide the vehicle across the icy highway. The black ice sent her fishtailing across the wide roadway, and the vehicle did a complete 180-degree turn before veering into a ditch. It was a slow-motion nightmare as she went sliding off the roadway and nose-first into a snowdrift.

She checked her passenger, but Gabrielle seemed to have weathered the excitement with no ill effects. In fact, she had slept through the entire episode.

Angelique took a moment to give thanks for their survival. She heaved a huge sigh, her heart still trying to beat its way out of her chest.

Okay, now to get back on the road, but not as fast this time.

The motor was still running, so she shifted into reverse and looked over her shoulder before applying a little gas. *Slowly now.*

The wheels spun in the snow, but the vehicle did not move. She pressed the gas pedal again, but again the wheels spun without actually moving the car.

She rested her forehead against the steering wheel. *No. Not when I've come so very far.*

Angelique refused to give in to self-pity. She sucked

in a deep breath and, at the same time, pressed her lips together. Pulling her scarf around her head and buttoning her jacket, she tried to drum up a fresh dose of optimism. Too bad she didn't have the proper clothes for this weather.

She opened the door, pushing hard to dislodge it from the snow. When she stepped out, her shoes sank into almost a foot of the white stuff.

It's crunchy. Somehow she had thought snow would be soft and mushy like a marshmallow. *And cold.* It was as though her feet had instantly frozen.

Angelique looked up and down the highway. Although it was quite a well-kept four-lane route, there was no traffic. *Probably all the smart people around here are huddled by a roaring fire in their homes.*

Her eyes watered, and it felt as though the cold was abrading her cheeks.

Glancing up at the gray sky, Angelique wished she had hung out a little longer at that Mexican restaurant in Langston. It had been brightly decorated with strings of tinsel, and a large Christmas tree sat in one corner, adorned with very colorful decorations.

There was canned music. Mexican Christmas songs were playing, and all the patrons seemed to be pretty jolly. Perhaps it was the small-town vibe…or it might have been the seasonal cheer and the fact that quite a few of the diners had chosen a bottle of beer to wash down their lunch. "*Feliz Navidad*," the voices sang. Now she had that tune playing in her head.

At least it was warm there, and the waitress was friendly. Milita, her name was. "*Feliz Navidad*," Milita had said. "*Y prospero año nuevo.*"

Angelique wanted to have a prosperous new year and to be able to enjoy the holidays without looking over her shoulder. She had too much at stake, for herself as well as the one she loved. *My Gabi.*

Milita had given Angelique directions to her destination. The place where she hoped they would be welcomed. It was almost Christmas, after all.

Angelique saw a vehicle coming her way. It must have been coming from or at least through Langston. She was torn between hoping for a savior and fearing for her safety. The total isolation of her situation was just dawning on her. *Oh, please…*

The vehicle was a truck…a pickup truck.

She stood frozen in place, and, in fact, she felt frozen. She turned her back on the strong breeze, her hands tucked in her jacket pockets.

As the truck neared, the driver slowed down. Her heart fell when he passed her by, but she realized he was pulling over on the shoulder just ahead of her snowbound vehicle.

Angelique pressed her lips together, hoping this person could help her.

The driver's side door swung open, and a man got out. He looked like the consummate cowboy. Boots and denims, topped off with a cowboy hat. He was wearing a tan suede jacket lined with fleece and leather gloves. He was tall and looked like a giant Y coming toward her, with broad shoulders, tapering down to long legs.

He appeared to be pleasant as he approached, his breath coming out in wisps of white streaming behind him. He had sandy-blond hair and brown eyes.

"Hey, little lady. Looks like you're in a jam."

"Um, yes. Well, the road was really slick." She sounded defensive, even to her own ears.

"Yeah, that happens a lot around here this time of year. The road crew hasn't gotten out this far to spread sand on the highway." He pointed to his truck. "We mostly drive with all-weather tires."

"Oh no. I have to wait for sand?" Desperation was taking over her psyche.

He raised his gloved hands. "Not at all. I can pull you out of the snowbank, but we have to see if your car is drivable. You may have twisted something underneath."

Angelique wrung her hands together. "How can I tell?"

He grinned, and she realized how handsome he was. The big brown eyes were gazing at her as though they found something worth looking at.

She felt her color rising. "What do I need to do?"

"Well, you better get back in your car, because it's cold out here and that jacket doesn't look near warm enough." He gestured toward her car, tilted into the ditch. "Let me help you."

He took her elbow, walked her to the vehicle, and opened the door for her.

She turned to gaze up at him. "I can't thank you enough for helping me."

He flashed another killer grin. "Don't thank me yet. Let me see if I can get you out of here. Now, climb in out of the cold." He closed her door and walked back toward his vehicle.

All of her windows had immediately fogged up, so she turned on the defroster and rolled the front two side windows down and back up quickly to clear them.

Angelique watched him return to his truck and back it up toward her rear bumper. *What if he pulls the bumper off? What will I do then?*

He dug around in a big toolbox affixed to his truck bed and dragged out a heavy chain with a big hook on each end. He hooked one end on something under the front of his truck and had to lie down in the snow to hook the other end to some part of her car's undercarriage. He climbed out, snow clinging to his jacket, and gave her a thumbs-up before returning to his truck.

Angelique gripped the wheel, staring into first one and then another of her side view mirrors, but her rear window was totally frosted over.

She felt the car jerk when the chain was taut, and after that, the car began moving backwards. Her car bumped back onto the pavement in reverse. She released a breath she hadn't realized she'd been holding.

The man left his truck idling and came to unhook his chain. He stopped by her door, and she opened the window.

"Thank you," she said. "Thank you so very much. I-I have some money to pay you." She reached for her purse.

"No, don't even think about it. Which way are you headed?"

"I was going the same direction you were, but the car spun into the ditch."

He nodded. "Try to turn around slowly, and if you're able to steer, I'll follow along behind you for a while to make sure you're okay."

Angelique couldn't believe how kind this stranger was. "Thanks again, Mr…?"

"Derrick. My name is Derrick Shelton."

"Thank you, Derrick. I'm Angelique."

"Nice to know you, Angelique. Now, be safe. Y'hear?" He grinned and gave her a two-fingered salute off the brim of his cowboy hat, then climbed back into his truck. He waited until she very slowly managed to turn her car around and then fell in a comfortable distance behind her.

When she saw the odd horseshoe-shaped gate with the name Garrett emblazoned overhead, she turned off the highway, giving him a wave before she bumped over the cattle guard and entered the property.

He tooted his horn at her and went on.

For a moment, Angelique felt abandoned, but then she lifted her chin a bit, knowing that somewhere on this road, she would find the answers to questions that had plagued her all her life.

"Dad! Are you expecting someone?"

Big Jim Garrett came to the front of his ranch house and found Tyler, his middle son, peering out one of the windows flanking the front door. "Not expecting anyone, but it's Christmastime. People know they can stop by." Big Jim stepped to the other side of the door and saw a black SUV pulling up close to the house. It looked stark in contrast to the whiteness of the snowy landscape. "Maybe there's a religious pamphlet they think I just gotta have."

It appeared that a dark-haired woman was behind the wheel, and she was sorting through something. In time, she climbed out of the vehicle and wound a scarf around her head, then began to plod her way through the snow and up onto the porch. She stood for a few moments, as though uncertain.

"Open the door, Son. Let her inside," Big Jim urged.

Tyler swung the door open, startling the woman, who let out a little gasp of surprise.

"Come right in, young lady," Big Jim invited.

Tyler stepped back and waved her inside.

"I—I'm looking for James Garrett. I got directions in town, and I think I've got the right place."

"You found me," Big Jim said. "I'm James Garrett. What can I do for you?"

She gazed at him with eyes as blue as his own. "I—uh… I need to get my daughter out of the car. Is that okay?"

"Well, sure," Big Jim said. "Let me help you." He strode out beside her, holding her arm as they stepped off the porch. His boots sank into the new-fallen snow. "Watch yourself. This walk gets slippery."

The woman leaned into the vehicle and released a small child from a safety seat. When she turned, Big Jim held out his hands to take the child. He lifted the little one against his chest so she could see over his shoulder. "Hey, little lady."

The little girl's lips trembled. She gazed around, making sure her mom was nearby. She reached out a hand to her mother. "Mommy?"

"It's okay, my precious. I'm right here." Angelique stroked the child's hand.

Big Jim held his hand out to the young mother and escorted her up to the porch and into the house, while Tyler held the door open for them.

Big Jim showed the woman into the room his beloved deceased wife, Elizabeth, had called the parlor. He wasn't sure what that was supposed to be, but he kept it neat in her honor.

The parlor was a cheery room, with framed family pictures and chintz fabric on the settee. Big Jim had not had the heart to change a thing since Elizabeth had passed on. Even the sheet music on her piano remained as she had left it.

Big Jim gestured for the woman to be seated before he took the nearest chair. Tyler lounged against the door frame, his arms folded across his broad chest.

The child was bundled up in a one-piece quilted outfit with zippers. Big Jim let the hood fall back and was staring into the child's eyes—eyes everyone around the Langston area called Garrett blue. These were the same kind of blue eyes his three sons had inherited from him. And most of the cousins had the same familial characteristic. Unusual turquoise-blue eyes with a darker ring around the edge.

Garrett blue.

Tyler's wife, Leah, entered the room, smiling. "I thought I heard some voices up here. Do we have company?"

Tyler put his arm around her shoulder. "Apparently."

Big Jim was staring at the young woman. "I didn't catch your name."

She cleared her throat. "My name is Angelique Guillory, and you're holding my daughter, Gabrielle."

Big Jim's brows furrowed. "Guillory? I knew someone with that name a long time ago." He recalled one of his first girlfriends, the beautiful Sofie Guillory.

"Yes, you did." The color in Angelique's cheeks heightened. "I believe you're my father."

Derrick Shelton strode into the sheriff's office in Langston. He took off his leather gloves and suede jacket as he walked. Shep Collier, the new deputy, always had the gas heater turned up so high Derrick had to peel off layers or pass out.

"Hi, Sheriff," Shep said. "How was your trip?"

"Fine, I guess."

Breckenridge T. Ryan, the only lawyer in Langston, had called on Derrick to appear in a court case. The drive to the courthouse in Amarillo had been eventful, with the opportunity to help a beautiful damsel in distress.

Derrick shoved his gloves in a pocket of the jacket and hung it on the bentwood coat-tree near the door. "Anything happen while I was gone?"

"Um, no, sir." Shep shuffled through the messages. "I took a report from old man Shaw. He said there were some stray goats wandering on the road out by his place."

"I'll tell you what, Shep. Why don't you go out and help round up those goats? The only person I know who owns goats around here is that woman who makes cheese. She lives a little farther down the road from the Shaws."

Shep was scrambling into his jacket and hat. He wrapped a scarf around his neck and was halfway out the door before he turned. "Thank you, sir. I appreciate you letting me go. I'll make you proud, sir."

Derrick tried to remember if he had ever been this

annoying. “Good man. Wish them a Merry Christmas from the department.”

“Oh yes, sir. I’ll do that.” Shep rushed out the door.

Derrick turned the gas stove down and went to his desk. Taking over for the old sheriff had come at a price. He stared at the folders on his desk and sighed. Paperwork was not his forte. He poured himself a cup of coffee and settled into his chair. Shoving the papers aside, his thoughts returned to the dark-haired beauty he had encountered earlier.

Angelique. She said her name was Angelique.

But that was all he knew. He had been surprised when she turned in at the Garrett ranch. Maybe she was visiting for the holidays.

Those amazing eyes. She could be a relative. A cousin, or something.

He sipped the coffee, trying to think of an excuse to call on the Garretts.

Tyler Garrett stared at the woman in shock. She couldn’t be saying what he thought he had heard. That would make her his sister. And that absolutely could not be true.

Leah had no such doubts. “Yes, I can see it now. There’s quite a family resemblance.” She crossed the room to offer her hand. “I’m Leah Garrett, and this is my husband, Tyler.”

The woman looked a bit bewildered, but accepted Leah’s hand. “Pleased to meet you, I’m sure.” She took Gabrielle from Big Jim and drew the little girl close.

“What a precious little girl.” Leah stroked the back

of her fingers over the child's cheek, eliciting a dimpled smile from the child.

"Thank you," the woman said. "Please call me Angelique." She heaved a big sigh. "Or Angel. People back home call me that… At least my mama did."

Leah looked delighted. "Why, that's lovely. It sounds magical." She sat down beside this Angelique person and continued to chat.

Tyler turned to his father. Big Jim appeared to be in a state of shock. Tyler couldn't recall a time when his dad was at a loss for words, but he sat staring at Angelique with his mouth slightly agape.

Tyler caught Big Jim's eye and cocked his head toward the door. "We're going to get you ladies something to drink. Coffee?"

Leah looked up at him, her lovely face smiling. "Thanks, sweetheart. I made a pot of hot cocoa. Could you please bring me a cup of that…with a couple of marshmallows?"

Angelique perked up. "Homemade cocoa? Oh, that sounds great."

"Sure thing," Tyler said and motioned to Big Jim. "C'mon, Dad. Let's get some cocoa to warm up the ladies."

Wordlessly, Big Jim got to his feet and followed Tyler to the kitchen.

Once in the kitchen at the back of the house, Tyler turned, grasping his father by the shoulders. "What the hell, Dad? Who is this woman? Can there be any truth to what she's claiming?"

Big Jim raked his fingers through his thick head of silver hair. Heaving a huge sigh, he leaned against the counter with both hands, staring off into space. "I-I knew Sofie Guillory when I was in college. We..." He swallowed hard. "She was a pretty girl from New Orleans...really pretty and sweet. We...uh..."

"Okay, I get the picture, Dad." Tyler felt as though he'd been sucker punched. He couldn't believe his father would turn his back on any responsibility, let alone something as important as a pregnant girlfriend.

"Sofie went home for the summer after freshman year and didn't come back the next school year." Big Jim looked as though he was in a daze. "She'd said that her parents wanted her to go to LSU, so I figured she had transferred." He shook his head.

Tyler put his hand on Big Jim's shoulder. He couldn't count the times his father had comforted him, but this was the first time in their relationship that he was called upon to return the favor. "This—this Sofie... She didn't get in touch with you after...after...?"

"Not a word. I stayed in college and got engaged to your mama the summer between my junior and senior years." He kept shaking his head. "To tell you the truth, I never once thought about Sofie until today. We were just two young people screwing around."

Tyler let out a badly timed snort. "Yeah."

Big Jim jerked his head up, his Garrett blue eyes lasering their way into Tyler's soul.

"I-I mean..."

"I heard ya." Big Jim huffed out a sigh. "And it's the goldarned truth. All them young hormones getting together. It was just..."

Tyler tried to imagine his father as a young stud... *Couldn't*. "Didn't you use any protection?"

"Sofie was on the pill, or so she told me." Big Jim shrugged. "I don't know why she didn't get in touch with me. I would have done the right thing."

Tyler leaned back against the large double-door refrigerator. "And then what? You wouldn't have married Mom, and you wouldn't have Colt, Beau, and me."

Big Jim cringed. "I know. But I wouldn't have known anything else. I'm just hornswoggled."

"Sorry, Dad. It's hitting me pretty hard too."

Leah came into the kitchen. "What's going on, guys? Need some help?" She stopped short when she caught sight of Big Jim's face.

"We'll take care of it," Tyler said. "Just go back and entertain our…guest."

Leah shot him an uncertain look before she returned to the parlor.

Tyler clapped his dad on the shoulders. "Okay, we need to get some cups."

Chapter 2

ANGELIQUE GUILLORY SAT HOLDING GABRIELLE AND trying to appear calm. In truth, she was shaken to the core. To come face-to-face with the man who had impregnated her mother so many years ago left her quaking inside.

She gnawed her lower lip. It hadn't happened the way she had rehearsed in her head. *No*… She hadn't expected to stand on that porch and have a man throw open the door and gaze at her with the same eyes that she had grown up wondering about. With all the dark-eyed people in her family, she was the one who stood out. That the trait had been passed on to her daughter was remarkable.

Now she had found a man and his son with those same eyes. *My brother.*

Angelique shook herself out of her reverie just as Leah entered the room.

Gabrielle was still sleepy, opening her mouth wide to deliver a huge yawn. She leaned her head back against Angelique's breast. Maybe it was good that she was worn out from the trip. Otherwise, she would have been all over the place.

Leah glanced back over her shoulder and then fixed a determined smile on her face as she returned to take a seat beside Angelique. "Those silly men don't know how to make hot cocoa properly. Hope we can stand to drink it."

"Oh, I'm sure it will be okay." Angelique flashed a nervous smile. "I'm not particular."

Leah gave a reassuring nod. "So, I heard you're from New Orleans. That was a long trip to take with your little one. I don't think I could have done that by myself."

Angelique felt a tightness in her chest. *Well, you didn't have the hounds of hell on your heels.* She swallowed. "It was a long drive, but I-I only wanted to find my father."

"I can understand that, but we're a family, and if you're a Garrett, you're part of the family."

To her embarrassment, Angelique was unable to keep it together. As silent tears welled up in her eyes and rolled down her cheeks, she kept her gaze fastened on her daughter, so innocent and so worth whatever trials Angelique had to go through to keep her safe.

Leah moved closer and slipped an arm around Angelique's shoulder. "Oh, it's okay to feel your feelings. Don't worry. You can express yourself."

Angelique held her breath, trying not to start weeping openly. She nodded furiously, and Leah responded by vigorously patting her shoulder.

"Let me bring some tissues." Leah jumped up and left the room abruptly, giving Angelique a chance to sniffle in private.

That was when the two men, her father and her half brother, came back into the room.

Angelique kept her gaze down, fussing with Gabrielle's soft and curly dark hair.

"Here you go, young lady," Big Jim said. "This should warm you right up." He set the tray on the coffee table and picked up one of the cups to hand to her.

Angelique heaved a sigh and accepted the mug, locking eyes with Big Jim. She saw the concern on his face when he realized she had been crying. She sniffled and blinked, but Leah returned, offering a handful of tissues. "Thanks," she whispered.

Big Jim's brows drew together in a frown. "Now, looky here, young lady. You got no reason to cry. I'm glad you got yourself and your little girl up here to the ranch. I'm not denying that I'm your father...an' I'll do whatever I can to help you out."

This statement was the final straw. Angelique's shoulders began to shake as she dissolved into tears. Big Jim crouched down beside her, embracing her and giving her clumsy pats on the back. Gabrielle chose that moment to add to the din, so both mother and daughter were wailing. There were not enough tissues in the world to stanch their tears.

Big Jim's eyes were wet, but he blinked the tears away while trying to comfort Angelique and Gabrielle. "There, there," he said.

Now Leah was weeping and Tyler held her, patting her back. "It's okay, honey. Everything is okay."

Angelique looked around at the tearful Garretts, and suddenly it all seemed funny. She started laughing, with tears streaming down her cheeks. Gabrielle was squirming to get down, but there were so many fragile keepsakes on the little tables that Angelique was afraid to let her daughter go. Gabrielle's fussing continued, but she stopped trying to get down.

Big Jim broke into a relieved smile, and Leah blotted her eyes.

"I'm sorry," Angelique said. "It's been an emotional day for me. I'm so glad to have found you."

Big Jim shook his head. "I'm sorry you waited so long."

"I just found out your name," Angelique said. "My mom finally told me on her deathbed."

Beau Garrett stared at his wife in disbelief. He stood with his boots planted in a wide stance, his hands fisted at his waist, and his gut in a twist. "Say that again."

Dixie, his redheaded wife, spread her hands, strewing tinsel at her feet. "I know. It's hard to believe, but Leah called to tell me, and you know she would never embellish the truth."

Beau continued to frown at her. "Seriously, Dixie..."

Dixie arranged a few strands of tinsel on the tree. "Leah told me this woman showed up at Big Jim's doorstep and claimed to be his daughter... His love child."

Beau sucked in a deep breath, trying to control his emotions. "I don't believe it for one minute. My dad would not get some woman pregnant and then walk away. He would do the right thing."

Dixie turned around. "Look, lover... I didn't make this up. I'm just passing it on." She put the rest of the tinsel in a ziplock bag. "It's probably a scam. Don't a lot of scams take place around the holidays? You know, when people might be more emotionally vulnerable?"

"Maybe." He tried to wrap his head around the news Dixie had just shared. She was right. It had to be some kind of scam. He threw himself down on the sofa and patted the space beside him.

Dixie flipped on the Christmas tree lights and crossed the room to sink down next to Beau.

He circled her with his arm and stared at the tree. He tried to give all his attention to his wife's handiwork. "Looks great, baby. You got it done all by yourself."

"I need to balance it a little. There are some bare spots."

This was a special time they shared. When Beau and Dixie had tucked their daughter, Ava, into bed, they spent some time together, catching up and sharing the events of the day. Dixie was running the feed store her father left her, while Beau was running their ranch. The land had been part of Dixie's inheritance, as well as the ranch house she had grown up in. Added to that was the significant amount of prime pastureland that had been Big Jim's wedding present. Each of them had plenty of responsibilities, but the most important was the redheaded little girl asleep in her room.

Beau, the youngest of Big Jim's sons, was nonetheless a responsible husband and father. He couldn't imagine any reason his own father would shirk his responsibility. No, this woman, whoever she was, must be mistaken or, as Dixie suggested, running some kind of scam.

Dixie climbed out of his embrace, intent on decorating the perfect tree. The day the shipment of Christmas trees had arrived at the feed store, she had gone through the stock as it was being arranged and made sure the very best tree had been tied to the roof of her SUV. Now, that perfect tree would be perfectly decorated.

Beau had given up on telling her how good it looked

at various stages of its adornment. Dixie was a perfectionist, as proven by the way she dressed Ava and the care she was taking with the slow but sure remodeling projects she was working on around the house. Of course, her grand plans always included her husband's considerable muscle and talent.

"You know," she said, "your dad is worth a ton of money, so it's reasonable that some con artist would try to take advantage of him."

Beau swallowed hard. He would get with his older brothers and together they would get to the bottom of this farce. "Not if I can help it."

Big Jim lay awake, staring up into the darkness. He somehow felt as though he were being unfaithful to Elizabeth because he had been thinking about the beautiful Sofie Guillory.

He and Sofie had said the words *I love you* a thousand times. But had it been love or a side effect of their frequent coupling? It seemed there had been a lot of love going on back then. All his fellow Agriculture students had girlfriends. On weekends, when he and Sofie showed up at one of the country-western dance halls, they would meet up with their friends, have a beer or two, and dance.

Perhaps it was the dancing—hot-and-heavy body contact—that had resulted in them stripping down and making more hot-and-heavy body contact in his truck.

Sofie Guillory, the beautiful girl with dark, almost black, wavy hair and huge dark eyes, a contrast to her milky-white skin. She had caught young James Garrett's eye the first day in freshman English class.

He fell asleep dreaming of the beautiful dark-eyed girl who had stolen his heart as a young man. Now their daughter and granddaughter had appeared to steal his heart again.

Colton Garrett was furious. He was the oldest of Big Jim Garrett's sons, and he was determined not to allow his father to be taken advantage of. He had called his brothers to meet him in his barn, a male domain where he had filled a cooler with longnecks despite the cold weather. He had arranged three wooden chairs in a circle close to an electric heater. The Adirondack chairs had been stored in the barn for the winter, so Colt had dragged them out to the center near an electric outlet where the heater was plugged in. He was ready for Tyler and Beau to make their appearance.

Colt leaned against the open doorway and gazed out at the beautiful countryside. He loved to awaken to new-fallen snow, but this morning his focus was not on the scenery.

Misty, his wife, was at work. They had breakfasted together, and then she drove off to her job in the town of Langston. She was the office manager for Breckenridge T. Ryan, the only lawyer in the area. Breck handled everything from wills to bail hearings, but he relied on Misty Garrett to keep him organized.

Colt figured that Beau would not have any trouble meeting with his brothers because Dixie would also be in Langston, managing the feed store she owned.

It was Tyler, his middle brother, who might have trouble getting away. Leah was a stay-at-home mom.

Their nine-year-old daughter, Gracie, was home from school for the Christmas break, and they had a one-year-old baby who took up a lot of his mother's time and attention. Tyler was staying close to home so he could load up on family time…time he missed when he was touring as a country-western singer with his band.

Leah was the ultimate super wife and mom. And she was the one who had actually met and interacted with Big Jim's supposed love child the most.

But Colt was surprised when he saw Tyler's truck heading up to the barn. He was apparently the first to arrive. He parked and swung out of the truck, tromping through the snow to the barn. "Hey, Big Bro. Here I am. What did you want to talk about?"

Colt snorted indelicately. "As if you didn't know."

"Well, I thought I would do you the honor of laying it all out for me."

"Come on over to the heater. Take a load off." Colt indicated the chairs.

"Hah! Just what I need. Splinters in my butt." But Tyler ambled over to the cooler and removed a longneck before placing said butt in one of the wooden chairs. "Is Beau on his way?" He flipped off the bottle cap and took a sip.

"I hope to hell he gets here pretty quick." Colt went back to peer out the barn door. "He's driving up now…but he's got Ava with him." He turned to Tyler. "Be careful what you say in front of her. Little pitchers have big ears."

Tyler shook his head and took another sip of beer. "Where do you get these things? You sound like Mom when we were little. She had a thousand of those old sayings."

Colt flapped a hand at him. “Be cool, man.”

Tyler laughed. “I’m always cool, Big Bro.”

Beau got out of his truck and lifted Ava from her car safety seat. He carried her into the barn. “Here’s Ava. She came to see her favorite uncles.”

Colt shot him a dark glance, not believing that his youngest brother would bring his preschool daughter to a serious discussion involving their father.

“Don’t worry,” Beau said. “We got this.” He seated himself in one of the Adirondack chairs and settled Ava in his lap.

Colt noticed the little girl wore a bright-pink set of headphones, almost invisible against her bright-red curls.

Beau produced his cell phone and plugged her headphones in. “Now, what did you want to talk about?”

Colt had to laugh at that. “Pretty slick, Bro.”

Tyler tipped his longneck back and drained the bottle. “Colt wants us to get rid of this new sister of ours. Maybe tar and feather her…and her beautiful little girl too.”

Beau raised his brows, looking at Colt questioningly.

Colt scowled back. “No, I’m concerned—and rightly so—that some woman shows up and claims to be Dad’s long-lost illegitimate daughter. Aren’t you fellows the least bit suspicious about that?”

Tyler sat up, glaring at Colt. “You should wait and meet the woman. One look and you can see the old man staring right back at you.”

Colt felt the muscles in his shoulders tighten up. He took a moment to try to relax, starting with uncurling his fingers from his tight fists. “Now, look here, Little Brother, lots of people look like Dad…like us. Dark hair can come in a bottle, and blue eyes may be contacts. Looks don't mean a thing."

"You think a woman would poke contacts in her little girl's eyes?" Tyler shook his head. "Reserve your judgment until you meet her."

Beau tilted his head to one side. He barely missed getting clocked by his daughter's headphones as she suddenly threw herself back against his chest, singing a little song, her gaze fastened on the cell phone. "I haven't met this person, but I can't understand why she would wait so long to get in touch." He shrugged as best he could. "I mean, Dad's been here all his life. She could have shown up at any time. Why now?"

Colt's eyes narrowed to slits. He hit his fist against the palm of his other hand. "Exactly! I wonder what caused this mystery daughter to crawl out of the woodwork now?"

Tyler had leaned back in the chair, stretching his long legs out in front of him, crossing one boot over the other. He heaved a slightly irritated sigh. "Angelique said her mother only told her the name of her birth father recently, on her deathbed. I don't think most people would lie about that."

Colt made a scoffing sound in the back of his throat. "You are so gullible, Ty. You bought any prime swampland lately?" He shook his head.

Beau's head swiveled from brother to brother.

Tyler crossed his arms over his broad chest. "You don't need to be an ass, Colt. Your opinion is just that. Your opinion. But you're operating from pure ignorance."

Beau held up one hand to calm Colt. "Simmer down,

both of you." He adjusted Ava so he could turn to face both brothers. "First of all, what is it you're afraid of, Colt?"

Colt tried not to roll his eyes. He knew Beau was trying to keep the peace, but his patience was stretched to its limit. He couldn't understand why these two weren't up in arms, ready to protect Big Jim. He blew out a deep breath. "I'm concerned that this…this woman is a fake. I think she is some kind of scam artist out to take advantage of a sweet old man."

"Okay, I get that," Beau said. "Now, let me hear from Ty. Why do you think this woman's claim is valid?"

Tyler shook his head. "You had to be there. If you could have seen Dad's face, you would get it. He knew this woman's mother and didn't deny it for a second."

Beau took his daughter's headphones off and struggled to his feet with Ava in one arm. "Say goodbye to your favorite uncles, Ava. We're gonna go home." Ava held out her arms to Tyler and then to Colt, each of whom gave her a hug and kiss on the cheek.

"Wait!" Colt said. "Why are you leaving? Nothing's been settled."

"Colt, this is nothing we can settle in a day." Beau snugged Ava's quilted coat around her and arranged the hood over her curls. "And I'm not sure this situation is anything we have a right to be involved in." He carried Ava to the barn door and slid it open. "After all, this is about the relationship between our dad and the woman who wants to be accepted as his daughter. Let 'em work it out."

Colt and Tyler stared after their little brother, who seemed to have had the last word.

Angelique had gotten up a couple of times during the night. She had checked on Gabrielle, and then later she had jerked awake, fleeing from a dream she couldn't remember but that haunted her anyway.

She had lain awake in the dark, curled into a defensive position with every muscle in her body tensed. She could tell herself to relax…that she was in her father's house and it was secure.

But she had not been forthcoming with him. He had no idea what had caused her to undertake this desperate mission to find a safe haven for herself and for her most precious daughter. Gabrielle must be safe.

In time, the sky grew lighter, going from total darkness—a black sky strewn with a million stars—to varying shades of gray.

Angelique had crept to the window from time to time to check the rural domain belonging to the man she hoped would allow her to stay. The Garrett ranch appeared to be really large. There were quite a few outbuildings and several fenced-off areas. Being a city girl, she had no idea what these spaces were used for, but the ranch was the complete opposite of the small apartment she had occupied in New Orleans.

Now she was up and dressed and sitting on the edge of the bed, her hands clasped in her lap. She appeared to be calm, but her muscles were tensed and her hearing was magnified a thousand times.

She jumped when a soft knock at the door broke the silence. She rose without waking her daughter and crossed to open the door.

Big Jim Garrett stood in the hallway, fully dressed in his cowboy regalia. "I made breakfast. Don't know what you're used to, but I set out food for you and the little one. I got a booster chair out of the attic, and it's pulled up to the table, so Gabrielle should be fine."

"Oh, that was so nice of you." She heard the pitiful quaver in her voice and cleared her throat.

"Uh, I need to go out and tend to the stock. I didn't want you to get up and wonder why I had abandoned you." He frowned. "Bad choice of words."

"Oh, no. My mom said you had no idea I even existed." Angelique swallowed against the boulder at the back of her throat. "Please don't think I blame you for anything. I just wanted to know…"

Big Jim looked embarrassed. "I'm going out now. Be back in a while."

She nodded. "Thanks for everything."

Big Jim gave a nod of his own and walked down the hall.

Angelique gathered Gabrielle and changed her diaper. They were working on potty training, but there was no way Gabi could make it through the night.

Angelique found her way back to the kitchen, walking hand in hand with Gabrielle through this huge maze of a house.

The kitchen was bright, and though the sky outside was overcast, plenty of light poured in through the far wall of windows.

The table was set for one, but there was a banquet of food on the countertop.

"I hope you're hungry, Gabi. Do you want some eggs?"

Gabrielle rubbed her eyes. "Un-huh…eggys." She pointed to the array of food above her head.

Angelique helped Gabrielle climb onto the booster seat, then picked up her plate and turned to face the feast. She selected bacon, eggs, and toast for herself and put some scrambled eggs on a saucer and oatmeal in a cup for Gabrielle. She placed these on the table and followed her nose to the coffeepot. There were man-sized mugs looped on a tree of sorts by their ears. Selecting one, she poured the dark, fragrant liquid and sniffed appreciatively.

Angelique found herself smiling when she saw a yellow sippy cup with milk in it. Big Jim knew what it took to care for a young child.

She returned to the table to take her place beside her daughter. "Good morning, sunshine. Here's your eggs." Angelique handed Gabrielle a spoon and scooped a bite of scrambled egg into her own mouth. "Oh, these are good."

Gabrielle reached for the spoon and filled it with her own food. "I eat my eggys."

Angelique scooped more eggs and followed with a strip of bacon. She had forgotten how good it felt to sit at a table and eat a real breakfast. Being on the run had changed her eating habits, but she did manage to make sure her daughter ate well. She continued to feed herself while Gabrielle cleaned her plate. She must have liked the fluffy scrambled eggs because she picked up the little plate and licked the last morsel off.

When Angelique looked up, she saw Big Jim leaning against the doorframe leading to the back entry and laundry room. He had a big grin on his face.

"This little Gabi sure has mastered the art of feeding herself." He picked up Gabrielle's little plate and added a couple more spoonfuls of eggs before placing it before her.

Gabrielle clenched her teeth together in a fierce grin and waved her spoon. "I got more eggys!"

"Good girl. I would be wearing half that food by now." He shook his head and gave Angelique a wink.

She smiled back at him. "Somehow, I doubt that. You seem to have a handle on just about everything around here."

He went to the coffeepot and poured himself a big mug of the coffee before approaching the table. "May I join you young ladies?"

Angelique gestured to the chair across from her. "Sure. It's your table."

He pushed the chair back and sat down. "Did I make the coffee to your liking?"

She nodded. "It's good, but different from the coffee I'm used to. In New Orleans we drink our coffee with chicory. I guess it's an acquired taste."

Big Jim smiled. "I remember Sofie telling me something about how during the Civil War, when the Union naval blockade cut off the Port of New Orleans, people used chicory to stretch their coffee supply."

Angelique stirred some cream into her coffee. "It was actually popular in France during Napoleon's time. There was a blockade of his own making, and the French began roasting and grinding chicory to stretch their coffee supply. So when French people migrated to the New World, they brought the chicory with them."

Big Jim was grinning at her, holding the mug with both hands.

Angelique felt the color rising in her cheeks. If he only knew how hungry she had been for exactly this kind of interaction. A normal father-daughter conversation taking place at the breakfast table. *Almost normal.*

"How old is your little daughter?" He gestured to Gabrielle, who was banging her empty sippy cup on the high-chair tray.

"I want milk," Gabrielle said, looking at Big Jim.

"My daughter, your granddaughter, will be two in February. She's an Aquarius." Angelique took the sippy cup and refilled it. "Here you go, Gabi." She offered it to her daughter.

"That sounds great." Big Jim lifted his mug in a salute. "So, are you planning on staying for a while, or are you gonna run back to New Orleans?"

That question caused tightness in Angelique's throat. *Does he want me to leave?* A muscle twitched near her eye. "Um…I haven't made plans yet."

"Good. I was hoping you could stick around for a while. You know, get to know your half brothers and their wives."

Relief flooded her chest. She needed to be here. If she never returned to New Orleans again, it would be too soon. She sucked in a breath and let it out all at once. "I can't tell you how much this means to me. I-I felt so lost after my mom passed on… And when she told me your name, I had to find you."

The smile he gave her radiated kindness. "I can't tell you how glad I am that you found me. I'm sorry I didn't know about you." He shook his head. "I missed out on your entire childhood."

She cast her eyes down at her empty plate. "It wasn't

all that good. I want to make sure my little Gabi has a better life."

A furrow appeared between Big Jim's brows. "I thought Sofie came from a pretty good family."

Angelique stirred the coffee in her almost-empty cup. "She did. But my mom defied them and there was…an estrangement." She looked up to meet his gaze.

"Sofie had a strong personality. I can't imagine anyone making her do anything she didn't want to do." He looked thoughtful.

"Well, her parents sent her to a Catholic home for pregnant girls, thinking she would give me up for adoption… but she wouldn't." Angelique flashed a grin. "She said it was love at first sight, and she refused to hand me over."

"Then what happened?" Big Jim asked.

"My grandparents weren't exactly thrilled to have an illegitimate granddaughter so they hid me away. But my mom was a born rebel and really wanted to find a way to support me by herself. She went down to the Quarter and got a job in a shop there. She didn't make much money, but she got a little efficiency apartment upstairs and we lived there for a while. She made some friends, and we got by."

Big Jim stared hard.

Angelique couldn't tell what he was thinking, but he sure was thinking hard. She pushed back from the table and started gathering the dishes and eating utensils. "Let me wash these. It will only take a minute."

She rinsed the dishes and slipped them into the dishwasher. Glancing back over her shoulder, she saw Big Jim deep in thought. Perhaps she should not have told him so much. Perhaps she should not have told him anything at all.

Chapter 3

Big Jim clutched the almost-empty mug. It seemed to be the only thing he could hold on to. His entire reality had taken a hard turn. The first woman he had cared for had given birth to his child and raised her without his knowledge.

He felt guilty for wishing things had been different…because he really didn't. He knew that graduating and marrying Elizabeth had been the most perfect path he could have taken. He had loved his wife deeply, and the birth of their three sons had only enriched their lives.

Big Jim had been devoted to his family and had worked hard to build a good life for them. The boys had grown to be good men. Good family men.

But as he gazed at the lovely dark-haired woman across the kitchen, he had regrets.

Just then, Angelique's daughter put her hand on Big Jim's sleeve. She gazed up at him with her wide Garrett blue eyes, looking so pretty and so innocent.

Angelique had said her name was Gabrielle Guillory. Did that mean Angelique had never married?

"That's your grandfather, Gabi."

Big Jim put his hand on Gabrielle's arm. "It's good to have you here, Gabi. Can you call me Grandpa?"

Gabrielle continued to stare at him, her big blue eyes

examining every aspect of his face. She turned to look at Angelique and grinned. "He gots blue eyes too."

Angelique smiled back. "Yes, he does. He wants you to call him Grandpa. Can you do that?"

"Gwampa," Gabrielle pronounced.

"That's perfect," Big Jim said. "Just perfect."

Big Jim was reluctant to ask Angelique about her child's birth. He supposed that she would eventually tell him her story. He wouldn't push her.

Angelique turned from the sink, dried her hands on a linen towel, and hung it back on its hook. "You have a great place here, Mr. Garrett. It sure is different from where I've lived." She shrugged and slid into the chair next to Gabrielle in her booster seat. "I mean, winter is cold and wet in New Orleans, but it hardly ever snows there."

Big Jim reached to take her hand. "First of all, I don't expect you to call me Dad, but at least you can call me Big Jim."

She grinned at him. "I can see how you got that name...Dad."

Her hand felt small and boneless wrapped in Big Jim's big paw. "Good thing you took after Sofie when it came to your bone structure."

"Well, I'm taller than my mom was, so I got my height from you."

"Tell me about yourself." Big Jim beamed at her. "What do you like to do?"

She smiled and dimpled. "I'm a pretty quiet person. I like to take care of Gabrielle. Cook—I like to cook. And I like to draw. I have a bunch of sketches of Gabrielle, mostly when she's sleeping because that's when she's still."

Big Jim mulled this over. "Do you ride?"

Angelique laughed out loud. "I ride the trolley sometimes. If you're talking about anything with four legs, the answer is no. I have never been on a horse in my life."

Big Jim chuckled. "We'll have to fix that. I've got a sweet little mare that would love to have you in the saddle…as opposed to one of us big galoots on her back."

Her eyes opened wide. "Oh no! I would be terrified. And what about Gabrielle?"

Big Jim's eyes twinkled. "We'll get Gabrielle her own horse."

She realized he was teasing and dissolved in a fit of giggles. When she recovered, she sat grinning at him. "I never dreamed you would be so nice."

It struck him that maybe Angelique had not been treated well by the people in her former life. "I sure do hope you're planning on stickin' around, Miss Angelique Guillory. This is about the best Christmas present I've gotten in a long time."

Misty could tell by the set of Colton's jaw that something was really bothering him. At first, she had thought he would share it, but as the evening wore on, she'd had her fill of single-syllable responses in return for her attempts at conversation.

After dinner, she left her younger brother, Mark, at the table with a slab of store-bought cake and drew Colt into their bedroom.

"What's up?" he asked.

"Exactly! I want to know what the heck is bothering you." Misty put on her tough don't-mess-with-me face. The one she had used on Mark when he was younger.

A muscle near Colt's mouth twitched. "Nothing."

"Well, you better spell out that nothing and stop moping around here like a storm cloud. I want my husband back and not this snarly thing." She stood glaring at him with her hands on her hips.

Colt heaved a huge sigh and ran his fingers through his thick, dark hair. "Sorry, baby. Someone is trying to take advantage of Dad, and I'm not getting any cooperation from my brothers."

Misty sat down on the bed and patted the space beside her. "You better let me know what's going on. I can't imagine anyone getting the best of Big Jim Garrett."

Colt sat down, bouncing Misty with his weight. "How about a really pretty woman showing up at the ranch claiming to be his long-lost daughter?"

"What? That sounds fishy to me."

"Thank you. Ty met her and thinks she is telling the truth. And Beau thinks we should all butt out."

Misty sat staring at him in disbelief. Of all the things she could have imagined, this was not on the list. "Well, what are you going to do about it?"

"I haven't decided yet. But I'm going to do something."

"Why don't we go to visit Big Jim? It is the season, you know."

He frowned down at her. "What do you have in mind?"

"Well, I could bake something and we could take it over."

Colt's frown turned into a smile. "Babe, you're not known for your baking."

Conversely, Misty's smile turned into a frown. "Shut up." She crossed her arms over her chest. "I'll get a recipe from Leah's grandmother. She's always willing to teach me something. She says she's sharing the family recipes."

Colt was silent for a moment, then nodded. "That should work."

"I'll call her now, before she goes to bed."

Colt agreed that they would take whatever Leah's grandmother came up with to the Garrett ranch house after Misty got off work the next day, and they would take Mark with them since he would be eager to talk to Big Jim.

"Sounds like a plan," Misty said. Now she hoped Leah's grandmother had a really easy recipe and that she would be able to make it.

Big Jim opened the door with a big grin on his face. "Well, surprise! It's three of my favorite people. Come right in here and warm yourself up." He opened his arms wide, and Mark threw his arms around Big Jim's torso.

Misty appreciated that Big Jim took an interest in her brother, since he had never had a good male image to follow.

"We brought dessert," Misty announced.

"Well, how 'bout that?" Big Jim looked a little confused. "Come back to the table. We was just finishing up."

Misty and Colt exchanged a glance. *So that's how it is.*

Big Jim led the way with his hand on Mark's shoulder.

When they entered the spacious open area that housed the combination kitchen, dining, and family room, it was impossible to ignore the beautiful woman seated at the table. There were dishes in place, but it appeared the food had been eaten.

"This lovely young woman is Angelique Guillory, my daughter. Angelique, honey, I want you to meet my oldest son, Colton, and his wife, Misty."

Misty felt Colt stiffen beside her, but she smiled, hoping to deflect his reaction.

The woman stared at the trio, seemingly speechless, but then recovered. "Hello. It's nice to meet you."

Big Jim urged Mark forward, hands still on his shoulders. "And this is Misty's little brother, Mark." He was grinning proudly as Mark offered his hand.

"Pleased to meet you, ma'am."

The woman shook his hand, but appeared to be puzzled. "Nice to meet you, Mark."

Misty stepped forward bearing the dessert she had made. "Gran gave me her recipe for buttermilk pie. We thought we would share our dessert with you."

"Hot dang!" Big Jim clapped Mark on the shoulder. "Let us get some plates and forks." The two of them headed for the kitchen area and busied themselves gathering utensils and small plates.

There was a toddler sitting at the table on the booster seat Big Jim had gotten for his grandson, Leah and Tyler's baby, James Tyler Garrett. Now a strange child with large turquoise-blue eyes and dark curls stared at the newcomers from this throne, banging her heels against the base of the booster seat.

"Um, what a pretty child, Angelique," Misty said.

The woman nodded. "This is my daughter, Gabrielle."

Big Jim and Mark returned, sporting the dishes, which they placed on the table. "Let's all sit down and have some of Misty's pie," Big Jim said.

Colt held a chair for Misty, seating her next to Angelique, and took a seat beside his wife. He seemed to have his full attention fixed on his so-called half-sister.

When they were all seated, Misty served the pie and took a bite for herself. She was pleased that the people gathered around the table were making approving sounds as they tasted the creamy, custard-like pie. This was her first attempt at pie, and although it had smelled wonderful while in the oven, and it looked perfect, she had the horrible fear that it might not taste that good.

"This is great, babe," Colt spoke for the first time.

"Yes ma'am!" Big Jim crowed. "Danged good pie, Misty."

"It's delicious," Angelique agreed, scooping a little of the custard into a spoon for her daughter.

Misty felt her cheeks burn. She rarely received rave reviews for her cooking. *Maybe I'll have to go to Gran for more easy recipes.*

After they had eaten, Big Jim pushed back from the table and invited Mark to help clear the table with him. Colt offered to help, so Misty was left alone with Angelique and her daughter.

"So, Angelique," she said, leaning closer. "What do you do?"

"Do?" Angelique looked surprised.

"You know, for a living? I work as office manager for the local attorney."

Angelique sucked in a deep breath and huffed it out. "I-I worked in a, uh, restaurant back in New Orleans."

A waitress. That figures. Misty cleared her throat, searching for something to chat about. "I understand the food in New Orleans is fantastic."

Angelique actually smiled at that. "We like it. With the nearby Gulf of Mexico, we have access to a lot of fresh seafood year 'round."

"Yum. That must be nice. I love seafood. Here in ranch country, we eat a lot of beef, of course. Big Jim is a master of the barbecue grill."

Angelique's large blue eyes opened wide. "You only eat beef?"

"We eat chicken and pork, too, but this is ranch country so every rancher around here has a side of beef in his freezer."

Angelique smiled. "That sounds great."

"Your little girl is lovely. Is your husband still in New Orleans?" Misty had planned this question, hoping to gain some kind of background information on the woman Colt thought was out to scam his dad.

"Oh, I'm not married." Angelique didn't hesitate with her response.

Loud and proud. "I see."

Angelique leveled her gaze on Misty. "I only came here to find my father, and I wanted him to meet his granddaughter."

"Of course. He seems to be enjoying your visit." Misty moistened her lips, glad to see Colt returning.

"Ready to go home, babe?" He gave a little nod toward the front of the house. "Mark wants to stay here so he and Dad can work the horses first thing in the morning."

She took her leave, telling Mark to call her when he was ready to go home.

Dixie Garrett's husband, Beau, was the youngest son of a rich and powerful rancher. She had gotten off to a rocky start with Big Jim Garrett, but had since come to love and respect her father-in-law.

When Beau had been summoned to a private meeting by his oldest brother, she'd figured it had something to do with Christmas. Maybe they were planning some sort of special family event. Or maybe it was a brothers-only shopping trip. But since his return, Beau had been withdrawn and somewhat terse when she tried to draw him out.

Now, with Ava fast asleep in her room, Beau lounged in front of the television, pretending to be watching the news, but his troubled brain was mulling over something that seemed to be eating away at his soul.

Beau was the most positive person Dixie had ever known, but something had gotten to him.

Definitely not in the holiday spirit.

She approached him, determined to ignore the storm cloud hovering over his head. "Scoot over, cowboy. I need some cuddle time."

He looked up at her and then made room on the sofa. He lifted his arm and reached over to her in an invitation. "Sorry, babe. Come on over here." He used the remote to mute the news.

Dixie sat next to him and snuggled close as he drew his arm around her. This simple act gave her hope that he would get back to his usually good-natured self soon.

"I had a pretty good day," she said.

No response at all.

"I worked on the books and got everything ready to send to the accountant at the end of the year."

He heaved a sigh. "Sounds awful to me."

Encouraged, she went on. "Oh, no. It's really exciting to see how the feed store has improved financially over this last year."

He nodded absently. "Good job, babe."

"No, really. I had a chance to analyze the sales, and I can tell what the best sellers are and what time of year to order from the wholesalers."

He gave a chuckle. "Like, order Easter bunnies and ducklings in the spring?"

Dixie grinned at him. "Something like that." She made a kissy face at him, and he leaned closer to give her a quick kiss, but she cupped his face in her hands, insisting on a better kiss.

When he drew away, he gave her a quizzical look. "Something on your mind?"

She flashed a smile. "As a matter of fact, yes. I demand that you tell me what happened when you met with your brothers. You've been Mr. Grumpy Face since you got home."

Beau blew out a long sigh. "Have I? I'm sorry." He sat up and pulled his boots off, wiggling his toes, a ritual that followed the removal of his footwear.

"Well? What's going on?"

"I really hate to get back into it." His brows drew together in a frown. "Honestly, honey. Colt is all in a dither over the woman who is staying with Dad."

Dixie sat up straight, her mouth agape. "The woman

Leah told me about? She's staying with your father? Well, is she who she says she is?"

Beau shook his head. "I have no idea, but she claims to be..." He heaved out another sigh. "She says that she is Big Jim's long-lost daughter, and Dad seems to be backing her up."

"I'm having trouble believing that. Your father would never have cheated on your mother."

Beau looked disgruntled. "No, he didn't cheat. She claims that Dad and her mother were college sweethearts and that she got pregnant but didn't tell him."

"What was Big Jim supposed to be? Blind?" Dixie made a scoffing noise in the back of her throat. "He didn't notice that his girlfriend was putting on a little weight?"

"The way I heard it, this girlfriend went back to New Orleans...that's where she was from." Beau shook his head. "It was the end of the spring term, and she went to New Orleans, while Dad came home to the ranch for the summer. That was the last Big Jim saw of her. He never knew she was pregnant."

"If indeed she was." Dixie crossed her arms over her chest, outraged that some woman would make such accusations against her father-in-law.

"The thing is, I'm sorta caught in the middle." Beau spread his hands, palms up. "Colt is convinced she's a scam artist who is preying on Dad. He said the holidays bring out lots of scams."

"That's probably right. I'm sure Colt won't let anyone take advantage of Big Jim."

"That sounds like you think I would let that happen." His voice had taken on an edge.

"No, dear one. I'm sure you wouldn't, but what's the problem?"

"Well, Ty is just as convinced that she is the real deal. He and Leah were with Dad when the woman showed up."

"What would make him think she was for real?" Dixie couldn't imagine any rift between the Garrett brothers.

Beau leaned back against the sofa. "Ty says the woman has the same eye color as all the Garretts. You know nobody around here has eyes like these unless they're a Garrett. Cousins out the ears, but almost all have this same shade of baby blues." He batted his eyes at her.

"Oh!" Dixie leaned against Beau's shoulder. "That does sound odd. Do you suppose she could be for real?"

"I dunno, but Ty said Leah spent some time talking to her, and they believe she is Dad's daughter." He swallowed hard. "That would make her our sister."

Dixie stared up at the ceiling, wondering how this would play out.

Beau nudged her. "Did I mention she has a little girl with Garrett blue eyes too?"

Chapter 4

On Sunday, Big Jim loaded his daughter and granddaughter into his truck and drove them to church in town. He let them out in front and then went to park. Since it was the Christmas season, there were more worshippers than usual so his parking place was farther from the church.

When he walked back to the church, he found Angelique inside chatting with Leah and Tyler.

Gabrielle gazed up at the adults, very interested in the baby Tyler was holding. She kept touching his feet inside the flannel onesie. She touched one foot and he kicked, so she touched the other to receive the same treatment. She giggled and this made the baby laugh.

Leah was laughing with them.

Big Jim was so grateful that his middle son had married this sweet, kind woman. He walked over to the group and spread his arms wide to offer a group hug to both women.

"Good to see you folks," he said.

"We were introducing Angelique and Gabrielle to our kids," Tyler said. "Gracie is in the fourth grade this year, but school's closed for the holidays." He pulled Gracie close for a hug.

"And how old is your baby?" Angelique's smile was beautiful, reminding Big Jim of Sofie.

"Our son, JT, will be one year old soon. He was born just before Christmas last year." Leah took her son from Tyler and arranged him over her shoulder. "Let me show you to the nursery," she said. "You'll love the ladies who care for the little ones. Come on, Gracie." She escorted Angelique and Gabrielle to a hallway in the back that led to the children's Sunday school classes and the nursery.

"That's some woman you got there, Son."

Tyler nodded. "My Leah is one in a million."

Big Jim and Tyler went to the pew usually lined with the entire Garrett family and found that Misty and Colt were already in place.

Big Jim greeted them, but noted that there seemed to be some kind of tension between his two older sons.

Tyler remained standing beside Big Jim. When Leah and Angelique returned from the nursery, Tyler took a seat with Leah on the opposite end of the pew from where Colt and Misty were sitting.

Big Jim figured he would eventually hear all about the problem between his two older sons. At least he had a heads-up. He seated Angelique beside Leah and was ready to take a seat when he spotted Beau with his red-headed wife and daughter. Big Jim waved them over.

"Hey, Dad." Dixie stretched up to give him a kiss on the cheek, while Ava leaned out of Beau's arms and into Big Jim's.

"Hi, Grampa." Ava squeezed his neck and planted another kiss on his cheek.

Damn! I love these two. "I want you to meet Angelique. You may have heard that she's my daughter."

Beau leaned down to clasp Angelique's hand. "I'm so glad to meet you. I guess you're my sister."

Angelique's eyes teared up. "Oh, you don't know how good that sounds to me."

Beau patted her hand. "This beautiful woman is my wife, Dixie, and this is our adorable daughter, Ava. Don't worry. We'll all get to know each other."

Dixie smiled and waggled her fingers. "Let me take Ava to her Sunday school class and I'll be right back."

Big Jim set Ava on her feet and waved as Dixie led her to the back hallway. He glanced around at his family and felt his chest swell with pride. *Damned good-lookin' folks.* He sat down beside Angelique and stretched his arm over the back of the pew.

Angelique leaned closer to whisper in his ear. "Can you tell me who that man is?" She was pointing to a familiar figure.

"That's Derrick Shelton. He's an old friend of my sons'. Why do you ask?"

A little smile graced her lips. "I had some trouble when I was on the road. I spun out and drove into a snowbank. That man pulled my car out."

Big Jim nudged Beau. "Son, will you ask Derrick to come over here?"

In a few minutes, Beau returned with Derrick Shelton in tow.

Derrick was totally focused on Angelique, a wide grin on his face. "Hello, Angelique. I was hoping we would meet again."

Angelique's cheeks took on a very attractive blush. "Me too."

"Sheriff, I hear you rescued my daughter." Big Jim clasped Derrick's hand in a hearty shake.

Derrick's face registered surprise bordering on shock. "Your daughter, sir?"

"Long story," Big Jim said. "But thanks for taking care of my girls."

Derrick's brows rose. "Your girls?"

"My daughter and granddaughter." Big Jim broke into a broad grin. "That lil' Gabrielle is just as purty as her mama."

Derrick looked at Angelique. "Oh, is your husband here?"

She shook her head. "No husband."

It may have been his imagination, but Big Jim thought Derrick looked relieved.

"I sure hope you're going to be sticking around for a while, Angelique." Derrick's voice dropped a level. "At least through Christmas."

Angelique's dimples flashed. "Oh, I hope so too."

"What do you mean, you can't find her?" The veins on Alphonse Benoit's forehead stood out, and his face reddened. He could not imagine that two of his best men had failed. "Where is she?"

"Um, she disappeared. We're still searching, Mr. Benoit."

Silence. Benoit took a moment to get control of his anger. If Buford Fontenot were in his presence, Benoit would have his fingers wrapped around the man's throat. If he were to be found floating in the Mississippi, no one would miss him.

Benoit's voice dropped to a lower register. "You will

find her…and you will find my granddaughter…and you will bring them to me."

"Yes, Mr. Benoit."

"Just so we're clear, Mr. Fontenot…you understand what will happen if you and Mr. Breaux fail me?"

"Yes, sir. Don't worry. You can count on us, sir. We'll find her."

Benoit disconnected, his hand lingering on the phone. *Trust.* It was something he valued greatly…and if his trust was betrayed, he would go to the ends of the earth to exact revenge.

After the church service had ended, and the children had been retrieved from the nursery and Sunday school classes, Big Jim gathered his family and arranged for the various members to meet up at Tio's Mexican Restaurant. And he had called ahead to ask Milita to reserve the big table in the back corner.

Derrick Shelton hung out on the edge of the group, hoping to get an invitation. When Angelique and Leah returned from the nursery, each with a child, he was somewhat stunned. It was as though Angelique had been cloned. Her little one had the same dark hair and blue eyes…the blue eyes that all the other Garretts sported.

He leaned over to touch the young girl on her arm. "She's a beautiful girl," he said. "She looks like you."

The child examined him and then flashed a dimpled grin as though he had passed muster.

Angelique's pale cheeks took on a tinge of very attractive color. "Um, thanks."

He spoke in a lower tone. "You sure do look pretty today."

She smiled. "Better than when I was freezing my tail off out in the snow?"

"You looked pretty then too." He could tell she was pleased.

"Hey, Derrick!" Tyler slapped him on the shoulder. "Why don't you join us for lunch at Tio's. We're all going to strap on the feed bag."

Derrick tried to look as though he was considering this offer. "Yes, sure. I could always eat Mexican food."

"See you there." Tyler put one arm around Gracie and the other around Leah, ushering them to the exit.

Derrick stepped closer to Angelique and asked if she would like to ride to the restaurant with him, but she explained that the child safety seat was in Big Jim's truck.

"It's only a couple of blocks, isn't it?"

"Um, yeah. Sorry." Derrick felt like an idiot for suggesting she go in his truck, but he wanted to spend time with her without the entire Garrett clan looking on.

She smiled though. "I'll see you at the restaurant."

Derrick nodded and went to find his truck among all the others parked near the church. With a little luck, he would at least be able to sit next to Angelique at the restaurant.

But when he arrived, there were members of the Garrett tribe assigning seating. It was Colt who grabbed him by the arm.

"Hey, Derrick. Glad you could join us. Come sit right here by me."

The only good thing about this arrangement was that

he wound up sitting right across from Angelique. She, in turn, was flanked by Big Jim on one side and her daughter in a booster seat on the other side. Leah was next to her, and her daughter, Gracie, was seated between her mom and Tyler, her dad.

It didn't take a genius to figure out that Colt and Tyler were at odds.

Colt, never one to hide his feelings, refused to look at Tyler at all. Tyler, on the other hand, seemed a bit amused by his older brother's stance.

Derrick had played high school football with Colt, but had been in league with the two younger Garrett boys as well. In their history together, he had never known them to disagree over anything major, but these two seemed to have dug in.

Milita Rios, the owner's daughter at Tio's Restaurant, brought water to the table on a little rolling cart, along with a stack of menus. "Good afternoon, Garrett family…and Sheriff. How many iced teas?"

There was a show of hands, and then she asked who wanted coffee and made a note of both.

"How about Ranchero Platters all around?" Big Jim made a circling motion with his hand.

"That's a lot of food, Dad," Leah complained. "I'll take the Señorita Platter. That's plenty for me, and Gracie wants the beef enchilada plate."

Big Jim seemed deflated. "Sorry. You're right. My dear departed Elizabeth would smack me down for wasting food." Then he brightened. "How about Rancheros for the men at the table?"

His suggestion was met with nods and grunts of assent from the males.

When Milita had taken orders from Misty and Angelique, she left, promising to return with their drinks.

There was a full minute of silence while everyone retreated into their own thoughts. Derrick was focused on the lovely woman seated across from him.

She was definitely aware of his attention, but was having trouble meeting his gaze.

"So, what do you think?" Colt had leaned close to whisper in Derrick's ear.

"About what?" Derrick turned to stare at him, but apparently Colt was dead serious about something.

"About this scam?" He nodded toward where Angelique sat listening to Big Jim tell one of his tales.

"What are you talking about?"

"Oh, come on! Don't tell me she's taken you in too?" Colt glowered at him.

"She?" Derrick frowned back. "Are you talking about Angelique?"

Colt's lips turned up in a snarky smile. "So that's how it is?"

Derrick pushed his chair back and motioned for Colt to follow. "Excuse us, folks. Me and my buddy here are going out for a smoke."

Those gathered at the table exchanged puzzled looks.

"But neither of them boys have ever smoked." Big Jim stared after them as they strode to the parking lot.

Beau snorted. "I'm sure they're smoking, Dad. But not tobacco."

Once outside, Derrick slued around to face Colt. "What the hell's the matter with you, anyway?"

Colt took a wide stance. "Me? You're the one who's drinking the Kool-Aid. Get your head outta your ass, man." He crossed his arms over his chest. "I know she's a pretty woman, but there's definitely something going on here. Don't you think it's strange that this mysterious, long-lost daughter suddenly shows up right before Christmas?"

"What do you think she's up to?" Derrick spread his hands. "She's just a woman with a little girl, and she's a long way from home."

Colt's eyes narrowed. "And that's another thing. It's Christmastime. Shouldn't she be with her own family and not mooching off my dad?"

Derrick stepped back, setting his fists on his hips. "Whoa! That's quite an accusation. What is it you think she's doing here?"

"She's a scam artist. Can't you see what she's doing?"

"Apparently not." Derrick scowled at his friend from childhood. "Have you looked in the mirror lately? She looks just like you. Just like Ty and Beau." He turned away, taking a few paces down the walkway. When he faced Colt again, he tried to reason with his friend. "Angelique looks like a feminine version of Big Jim Garrett himself."

Colt's brow furrowed. "I know, but it has to be faked. Hair can be dyed. Eye color can be changed with contacts. It's just so…so…"

Derrick expelled a long and exasperated breath. "Colt, give it up. What is it you're afraid of, anyway?"

"You don't understand, Derrick. I can't let anyone take advantage of Big Jim." His voice took on a strident note. "I mean, he's my dad."

Big Jim was just about to get out of his chair and go outside to find out what the heck his oldest son and the sheriff were fussing about. It was pretty obvious they were at odds, and this encounter had everyone at the table on edge. It wasn't clear whether or not they would throw down or walk away.

Then, as suddenly as it had begun, both men came through the front door of Tio's, apparently just as good friends as they had always been.

Big Jim took a deep breath and released it, and it was as though the others at the table did the same.

"So, how was the smoke?" he asked.

"Very enlightening, sir." Derrick pulled out his chair and seated himself just as Milita returned with their tea and coffee.

Colt looked like a thunderstorm, but headed for the restrooms. "Gotta wash my hands," he muttered.

Okay, something's up, but they're not gonna spill it in front of the family.

Big Jim tuned in to all the individuals seated at the table. Misty was on edge, and when Colt returned to the table, she whispered something behind her cupped hand. Colt shook his head, not wanting to talk about whatever had transpired between him and the sheriff.

Beau was keeping an eye on both his brothers, and Dixie appeared to be tuned in as well. Beau had always been the peacemaker, often keeping his brothers from coming to blows. Now, he and his bride were being watchful, but not taking sides. Ava was seated between them, but they were exchanging glances and spoke in low whispers.

Thankfully, Leah was keeping Angelique occupied

as they concentrated on feeding their children and chattering together.

Big Jim was especially glad Tyler, his rebellious son, had brought Leah and Gracie into the Garrett family.

Angelique was stuffed. She had eaten far too much, lingering over a meal that seemed endless.

There were some strange tensions at the table, but Angelique didn't know these people well enough to make any assumptions. Her position was so tenuous that she was afraid to question anything and afraid to be questioned. Good to let the past be hidden…at least her own past.

Glancing quickly at Big Jim Garrett, she had to smile. He was just as handsome as her mother had claimed. When he was young, he must have been a heartbreaker.

She wiped at her daughter's face with a paper napkin, and then Gabrielle held out her little hands to be cleaned. "Did you like your chicken?"

"Um-hum." Gabrielle nodded her head vigorously. "I like it."

Surreptitiously, Angelique checked out the three brothers. Each one was a hottie in his own right.

Colton, the oldest, had a rugged look, much like a younger version of Big Jim. Strong jawline and, of course, those blue eyes. His stature was like his father's, well over six feet and broad across the shoulders. And his wife, Misty, had dark hair and eyes and very fair skin. The two of them had been very standoffish, so Angelique didn't have a handle on their personalities. Or maybe they were just snobs.

Tyler was cut from the same cloth, but his appearance was more polished. She had heard that he was a country-western singer of some note. She preferred the blues or some zydeco. But she could imagine Tyler standing up on a stage performing for his audience. He seemed to be the perfect partner for Leah. His dark hair was a good foil to her blondness.

The youngest son…her brother Beau… He had the same kind of good looks and a similar stature, but he had a different attitude. Like he was generally amused by life. His redheaded wife was gorgeous, but she seemed to have a more polished, almost city-girl vibe going on. Their little girl, Ava, was a clone of her mom, except for those brilliant blue eyes, a gift from her father.

All in all, a very attractive family. Angelique didn't quite feel a part of it yet, but at least Big Jim had admitted that he was her father. She had expected to be rebuffed, so his acceptance was more than she could have hoped for.

She turned to look at him and found him regarding her with amusement.

"So, what do you make of this rowdy bunch?"

She couldn't keep her eyes from moistening up. Blinking rapidly, she reached for her water and took a sip. "I think I'm the most fortunate woman in the world. I am so very happy to be here, and to have my little girl here with me. I have never had a real family…just my mom and myself, and then Gabrielle."

Big Jim placed a hand on her shoulder. "Listen here, little lady. You will always have a place right here at this table and as a part of this family. You are my daughter. I don't deny it. I'm sorry I wasn't there for you." He squeezed her shoulder. "But I'm gonna try to make it up to you."

Angelique struggled to blink away her tears. She couldn't break down in front of all these people, even if her father was assuring her she was welcome.

Fortunately, Milita came pushing a cart, followed by her father, the owner and cook, with an additional tray. She began to expertly deal out the plates among the Garretts and guests.

Angelique stared at the serving of flan in front of her. She had been told it was a delicious custard-type Mexican dessert. She had been filled to the brim before setting eyes on this treat, but she thought there would be room enough to enjoy a few bites. When she looked up, she locked eyes with Derrick. His brown eyes were fixed on her, and there was a question in his expression.

Derrick had trouble keeping his eyes off Angelique Guillory. He was considering what his friend Colt had told him, and how impassioned his argument had been.

Yet Derrick was having trouble considering the lovely Angelique as a coldhearted scam artist. Or perhaps it was that he didn't want her to be a scam artist.

Colt seemed convinced that Angelique would take advantage of his father. Derrick could understand the desire to protect one's parent. Or was Colt operating from greed? Was he afraid that the Garrett estate would be shared with another heir?

Angelique pushed back from the table, stating she was taking her daughter to the restroom. She helped the little girl down from the booster seat, and they walked hand in hand to the back.

Derrick looked around the table at all the people engaged in pleasant conversation…except for Colt and Tyler. Tyler seemed to be somewhat amused by his big brother's snit.

It was usually Colton, the strong older bro, who was the one to have the cool head. Derrick could recall many times when Colt was the one to settle disputes among his siblings.

Now, it seemed that Colt was trying to get Derrick to choose sides, but he didn't want to offend either brother; nor did he want to speculate on Angelique's motives for appearing at the Garrett homestead so near to Christmas. It did seem timed to tug on the old man's heartstrings.

Gabrielle came running toward Big Jim, with a grinning Angelique trailing behind.

"I go potty all by myself!" Gabrielle shouted.

"You do?" Big Jim drew her into his lap. "That's great. Does that mean you're a big girl?"

Gabrielle nodded vigorously. "I a big girl."

Big Jim appeared to be delighted.

Angelique returned to her seat and turned her attention to Big Jim.

Derrick surreptitiously kept an eye on the interactions between Angelique and Big Jim, who seemed to be totally enraptured by the woman. He was chatting with her and gazing at her and her little girl fondly. In fact, Big Jim seemed to be totally unaware of anyone else at the table.

He realized Big Jim looked like any father communicating with his daughter and granddaughter.

Chapter 5

Angelique was wearing a coat Big Jim had unearthed from a closet. It was a little large on her, but it was really warm, and she couldn't complain. Certainly it was a better choice than the thin jacket she had brought from home…from New Orleans…

She was riding home in Big Jim's truck, or if not home, they were headed to the Garrett ranch, Gabrielle's safety seat securely strapped in behind her with Gabi singing at the top of her lungs.

For his part, Big Jim couldn't stop grinning.

Funny how much difference a few days could make in her life. Angelique had been so very afraid when she had left New Orleans. Now she was actually verging on being happy…and somewhat relaxed. She had been looking over her shoulder for so long now that it would be hard to relax completely, but she was beginning to think this decision to find her father was going to work out for the best.

Big Jim seemed to have accepted her, and there was Leah, who was so kind and friendly.

Now she had to wonder about her three half-brothers. Would they accept her as a part of the family? The one named Colt seemed to be particularly distant, and his wife seemed almost hostile.

She couldn't figure out what the youngest brother,

Beau, was thinking. He seemed to be pleasant enough, but kept to himself, never really voicing an opinion. His wife definitely kept to herself as well.

Angelique had been told that Beau and his family did not live on the Garrett ranch. That might have been why they were a bit more subdued.

She hadn't expected to gain immediate acceptance, but Big Jim's positive attitude was a blessing indeed. *He's my father.*

Where is she? Where is that little tramp, and where is my granddaughter?

Alphonse Benoit poked at the fire in his fireplace. The house was darkened but he stared into the fire as though he could find the answers he was seeking within the flames.

The huge mansion seemed particularly empty that evening. Most of the staff was off, busy with their own little Christmas preparations. Busy with their own little families, leaving Alphonse alone to rattle around in his home. Alone and missing the people who had ripped his heart right out of his chest.

He was obsessed. He had been haunted since the death of Remy, his only son, his progeny. How could a young man so virile die? How could he be taken from this earth, especially when his father had such huge plans for him?

Remy's death had been a double blow to Alphonse. He mourned his son, and he mourned the end of his bloodline. There would be no Benoits to carry on his name.

Last of the line.

Alphonse hung the fireplace poker on a rack with other tools. He was also mourning the loss of his beloved Sofie, his passionate and beautiful lover. The only person other than his son who had dared to say no to him. While he did not delude himself into believing that she was in love with him, she was in love with how he loved her…with the things he had provided for her. It had pleased him to please her.

Now she was gone…and he was alone.

The depths of his loneliness knew no boundaries. He seemed to sink farther and farther every day. His depression gave birth to intense anger. He was angry with everyone about everything. His household staff was tiptoeing around trying to anticipate his needs. Trying to avoid his ire.

The anger burning in Benoit's gut could only be assuaged by securing the presence of his only other living relative. The young girl his son had conceived with this Guillory woman. His beloved Sofie's daughter and granddaughter.

When Sofie was alive, her daughter remained by her side, but soon after Sofie had been interred, this ungrateful young woman had taken his only granddaughter and fled.

Benoit clutched his hands together until the knuckles turned white. He could not allow this child to be raised by Sofie Guillory's illegitimate daughter. This child—the child who should rightly be under his care—should receive the best education. She would be the belle of New Orleans, introduced to all the right people. Not raised in a small apartment in the Quarter. Not raised by a skinny little rag of a woman.

He blew out a deep breath, trying to clear his brain. He hadn't dreamed this Angelique would disappear. How could she? She had no money, no resources. Most of all, no friends… At least no one who would help her. Everyone knew Benoit was looking for her, and they wouldn't risk crossing him.

He hadn't heard from either of those idiots Breaux and Fontenot. They probably didn't have one sober brain cell between them.

There had to be another way to find her. She had to be hiding somewhere in the Quarter. There must be some friend he didn't know about who had given Angelique and Gabrielle shelter.

Benoit's stomach was in a clench. He couldn't bear to think of his granddaughter—of Remy's daughter—not living with him now that Sofie was gone.

He would find Gabrielle. He would save her. He would give her the life of a princess. Remy's daughter deserved no less.

Early the next morning, Tyler drove Leah, her grandmother, and Gracie to his father's ranch house.

Big Jim welcomed them with hugs, ushering them inside and out of the cold.

Tyler brought baby JT, in his safety carrier and bundled up so he could hardly move.

Big Jim took the little one from Tyler. The look on his face warmed Tyler's heart. He was glad that they had named their son James Tyler, a name Leah had come up with. She wanted to honor the two most important men in her life, and it made both of them feel great.

"Glad to see you folks." Big Jim gave Leah's grandmother special attention. "Miz Fern, you sure are lookin' mighty fit. And how's my little Gracie?"

Tyler watched his father spread his special kind of love on the three females Tyler himself loved beyond reason.

"What brings you all out so early?" Big Jim asked.

"We wanted to spend some time with you, Dad," Tyler said.

"And it's almost Christmas, so we wanted to make some plans to celebrate with the entire family." Leah slipped out of her coat and brushed a few snowflakes out of her hair.

Gracie hung on Big Jim's arm. "It's so fun to have a big family."

Big Jim kissed her on the forehead. "You are so right, Gracie. We're a very lucky bunch. There are some poor people who got nobody in their lives."

Gracie made a face. "Aww, that's sad, Grampa."

He patted her shoulder and leaned down for another hug. "It is, baby. It is."

"We come ta make sure you got in the Christmas spirit." Gran was grinning as she held aloft a tin of cookies she had baked the night before.

Big Jim's eyes opened wide. "Why, Miz Fern. You sure do know how to make an old man happy."

Tyler loved that his father made a special effort to give attention to Gran. He could tell she was pleased, and that pleased him as well.

Mostly, he and Leah had made the decision to pay this visit so Leah could check out Angelique's needs. She planned to make a shopping trip to Amarillo to finalize her Christmas gift stash.

"You all come back to the kitchen. We were just clearing away the breakfast dishes."

When they had all trooped to the back of the house, where the cavernous open space housed the kitchen, dining room, and den, they saw Angelique at the sink, rinsing dishes and stacking them in the dishwasher.

She turned, smiling prettily. "Oh, hi, folks." She reached for a dish towel to dry her hands. "I didn't know you were coming over."

Gabrielle was seated on the floor nearby, nesting plastic containers and rearranging them.

Leah laughed. "It was a sneak attack."

"My family is welcome to this home anytime they see fit." Big Jim was smiling, but Angelique took it as a rebuff.

"Oh, I'm sorry… I didn't mean…" Her face flushed and she kept her eyes on the floor.

"Not to worry," Big Jim said. "It's just that my home is open to all my kids, and that includes you and Gabrielle."

Leah rushed to her side, putting her arm around Angelique's shoulder. "We're all so casual around here. Half the time I forget to lock the door. Don't worry. We're all here for you."

Tyler wished that were so, recalling Colt's tirade. Looking at Angelique, with her incredible resemblance to the rest of the Garrett clan, he could not understand Colt's attitude. *Nobody could fake those eyes.*

"How about some coffee?" Big Jim invited, gesturing toward the table.

"That would be great," Tyler said. He took the baby carrier from his father and sat down at the table before he began removing layers of warm clothing from his son.

JT stared at him with the same eyes as Angelique's child, who had come to watch what Tyler was doing to his son.

Big Jim looked on as Tyler stripped his son down to a one-piece fleece outfit. "There's my boy." He held his hands out to take the squirming baby.

JT gazed rapturously at his grandpa and grunted several times.

Big Jim was delighted, certain that JT was talking to him, but Tyler figured he was filling his diaper.

Gabrielle was gazing at JT with a wide dimpled grin. "He gots eyes like me."

"And me," Big Jim said. "You got the same eyes as me too."

When they were all seated around the table with coffee or cocoa, Leah made it a point to engage Angelique in a low conversation meant to be "girl talk," but Tyler was close enough to hear.

Leah leaned close to Angelique. "So, how is it going? Are you getting settled in okay?"

Angelique smiled. "Well, I'm really so happy to be here, to have found my father. I never thought I would know him."

Leah reached out to squeeze her hand. "That's really wonderful. We're so glad you're here with us, especially at Christmas. Family should be together for the holidays."

Angelique nodded fiercely, maybe to keep from tearing up.

"Do you have everything you need?" Leah shrugged.

"Sometimes when Ty goes on tour with his band, I go along. It's a real family adventure, especially with the baby. Somehow, I never remember to bring everything I need."

Angelique sucked in a breath and huffed it out. "I had to make some choices when I left New Orleans. I could only fit a few things in my car, so I made sure I brought along the things I cared about the most." She spread her hands. "I mean, if I never go back, I wouldn't miss the rest of the things I left behind."

Tyler couldn't understand this kind of thinking, but Leah seemed to understand completely.

"I know what you mean," Leah said. "When I came here, I was running away from a bad situation, so I grabbed the essentials and hit the road." She turned to look at Tyler. "And then I met the most wonderful man in the whole wide world. He…he gave me what I needed most."

Tyler leaned close and whispered in her ear. "No, baby. You gave me what I needed most." He brushed a kiss against her cheek, and when she turned to face him, he kissed her lips.

They sat smiling at each other, Tyler wondering how he could have found this perfect woman.

"Those two are just crazy 'bout each other," Gran said. "Don't you pay 'em no never mind." She was laughing, her face crinkled into a thousand wrinkles.

Angelique nodded. "I think it must be wonderful to have someone love you like that."

Tyler heard this quiet exchange and wondered about Angelique's child. Did someone love her? Where was that someone now?

Leah turned back to Angelique. "So, am I understanding that you aren't planning on returning to New Orleans?"

Angelique seemed genuinely disturbed by this inquiry. "Um, I don't plan to go back. I hope I can stay here… I mean, around here. Maybe I can find a job?"

Leah's face contorted into a frown. "Really? What kind of job would you look for?"

Angelique shrugged. "I've been a waitress, and I was a bartender before that." She shrugged again. "I know it's not much."

"Don't be silly," Leah said. "I'm sure you were a wonderful waitress and bartender." She reached out to squeeze Angelique's hand. "I don't think you need to worry about it right now. It's almost Christmas. Just relax and enjoy the season."

"I'm trying."

"I'm going to go to Amarillo to shop for Christmas presents, and I thought you might like to go with me." Leah grinned her encouragement. "We could make a day of it. Want to come?"

Angelique's cheeks took on some color. "Oh, I-I don't have much money."

"Not a problem. You can come with us and have lunch in the city. Learn about the area."

Angelique gnawed her lower lip. "Well, I guess I could do that."

Big Jim leaned closer. "I'm so glad you two girls are gettin' along so well. It makes an old man's heart swell up to see two of my favorite ladies makin' friends." He beamed at both of them.

"Well, Big Jim, these two are gonna run off to Amarillo to do some Christmas shoppin'," Gran offered.

Big Jim's brows rose. "They are? Well, Ty, I'm a-gonna let you change your son's poopy diaper, and I'm a-gonna go get a little something to help these girls do their shoppin'." He passed JT to Tyler and rose from the table.

Tyler chuckled and carefully took JT to change the offending and odorous diaper. When he returned, his dad was just getting back to the table.

Big Jim took his place at the head of the table and flipped a card to each of the two young females. "Here you go. I want you girls to have a good time. Buy yourselves something nice, have a great lunch, and get the presents you want to give out."

"Oh, Dad," Angelique said. "I couldn't possibly use your card. People will have to understand that I can't afford to buy presents this year." She pushed the card back toward him.

Leah held out the card he had given her as well.

But Big Jim held his hands up and shook his head. "You two can most certainly accept a little shopping spree on your old man. I would consider it an insult if you don't take these cards and have yourselves a great day."

Angelique sat frowning and gnawing her lower lip, but Leah grinned and nodded. "I hope you have a lot of money to pay this off, Dad. I'm going to make you cry."

Big Jim rolled his eyes and hooted with laughter. "You go ahead on, young lady. Miz Fern and I will be your babysitters while you're out spendin' me into the poorhouse."

Gran laughed and clapped her hands together. "You betcha we will."

Tyler smiled, bouncing his son on his lap. He figured this was his dad's way of making sure Angelique had some spending money for Christmas presents, knowing that Leah would be on hand to steer Angelique's spending. *Way to go, Dad.*

~

Angelique had lots of reservations about this proposed shopping trip. First of all, she was not feeling comfortable about accepting Big Jim's credit card. Nor was she really comfortable leaving Gabrielle in anyone else's care. But Leah was so excited about having a girls' day out with her.

It felt good to have someone welcome her to the family with open arms. Angelique appreciated that Big Jim and Tyler accepted that she was truly a blood relation, and she found it amazing that Tyler's wife seemed to want to be best friends. Angelique had never really had a best girlfriend.

There had been Remy. He was always her best friend, until…until…

"Are you ready?" It was Leah, looking very ready herself.

"Um, yes. Just let me grab this coat that Big Jim lent me." Angelique shrugged into the coat. "I don't know who it belongs to, but it's nice and warm. I hope the owner doesn't mind me wearing it."

Leah tilted her head to one side. "From the hall closet?" At Angelique's nod, she sucked in a big breath and blew it out. "I think that coat belonged to Elizabeth, Big Jim's wife…Ty's mother."

"Oh, no! I shouldn't be wearing it." Angelique started to take it off.

"No. It's only a coat. I'm sure Big Jim wanted you to be warm." Leah made a motion for her to follow. "Let's get on the road."

Remembering her nosedive into the snowbank, Angelique shuddered. "Um, do you think the road crews have put sand on the road?"

"It's not a problem for us. We have snow tires on the truck."

Angelique wasn't sure what that meant, but Leah sounded so assured, she felt safer and followed her outside to the truck. She was surprised to find Tyler in the driver's seat and the truck running.

Leah opened the front passenger door and told Angelique to climb in.

"I didn't know we had a chauffeur," Angelique said.

"I'm just along to carry your packages and drop you by the door," Tyler said. "I'm here to serve."

"Don't you want to sit up here by your husband?" Angelique asked.

Leah grinned. "I want you to sit up there by your brother." She hoisted herself up into the seat behind the passenger seat.

Angelique had to flash a grin. To be acknowledged as Tyler's sister was a major step. She stepped up on the running board and seated herself next to Tyler, thankful that the heater was going. "Hey, Bro."

Tyler gave her a little salute. "Strap in, Sis."

Derrick thought he should have called, but at the end of the day, he found himself taking a detour on his way home. He pulled in at the Garrett ranch and his tires bumped over the cattle guard. The trees that grew close to the road were bare, giving punctuation to the starkness of the landscape. Fence posts lined the fields on either side of the private road. When he came to a stop in front of Big Jim Garrett's ranch house, he was still trying to come up with a reason for his impromptu visit.

Derrick was the sheriff now. He had a standing in the county, and he didn't want to do anything to mess that up. Certainly not anything to offend one of the most powerful men in the area.

While he was sitting in his truck, the motor idling, someone turned on the outside light. *Busted.*

Derrick killed the motor and got out. He climbed the steps to the porch.

"Hey, Derrick." Big Jim held the door open. "C'mon in and get warm."

"Thanks a lot." Derrick stamped off his boots before stepping inside.

"Glad to see you, but I hope you're not here on official business."

"No, sir. I was driving by and thought I'd check in." He followed Big Jim into the kitchen. "And I might as well confess I was hoping to catch sight of your beautiful blue-eyed daughter."

Big Jim grinned from ear to ear. "That's not a bad thing. She is a beauty, isn't she?"

Derrick huffed out a big sigh. "That she is, sir." He took off his leather gloves and stuffed them in the pocket of his jacket, but shed the jacket, placing it over the back of one of the kitchen chairs.

Big Jim gestured for him to take a seat as he brought

the coffeepot and another mug. "This should fix you right up."

"Might I inquire as to the whereabouts of the lovely Miss Angelique?" Derrick accepted the mug of steaming coffee gratefully.

Big Jim sat down and lifted his own mug in a salute of sorts. "My beautiful daughter and beautiful daughter-in-law have gone to Amarillo to shop for Christmas presents."

Derrick felt his brows draw together. "It's getting dark, Big Jim. Do you think they're okay?"

Big Jim smiled and sipped his coffee. "I'm pretty sure they're having a good time with Tyler to herd them around. He drove them into Amarillo and will make sure they come home after they've shopped the stores out."

"Then they're in good hands." Derrick's gut relaxed. Surely the ladies would be well taken care of with Tyler along.

The two men silently sipped coffee.

Finally Big Jim set his mug on the table and leaned back, crossing his meaty arms over his chest. "So you like my daughter?"

Derrick managed to swallow his coffee without choking. "Yes, sir. I think she's really nice."

Big Jim nodded. "I think so too. Maybe you want to get to know her better?"

Derrick's throat felt dry, and his voice sounded raspy. "That would be great."

"Well, you know I think the world of you, Derrick. You're a good man."

"Thank you, sir."

"But this whole thing…you know, being father to a

daughter? That's all new to me, and I'm feelin' pretty protective."

"I understand, sir." Derrick thought he would be asked to leave soon.

"So, I want to get it out in the open, right up front…"

Derrick braced himself.

"If you hurt my little girl, I will have no problem burying you so far in the ground even the wild hogs won't find you."

The threat hung in the air between them.

Derrick wondered if Big Jim realized he had just threatened an officer of the law. *Probably not*. He eased out a breath. "You must know I would never do anything to hurt Angelique. I'm not that kind of man."

"Didn't think so." Big Jim finished off his coffee and reached for the pot. "Need a refill?"

Derrick offered his mug and watched Big Jim pour. "Thanks."

That's when the front door burst open and the noisy shoppers entered the house. Angelique and Leah rushed into the kitchen, giggling.

"Oh, you're going to be so sorry you gave us these cards, Dad." Leah was grinning and her cheeks were rosy.

Also rosy-cheeked, Angelique looked surprised to find Derrick there, but smiled. "Where is my baby girl? I'm never away from her for this long."

Derrick thought she looked even more beautiful than he recalled. He winked at her and she nodded shyly.

"Leah, your grandmother was tired so she and both babies are bedded down together." Big Jim rose from the table and hugged each woman in turn. "You ladies must have emptied the stores."

"We did," Leah said, but offered up both cards.

Big Jim held them up to his ear. "Oh, tell me about it." He feigned a worried expression. "Oh, the poor little things are crying."

This sent both women into another fit of giggles.

Tyler came into the house then, laden with bags. "Here comes Santa Claus…" he sang out. "This is just Angelique's stuff. My little darling has her stash in the truck."

"We need to get home," Leah said. "I came in to give you the wonderful magic cards and to gather Gran and my children."

Big Jim gave her a hug and kiss on the forehead. "Your daughter is watching television, and your son is snuggled with your grandmother in her old room."

Angelique and Leah went to find their children, and Tyler set the bags and packages down on the table. "Night, Dad. See you, Derrick. I'll probably have to carry someone."

Derrick gave a wave from his place at the table. He felt a stab of unaccustomed envy for his friend, the happily married family man. Beau was also happily married with a daughter. Only Colton remained childless, but he seemed to be happy with his wife, and Derrick supposed they would procreate at some point in time.

He had been content to take on the challenges of his job, but hadn't really had time to search for that perfect woman with whom he could spend a lifetime. At least that was the excuse he gave himself.

He usually showed up at the Eagles Hall on a Friday or Saturday night when there was a live band, and he was known to dance with a few of the local ladies, but no one had snagged his attention. At least not to the extent that little Miss Angelique Guillory had. For the first time ever, he was thinking how nice it would be to have a sweet little one like Angelique's daughter, Gabrielle.

Derrick swallowed hard. What was he thinking? He hadn't spent much time with this woman, so he must be enamored by her beauty and her seemingly sweet personality.

Just then, she came into the kitchen, a broad grin on her face. "My precious little one is asleep in her bed. You and Leah's grandmother must have worn her out."

Big Jim gave her a hug and gestured for her to take a seat. "Did you have dinner?"

"Sure did." She rubbed both hands over her middle. "Stuffed, in fact."

"Well, it sure does look good on you." Big Jim started to sit down and then stopped himself, meeting Derrick's eyes. "Um, I think I need to go check on something in the barn. Angelique, will you entertain Derrick for me?"

She looked puzzled but nodded.

"I'll be back in a while." Big Jim shrugged into his jacket and left by the back door, pulling on his leather gloves.

Derrick understood that he was being given a chance to spend time with Angelique, without an audience for a change. "He sure nailed it."

"Nailed it?" As she stared at him with her incredible blue eyes wide open and those luscious lips parted, Derrick had an overwhelming urge to kiss her.

"He said you look good, and I'm agreeing with him."

She blinked and looked down at her hands. "Oh, well...thanks."

"Angelique, I'm about to ask you out on a date, but I'm a little nervous because I don't know if you've got someone special in your life." He reached out to take her clasped hands in both of his.

She looked stunned.

He exhaled, just then realizing he was holding his breath. "I would like to take you to the Eagles Hall Friday night. There's a live band out of Dallas, and they're having a party to benefit a children's facility."

Angelique pressed her lips together for a moment, which caused her dimples to flash. "I-I can't go out with you. I can't leave my daughter."

He held her hands and gazed at her, wondering how anyone could be so unassuming. "We can bring Gabrielle. The Eagles Hall is kid-friendly." He stroked his fingertips over the back of her hand. "That is, if you would like to go out with me."

"Oh, um…well, I haven't been on a date in some time." The beautiful grin returned. "I'm not sure I'm exactly datable."

He raised her hand and brushed his lips over the back. "I would like to date you."

Her cheeks took on more color. "I can't imagine why…but I guess that would be okay."

"So, I can pick you and Gabrielle up about six on Friday, and we can grab a bite at the Eagles'."

"Um, sure." Again the lips pressed together.

He hoped she would be able to relax and have a good time. He stayed at the table, holding her hand and chatting, until Big Jim returned from his supposed late-night errand.

Derrick took his leave and drove to his own much-smaller ranch, grinning all the way home.

Chapter 6

By Friday, Angelique was a bundle of nerves. She had no idea what to wear, or why it was okay to bring Gabrielle, or if she should be going on a date anyway. It was less than a year since Remy had… No, she couldn't even think about the fact that he was no longer with her—or about the reason he was gone.

But the entire Garrett clan seemed to think it was a good idea. Big Jim informed her that most of the family would probably show up at the Eagles Hall. It was apparently the thing to do on a Friday night.

She tried to quiet the uproar going on in her stomach. Surely, things would go well if everyone was going along.

Leah was excited for her. "That's great! Derrick is such a babe, and he's a really nice man."

Gran grinned broadly. "I knew that young sheriff feller was sweet on you!"

Angelique had a little trouble thinking of Derrick as the sheriff. The lawmen she recalled in New Orleans were all bought and paid for by Alphonse Benoit, her beloved Remy's corrupt father. She didn't know how such a wonderful and kind man could have been sired by someone as evil as the elder Benoit.

And now, this tall, broad-shouldered sheriff wanted to date her. How did that happen? She wasn't sure she still remembered how to be "dated."

"I brought you a pair of my jeans," Leah said. "I don't mean to be pushy, but you would probably feel more comfortable in denim."

"Oh, thanks." Angelique held up the pair of jeans, and thought the size should be fine, but wasn't sure why they would be appropriate. She hadn't brought much in the way of wardrobe, in favor of grabbing more useful things in her hurried escape from the Big Easy.

"And I didn't know what your shoe size was, but I brought a pair of my old boots."

Angelique swallowed hard. Now what? She gazed at the somewhat scuffed footwear. "I wear a seven-and-a-half shoe."

"Cool. These are an eight. Just wear a pair of thick socks, and you should be fine." Leah was grinning. "I doubt that Derrick will stomp on your toes, but better safe than sorry."

Angelique nodded, totally confused as to the goings-on at this Eagles place. Sounded awful so far.

But by six o'clock, she was decked out to Leah's satisfaction, and a bit nervous.

When Angelique emerged from her bedroom, Leah ushered her to the kitchen, where Big Jim, Tyler, and most important, Derrick sat around the table.

Derrick jumped to his feet, but Big Jim and Tyler greeted her with applause.

"You ladies look extra lovely tonight," Big Jim said.

Tyler let out an earsplitting whistle. "Hot! They look hot, Dad."

Judging by Derrick's expression, he agreed.

Gabrielle was standing by her grandfather. "I gots a cookie!" she shouted and held up a sticky hand holding a mauled cookie. She was gnawing on it and rocking back and forth, holding onto Big Jim's hand. She looked so content, comfortable with her grandfather...the good one.

"Hi, Angelique," Derrick said softly. "You look... amazing."

Everyone was grinning at her, so Angelique thought she must pass muster. "I'm ready if everyone else is. What time does this thing start, anyway?"

Big Jim let out a loud guffaw. "This 'thing' is ongoing. The Eagles serves great burgers and other refreshments. They close the kitchen about seven thirty, and the band tunes up at eight."

Derrick reached out to take her arm. "You'll have a good time, Angelique. I promise."

They all bundled up and climbed into their various vehicles.

Angelique and Gabrielle rode with Derrick, and they got to chat along the way. Derrick told her about growing up on a ranch, and Angelique gave very little information about her past life in New Orleans. It was best that way.

Since they were fairly early, Derrick found a parking place close to the entrance. He climbed out and trudged through the snow to open the passenger door for Angelique. She stepped down into his arms, realizing she was standing way too close to a man who was gazing at her like she was the last cookie in the tin.

"We better get Gabi out of her car seat," she said.

Derrick gazed down at her, his expression combustible. "Sure."

Angelique flashed a smile and slipped her arms

around his neck. "Oh, just kiss me before we both freeze."

"Yes, ma'am." Derrick drew her closer and brushed his lips against hers. His kiss started out gentle but deepened.

It had been a long time since she had been kissed, especially by someone who made her toes curl up in her borrowed boots.

When he drew away, Angelique realized the tempo she heard was her own heart trying to beat its way out of her chest.

Derrick gazed at her and tipped his hat before going to remove Gabrielle from her car seat. He carried the little girl and reached to take Angelique's gloved hand. "Let's get you ladies warmed up."

Angelique couldn't imagine how much warmer she might be without exploding. And yet, when she saw her daughter with her arms around Derrick's neck, her heart warmed even more.

As they approached the Eagles Hall, she noticed that the exterior was decorated with Christmas lights but they weren't turned on yet, as it was still daylight.

She tried to rouse her Christmas spirit, but she had been operating on fear for too long. Maybe if she could get through this one, she might believe in all this jolly stuff.

But somehow, seeing her precious daughter clinging to the neck of this gentle giant gave her hope.

Maybe, if she had escaped New Orleans, there might be a way to reinvent Angelique Guillory and find her real home in the heart of all this family.

Derrick held on to her arm as they climbed the steps to the Eagles Hall, but he stopped to stomp the snow off his boots, so Angelique followed suit. Once inside, he handed cash to the woman sitting at a card table by the door. She tore off two tickets for him, and they walked into the cavernous hall.

It was a huge space with a dance floor in the middle and long tables arranged around the room. There was a raised stage on the left, and Angelique could see a kitchen on the far side of the hall. Recorded Christmas carols were playing through the sound system.

"There they are," Derrick said, and when Angelique followed in the direction he indicated, she could see Big Jim and Gracie and Fern Davis holding down a long table close to the dance floor.

Big Jim waved them over, a grin on his face. "C'mon over here, folks. We've snagged this table. Leah and Ty are getting us some hamburgers."

"And I'm really hungry," Gracie announced.

"She's a growin' girl." Fern gave her a hug.

Angelique peeled out of her borrowed coat and arranged it over the back of a chair, then removed Gabrielle's knit cap, fluffing her dark curls.

"Here," Big Jim said. "Let me have my little Gabi." He reached for Gabrielle, but she clung to Derrick's neck. Big Jim drew back, frowning.

Derrick turned to Angelique. "Let's go order some food. I think Gabi would like some dinner."

Angelique had fed Gabrielle prior to Derrick's arrival at the ranch, but thought it best not to mention it right then. "Oh, good. I'm really hungry." She tucked her hand in the crook of Derrick's arm, and they went to the kitchen area. It had a wide counter, and a few people were in line ahead of them.

"Look! It's Angelique and Derrick." Leah tugged on Tyler's sleeve. "And doesn't little Gabrielle look adorable?"

Angelique gave a little finger wave. "Hello, you two. What's good to eat?"

Leah stepped closer. "It's a very limited menu, but everything they serve is delish. I ordered a cheeseburger and fries." She gave a little giggle. "Ty ordered two."

Tyler patted his very flat stomach. "Big man needs big meal."

Derrick nodded. "What he said."

When they were able to order, Angelique chose her own cheeseburger with a side of potato salad, while Derrick got a couple of burgers with fries.

Derrick very seriously read part of the menu to Gabrielle.

"Finch fwies," Gabrielle insisted.

By the time they returned to the table with their food, Tyler and Leah were dealing out the goodies to the others.

Angelique was digging into her food when she felt a presence. She looked up to find Colton and Misty Garrett staring at her, not quite frowning but definitely not smiling.

Cold. That best described their expressions.

Suddenly, Angelique's food lost its appeal. She tried to swallow, but her throat felt tight.

"Over here, Son." Big Jim was waving at the newcomers.

Thankfully, Colt's attention was diverted and his stony expression morphed into one more pleasant as he ushered Misty toward where Big Jim was pointing.

Angelique heaved a sigh, but when she turned around, Derrick was frowning.

"Don't let them get you down." He watched Gabrielle grab a crinkle-cut french fry and cram it in her mouth. She was seated on his thigh, within grabbing distance of her food. "Want some ketchup on that, Gabi?"

Gabrielle held up the remains of the fry, looking hopeful.

Derrick selected a different fry and dipped it in a little ketchup, while Gabrielle ingested the rest of the one in her hand.

Angelique resisted the urge to wipe Gabrielle's face, because to do so would interfere with the bonding process going on before her eyes.

"Colt's trying to protect his dad," Derrick continued in a low voice. "He's always been the big brother, protecting the younger ones. Now, he's under the mistaken impression that he has to protect Big Jim from you." He looked up to meet her eyes.

"Me? What's there to be afraid of?" A flicker of anger roiled in her gut. "Doesn't he understand how thrilled I am to finally know who my father is…and to know that he didn't know about me? I always figured he was some weasel who dumped my mom when she got pregnant." She dropped her gaze and blinked furiously.

Derrick reached over to squeeze her tightly fisted hand. He had given Gabrielle another french fry, so his fingers were a little greasy.

This struck her as funny, so she had to smile.

"You better eat that cheeseburger, because the band is going to be tuning up soon and I'm gonna want to dance." He winked at her.

She handed him a napkin. "Well, I suggest you wipe Gabi's face, or you're going to be wearing all that on your nice shirt."

Fortunately, Gabrielle submitted willingly to Derrick cleaning her face and held out her little hands to have them wiped as well.

Angelique ended up taking Gabrielle to the ladies' room to give her a wash-up. She was totally involved with her daughter, but when she turned around, she found Misty Garrett leaning up against the bathroom door, barring her exit.

Angelique put Gabrielle on her hip and took a few steps toward the door. "Excuse me."

But Misty didn't budge. "I want to know what you're up to. Why are you trying to scam my father-in-law? He's a very nice man."

Angelique inhaled and blew out a breath, trying not to upset Gabrielle. "He is my father. I don't care if you don't believe me. He knows the truth, so if you will please let us pass…"

There was a knocking at the door and someone was pushing on it.

Misty moved to one side, but stood with her arms crossed over her chest, still glaring.

"Oh!" It was Leah who pushed into the restroom. "What's going on, girls?" Her head swiveled from Angelique to Misty and back again.

Silence!

Leah turned on Misty. "Listen, you have to stop being so mean. You and Colt have no right to be such asses."

Misty's mouth dropped open. "I cannot believe you said that. What's the matter with you?"

Leah shook her finger at Misty. "What is the matter with you? Are you jealous that Dad's got a daughter?" She fisted her hands on her hips.

Misty made a sound that was more like a squawk. "How could you even think I would be jealous?"

"Because that's what's wrong with Colt. He's jealous that Angelique and Gabrielle make Dad so happy. Can't you see that he's just thrilled that she found him?"

"Wait! Please don't fight." Angelique clutched Gabrielle close to her chest. "I don't want to be the cause of any fighting in the family." She wasn't able to keep the tears from spilling down her cheeks.

Leah slung her arm around Angelique's shoulders. "Not worth getting upset about. I'm sure Misty and Colt will come to their senses."

Misty emitted a huff and gazed at the ceiling.

"Because..." Leah paused for dramatic effect. "I'm sure they don't want to ruin Christmas for everyone."

Misty rolled her eyes and huffed out another huge sigh before slamming out of the restroom.

"Let me hold Gabrielle while you mop up your eyes. I'm sure you don't want Derrick to be concerned." Leah reached to take the child. "He and Colt have been friends since they were kids."

Angelique let that sink in as she pressed a damp paper towel to her eyes. She figured that Derrick would have to side with one of his close friends over a relative stranger, even if he seemed to be attracted to her.

When they got back to the table, she saw that Misty was still frothing mad, but she sat beside Colt, gripping his arm. They had chosen to sit as far from Angelique as possible.

Big Jim seemed to have pulled back into himself, as though evaluating the situation.

Derrick stood as she approached, pulling out her chair. He reached to take Gabrielle, who also stretched her arms out to him. It seemed they had formed a pretty solid bond.

Having the handsome sheriff acting the gentleman made Angelique feel appreciated. For a woman who had been taken for granted most of her life, this was heaven.

Leah sank onto the chair next to her husband. She leaned against him, resting her head on his shoulder. Tyler gave her a kiss on the forehead. He held their baby son.

It pleased Angelique to see the strong men treating the young ones with such tenderness. She took a sip of her soda, realizing how tense she was.

Derrick reached over to take her hand. He looked at her questioningly.

She was reluctant to tell him about the confrontation in the restroom. "Everything looks so festive." She forced herself to focus on her surroundings.

There was a giant and brightly lit Christmas tree sitting in a niche beside the raised stage platform. There were Christmas lights strung around the walls too.

She noticed several men setting up equipment for the band. She liked music. She had loved to listen to the jazz and blues musicians New Orleans was famous for. She also really enjoyed zydeco, the spirited tunes always lifting her spirits.

At the moment, her spirits had been slapped in the face.

Angelique stole a furtive glance at the other end of

the table. Big Jim and Colt were deep in conversation, while Misty sat tight-jawed and silent.

The canned Christmas music had been shut off. The musicians began playing something jaunty, and many couples took to the dance floor.

"Let me take our trash and dump it." Derrick stood and picked up the tray with wrappings from their burgers and fries. She reached for Gabrielle, but Derrick shook his head. "I got her."

She watched him skirt the dance floor until he disappeared. Then he reappeared on the other side, heading back to the table...but he went to the other end and passed Gabrielle to Big Jim.

For his part, Big Jim was beaming from ear to ear, but Angelique's insides hit the panic button. Derrick exchanged some pleasantries with Big Jim and Colt before returning to where Angelique waited. She looked up at him. "Why did you hand Gabrielle to Big Jim?"

He sat down beside her and gathered her hands in his. "For two reasons. First, I wanted Colt and Misty to get a good look at Gabi and to see how much Big Jim loves her."

So, he knows. Angelique bit her lower lip and glanced to where Big Jim sat making silly faces for a laughing Gabrielle. She noted that Colt and Misty were paying close attention. "What's the other reason?"

He kissed her hand. "I want to dance with you."

Gabrielle was giving Big Jim sloppy kisses. "My gwampa!" she assured Colt.

"Isn't she the sweetest little thing?" Big Jim asked. "Just

look at those curls and, of course, her eyes. She's gonna be a heartbreaker, just like her mother and"—he swallowed hard—"her grandmother. She was a beauty too."

A muscle in Colt's jaw twitched. Misty squeezed his arm, but she looked upset as well.

Big Jim knew there was tension between his sons, but he refused to buy into it. They would have to work it out between themselves… At least that's what he was thinking.

"Dad, you seem to have bought into all this…this…"

Big Jim turned to give his oldest son a stern glare. "Be careful what you say, Son." He held up one of his large hands, cradling Gabrielle in his other arm. "I do not know why you've got a stick up your—" He glanced down at the young one in his arms. She was gazing at him, her big blue eyes fixed on his face. He lowered his voice. "Up your rear end… But I suggest you reel it back while you're still in the will."

"Dad, I—"

"Let me explain it to you. I was really in love with Sofie Guillory when I was in college. We had…relations. Can you get that through your thick skull?"

Colt stared at Big Jim, but he remained silent.

"I have no doubt that Angelique is my daughter and Gabi is my granddaughter… No doubt at all. Do you understand?"

"Yes, Dad. I understand." Colt's mouth was tight, and Big Jim figured he was not convinced.

Big Jim watched as Derrick led Angelique out onto the floor and they danced to a slow song. It was easy to see that Angelique was new to country-western dancing. But she seemed to be confident in Derrick's arms.

A slow smile stretched across Big Jim's face. It seemed that Derrick really liked his daughter. Big Jim knew Derrick was a good man, but he also knew that Angelique was vulnerable. He had not asked her any questions about the father of her child. He figured she would confide in him when the time was right.

But it seemed that Derrick Shelton was falling for his daughter and granddaughter at the same time.

Derrick was from a good local family, and he had a little ranch, but Big Jim wasn't sure he should be encouraging this relationship. She had only just arrived in the neighborhood, and Derrick was the first man she'd met. She should take it slow. She was so beautiful she'd have the pick of the local bachelors. No need to make a swift decision. Besides, he wanted her and Gabrielle all to himself for a while.

He surveyed the couple whirling in circles around the dance floor. The grin on Angelique's face warmed Big Jim's heart.

Maybe he would give Derrick a chance. Maybe the sheriff wanted to entertain Angelique? Maybe he wasn't serious about the relationship? Maybe he was just being nice to the newest members of the Garrett family?

But Big Jim couldn't ever recall seeing Derrick Shelton with any particular girl before. Maybe his intentions were sincere.

Angelique was having a great time. Derrick didn't seem to mind that she stumbled sometimes, but she was getting the hang of it.

Although having Derrick's strong arms around her

made her feel protected when they were dancing to a waltz or what he called a two-step, she most enjoyed a funny stomping and shuffling dance called the "Cotton-Eyed Joe."

Derrick danced beside her and led her around the floor, kicking and stomping alongside. It was a lively tune, and she was laughing by the time the song ended. She collapsed against Derrick, giggling. "That was so much fun."

He twirled her into a dip, and when he raised her back up, he kissed her. It wasn't a passionate kiss. It was a fun kiss. But it was still a kiss.

Derrick walked her back to the table, his arm around her.

Angelique glanced over to see that Big Jim was watching them. She didn't think he looked too pleased. But Leah and Tyler were grinning, while Colt and Misty glared. No guesswork needed with this family.

Angelique told Derrick she needed to check on Gabrielle.

Big Jim gave her up grudgingly. "But we're getting along so good."

Angelique laughed out loud. "Well, if you would like to take her to potty…"

Big Jim held his hands up in surrender. "No, thanks. I did my share of potty duty with the three boys."

Leah walked with her to the ladies' room, JT in her arms. "Good idea."

Angelique sighed. "It's gotta be done." She pushed into the restroom with her backside and held the door open for Leah to enter.

There was a changing station, and Leah nodded and placed JT on it. "Going for it."

Angelique peeled Gabrielle out of her fleece leggings and placed paper towels on one of the toilet seats. Then she held her daughter in place while she relieved herself.

Leah changed JT while Angelique washed her hands as best she could, one at a time. "I'm glad to see that you and Derrick are getting along so well."

Angelique laughed. "You could say that."

"It sure looks like it. I wanted you to know that Ty and I are happy for you."

Angelique shrugged. "I don't know what I am. He seems to be such a nice guy."

"That he is. Ty and his brothers have known him since childhood. Ty said he had never known Derrick to be so openly…uh, affectionate."

That pleased Angelique. But with all the things she had left behind in New Orleans, she thought maybe she had left behind her ability to care deeply… *Do I have the capacity to love again?* She tried to search herself but couldn't find an answer for this question.

"Well, you do like Derrick, don't you?"

Angelique sucked in a deep breath and released it. "Of course. What's not to like? He's a thoroughly beautiful specimen." She nuzzled nose to nose with her daughter, delighted when she giggled. "I'm so new here. I need to find some kind of job. I can't stay with my father forever."

Leah frowned. "I'm sure Big Jim is completely happy to have you there. It's such a huge, rambling house. He gets lonely by himself. The brothers try to make sure to spend time helping out around the ranch. Lots of jobs to do."

"I'm sure. Glad they're around to help."

"I mean, Big Jim isn't all that old. Mid-fifties, I think. And he's very healthy and active." Leah bit her lower lip, then shrugged. "He was dating someone last year…a teacher in Langston. I thought it might lead to something, but it sort of fizzled out."

Angelique tried to think of Big Jim going out on dates. He was a very attractive man. He looked like his sons, who were all very handsome. They all shared the same unusual eye color as Angelique and Gabrielle, and all four men were tall and broad-shouldered with thick hair. But Big Jim's once-dark hair was now silver. All in all, a very fine-looking man. Angelique could understand why her mother had lost her heart to him.

"Shall we join the gentlemen?" Leah had gathered JT and was heading for the door.

"Coming." Angelique followed her back to the table, wondering if the relationship between her father and the schoolteacher could be rekindled.

Chapter 7

DERRICK AND TYLER HAD BEEN CONVERSING WHILE their ladies were in the restroom together.

Tyler seemed to be truly happy that Derrick was seeing Angelique. He had reminded Derrick that his Leah had had a daughter when they had first met and that he had adopted Gracie after they had married. "It worked out fine. I love Gracie like she was my own."

Derrick had punched Tyler's arm. "Are you trying to tell me something, bud?"

"Naw. Just wanted to let you know that marrying a woman with a child could work out really well. It sure has for me."

"So I see. It's a little early in this relationship to be shopping for rings." Derrick smiled as he saw Angelique and Leah emerge from the ladies' room. He was glad that Angelique had a friend. She needed one.

He stood up and reached to take Gabrielle from Angelique while also pulling out her chair. With all the adults milling about he was afraid Gabi might get stepped on.

Gabrielle reached for him as she was being handed off. For some reason, the smile and reaching of small arms never failed to stir him.

Gazing at her, Derrick could imagine becoming her father and watching her grow up…with Angelique by his side. He tried to wrap his brain around that… *Couldn't*. He'd been a bachelor too long.

Maybe he needed to slow things down. But there was something about this woman that made him want to be with her all the time. When he was not with her, he was thinking about her.

"I don't know how long this evening is supposed to go on, but Gabi is yawning and I'm used to going to bed pretty early. Would it be dreadful to leave early?" She gazed up at Derrick, her big blue eyes imploring him.

"Of course not. Let's tell Big Jim that we're leaving. He may have something to say about it." In his mind, he wondered if Big Jim would want them to be alone in the ranch house. He had caught Big Jim's expression but couldn't read it.

Angelique pushed her chair back and stood, ready to call it a night.

Derrick scrambled to his feet, helping Angelique into her coat and finding Gabrielle's knit cap, jacket, and blanket.

They said good night to Leah and Tyler and then braved the crowd at the other end of the table.

Big Jim had been observing their preparations, his countenance unreadable. But when they approached, he stood, embracing Angelique and Gabrielle in one big bear hug. "Aww, you folks aren't gonna be party poopers, are you?"

Angelique planted a kiss on his cheek. "Sorry, Dad. I'm really tired."

"Well, the back door is unlocked," Big Jim said. "Be careful driving my daughter home, young man." He offered a hand to Derrick, though his grip was very firm when they shook. If ever a handshake could convey a threat, this was it.

"Yes, sir. I'm always careful." Derrick grinned at him. "I'm the sheriff now, remember?"

Big Jim slapped him on the back, seemingly jovial. "Oh, yeah! I forgot that you replaced our old sheriff. We got some young blood now."

Derrick couldn't tell if Big Jim was joking or being sarcastic. He suspected the latter. He ushered Angelique to the front of the Eagles Hall and left them while he trudged through the newly fallen snow to the truck. The motor growled into wakefulness, protesting the cold. "Atta girl," he muttered. "We have some very important passengers to pick up." He let the engine idle a few moments and then turned on the heater and defroster.

When he drew to a stop in front of the hall, he left the truck idling while he brought Angelique and Gabrielle outside, carefully installing the child in her safety seat.

"Oh, it's snowing," Angelique commented as she climbed into the passenger seat.

"Just a little." Derrick rounded the vehicle to take his place beside her. "Just relax and I'll have you home in no time."

But Angelique was wide-eyed, making comments about the feathery snowflakes. "I don't ever recall it snowing in New Orleans."

Derrick chuckled. "Well, it always snows here in north Texas. We usually always have a white Christmas."

"Really?"

"Sure. We enjoy each of the four seasons in turn, and each has its special beauty."

When they arrived at the ranch house, Derrick went around to the unlocked back door and walked through the eerily quiet house to admit Angelique and Gabrielle through the front. Gabrielle had fallen asleep during the drive, so he carried her inside and to the bedroom Angelique directed him to. She removed the child's outer layers and arranged her comfortably before quietly tiptoeing out of the room.

"Thanks for a wonderful evening, Derrick," she said. "I'm sorry I flaked out so early. I guess the past few days have finally caught up with me."

"Thanks for spending the evening with me." Derrick leaned over to deliver a quick kiss to her cheek. "I hope we can do something together again soon."

"Me too." She stifled a yawn.

"You get some rest. I'll let myself out." He turned to leave, but she caught him by the arm.

"More kisses, please."

Big Jim had been seething since his lovely daughter, Angelique, had left the Eagles Hall with Derrick Shelton. Derrick might be the new young sheriff, but that boy had been a running buddy of his son Colt. His two younger sons had tagged along.

What a ragtag crew! He recalled their summer faces, suntanned and usually a bit dirty, considering what boys can get into… Derrick had been a part of his own sons' exploits, so he had grown up as an almost-Garrett son—like an extension of the family.

Big Jim clenched the steering wheel, his knuckles white with the force of his grip. His jaw was tight as he drove toward the ranch house. It was late, or early morning, whichever way he considered it, but he'd had both Colt's and Tyler's families at his table and couldn't really leave them any earlier.

The moon shone white and full in a black, starry sky, lending an opalescent glow to the countryside. The new-fallen snow embraced the landscape like a fleece blanket.

He hoped Angelique was all right, alone at the ranch by herself, with Gabrielle for company. At least he hoped they were alone. What if that Derrick Shelton had taken liberties? Derrick was a good-looking young man by anyone's standards. It would be easy for him to take advantage of Angelique. He was obviously taken with her. But what if he had made unwanted advances in the absence of any other family members there to protect her?

He thought about Derrick as a young boy, always polite and ready for fun with the three Garrett sons. And even though he liked and respected Derrick Shelton as a man and as the recently appointed sheriff, Big Jim wasn't about to trust him with his newly discovered daughter.

Big Jim knew he had a lot to make up for, having had no knowledge of her existence until recently, but he found that all his fatherly emotions were coming to the fore.

Sure, Angelique was a grown woman with a child of her own, but Big Jim was experiencing a delayed feeling of their relationship and a certain sense of protectiveness.

That emotion had been present when his boys were younger, but since they had reached adulthood, he had allowed them to fight their own battles…mostly.

But Angelique was a whole different story. She was a girl and, as such, deserved to be treated with respect. She exuded a sense of vulnerability, an aura of fragility as though she was afraid of something…something bad.

Big Jim turned off the highway and drove through the big horseshoe-shaped arch over the entrance to the Garrett ranch. The tires of his truck bumped across the cattle guard, jarring his back teeth together. It was a long drive to the Garrett ranch house, with Colt's and Tyler's much newer houses erected further back into the property.

When he first sighted his own house, Big Jim was filled with a sense of fury. *That damned Derrick Shelton is still there inside my darkened house.*

He was filled with thoughts of all he was going to do to that young rascal. *How could he take advantage of my Angelique?*

Big Jim slammed to a stop and climbed out, in a near-murderous rage. He charged up to the house, finding the front door locked. *Danged asshole is shacked up with my daughter, and I'm gonna break his fool neck.*

He unlocked the door and crept inside in stealth mode, imagining the worst. But when he stepped into the den, he found Derrick alone and asleep. Thank heavens the young man was fully clothed and didn't appear to have removed anything other than his leather jacket and Stetson.

Big Jim heaved a deep sigh, allowing all his anger to slide away. He approached the sleeping man and touched his shoulder.

Derrick stirred and opened his eyes. "Hey, Big Jim," he said in a sleepy voice.

"Hey, yourself." Big Jim gestured to the back of the house. "You wanna stay over? It's pretty late."

"No thanks, sir. I better be getting home." He stretched his long arms and legs. "I didn't want to leave Angelique and Gabi all alone out here. I know it's unlikely that someone would come way out here to break in, but somehow I didn't want to leave them." He rose and gathered his jacket and hat.

Big Jim gave him a couple of pats on the back as he walked the young man to the front door. "You did the right thing, son. Thanks for takin' care of my girls."

Angelique lay in bed, relaxed and comfortable for the first time in so long she couldn't recall when she'd felt so good.

It was hope that was flexing its muscle deep inside her. She hadn't dared to feel hopeful in a long time… maybe never. Maybe there had always been that skinny tightrope underfoot, and maybe her life had always been teetering on the edge.

She stretched her arms and legs, flexing her wrists and ankles. The sheets felt cool in the places where her body had not warmed them. It was still dark outside. She craned her neck to see the small clock on the nightstand. It was just after four in the morning, but considering that she had fallen in bed relatively early, she wasn't ready to roll over and go back to sleep. She crept out of bed, placing her bare feet on the soft carpet, and made her way over to the small twin-size bed. Gabrielle was on her back, her little mouth agape. She looked very angelic in the soft moonglow.

Angelique pulled the blanket up around her child,

although the leggings and knit top she'd worn the night before were probably keeping her plenty warm.

The window looked out on the land to the north side of the Garrett house. Angelique leaned against the windowsill and gazed out at the scene. It didn't look real. It was as though someone had created it using a roll of quilt batting over everything. The snow was deep and fresh. It glistened as though it was paved with diamond dust.

She looked at the moon, sitting in the blackest of skies. Only a few of the brightest stars were visible, causing her to wonder where the rest of the little twinklers were hiding.

The house was quiet, but not eerie. It was snug, like a fortress, impenetrable by the enemies who sought her. Those who did not wish her well.

Angelique stifled a shudder. Although she was feeling safe at the moment, she must not let her guard down. She couldn't pretend that Alfonse Benoit would ever give up. He would eventually find her, so great was his evil reach. The best she could hope for was to embed her daughter safely within the Garrett family. Perhaps if Benoit could punish Angelique, he might overlook Gabrielle.

And then there was Derrick. Such a sweet man.

Angelique heaved a huge sigh. Too bad nothing could come of it. The first sweet man she had fallen in love with—the man who had fathered Gabrielle—had lost his life, and it was her fault. At least according to his father.

Still, Derrick was a charming and honorable man. He had no problem giving her a kiss good night and letting her take her child to bed. No demands. No pressure. He truly did seem to have all the qualities one could attribute to a Southern gentleman.

Like Big Jim.

Her father was a Southern gentleman, and she was certain he would have married her mother if he had known she was pregnant with his child. She wondered how her life would have been different if she had grown up here on the Garrett ranch, with Big Jim and her mother as parents. How would it have been to have a protective father?

She heaved another big sigh. Too late for what-ifs. She had survived her childhood and adolescence without a father. And with no brothers. But now the kaleidoscope had twisted into a new pattern. She had a father and brothers, some of whom acted as though they liked her. She had at least one sister-in-law who liked her. One did not, and the third was unknown. But most important, Gabrielle had a grandfather who adored her. Angelique's daughter would be safe here in the Garrett compound. If worse came to worst, Angelique could go away. She could lead her pursuers away from the child she would give her life for.

For Derrick, mornings started early. His first task was to open a can of cat food for the twenty-pound cat he had inherited when his parents had moved. Meow, so named because she was quite talkative and seemed to be saying "now" when she demanded attention.

It was his custom to grab a cup of coffee on his way to the barn. His herd of cattle were more pets than profit. He let them graze and supplemented their feed with a grain mix recommended by Jenna Kincaid, the local veterinarian. But it was winter now and the pastures were covered with a blanket of snow, so Derrick rolled out bales of hay to feed his bovine friends.

This morning, though it was still dark, the herd had gathered close to the fence where a feeding trough had been placed. Streams of white vapor arose from their nostrils as they snorted in the chill morning air.

Freddie, the longhorn bull and patriarch of this bovine family, pushed forward, offering his nose in greeting. There were younger bulls, Freddie's offspring, but the old man kept his place as boss of the herd.

Derrick rubbed Freddie's nose and scrabbled his way up to the wide space between the bull's eyes, a favorite spot for scratching. "Hey, old fellow. You been keeping the ladies satisfied?"

The large brown eyes blinked, perhaps confirming that he was doing his duty to the cows.

"Atta boy." Derrick scooped grain into the feed trough and watched as his four-hooved darlings gathered around the dinner table.

Satisfied, he took a step back to watch the first lightening of the sky to the east. It was always a thrill, no matter how many times he experienced it. Morning came to call at his ranch every day, and every day it was welcomed with proper awe and reverence.

As a man who had been raised to respect nature and love the land, he tried to take nothing for granted. With all the talk of global warming, he always did his part to conserve natural resources.

His next stop was the stables. He only had three horses. A mare, a stallion, and a foal, the product of their coupling. He knew his neighbor, Big Jim Garrett, spent a lot of time and energy making sure each and every colt was the perfect pairing of his equine genetics. But for Derrick, it was a much smaller microcosm of flora and fauna. He was proud to be able to farm enough to provide silage for his own animals. He planted oats and grain sorghum, and in the fall rye grass. Just seeing the small herd of Texas longhorn cattle living on and enjoying his land gave him great satisfaction.

It took him no time at all to feed the horses and muck out their stalls. They needed exercise, but the sheriff had to drive into town. It was with regret that he turned the horses out into the corral. "After work, I promise."

Derrick pulled off his work boots by the back door and set them just inside to dry. Then he headed for the shower to make himself presentable to meet his constituents or whoever might need him this fine winter day.

Colton Garrett was trying to keep from letting his feelings about his supposed half-sister ruin his Christmas spirit. He'd gotten up early and cooked bacon while the coffee brewed.

Misty was getting ready for work, having an immense loyalty to Breckenridge T. Ryan, her lawyer boss. He seemed to be comfortable with her running the office and keeping his clients and their information intact, leaving him free to defend his clients at the county courthouse, arrange bail for some and create wills for others. All this while spending time as a gentleman rancher, also a time-consuming business.

"I'm late." Misty came bounding around the corner

and into the kitchen of their ranch house, which occupied a lovely site on the Garrett ranch compound.

"Hang on," Colt said. "The weather is crappy. I really doubt there is a line of people waiting to get into the law office."

Tilting her head to one side, she pursed her lips. "Maybe, but I still need to get there and open up."

Colt handed her a cup of coffee with just the right amount of hazelnut creamer in it…her favorite. "You can take a moment to enjoy this nice breakfast I'm making for you. Now sit down and relax."

Closing her eyes, she inhaled the fragrant aroma of the coffee. "Ooh, I don't have time."

Colt frowned at her. "You are not encouraging me to get up and make breakfast."

Misty smiled and leaned in for a kiss. She stroked his cheek with one hand. "Okay, but sit with me. I'll have some bacon."

Colt shook his head in defeat, but placed the plate of bacon on the table and took a seat beside her. "Seriously, honey. Give the sand trucks a chance to get out on the road."

"You put those amazing snow tires on my truck," she said. "I'm perfectly safe, especially if you let me get on the road soon." Misty picked up a slice of crispy bacon and munched it emphatically.

"Don't you want me to drive you? I can pick you up later."

Misty gazed at him silently.

Colt could feel her unspoken hostility. "Is there a problem?"

She drew in a deep breath and set her coffee mug

down on the table. "I feel distinctly insulted when you reveal how little confidence you have in me."

"Aw, baby. You shouldn't feel that way. I have all the confidence in you. You know that."

Her lips tightened. "Well, you don't seem to think that poor little me could drive herself to work on a perfectly clear winter day."

"No, that's not..." He started to get to his feet, but she was faster.

She shoved her chair back and grabbed another slice of bacon. "I'll see you later."

And Colt was left to watch his wife storm off in a snit. Not what he had planned. He had intended to serve her a sumptuous breakfast for which he had thought she would be appreciative.

He just caught up with her before she pulled out. "Wait, Misty. I'm sorry." He opened the driver's side door and gazed at his totally irritated wife.

She heaved a sigh and turned off the ignition. "You're really sorry?"

"I—I'm sorry if you thought I was putting you down. I love you, y'know?"

Her expression softened. "I know."

He reached to stroke her cheek. Then leaned in for a kiss. "Sorry if I hurt your feelings. I wanted to protect you. I'm an ass."

She flashed her dimpled grin. "Yeah, sometimes... but you're *my* ass."

When she drove away, Colt stood in the snow, fists on his hips, considering how to take his wife's words.

Chapter 8

"Dad, you don't have to always cook for me." Angelique flashed a grin at Big Jim as he placed a plate with way too much food in front of her. "I can cook, y'know? In fact, I'm a damned good cook." She scooted Gabrielle up to the table, ensconced on the booster seat like a princess on her throne.

"I'm sure you are." Big Jim sat down at the table beside her, bearing his own plate piled high with bacon and sausages, eggs, a potato casserole, and toast. "But humor an old man. I'm making up for all those years I didn't get to cook for you."

A tightness in her throat kept her from responding. She pressed her lips together, biting her inner cheek to keep from tearing up. She didn't know why she had suddenly become so sensitive about the subject of her one-parent childhood. It had been tough growing up without a father. She had been bullied in school, but Remy had always stood up for her.

Remy had been her hero, in grade school and all the way through their troubled relationship. Not troubled by Remy, but by his parents, Alphonse and Cecile Benoit.

They lived in a beautiful mansion in the Quarter. Angelique had thought it was a palace, especially when compared to the cramped apartment she shared with her mother.

Angelique had always felt the Benoits' contempt. It was understandable. After all, her mother was among the working class…the poorer working class.

"So, how is it?" Big Jim broke into her reverie, leaning a bit toward her.

She looked at him in confusion. "What?"

"The eggs? The potatoes? Did I get them right?" He gestured to the small plate he had set in front of Gabrielle. "Gabi seems to like 'em okay."

His granddaughter was using a spoon and her fingers to feed herself the delicious morsels.

"Oh, um—yes. It's fabulous." She scooped some of the potato mixture into her mouth. She tasted the concoction and realized it truly was fabulous. "It's delicious."

Big Jim chuckled. "Glad you think so."

"What's in this scrumptious stuff?"

"Lots of good things. My boys loved it growing up."

Angelique kept eating but wondered how it might have been, growing up here on this sprawling ranch with a father who loved her…and cooked for her.

After breakfast, Big Jim told Angelique to get herself and Gabrielle bundled up. When they were properly attired, he wrapped Gabrielle in a wool throw and carried her outside.

Intrigued, Angelique followed, her feet sinking into the crispy white snow. She tried to step in the tracks made by Big Jim, but his stride was too long for her shorter legs.

"Here we go, ladies." He opened a door in the side of a wooden building, holding it wide for Angelique to enter.

She stepped up into the interior, noticing immediately a strong odor. “Phew! What is that horrible smell?”

He grinned, closing the door behind himself. “That’s perfume to a cowboy, Angelique. This is the stable, and what you smell are my beautiful black Arabian horses. I haven’t cleaned out their stalls today, or let them out into the corral. They need the exercise.”

Angelique sucked in a breath, making a face. “You do this every morning?”

“Sure do. I love these horses. Arabians are a special breed.”

“You ride them every day?” She was fascinated as she heard the sound of hooves stamping and horses snorting and making a sound.

“Of course I do. These are my beautiful little babies.”

Angelique let out a laugh. “Are you kidding? The horses are huge. I would be terrified to get up on one.”

Big Jim gave her a look she thought was amused, but maybe a little sad too.

She swallowed hard. “I-I guess if I had been raised here I would be riding horses from the time I could walk.”

Big Jim nodded. “I was thinkin’ that very thing.” He gave her a one-armed hug. “But I think you turned out pretty good without me.”

A rush of tears filled her eyes and spilled down her cheeks. If only she could tell him how totally screwed up her life had turned out. “Thanks.” She wiped at her tears, but smiled. She felt safe wrapped in this big man’s arm.

Gabrielle reached over to pat Angelique’s hair. “Don’t cwy, Mommy.”

This struck her as funny, and she began laughing and couldn't stop. It was hard to breathe, and soon she was giggling and gasping for air. "Oh, I don't know what's wrong with me." She kissed Gabrielle's hand and held it.

Big Jim gave her a kiss on the cheek. "Not a damn thing."

It felt as though something that had been holding her back, some restraint, had broken away. She nestled her head on Big Jim's shoulder. "Thanks, Dad."

"Come on over here with me and let me show you these little darlings." He urged her to go toward the horse stalls. "This here's my Ebony. She's got a great bloodline."

The horse gazed at Angelique, large dark eyes alert and interested.

"She wants a treat."

Gabrielle reached out a hand to the mare, and Big Jim leaned down so she could touch the horse's nose. Gabrielle squealed in delight.

Big Jim stroked the horse's nose, and Gabrielle leaned back to do the same. "Horse. This is a horsey."

"Horsey!" she shouted.

Angelique watched, fighting down a sense of fear, telling herself that her daughter would be all right in the arms of her loving grandfather.

"Yessiree, little lady. Your grampa will make sure you learn to handle yourself on a horsey." He smiled at Angelique. "And you, my dear daughter… You will learn to ride too. I'll pick out a really gentle mare for you."

"Oh my! No, I'm not really the cowgirl type." She held up her hands as though surrendering.

Big Jim huffed out a single laugh. "Sure you are. You just don't know it yet."

She shook her head, but chuckled. "That's for sure. I have no idea how to be a cowgirl."

"Not to worry. That's what your old daddy is for. I'll be happy to teach you how to ride."

"What if—what if I'm afraid of horses?"

Big Jim drew back, an exaggerated look of shock on his face. "Afraid of horses? How could anyone be afraid of Ebony? Look at that sweet face."

Angelique had to agree the horse's face was sweet. "But I could never get up on her back. I would be terrified. They're so big."

Big Jim let out a snort. "These Arabs are only about five feet at the shoulder."

"They look bigger." Angelique shook her head. "I don't understand why you raise so many of these black horses if you can only ride one at a time."

"Because," Big Jim said with a smile, "they are so beautiful. They give me great pleasure." Big Jim became serious, his smile fading. "It's my job to help you feel at home in the saddle. Don't worry, honey. I won't ask you to do anything you're uncomfortable with."

Angelique released a breath she hadn't realized she'd been holding.

"But now I'm gonna walk you ladies back to the house and get to work cleaning up the stalls. I wanted you to get a look at my Arabs. I think they're almost as pretty as the two of you."

Derrick had a pretty good day at work. The deputies all reported in without any trouble. Derrick reasoned that it was the weather. Generally too cold for much in the way of crime to occur. The road crew was slow in making its rounds spreading sand on the slick roads. Not good for a speedy getaway.

On the other hand, there was an uptick in domestic disturbances, probably due to people staying home. One husband had been taken into custody for being drunk and disorderly, but he insisted it was his wife who had driven him to drink. His wife was unaware of this since she had been Christmas shopping with her mother in Amarillo.

So, as his work day was drawing to a close, Derrick was trying to figure out a way to see Angelique again without bombarding her with his presence…and he was pretty sure that Big Jim Garrett might also prefer that Derrick space out his visits a little.

Finally, before he left for the day, he called the Garrett ranch landline. Unfortunately, it was Big Jim who picked up the phone. "Um, hello, sir. It's…it's Derrick Shelton."

"Well hello, son. What can I do for you today?"

"I'd like to talk to your daughter, Angelique, if she's available."

Silence…

Then a deep sigh. "Well, let me see if she's… available."

Derrick heard Big Jim set the receiver down on something hard. He waited a while and then waited even longer. Finally the receiver was picked up again.

"Hello?"

Just hearing her voice caused his heart to squeeze up. "Hi, Angelique. It's me, Derrick." He rolled his eyes. *Dumb. Really dumb.*

"Hi, Derrick."

Another silence while he groped for something to say that didn't sound completely inane. "Um, I wanted to check on you. You were so tired the other night. Feeling better?" He cringed. She must think he was an idiot.

"How sweet," she said. "I'm feeling fine, thank you very much for asking."

Emboldened, he decided to go for it. "I was hoping you might be willing to let me take you out to dinner Friday night…you and Gabi, of course."

"Sure, as far as I know that will be fine. I'd like to see you again, Derrick."

He liked that she didn't play games. He liked that she wanted to see him too. "I'll pick you two up Friday about six, if that's okay. We can have dinner at the steak house or anyplace you like."

"Anyplace I like?"

"Sure thing. You pick the place."

She cleared her throat. "How about your place?"

Derrick sat up straight, not sure he'd heard her correctly. "My place?"

"Yes. Is that okay?"

"Of course it is." He was thinking he would have to do a serious cleanup of his bachelor house, which his mother referred to as his sty. "Whatever you want. I can pick up something for dinner."

Angelique heaved a sigh. "I want to cook. I need to cook." Another sigh. "My dad won't let me cook. He is so sweet. He keeps cooking all these really fabulous meals for me. I love him, but I really love to cook."

"Uh, sure. Whatever you want. I can shop for anything you need."

He heard her giggle. "Oh, that will be awesome. I'll make a list. Do you like shrimp?"

"Who doesn't like shrimp?"

"That's wonderful. I am going to make your taste buds sit up and take notice."

Derrick hung up, feeling dazed and confused. He had a date with Angelique, and they were going to spend an evening relaxing at his home instead of making polite conversation in front of the entire community, or as much of it as would fit in the steak house.

Angelique couldn't stop grinning. She was going to have a chance to get back into the kitchen.

Derrick's kitchen.

Of course he wouldn't have all the fabulous ingredients always on hand in Sofie's kitchen, but she would figure out something easy and maybe without all the ingredients she usually added.

She tried to think of something she could whip up to give Derrick a taste of New Orleans without all the fixings at hand. Maybe jambalaya...maybe étouffée? No, he wouldn't have all the spices and special ingredients.

Angelique heaved a sigh. She really wanted to have the chance to impress Derrick with her cooking skills. She pondered that for a moment, but quickly put it aside, unwilling to examine her relationship with the handsome sheriff too closely. It was enough that he liked her.

She checked out Big Jim's cupboards and found that he was well stocked with a number of the spices she would need. Since she had no way of knowing what was in Derrick Shelton's kitchen, she thought maybe she could mix up her own little bag of Cajun seasoning right here in Big Jim's kitchen…his manly domain.

Angelique set out some of the spices, lining them up in a row on the countertop and finding most everything she needed to whip up a righteous Cajun dish that would make her mother proud. She presumed these were the ingredients of Big Jim's super-secret barbecue dry rub.

Unexpectedly, Angelique's eyes teared up. Her mother's recent passing left a raw place that didn't take much to wound anew. So many things they would never again be able to share. The fact that Sofie would not get to see Gabrielle grow up was the greatest tragedy. Gabrielle had been the apple of her grandmother's eye.

And now, thanks to Sofie's deathbed admission, Angelique had been able to locate her father and flee to a safe haven.

She pressed her lips together, stanching the urge to break down. She had not taken the time to mourn truly, since without Sofie to intervene, Alphonse Benoit had made the move to take Gabrielle. Unfortunately, he had the law on his side, having bribed a local judge to declare Angelique an unfit mother so he could gain custody of his granddaughter.

Not gonna happen. Not while I'm alive.

"What are you up to, little missy?" Big Jim's deep voice jolted her out of her reverie. "Are you rearranging my cabinets?"

She managed a smile. "Nothing so ambitious. Besides,

everything looks good. I was checking on your spices and herbs. I might want to cook something someday."

Big Jim cocked his head to one side.

"You know, I'm from Louisiana. I cook Cajun and Creole recipes…like my mom. Did my mother ever cook for you?"

Big Jim's lips tightened and he looked sad, shrugging his shoulders. "We were kids then. She lived on campus in a girls' dorm, and I shared an apartment with another Ag student." He shrugged again. "We went to dances or to a country bar on the edge of town. That Sofie, she was born to dance."

Angelique nodded, recalling her mother's love of music and how music would cause her to sway, without being aware of the movement. "She had a great singing voice."

Big Jim shook his head. "I don't recall an occasion where Sofie was singing."

Angelique smiled. "Well, she had a remarkable singing voice. After I was born, she made a living for us by singing. She had a regular gig at one of the popular clubs down in the French Quarter."

"I'm sorry. I wish I had known."

"Aww, it wasn't so bad. When I was really little, one of Mom's friends took care of me while she was working, and we had daytimes together." Angelique shrugged. "And when I was a little older, I got to go with her. I grew up listening to her sing, and I grew to love the blues."

Big Jim reacted by raking his fingers through his thick silver hair. He heaved out a sigh. "I should have tried to find Sofie after our freshman year. When she didn't return, I figured she had other interests. You know? I figured she had transferred somewhere else." He fisted his hands at his waist. "Sofie was as smart as a whip. She could have been anything she set her mind to. You know, lawyer, doctor? She was that smart."

Angelique reached out to place her hand on his shoulder. "I'm sorry you two didn't end up together, but you have had a great life here. I mean, your family has done quite well. And me? I survived...at least I have so far." A shiver that could have set off the seismic charts coiled around her spine.

When Derrick picked her up, Angelique was in an exceptionally good mood. Her beautiful eyes sparkled, and her dimples flashed every time she grinned, which was often.

Big Jim was entertaining his granddaughter for the evening. Although he did give Derrick a stern look that seemed to imply he was to keep his hands off Angelique.

"I'm so excited," she said. "I hope you like my cooking."

Derrick reflected that she seemed to be more interested in cooking for him than actually being out with him. *She must be some kind of great cook.*

She directed him to drive her to the local grocery where they shopped, him pushing the cart. This felt very complicated to him, especially when he got nods and smiles from some of his constituents.

"Good afternoon, Sheriff," the preacher said. He was shopping with his wife. "I don't believe I know your... lady friend." He nodded toward Angelique.

Derrick took Angelique's hand. "Sir, this is my friend, Angelique Guillory. And Angelique, this gentleman delivers great sermons every Sunday, rain or shine."

Angelique dimpled. "I remember. I've been to a couple of services with my father."

The minister's brows climbed up almost to his hairline. "I saw you with Big Jim Garrett, but I didn't notice your father."

She cocked her head to one side. "Big Jim is my father."

Derrick was proud that she was so open and not embarrassed by the happenstance of her birth. He saw that the minister was floundering for a response.

"Oh, your father…" The minister's voice faded, but his eyes were wide open. His wife however, looked as though she had swallowed a sour pickle. Her lips were pursed, and disapproval was written all over her face.

"We'll see you on Sunday," Derrick called as he pushed the basket down the aisle. "What's on your list?"

"Well, I'm gonna make you the best jambalaya you've ever put in your mouth. We need some chicken breast and smoked sausage to start with. My mama would have her own broth, but I'm afraid we'll have to use some of the canned variety."

They meandered around the store, while she chose items and put them in the cart. By the time they arrived at Derrick's ranch house, it was around five o'clock. There was plenty of sun, but the temperature was dropping. He hustled Angelique into the house, his arms filled with groceries.

"You leave your door open?" she asked, twisting the knob and swinging it wide so he could enter with his load.

"Sure. I'm not exactly known for my vast wealth or worldly possessions."

"Oh, what a nice house." She did a complete turn, gazing around at his front room. "Very cozy."

"Thanks. I grew up here." He made his way to the kitchen and unburdened himself on the wooden table. He straightened the bags and turned to gaze at Angelique.

She was looking around his kitchen in apparent delight. "This is wonderful. It doesn't look like a bachelor pad." She set down the bag she carried alongside her handbag. "I mean, everything is so neat."

He chuckled, recalling the state of his house when Angelique had first suggested they dine in. "Well, I did straighten up a bit for your visit."

"Everything looks great. Like a picture out of a magazine."

At first he thought she was kidding, but he recalled that she told him she had always lived in a small apartment in the French Quarter. Maybe his place looked better than he thought. "It's nothing compared to Big Jim's place."

Surprised, she turned to him. "It's not a contest. The Garrett ranch is like a family compound. Both of the older two sons and their families live on the property, and it's got a lot of animals too." She started unloading the groceries from the bags. "I need a pot to cook the chicken in."

"Oh, no," he said. "I didn't mean to be making comparisons. I meant that you were used to a big ranch, and this is just a small family homestead."

She rinsed the chicken breasts and placed them in the saucepan he presented. "I think it's absolutely perfect. Family homestead, huh? So where is the family?"

Derrick emptied the rest of the items from the bags and put the empties in his recycle bin. "Family? Well, my parents retired and left me the property. They moved to San Antonio to take care of my grandma."

"San Antonio? Like the Alamo and all that?" Angelique was working efficiently, obviously used to being in the kitchen.

He settled at the table, where he could watch her and be out of the way. "That's the place. They've always loved the River Walk and downtown area. So they moved in with my mom's mother to make sure she's cared for. My dad was ready to turn the reins over to me."

"How cool. What a great family." She had chopped the onion and pepper and was now slicing the smoked sausage.

"It's my family. I have a sister who married a Marine. They move around a lot."

"Sounds wonderful to me." Her face was averted, and somehow her mood had fallen. "I-I never had that experience. It sounds like something I may have read about in a book."

He regarded her steadily. "I'm sorry you didn't have the picture-book family growing up, but you turned out great. Now you're connected to your real father and he is crazy about you."

She turned, with what he thought was a hopeful expression. "You think?"

"I know."

When the meal was on the table, Derrick was amazed at how beautifully presented it was. Angelique had even garnished the jambalaya with a little cilantro. He inhaled an appreciative lungful of the aroma.

She was seated beside him, looking anxious, as though it was important to her that he enjoy her handiwork. “Try it, please. I didn’t add as much of the hot sauce as usual, because I didn’t know how you like your food.”

He scooped up a big spoonful, hoping it wasn’t lethally hot. “Hey, this is delicious.” He could taste the mélange of all the delicious flavors. The chicken and smoked sausage complemented each other as the vegetables and spices melded together to create a tasty dish. “You should open a restaurant. We only have a couple of places to eat out here in Langston. You could make a mint serving up food like this.”

Angelique was grinning. “Glad you like it. I love to cook, but Big Jim does, too, so he is always cooking for me. It felt so good to be able to have some time in the kitchen again.”

Derrick reached for her hand and brought it to his lips. “My kitchen is your kitchen. Any time you need to flex your cooking muscles, just let me know. Call me and I’ll pick up whatever you need in town.” He released her hand so they could gobble the delicious meal. He was happy that she was happy. He sensed that this beautiful woman needed to fulfill herself, and he was willing to be there for her to help make sure that happened.

Chapter 9

Angelique felt as though she was floating on the ceiling. Somehow, seeing Derrick gobble up her jambalaya made her feel accomplished. Yes, it was tasty. Not her best, but she would have to acquire a full array of her usual fixings, the things that were standard in Sofie's kitchen. As long as Angelique kept her mother's recipe alive, it was as though a part of Sofie's legacy lived on.

Angelique would teach Gabrielle these recipes, and she would teach her children. The descendants of Sofie Guillory would carry on the traditions built around food.

"Seriously," Derrick said, "this is the best food I've eaten in a long time. You *should* open a restaurant."

Angelique chuckled. "Yeah, I'll take that bag of money I keep in my back pocket and open a restaurant, with a little chair in the corner for Gabrielle."

Derrick shrugged. "I'd eat there all the time."

"Nice, Derrick."

When they had finished their meal, Derrick helped clear the table. He loaded the dishwasher while she put the rest of the jambalaya in a covered container and stored it in the fridge.

When she turned around, Derrick was right there, smiling. She was glad the refrigerator was at her back, because the warmth radiating from his expression made her feel swoony. But she didn't want him to think she wasn't ready for whatever was to come, so she reached for him, wrapping her arms around his neck and pulling him close.

Derrick lowered his lips to hers, slowly.

Her heart was trying to break out of her chest, echoing in her ears. Then their lips touched and the swoony feeling took over. The kiss deepened and Derrick's strong arms circled around her, drawing her away from the sturdy appliance and crushing her against his rock-hard chest.

It had been so long since Angelique had felt any reaction to a man other than fear. And now she was wrapped in the arms of a strong, healthy, and totally delicious man.

Derrick's hand slowly swept over her backside, giving one of her cheeks a squeeze. Oh, yes! If the bulge in his Wranglers was any indication, this night was going to progress to sweet loving.

Angelique was ready to climb up this tall and hot cowboy, when he abruptly let go and stepped away.

He stood with his back to her, hands on hips and breathing heavily.

"Wha—what's going on? Why did you stop?"

Derrick swallowed hard, shaking his head. "I'm sorry. I would never do anything to disrespect you. I-I'm just way too attracted to you."

Angelique stared at his back—he was still breathing hard—wondering if he had made some vow of celibacy. "And that's a problem?" She reached out to touch his shoulder and he turned back to face her.

"You know I like you… Hell, I'm pretty sure I'm falling in love with you…" He shook his head.

"In love with me?" Angelique's insides were soaring.

He cupped her cheek in one hand. "You have to know I've been crazy nuts about you since I first found you in that snowbank." He brushed a soft kiss against her lips.

"I-I feel the same way, but if we really care about each other—"

"But your old man would kill me if..."

Stung, Angelique stepped back. "You don't mean that. I mean, we're not kids, Derrick."

He pulled her against his chest. "No, but let's give it a little time. What I feel for you is not some passing thing. I want to be sure neither of us has anything to be sorry for."

"You mean, if it doesn't work out?"

He placed a kiss against her hair. "Honey, you just got here. Some of us have to live here in this community. It's good to let things roll out nice and slow."

Angelique contented herself to be in his arms, but wondered what kind of power her newfound father had over this man who claimed to be falling in love with her.

That night, Angelique lay awake...in her own bed. Well, it was the bed she had been given in her father's home.

Derrick's abrupt rejection was still preying on her mind. Not to mention her libido.

She had not been interested in any man since she had lost her beloved Remy. Now she had met a man worth falling in love with—a really good man—but he was not that interested in her. Or maybe he was afraid of her father.

A shiver wracked her body, causing her to pull the

quilts up around her head. But it wasn't the cold that chilled her. It was the thought that her father—the man whose blood ran through her veins—might be as vicious as Alphonse Benoit.

Everyone who had heard the Benoit name knew he was a fearsome man. A man who had no empathy. No ability to care about anything or anyone but himself… and Remy. His son was his obsession. How could such a wonderful and kind man have sprung from the loins of a monster?

Could Big Jim Garrett also spark that kind of fear? *Surely not.* Big Jim cared about so many people. About his family and about his horses…

But was he capable of violence? Would he hurt someone who crossed him…or worse?

Angelique swallowed hard. Her throat seemed to be constricted. Perhaps it was just her karma to be caught in the web of brutal men.

Big Jim lived up to his name. He was well over six feet tall and built like a Mack truck. Broad-shouldered and strong. He worked, so it was reasonable that he was strong. Not like Alphonse. His strength was in his fear factor. He could bring about a disappearance with a single phone call.

Alphonse had put up with her friendship and eventual love affair with his son and even expressed joy over the birth of Gabrielle. But he had become withdrawn after Remy's death.

A wave of fresh pain washed through Angelique, reminding her of all she had lost in the past year. First her beloved Remy had been wrenched away from her, and then Sofie, her mother, her source of comfort.

After Remy's death, she had returned to live with her mother. Between the two of them, they had managed to take care of Gabrielle and keep themselves going.

That was when she had realized that there was something going on between her mother and Alphonse. Sofie dismissed it, saying that it was nothing but a fling; however, that was untrue. It was obvious that Alphonse worshipped Sofie.

When she revealed that she was suffering from cancer and had only a few months to live, Angelique had been heartbroken, as had Alphonse. But while Angelique had been on hand to tend to her mother's needs, Alphonse had grown more and more bitter. Jealous of every moment she spent with her mother.

And then, at the end, when Sofie had revealed the name and location of Angelique's birth father, Angelique had slipped away, taking Gabrielle and without saying goodbye to Alphonse.

He would have considered that the ultimate betrayal. Sofie had left him, and he had no recourse. He turned his anger on Angelique, intending to take Gabrielle from her. He first tried to buy the child from her, but Angelique was horrified, rejecting all offers. Next, he got a local judge to state that she was unfit to raise a child. That was when Angelique left New Orleans, determined to track down this mysterious James Garrett, hoping to find a place where she and Gabrielle could be safe.

Derrick had taken Angelique back to the Garrett ranch, walked her to the front door, and given her a remarkably restrained good-night kiss. She had been quite reserved since he had stepped away from the passion they both felt. He knew he'd hurt her feelings.

What kind of man would turn down the beautiful and willing Angelique Guillory? He'd returned to his home, frustrated and on edge.

He paced around, finding things to pick up, but his house was neater than usual due to his hasty cleaning session prior to bringing Angelique there. Finally, he threw himself down in front of the television and watched figures prance across the screen without following the stories. He absently stroked Meow, who seemed to be questioning him, her large yellow eyes offering comfort. The large black cat crept onto his chest to provide a massage, complete with acupuncture. *Love hurts…*

Angelique doesn't understand. She's a city girl. New Orleans is a whole different world.

He heaved a deep sigh.

Langston was a small town. Derrick had grown up with Big Jim as a role model. He had played basketball with Colt. He'd been an Eagle Scout, working with both Colt and Tyler on projects. They had all gone to church together forever.

How could he have thought he could date Big Jim's daughter and not have it affect his relationship with the entire Garrett clan?

"Oh, dammit to hell! I'm in love with her." His voice sounded harsh against all the hard surfaces.

Meow stared intently.

"It's okay, girl. I'm an idiot." He ruffled Meow's luxuriant fur. "I screwed up with the most wonderful woman on the planet."

Meow laid a comforting paw on Derrick's knee.

"That's a good girl. I think we should stick to what we know. The law and this ranch. That should keep us out of trouble."

"So you cooked dinner for Derrick, huh?" Big Jim eyed his daughter critically.

She nodded, eyes cast down.

Was that guilt or shame?

Angelique sat at the breakfast table, absently watching her daughter poke spoonfuls of oatmeal and scrambled eggs into her own mouth. Her mood was definitely down.

Damn! She needs a woman to talk to. I'm no good at this bonding thing.

Big Jim arranged a smile on his face and took a seat at the table, bearing his own piled-high plate. "Any more plans I should know about?"

She gave him a sharp glance.

"I mean, in case I need to babysit anytime soon." He buttered his toast with great concentration.

"Mmm…I don't know." Her shoulders dropped a bit. "Probably not."

The seeds of anger raged in Big Jim's chest. *He hurt her. That little weasel! I'll kill him.*

"Did something happen last night? I mean, you seem a little…uh…upset."

She blinked rapidly. "Oh, um…well… No, everything was fine. He really liked my jambalaya." She straightened her shoulders, sitting up straighter. "We had a great time. I cooked. We ate. He brought me home. That's it."

"Uh-huh." *I'll definitely kill him. Derrick Shelton, you're a dead man.*

Derrick Shelton started the day feeding his livestock. Meow picked her way through the snow beside him, using a prancing motion. It was cold and dark, but the small cluster of longhorn cattle were gathered by the fence. He cut the baling wire securing two small bales of hay after heaving them into the feeding trough. He would follow up with some grain later, but this was a solid breakfast for his stock.

Horses came next. Feeding them took no time at all, and soon Derrick was trudging back to the ranch house, Meow prancing along by his side. "Good girl."

Derrick fed Meow and left her in the house before driving toward town. He called in on his cell to let his office know he was going to make a safety check on an older couple before coming in. He had called their home but received no response. Now he needed to follow up and make sure they were okay.

He drove up to the small farm. The elderly couple's twenty-year-old Ford pickup was parked in front, close to the house. Derrick parked and strode up to the porch. He knocked on the door, and again, louder, with no response. "Mr. and Mrs. Lawson! Are you all right?"

A dog barked but there was no other response. Now he heard the sound of small paws scratching frantically on the door.

He knocked again, this time twisting the doorknob. The door opened, squeaking a bit as it swung wide.

"Hello?" Derrick called out. "Mr. and Mrs. Lawson? It's Sheriff Shelton. I'm coming inside."

Cautiously, he stepped across the threshold. He realized the heat was not on inside. A small black dog was dancing around his boots. "Hey, fellow."

"Help!"

He heard a feeble voice call out and followed it to a back room.

There he found the elderly couple. The woman was lying in bed, covered with blankets and quilts. She opened her eyes and moaned softly.

Her husband was lying on the floor. The dog kept barking excitedly.

Derrick squatted down to make sure the man was alive. The old man's eyes fluttered open. "M-mother's sick."

"I see. Let me get you some help."

"I tripped over Smokey here. Couldn't see him in the dark."

Derrick lifted the old man into a chair beside the bed. "How long you been lying there, Mr. Lawson?"

The old man raked his fingers through his thatch of white hair. "I reckon it was yesterday I fell."

"Why is it so cold in here, Mr. Lawson?"

"Dang it. We ran out of propane, and I couldn't get to the phone after I fell."

"Well, let me get you two some help."

Derrick called for an ambulance and stayed with the couple until they were safely on their way to the hospital.

He secured the house and looked down at his feet. "Well, Smokey, what am I going to do with you?"

Smokey gazed up at him, his eyes alert.

"I suppose you're going to be coming with me." He headed for his truck, making kissy sounds on the way. Sure enough, Smokey came with him and jumped up into the truck, settling on the passenger side.

Derrick sincerely hoped Smokey would be in the mood to adapt.

Angelique tried to keep her chin up. It really didn't matter that she had been rejected by the man who claimed to be falling in love with her. She was confused, and had no idea how to discover the truth.

If it were true that Big Jim Garrett was a threat to a man she was dating, a man who stirred her passions... If that were true, then Big Jim was not much better than Alphonse Benoit. That thought was terrifying.

Angelique was so glad to have Leah as a friend. The fact that they were both mothers was a plus. Leah was someone who understood the challenges of motherhood. But even with Leah, she could never share the secrets she was hoping to bury in her past.

She felt confident that Sofie had not told anyone else Big Jim's name, and her birth certificate said "father unknown." She was counting on time and distance to keep her safe...to keep Gabrielle safe.

But when Leah dropped by after breakfast with both her children and announced that Big Jim was going to be the babysitter for the day, with Gracie to assist, Angelique gladly turned Gabrielle over to her grinning grandfather.

"You just come to your ol' Grampa. We're gonna play until we all fall over in a heap."

Gabrielle ran to Big Jim's open arms and took a flying leap at him. She was rewarded with a soaring lift and twirl, where she spread her arms, looking like an airplane or giggling bird.

Gracie giggled at that. "Grampa, we have to feed them and play with them and let them have a little nap."

Big Jim raised his fearsome brows. "We do? Well, we better get to playin' then."

"Where are you taking me?" Angelique asked Leah.

"We're going shopping. The sun is shining, the roads are clear, and Amarillo is calling. We're going to help the economy."

Angelique shook her head. "Oh, I can't go. I spent Big Jim's money when we went shopping for Christmas presents. I got Gabi a nice warm outfit, and I need to get a job before I splurge again. I have no money to spare."

"Sure you do, honey." Big Jim reached in his billfold and pulled out a card, extending it to her.

She took it, surprised to see her name on a platinum Visa card. "What's this?"

"Thought you should have access to some funds. Knock yourself out. It's Christmas, and that's your money to spend any way you want."

She started to return it to him, but he held up his hand. "Seriously, Angelique. You need some warm clothes and so does my little Gabi, so you go get what you want and some presents if you feel like shoppin'."

Tears filled her eyes. She leaned forward into Big Jim's arms.

He patted her on the back rhythmically. "Now don't you go makin' a big deal outta this. I'm your daddy, and I'm treatin' you just the way I did my other kids.

You need something, and I want you to have it." He motioned to the door. "Now get on outta here so I can spoil my grandkids." He gave her a kiss on the cheek, and Leah grabbed her hand.

"Let's get on the road. Never know when it's going to snow again."

"Um, okay," Angelique said. "Let me find my jacket."

And with that, the two women were out the door and soon thereafter on the highway, with Christmas carols playing on the country station on Leah's truck radio. There were some country holiday songs that Angelique had never heard, but most were familiar carols sung by country singers with fiddle players accompanying them.

Leah was in high spirits. "Woo-hoo! We're going to have a great time. There's this great restaurant I want to take you to. It's home-style, but better than your grandma ever made." Leah sucked in a gasp. "Oh, I didn't mean to put your grandma down."

"Not a problem." Angelique thought about her mother's mother, the very wealthy woman who had been willing to cast her daughter and grandchild out with apparently no remorse. "Your grandma is adorable."

A wide grin spread across Leah's face. "She's the best."

"It must be nice to have had someone like that in your life growing up." Angelique's childhood had been relatively lonely. She wanted Gabrielle to grow up amid an entire clan of loving family.

"Well, I grew up in Oklahoma, but I spent summers with my grandparents here in Langston. It was the best time ever." Leah's grin echoed her statement.

"Must have been fun," Angelique said.

"How about you?" Leah asked. "How were summers in New Orleans?"

"Pretty good," Angelique said. "Hot and sultry. My mom was my everything. She was beautiful and creative. Always had some kind of artistic project going, and she had the voice of an angel. She sang in a blues club on weekends."

Leah turned down the heater. "That sound so glamorous."

Angelique smiled, thinking back to those days. "I hid under the table and listened to my mom. I would be asleep when she finished her last set, and she would carry me to the car." Angelique shrugged. "Not exactly a picture-book childhood."

Leah patted her arm. "I don't think either of us actually had a picture-book childhood. But the important thing is, we survived."

Angelique's brow furrowed. "I'm pretty sure your husband and his brothers had a pretty good childhood. Two parents who loved them and each other. They didn't have to wonder where their next meal was coming from."

"Yeah, pretty much. They had the security of a good family. All the good stuff. Going to church every Sunday. Staying in the same school system all the way through."

"And I'll bet they never stopped to think how lucky they were."

"What's the first thing you want to shop for?" Leah changed the subject abruptly, as though dwelling on her husband's childhood was somehow disloyal.

"I'm feeling guilty about accepting this money from my dad. I know he's used to spending on whatever he wants, but that's something I've never done. My mom and I had to think long and hard about every single expenditure." Angelique grimaced. "It's hard to shift gears just like that." She snapped her fingers.

"I know how you're feeling. Marrying into the Garrett family was a shock to my system." Leah heaved a sigh. "But I saw what you bought when we shopped before. Let me tell you that Gabi will need an entire winter wardrobe, not just the few things you purchased," Leah said. "I strongly suggest you get some warm boots. I'm sure it's no fun slogging through the snow and slush in those little flats."

Angelique turned to look at Leah. "That sounds expensive. Do you think it will be all right?"

"Your dad wants you to get geared up. He's not a penny-pincher. Buy some presents, too. I bet you want to get something special for Derrick Shelton. He's such a great guy…and not hard to look at."

Angelique tried not to react. "Nooo, he's not," she said slowly.

Leah glanced at her and then back at the road. "Am I hearing trouble in paradise?"

"No… No, we just…" She took a deep breath and blew it out forcefully. "We're taking a break. It really wasn't a big deal."

"Really? I thought the two of you made a great couple."

"Me too." Angelique turned to gaze out the window, hoping Leah would not have more questions.

Derrick drove into Langston and pulled up at the sheriff's office with Smokey sitting beside him, his ears perked up, seeming to enjoy the ride. The dog had been hungry and thirsty, too, but Derrick had made sure to hydrate everyone as best he could before the Lawsons were taken away in the ambulance. The dog was in better shape than the humans.

When he parked in front of the office and opened the door, Smokey jumped out with him. "Okay, boy. You gotta stay with me. I can't be responsible for losing the Lawsons' dog. Just hang out with me for a while and chill."

Smokey sat down in front of him, as though he agreed.

"Come on inside. You can stay warm in here." He thought about the Lawsons running out of propane and how there might have been a tragedy had he not decided to check on them.

Smokey followed him into the building, where the two deputies had to make a big deal about the dog. Carl squatted down to pet Smokey, while Larry was offering a piece of ham from his lunch.

Derrick noted a decent-size tree had been set up near the front door. It had several sets of lights, but not much else in the way of decorations. "You fellows been visited by some Christmas elves?"

"Aw, my mama wanted to make sure we had Christmas." Larry shrugged and offered a grin. "She sprang for the tree, and all of us rounded up the lights."

Derrick gave him a slap on the shoulder. "Good

idea." They stood admiring the tree for a few moments. "I think we need to check on all the elderly and ill people in the county," he said.

"How are we going to know who they are?" Larry asked.

Derrick gazed down at the two men now sitting on the floor with Smokey. "Start with people you know. Call the churches and ask for a list of their elderly people who might be sick and alone. I'm going to call Doctor Ryan. I'm sure her staff will get on board." Derrick patted his thigh, and Smokey followed him into his office and settled under his desk.

When he called Doctor Camryn Ryan's office, he spoke to her office manager, Loretta, and then to her rather crusty nurse, Reba.

"Thanks for the heads-up, Sheriff," Reba said. "But you can depend on Loretta and me to check on all our elderly and sick patients."

"That would be great, Miz Reba. We appreciate it."

"And Loretta said that she and I will do a phone check on all our patients. We're not that busy today. If we can't reach any of our especially delicate folks, we'll let you know."

"Good deal, Miz Reba. We appreciate your help."

Reba let out a less-than-ladylike snort. "We appreciate you giving us a kick in the pants. We should have thought of checking on our fragile patients first."

When he hung up, Derrick felt a little rush of pride for living in a community where people cared about people.

Chapter 10

"YEW YOUNG LADIES JES' SET YERSELVES RIGHT down there an' I'll fix us a lil' afternoon snack." Fern Davis gestured to the table in Leah's cheery kitchen.

Angelique took a seat and folded her hands on top of the table, which was topped with a Christmas-themed tablecloth.

"How 'bout a nice cup o' hot cocoa to start off?" Fern called.

"That sounds great, Gran," Leah said. "I'm still a mite chilly from hauling all our loot inside."

"Me too." Angelique rubbed her hands together. Her fingers were cold. Although Leah had insisted she buy some leather fleece-lined gloves, she hadn't worn them because she wanted to carefully remove the tags, afraid she might damage the gloves should she just rip the tags off.

They had brought all the packages they had purchased inside, hoping to wrap the presents before Angelique took her own haul to the Garrett ranch house. "Leah, your house is so lovely."

"Thanks. I never thought I would have a place so nice, but when we got married, Big Jim gave us the land, and Tyler immediately set about making sure we had a home to raise our children in."

"You have a good man there." Angelique felt a

twisting in her gut. She had had a good man in Remy, who unfortunately had an evil father.

And now she was losing her heart to Derrick Shelton, a man she thought was invincible, but he was afraid of Big Jim Garrett, her own father.

"Here we go!" Fern announced. "I made a batch of my muffins. Thought they would go purty good with hot cocoa." She placed a plate with muffins between the two young women and served each a cup of cocoa topped with marshmallows.

Angelique inhaled, sighing appreciatively. "Heavenly. Oh, that is heavenly."

Fern grinned, her face crinkling up in the process. "Jus' wait 'til you taste those muffins. Yer lil' taste buds gonna jump up an' down, they's so happy."

Angelique reached for a muffin. It was still warm and smelled of spices she couldn't identify. When she took a bite, she closed her eyes and uttered a soft moan. "Oh, this is delicious. What's in it?"

Fern took a seat across from them, her small hands cradling her own cup of cocoa. "Aw, this is my own special recipe. I always done 'em this way." She nodded at Leah. "Yore grandpa sure loved 'em."

"I remember," she said.

"I hope you'll share the recipe," Angelique said. "I know Gabrielle would gobble them up."

Fern giggled. "I'll send some home with yew."

After their snack, the three of them got busy wrapping the presents Angelique had selected for the various members of her new family, plus the presents she had selected for her daughter. She didn't let Leah know that one of the sweaters she had supposedly purchased for herself was intended for Leah, who had admired it.

When they got back in Leah's truck, they added a big trash bag filled with wrapped presents to the haul of personal things Angelique had purchased for herself and Gabrielle. She hoped Big Jim didn't fall over in a heap when he got the bill.

Big Jim was actually having a great time playing with his grandchildren. Only Ava was absent, but he knew she was being well cared for.

"Giddyup!" Gabrielle dug her little heels into his sides to demonstrate that she had indeed mastered the fine art of horsemanship...or piggyback-riding one's grandfather.

Gracie giggled. "Hold on, Gabi. That big horsey might be hard to handle."

"I widing my horsey," she insisted. Her hands were locked in a death grip around Big Jim's neck, and he had a good hold on her ankles.

He let out a remarkably realistic whinny and pawed the floor impatiently with his right "hoof."

"Giddyup, horsey!"

He took off again, giving her an exciting ride around the spacious den, and then they progressed through the dining area and on to the front entry. Then once around the room his wife had called the "parlor" and back to the den where Gracie was laughing while Gabrielle giggled hysterically. They finally stopped in the kitchen.

"Whoa!" he said. "This horsey needs a drink of water. Time to dismount, Miss Gabi."

Gracie helped remove Gabrielle from Big Jim's back, letting her slide to the tiled kitchen floor. Gabrielle was still excited and jumped around holding onto Gracie's hands.

Big Jim got a tall glass out of the overhead cabinet and filled it with ice from the door of the big refrigerator. He turned to see that Gabrielle was watching him in fascination. "Your horsey needed to take a break and go to the watering hole." He reached inside the refrigerator to remove a pitcher of tea and poured some over the ice.

He found it amusing that Gabrielle was so fascinated by this simple act. She had reached up to the countertop, her eyes wide as she followed his movements. He hadn't been the object of this much scrutiny since his sons had been that age. "Want some iced tea, Gracie?"

"No thanks, Grandpa. I was thinking about some hot cocoa, but I'll make it."

He watched as she set about gathering the necessary items. He felt a surge of pride that his adopted granddaughter was so completely at home in his house.

"Maybe in the spring you can pick out a calf to raise. You can show it if you want."

"Oh, Grandpa, that sounds great. My chickens are looking really good." She flashed a grin. "The Buff Orpington is really gorgeous."

He nodded. "That's a really showy breed, honey. Glad you chose that one."

"And the Hollands are doing well too." She gave him a knowing look. "They are supposed to be good layers."

They heard a clinking sound and turned in unison.

Gabrielle had pushed a chair in front of the refrigerator and was gleefully pushing the bar of the ice maker. Each time cubes were ejected, she giggled and then pushed it again, sending ice cubes crashing to the tile floor.

Big Jim jumped into action, closing the distance to reach Gabrielle in a matter of seconds. He scooped her off the chair and held her close. "No, Gabi! Don't climb on the chair." He scooted the chair back under the table. "The tile floor is hard. Don't wanna crack your pretty little skull, now, do you?" He set her on her feet.

Gabrielle's eyes welled up with tears, and her lower lip jutted out.

Gracie busied herself picking up the ice from the floor. "Oh, Grandpa. She doesn't understand what you're saying. Just tell her 'no-no.' Gabi knows that." Gracie discarded the ice in the sink and mopped up the water with a sponge.

Big Jim regarded his wise granddaughter with renewed respect. "How'd you get to be so darn smart, anyway?"

Gracie shrugged. "My mom says it's in my genes."

"She's probably right." He turned to Gabrielle and pointed to the chair. "No-no, Gabi. Don't climb on the chair… No-no." He fixed her with a stern expression.

She still looked pouty, frowning back at him.

"No-no. Climbing on the chair is a no-no."

"Hey, Gabi," Gracie called. "Do you want a cookie?"

Gabrielle's face morphed into a smile, and she happily accepted the cookie Gracie offered.

"That's a good girl," Gracie said. "Now, stay off the chair. It's a no-no."

Gabrielle pointed to the chair. "Is a no-no."

Big Jim chuckled. "It's in the genes, all right."

Derrick finished his chores at his own ranch and headed inside.

Smokey seemed to be adapting to his new temporary environment. He had stayed close to Derrick's boots as he made his way around, feeding the cattle and horses, bedding the latter down in the stable.

Derrick had checked on the Lawson couple. Mr. Lawson had been discharged to a rehabilitation facility to recover after his fall, but Mrs. Lawson remained in the hospital because she had become dehydrated. They expected her to join her husband when she was stable enough to leave.

Fortunately, Derrick and Smokey were doing well together.

Derrick made himself a pot of coffee and considered the contents of his pantry. Dismal at best. Then he remembered the leftover jambalaya in the fridge.

He swallowed hard. Recalling the last evening he'd spent with Angelique brought a tightness to his chest.

God, he wanted her!

Not only physically, but there was that, and it caused an aching emptiness in his core.

Her full, sweet lips were built for kissing. Her pale skin contrasted with her dark hair. She was a rare beauty, but the one feature that tore the heart out of him was recalling the look in her amazing blue eyes when he'd left her at Big Jim's door. Her pain was palpable… as was his own.

Like a robot, he removed the containers from the refrigerator and spooned leftover rice into a bowl, topped it with the leftover jambalaya, and nuked it briefly. While it whirled around in the microwave, he took a longneck out of the refrigerator and popped off the top.

He heard a growl and turned quickly to see Meow, her fur standing on end and back arched, growling at Smokey.

Uh-oh!

Although Smokey was larger, Meow was tougher, and her fur standing at attention caused her to appear even bigger. The poor dog was shaking, glancing anxiously back and forth between Derrick and Meow.

"Sorry, Meow. I should have realized bringing a dog into your house would upset you." He picked up the mass of fur, holding her to his chest. Her super-fluffy tail smacked against his side as he tried to calm her. "C'mon. Be a good hostess. This poor dog is a temporary orphan. His mom and dad are in the hospital, so we're babysitting. Calm down, girl."

He felt her slowly relax in his arms and eventually start purring. "See? You're still the queen of the castle. No harm done."

Derrick put the cat down and retrieved his food from the microwave. The taste of the jambalaya brought back all the pain of his parting with Angelique. At the time, it had seemed as though he had to choose between loyalty to the family he had been raised alongside and the woman he had fallen in love with.

But the three Garrett brothers he had grown up with had found their perfect mates and were happily married. Some with children. All living with Big Jim's blessings.

He had to wonder what happened to men who fell in

love with their best friend's sister. And why had Big Jim suddenly become the mega dad, frowning at the man who wanted to take her out…at the man who wanted her.

Unfortunately, he had slammed the door on that relationship. He scooped a spoonful of jambalaya into his mouth, wondering how he could get back into Angelique's good graces after being such an ass. Loneliness wrapped around him like a cold, dark blanket, bringing his spirits even lower.

Merry freakin' Christmas!

Big Jim had been surprisingly unconcerned when Angelique tried to return the Visa card. "When I get a job, I'll pay you back, Dad."

"No, you keep that card. It's for you to use, and you alone." He tucked it back in her hand and closed her fingers over it.

"But I kind of overspent… I mean, I've never in my entire life spent so much money at any one time."

"Honey, it's not a problem. I would have spent a lot more on you if you'd grown up here, so indulge me. Okay?" He spread his arms wide, inviting a hug.

Angelique hesitated for a second, then leaned in, allowing herself to be enfolded in a giant's arm span. It felt good. *Really good.*

"Now, I just gotta get you used to riding horses."

Angelique drew back, her mouth open.

"In the spring. We'll go riding in the spring, when the wildflowers are blooming. You won't believe how beautiful the place is when the bluebonnets are in bloom."

She swallowed hard. “Sounds beautiful.”

“And Indian paintbrush. They’re kind of a coral, and when I see them mixed in with the bluebonnets, it just makes me wanna cry, it’s so amazin’.”

“I can’t wait. Warm weather and wildflowers.”

He gave her a wide grin. “You betcha. What more can we ask?”

“I hope Gabrielle didn’t give you any trouble.”

“Nah! The little ones are taking a nap in the den, with Gracie playin’ little mama.”

Leah came bustling into the room, tossing her hair. “I rearranged the presents under the tree. Looks better now. Remember there are a bunch in the corner behind the tree, but I didn’t want people passing by to trip.”

Big Jim laid a kiss on her forehead. Actually more like on top of her head as she smushed him with a hug. “That’s really sweet, darlin’. I could have done that for you.”

“I better get going. Ty is going to be home soon.” She pulled on her down jacket and wrapped the scarf around her neck.

“Where has that rascal been today?” Big Jim asked.

“Dallas. He drove down to develop a project with his friend Will. They’ve been working on a new arrangement in Will’s sound studio. Ty’s on his way home now.”

“That’s good. I worry about him driving around in bad weather.” Big Jim’s brow was furrowed.

“But the weather is fine. Sunshine, even.” Leah pointed to the bright, sunny outdoors through the windows. “See, the snow is melting.”

Big Jim’s lips compressed in a thin line. He let out

a huff of displeasure. "If you don't mind, can you give me a call and let me know when he gets home? I'll be worried until I hear from him."

"Aw, Dad. I know you love us and worry about us like we're little kids." Leah hugged his neck and gave him a kiss on the cheek. "I'll make sure Ty calls you the minute he gets home." She gave Angelique a hug, too, and headed to the rear of the house to gather her children. She reappeared a few minutes later, carrying her son and with Gracie zipping up her puffy down-filled coat behind her. "Gabrielle is still sleeping."

"Bye, Grampa." Gracie gave Big Jim a hug. "You're going to love my present. I made it especially for you."

Big Jim returned her hug. "If you made it, I know I'll love it." He waved goodbye as Leah and her children headed out.

Angelique went to the back of the house to the combination kitchen, dining, and family room. It was a cave-like room, and Gabrielle was sound asleep on her back lying on a pallet on the floor. Angelique lay down beside her, content to be with her daughter after being apart for most of the day.

She reflected on all the events of the day. Shopping for needed items for herself and Gabrielle, and purchasing Christmas presents for her new family members. She had gotten presents for the oldest of Big Jim's sons, Colton and his wife, even though they seemed to resent her presence. She sighed and closed her eyes. Perhaps they would get over their anger in time.

A few minutes later, Big Jim crept in to cover the two females with a quilt. He stood for a moment, gazing down at them, so grateful to have them in his life.

Alphonse Benoit poured Courvoisier into a crystal glass. It was his favorite cognac. He always had a case in his home to comfort and relax him. It was a type of rich and complex brandy he was especially fond of.

"My friend," he whispered and raised the glass to his lips, letting the fine liquid roll across his taste buds and ease down his throat. Cognac had been served and celebrated at the opening of the Eiffel Tower in 1889. He figured it was worthy of his loyalty.

With due deliberation, Alphonse set the glass down on the fine oak table beside his high-backed chair by the fireside. One side of his face was warm, but his insides were raging.

He was livid. He had all of his worthless associates looking for Angelique Guillory and his granddaughter, and none of them had come up with a single clue. He considered all the possibilities, wondering if she was hiding out with a man.

Yes, she was beautiful, and could probably attract any man with a normal libido. He snorted. She sure sank her teeth into his son, Remy. His son couldn't see himself with any other female from the time they were in grade school. Now Remy was dead, and Alphonse's only remaining blood relative was adorable little Gabrielle.

When Alphonse got his hands on his granddaughter, he would make sure she had the best of everything. No granddaughter of his would ever want for anything.

He was set on getting custody of Gabrielle no matter the cost. Angelique could give up her rights the easy way, or he was prepared to make her disappear the way he had dealt with his various enemies. He drained his glass and reached to pour another.

One does not cross Alphonse Benoit.

"Hey, man. What are you up to?" Derrick had called Tyler on his cell.

"Hey, Derrick. I'm on my way home from Dallas. About fifty miles from home now. What are you up to?"

There was a long silence while Derrick considered options. "I, uh, I wanted to ask you…"

"Ask me what, Bro?"

"How do you feel about me dating Angelique? I mean, do you have a problem with it?"

"Why would I have a problem with you taking Angelique out?" Tyler made a sound like a bull snorting. "I think the two of you are good together."

Derrick sighed. "I thought so too." He absently scratched Meow's head, which caused her to jump in his lap and rhythmically knead his thigh.

"That doesn't sound good," Tyler said.

"I screwed up everything with her." Derrick eased Meow onto the floor, where she hissed at Smokey.

Tyler chuckled. "Well, you don't do anything half-way, do you, Bro?"

"Oh, hell no! When I screw up, I do it right."

"C'mon, Derrick. What did you do?"

"I can't even say, Bro. Just know that I'm an idiot." Derrick heaved out a big sigh. "I suddenly got this idea that she's your sister and Big Jim's daughter—and maybe you wouldn't want me getting serious about her."

"Yep."

Derrick gazed at the phone. "Yep?"

"Yep, you're an idiot." The sound of Tyler's laughter sounded through the cell. Then he blew out a deep breath. "Well, whatever asinine thing you've done… maybe you can redeem yourself tomorrow night."

"What happens tomorrow night?"

"I will be dancing with my beautiful wife at the Eagles Hall to a live band. In fact, the entire Garrett clan will be there."

"The entire…"

"All of us. Maybe you could find someone to dance with." Tyler chortled again. "I mean, you're ugly as sin and have the charm of a buffalo bull, but surely some kind female will take pity on you."

Derrick considered the number of people who usually turned out for a live band at the Eagles Hall. He had hoped for a less public venue to make amends… but beggars couldn't be choosers, so… "Thanks for the heads-up. I might see you there."

He hung up feeling a tiny bit less miserable. Perhaps Angelique would be the kind female who took pity on him. He reached down to scratch Smokey's head. "If I'm lucky."

Friday night found Derrick feeling antsy. He had polished his boots and wore his favorite western shirt, freshly starched and ironed.

Yes, he had shaved with care and added a little aftershave, so he smelled as good as he looked.

Both Meow and Smokey sat still as statues, watching him as he paced around.

Derrick didn't want to arrive too early, but he recalled how Angelique had wanted to leave early the last time the Garrett clan invaded the Eagles Hall, so he didn't want to arrive too late either.

He finally gutted up and drove toward Langston. On the way he rehearsed various apologies, hoping he got a chance to offer one. It hadn't snowed in a couple of days, so although the fields on both sides of the highway wore a blanket of snow, the roadway was a clear, black swath cutting through the whiteness.

Derrick glanced up at the black sky. A lot of stars shining above and the moon was in its waxing gibbous phase, almost full. Another week and it would be full round. As it was, the moonglow lit up the whiteness of the snow, making the countryside look like a black-and-white photo.

In time, he rolled into Langston, noting that the town itself looked like a Christmas card. All of the local businesses were sporting bright Christmas lights, and the town fathers had seen to it that strands of lights hung from the one stoplight to all four corners of that particular street.

He arrived at the Eagles Hall, parking in the crowded parking lot across the street. He hiked to the building festooned with holiday lights and a collection of blow-up figures in front. Santa and several of his reindeer greeted passersby.

Derrick stamped the slush off his newly polished boots, loped up the steps, and paid his way inside.

The band had started, and a man with a deep voice was crooning to a two-step rhythm.

Derrick edged his way around the room, keeping his eyes open for any member of the Garrett family.

He saw Beau Garrett on the dance floor, twirling around with his wife. Her red hair made them easy to spot.

He spotted Leah's daughter, Gracie, sitting beside Big Jim Garrett himself. Big Jim was rocking his young grandson in some kind of baby carrier. He appeared to be totally rapt, gazing with a loving expression at the one-year-old.

Derrick swallowed hard. Seeing the patriarch of the Garrett clan in what appeared to be a vulnerable moment made him seem far less formidable.

Standing on the sidelines, out of sight, Derrick searched the crowd for Angelique, but he didn't see her at the table. Maybe she was dancing? Or perhaps she had gone to the ladies' room.

He loitered in the shadows, but couldn't find Angelique. Finally, he saw Tyler and Leah on the dance floor. Derrick edged around to the opposite side of the room, and when they came near, he stepped forward enough to give a wave. When the song was over, they came to him.

"Hey, Derrick," Tyler said. "I lied to you, bud."

Derrick frowned. "Lied to me?"

Tyler shook his head. "Yeah. No Angelique. She decided not to come with the rest of the family."

Disappointment must have shown on his face, because Leah gave him a hug. "She didn't know you would be here. She told Big Jim she had a headache and wanted to go to bed early."

Derrick felt a little better. At least she hadn't stayed away because he would be there. "Thanks. I guess I'll have to find another way to contact her."

"Um, you could give her a call, or is that too pushy?"

"Yeah, maybe."

Leah looked to Tyler for affirmation. "We could invite her over for dinner, and you could visit with her at our house."

"No, I wouldn't want to put you two on the spot." Derrick tried not to show his emotions. "I'll figure out a way to apologize to her. You folks enjoy the dance."

He gave a little shrug, trying to make it appear it was no big deal, and left the hall. The music could be heard outside but muted as he stepped down into the slush. Dark skies overhead. Derrick slogged to his truck and climbed inside, sitting for a moment while he decided what to do next.

Chapter 11

Angelique had put Gabrielle to bed but couldn't sleep herself. She was restless and a bit sad. It seemed that the Garretts had a routine of sorts. They liked to go to the Eagles Hall on Friday nights for hamburgers and dancing.

She had loved dancing in Derrick's arms. He was probably at the Eagles Hall right now, holding some other lucky woman in his arms. Maybe he would kiss her. Maybe he would take her to his bed. Especially if she didn't have a father Derrick feared.

Was this charming rural community no better than New Orleans? Were there evil men who preyed upon others? Fearsome men who ruled the community, the mention of whose name sent a shiver down the spine of anyone within hearing distance.

Angelique had claimed to be too tired to go dancing with the rest of the family, but in truth, she was anything but tired. Antsy was her best description. She turned on the television, but couldn't seem to follow the story line of any program.

She turned off the TV and went to the kitchen. The refrigerator was a tribute to all of Big Jim's grandchildren. There was a photo of Gabrielle, as well as Gracie and JT and the grinning little redheaded girl, Ava, daughter of his youngest son and his wife. Altogether a very attractive array.

Angelique was grateful that her precious daughter was among the dearly loved grandchildren of Big Jim Garrett. She supposed this gave her child some protection from her other grandfather, Alphonse Benoit. Not that Gabrielle would have anything to fear from grandfather dearest. It's just that her life would be twisted to suit the Benoit way of life.

"No!" she said aloud. Her voice was way too loud in the otherwise empty house. She thought about making coffee or some cocoa, but figured she would not be able to sleep. She turned most of the lights off, leaving enough for Big Jim to find his way into the house.

As she headed for the bedroom, she tried to appreciate how lucky she was to have found her real father and that he accepted her without question. She was also grateful for Tyler and Leah, whose acceptance warmed her heart. It was only Colton who refused to admit that she might be his half-sister. He was so angry. She was pretty sure he would never think of her as deserving to be a Garrett.

She made sure the outside light was on to welcome Big Jim home, and started to go to her room…but there was a truck sitting outside.

Angelique's stomach twisted in a knot. It was Derrick's truck.

What was he doing there? What right did he have to hover around in the shadows?

She pulled the drapes aside, angry that he was haunting her. She didn't care if he saw her. She wanted him to know she wasn't hiding from him.

"Oh, no!" He was getting out of the truck and trudging up to the house. Did he have the gall to think she was inviting him in?

He climbed up onto the porch and stood outside the door, hands shoved deep in the pockets of his jacket.

Her stomach was churning. *Why doesn't he knock?* Her jaw tightened, and she threw the front door open. "What do you want?"

He stood silently, gazing at her. "I want to apologize to you."

She blinked rapidly to keep tears at bay. "You don't need to apologize for anything. Just leave us alone."

He took a step back. "I can understand how you feel. I was a complete ass." He shook his head. "It was a guy thing. I'm sorry." He started to turn away.

"What are you talking about?" she huffed.

He turned back. "It's an unwritten rule. Guys don't jump on their best friend's sisters. I had a moment of doubt." He shrugged. "I grew up with the Garrett boys. We were all male, and suddenly there's this gorgeous woman and I'm reacting to you..." His voice trailed off. "I'm sorry if I hurt your feelings." He turned back, as if ready to depart. He stepped down off the porch.

"Wait!" Her voice wavered.

And there was this man, standing in the moonlight, gazing at her with pain in his eyes.

"Wait... I don't want you to leave." She opened the door a little wider. "Please come inside. I'm getting chilled." A hopeful little smile touched her lips.

Derrick strode back up onto the porch and took her in his arms, delivering a kiss that warmed her all the way to her toes.

"If I go into the house, I'm going to be all over you, and the Garretts may be on their way home right now." He gave her a sweet kiss this time. "I'm going to ask you to go on a date with me tomorrow night. I'm going to do my best to seduce you in style, so be forewarned."

Angelique couldn't suppress a giggle.

"But it will be in my home, where we won't be disturbed. I want to be with you, Angelique." He brushed his fingertips across her cheek. "I want to show you how much I care for you."

"I, uh, I care for you too." Angelique's heart was trying to beat its way out of her chest.

"I'll pick you up about six, if that's okay."

She swallowed hard and nodded, seemingly unable to form words. *Tomorrow at six.*

"I been to New Orleans once." Leah's grandmother was scurrying around the kitchen. "It was a high time."

Angelique had been helping Leah sort her clean laundry. It was an excuse for her and Gabrielle to be out of Big Jim's house when Derrick came to call. She didn't want to ask Big Jim to babysit while she was having her way with the hot and handsome sheriff.

She was extremely grateful that Leah was willing to be her coconspirator in this crime of passion. Or perhaps it was a crime of omission. No, that was sin of omission. Whatever, Angelique couldn't keep the grin off her face.

She tried to keep her focus on sorting the socks, those belonging to all members of the family. Tyler's were easy to spot, but Leah's and Gracie's looked much the same, just a slight difference in size. Of course, Fern's were plain and JT's were tiny. Sorting and rolling the socks kept Angelique from pacing the floor and looking out the window.

"When were you in New Orleans, Gran?" Leah asked.

"It was when me an' my sweetie was first married." Fern turned to the two women folding clean clothes. "It wasn't exactly a honeymoon, but it was purty soon after we was husbin an' wife."

"What did you do in New Orleans, Miz Fern?" Angelique asked.

"We had a fine time," Fern said, slapping her hand against her hip. "Me an' my honey went dancin' every night…an' the food was sumpin' else. I musta ate my whole weight in shrimp. It was dee-licious."

"Really? You liked Cajun cooking, Miz Fern?" Angelique thought she might have an opportunity to cook something and be appreciated.

"Oh, sure did. 'Course, I was a lot younger then, an' I could stand all that spicy stuff." Fern placed her hand on her chest. "Now, when I eat somethin' like that, I get all upset an' gassy." She shook her head. "Most likely, nothin' like that is gonna cross my lips again."

"Oh, sorry." Angelique was disappointed, but hoped that Derrick would be her best customer.

"Looky what I found," Fern said. She held up two tiny wooden figures. "Bet you ain't seen them since you was a lil' bitty girl."

Leah broke into a wide grin. "Oh my! I thought those were lost."

"They was, but I found 'em." Fern chortled in delight before handing the small figures to Leah.

Leah's eyes filled with tears and spilled down her cheeks. "I love them so much." She turned to show Angelique. "My grandpa made these for me the first time I got to spend Christmas with them. He carved a complete set of nativity figures for me. This is Mary, and this is one of the Magi. See the turban on his head?"

Angelique examined the small carved item. It was only about four inches high, including the aforementioned turban. "This is lovely," she said.

"He painted them all himself." Leah's voice had a tremor. "I loved him so much."

"Yep." Fern's face crinkled into a wide grin. "Yore grampa was a fine man."

"Did you find all of the pieces, Gran?"

"Shore did. I thought mebbe you kin share them with Gracie and lil' JT."

Leah did a little bounce up and down accompanied by a squeal of joy. "Oh, I can't wait to show Gracie. This set will be something I will be handing down to her."

Angelique bit her lower lip, wondering what she would be able to hand down to her own daughter.

"It's unusual to find you by yourself, Dad." Colton was helping his father repair the door to one of the horse stalls in the stable.

Big Jim didn't reply, but drilled a hole for the new hinge to be installed. He was squatted down while Colt held the door in place.

Colt cleared his throat. "I mean, where is… Angelique? She's usually right there, sitting in the house where you and Mom raised me and my brothers." He heard the bitterness in his own voice.

Big Jim held two screws clamped between his lips, which appeared to be clenched especially tight. He glowered up at his oldest son, a furrow between his fierce brows. He spat the screws into his palm.

"Honest, Son! I don't know what it is that you got against my Angelique. She's just about the sweetest little gal ever born."

Colt couldn't suppress a derisive snort. "Is she, Dad? Well, how come she didn't make your acquaintance until now? Didn't it occur to you to check into her background? I mean, she showed up here without even a phone call."

"Now listen here, Son. I have no reason to doubt her. She is my daughter. She is the daughter of my college girlfriend. She is Sofie's and my child. I'm sorry I didn't know about her, but now that I do know, I will never deny her. Angelique and Gabrielle are very precious to me."

Colt pressed his lips together to keep from blurting out something else to anger his father.

"Just hold the damned door steady so I can get this hinge screwed on." Big Jim changed the drill bit to a screwdriver bit and drove the screws into place. He stood and gave the gate a shake to make sure it was fastened securely. "That oughta do it."

"Until the next time Thunder decides to kick it down."

"Well, when he does, I'll fix it again." It was obvious that Big Jim was barely controlling his anger.

"Look, Dad, I didn't mean to upset you. I was hoping to talk some sense into you before you make a huge mistake."

Big Jim turned on him, his face red and a vein standing out in his forehead. "Just what is it you're so fired up about? Are you afraid she's going to be in my will?

Are you so greedy for the land that you would begrudge your sister a share?"

Colt reeled as though his father had struck him. "I can't believe you said that. I'm not greedy. I just don't believe that she's in any way related to you."

"She is my daughter." Big Jim's voice was a whole octave lower in pitch and his jaw was tight.

"Okay, I know you believe that. You want to believe it." Colt took a wide stance and fisted his hands at his waist. "If you truly believe this woman is any kin to you, why don't you have a DNA test to make sure?"

Big Jim took a deep breath as though steeling himself. "Because I am sure." He swallowed hard. "Colton, I'm gonna ask you to leave now, and don't come back until you have adjusted your attitude. You are my son, and Angelique Guillory is my daughter. Get used to it." He gathered his tools and headed for the house, leaving Colton staring after him with a burning sensation in his chest.

When Derrick picked Angelique up at Tyler's house, she appeared to be shy. He figured she was embarrassed to be sneaking around when she was a grown woman, but she was living in her father's house, and he seemed to be less than enthusiastic about the budding relationship. Derrick hoped to be able to show Angelique that he was proud to be seen with her and wanted to deepen their ties.

"You're sure you want to keep Gabrielle tonight?" she asked Leah.

"Of course. Go on now. You deserve a night out." Leah made shooing motions with her hands.

When Derrick handed her up into his truck, he assured her that he would bring her back to Tyler and Leah's house whenever she wanted.

Angelique enjoyed the beautiful countryside as they drove toward Langston. The moon was rising, and it cast a glow on the snowy scenery. There must have been a million stars strewn across the night sky, and all of them were twinkling for her pleasure.

"Beautiful night," she said.

He glanced at her and reached for her hand, placing it on his thigh. "Not nearly as beautiful as you are tonight."

A flush of warmth filled her insides. "I'm glad you think so, Derrick."

He shot her an appraising look. "I swear…you don't actually have any idea how gorgeous you are, do you?"

"Me? I'm just…"

He shook his head. "In high school, there were a ton of girls who didn't have anything near to your looks, and they were so full of themselves. Always preening and posing… But you…" He heaved a deep sigh. "You're the real thing. You could be on magazine covers or the movie screen."

Angelique shook her head. "Oh, come on now."

"No, I'm serious. I spend all my time looking at you, wondering what you could possibly see in me when you could have any guy you want."

"Please, stop. You must be in love with me." She stopped short. "I mean…"

"You're probably right." They had entered the town of Langston, and in no time he was pulling up to the steak house. "Hope you're hungry." He got out to go around and open her door.

Angelique was stunned by his comments, and even more stunned by his admission that he might be in love with her. This was going to be an interesting night.

She enjoyed the meal at the steak house. Apparently the cook had been taking lessons from Big Jim, although this steak had a slightly different seasoning. Perfectly prepared as well as anything she had dined on in the city.

People stopped by the table to say hello to Derrick and be introduced to his companion.

She had to accept that this was a small town and people knew people.

After dinner Derrick drove her to his ranch, which he insisted on calling "only a small place." A little over one hundred acres sounded huge to her.

When he opened her door and held out his arms, Angelique felt as though she was committing something serious to this somewhat serious man. She slid down off the seat and into his embrace. He took a moment to hold her, pressing a sweet kiss against her lips, but then hurried her inside because of the drop in temperature.

When she sucked in a breath, it chilled her insides, but she was inside his warm house in no time.

There was a dog now, in addition to Meow, the cat she had met the last time she was there. The cat regarded her solemnly, but the small dog approached, wagging its tail.

"That's Smokey. I guess I'm dog-sitting for an elderly couple." Derrick gestured to the cat. "Meow is finally beginning to accept Smokey. It was touch-and-go for a while there."

Angelique thought it was a good sign that a man could

be bothered to take care of pets. In truth, he seemed to be taking care of a great deal of the county.

He helped her out of her outer layers and shed his gloves and fleece-lined jacket.

They stood looking at each other for one agonizing moment, and then he kissed her. Kissed her like he really meant it. Kissed her in a way that blazed a trail from her lips all the way to her girlie parts. *Oh, mama!*

And then her clothes began to fall off.

It seemed the kisses were causing them to fall in a heap at her feet. Angelique pushed away, gazing up at the man helping her out of her garments. "Wait! One of us is wearing entirely too many clothes. Start stripping, cowboy."

Derrick grinned and sat down on the sofa to wrest off one of his boots. "Getting out of the boots is the hardest part." He got the second one off and then stood up, but Angelique stepped forward to help him. Something about taking off a man's shirt was distinctly exciting, but she found that he had a thermal undershirt beneath it. The thermal knit clung to all his muscles, emphasizing his well-developed chest and arms.

"Nice," she purred. "Do you work out?"

He chuckled as he slipped it off over his head, treating her to a nice display of rippling muscles. "Like at a gym? The answer is no. I work, period."

Good answer.

He scooped her up and carried her to his bedroom at the rear of the house. When he placed her in the middle of his bed, he took a moment to remove the rest of his clothing before joining her.

He trailed kisses down her body and found her most

sensitive areas to pay special attention to, using his tongue to bring spirals of orgasm swirling through her body. She wanted him inside her. But she didn't want him to stop what he was doing.

He broke away to sort through a drawer in the bedside table, producing a condom.

She took it from him and applied it to his erection, thrilled that he was so well-endowed.

He entered her gently and quickly brought her to a full orgasm. But he wasn't finished.

It had been so long, she was ready to detonate fast, gripping him with her thighs and arms. She arched against him, her nipples taut against the light swirl of chest hair. By the time he climaxed, she had lost count of hers. She was damp and breathing heavily. "Yeah!" She wanted to say thank you, but thought that was not appropriate. Instead, she lay contented in his arms.

He snuggled the bedding around her, and pulled her closer. She wanted to clean up, but she wanted to be held more. Somehow, cuddling with Derrick Shelton felt like the best thing she had done in a while.

That night, Colt shared with Misty the exchange between himself and Big Jim earlier that day. They were watching television, but when he started relating the conversation, she turned it off.

She felt heartsick that her husband was so hurt by his father's words. "I can't believe he's being so obstinate. It's as though he's taking this Angelique woman's side against you, his own son."

Colt shook his head. "It's like he has blinders on."

Misty laid her head on his shoulder and tucked her hand in the crook of his arm. "You have to let him make a fool of himself, Colt. He's not going to listen to you or anyone else."

"I never thought my own dad would take some stranger's side over mine." He swallowed hard. "I mean, he always used to value my judgment."

Misty hated that Colt, always the big, strong man, let Big Jim's comments get to him. "I'm sure he'll come to his senses eventually."

"Did I tell you that he asked me to leave?"

She patted his arm. "Yes, you did. It's okay. I'm sure he didn't mean it."

Colt brushed her away, standing abruptly. "Yes he did. He told me not to come back until I, quote, 'change my attitude.' How am I supposed to react to that?"

Misty watched him pace around. She felt helpless, knowing her husband was as stubborn as his father. "Colt, it's almost Christmas. You don't actually think your dad is going to ruin Christmas over this, do you?"

Colt stopped his pacing, seeming to consider her words.

Encouraged, she went on. "Big Jim is like a kid at Christmas. He loves to make sure everyone has a great time. You know how he plans his little surprises for the children? And he's always made it a big deal that the family goes to church together. Tomorrow is Sunday, so do you think he's going to demand that we sit somewhere else in church? Think about it."

Colt heaved out a big sigh. "I guess you're right. I don't think he's going to make a scene at church."

"You'll see," she said. "I'll bet he's regretting his words. He'll be glad to let it all smooth over."

Colt just stood there frowning. He raked his fingers through his hair. "I hope you're right."

Chapter 12

Big Jim felt the emptiness in his huge, sprawling ranch house. He got up early, as usual, and took a shower. He shaved and got dressed for church. The silence in the house seemed to press in on him as he made coffee. When it was properly brewed, Big Jim poured himself a cup and sipped it as he strolled around his vacant domain.

He realized he was a people person. He was a family man. But what happened when that family grew up, found their mates, and didn't need him any longer?

Big Jim drew the heavy drapes aside and stood gazing out at the beautiful countryside. What had happened to his dream? Oh, yes. He and Elizabeth had planned to grow old together after the boys were raised, but who knew she would be killed in an accident aboard a church bus returning from a women's retreat?

When Angelique had appeared with Gabrielle, it was just what he needed. Some people who needed him. More family.

He finished off the coffee and rinsed his cup, leaving it in the sink. Then he donned his jacket and Stetson and headed for his truck.

Today he was especially mindful of his surroundings. As he headed for the highway, everything he was seeing belonged to him. The land, the trees, the little creek that was now iced over. All except for the land he had given to Tyler and Leah for their home…and the land he had given to headstrong and uncooperative Colton and his wife, Misty.

Big Jim was especially disturbed that Colt was so antagonistic toward his very vulnerable half-sister, Angelique. Colt was usually quite willing to espouse the underdog, but something about Angelique seemed to really get under his skin.

Could he be jealous?

Big Jim's lips tightened as he turned onto the highway and headed into Langston to attend the church he had been a member of since boyhood.

He considered the possible reasons for Colt's antipathy. Perhaps he was angry that Big Jim would include Angelique and Gabrielle in his will. Or perhaps he was infuriated that his father had a relationship prior to his marriage to Elizabeth, and that the relationship had produced a beautiful daughter. Maybe his feelings were related to his loyalty to his mother and thoughts that there should have been no other women in Big Jim's life other than her.

Big Jim was one of the first to arrive at the church. He parked close to the entrance and hiked up the steps. There was a light breeze blowing, and the chill nipped at his ears. Once inside, he greeted a few of his neighbors and one of the Sunday school teachers who taught Gracie's class. He realized he was being unusually gregarious due to his lonely state. Sad situation for an otherwise self-confident man.

In due time, Colt opened the door and followed Misty inside. Misty saw Big Jim and averted her gaze.

Okay, so that's how it is.

Colt, however, approached with his hand outstretched. "Hi, Dad. Glad to see you."

Big Jim was a bit taken aback. Was this the same sulking and angry man he had left in the stables only the day before? "Uh—good to see you too, Son."

Misty offered a weak smile.

"Why don't you two go on inside and stake out our usual pew?"

"Sure, Dad." Colt took Misty's arm and headed inside.

Slowly, people began to fill up the church. They entered stamping the slush off their boots or shoes and unwrapping scarves from their necks. Parents ushered children back to their appropriate Sunday school classes.

"Grandpa!" A redheaded comet burst into the building and headed for Big Jim Garrett. His granddaughter, Ava, made a crash landing, tackling him around the knees.

"There's my girl!" Big Jim picked her up, kissing her cheek in the process.

She squeezed his neck with great enthusiasm. "I love you, Grandpa."

He gave her a serious look. "I'm sure I love you much more."

"Aw, Grandpa. You're so silly."

He set her on her feet and greeted Beau and Dixie.

"We'll see you inside, Dad," Beau said. "Gotta get Ava to her Sunday school class."

Dixie lifted a foil-covered plate. "I made cookies with my own two little hands."

"And they are so yummy," Ava insisted.

Dixie was not known for her cooking abilities, so Big Jim was proud of her for her efforts. "Good for you."

Finally, Tyler opened the door and Leah entered, carrying JT, with Gracie and Fern Davis close behind. Tyler closed the door and made a beeline for Big Jim. He held Gabrielle in his arms. "Good morning, Pop. You're looking good."

"As are you." Big Jim leaned down to give Leah a hug and kiss, and then the same treatment for Gracie. "Oh, look at my grandson, all bundled up." He held out his hands, and JT reached for his grandpa. He was wearing a tiger-striped fleece outfit with ears on the cap. "Come here, my little tiger boy."

Big Jim's chest warmed with joy. His family was here. Well, almost all of them. "Where is Miss Angelique this fine morning?"

Leah and Tyler exchanged a glance. Both shrugged in unison.

Big Jim frowned. "What's that supposed to mean?"

They both smiled and headed inside the church.

"Come on, Dad," Tyler said. "Let's get settled."

Big Jim followed with JT, concerned, but since both Leah and Tyler seemed amused, he tried not to worry.

He took a seat next to Misty, noting that she was unusually quiet. She gave him a faint smile, but clung to Colt's arm.

Big Jim let that fact settle in his brain as he unzipped JT's tiger suit and peeled the boy out of his fleece layer. His fine, dark hair swirled around his head like a cloud of fluff. Big Jim smoothed it a bit before dropping a kiss on top of JT's head.

Leah took Gabrielle from Tyler and sat down next to Big Jim. She began removing the girl's outerwear too.

Gracie squeezed in between Leah and her grandpa, grinning as she snuggled under Big Jim's arm. "Love you, Grandpa," she whispered.

He dropped a kiss on her forehead. "Love you more."

Almost all of the church was filled. People were still taking kids back to classes, and some were milling around, greeting friends.

Big Jim wondered if Angelique was ill or perhaps she was only sleeping in. He twisted around in time to see Angelique enter the church…with Derrick Shelton, and he had his arm around her. They were both grinning and looking all googly-eyed at each other.

Suddenly the whole picture was clear.

Angelique Guillory had spent the night with Sheriff Derrick Shelton, and they were basking in the afterglow. Anyone who had eyes could see it, yet Derrick waved and greeted the many fellow churchgoers. He was acting all proud of himself and of Angelique. He introduced her again and again, all the while keeping an arm around her.

Big Jim saw the joyful expression on Angelique's face. She was truly happy to be wrapped in Derrick's embrace…and whatever they had done the night before had brought about that happiness.

Big Jim released a big sigh. He was her father, and she was happy. That was all that mattered.

Her face was glowing as she leaned over to give Big Jim a kiss on his forehead. "Good morning."

Big Jim composed himself quickly. "Good morning to you, my daughter." He added the last for Misty's benefit. He reached out a hand to Derrick. "And to you, Derrick. You're looking good this morning. Sleep well?"

Derrick's eyes locked with Big Jim's. "Yes, sir. Like a baby."

Sunday morning in the Big Easy. The bells of St. Louis Cathedral rang out to welcome parishioners, as they had for almost three hundred years. Of course, the original building had burned down, but the site was designated for the church in the early 1700s by French engineers. The beautiful building towered above its neighbors, the Cabildo and the Presbytère. The cathedral overlooked the square with the bronze statue of General Andrew Jackson and the Pontalba Buildings with their frilly wrought-iron grillwork. Truly, this was the heart of old New Orleans.

Alphonse Benoit slouched in his high-backed chair, listening to the church bells.

His boyhood had been spent in Catholic schools, generally on his knees and memorizing Latin phrases. *Et cum spiritu tuo.*

His parents had punished him when he had acted out at school, and they had brought him to the cathedral every Sunday. The tolling bells were calling to him, but he refused to answer.

Perhaps when he had recovered his precious grandchild… Perhaps when he could take Gabrielle, he would return to his roots. He would be a good grandparent. Not the fearsome Alphonse Benoit whose very name brought a chill to those who knew of his exploits.

The housekeeper brought his coffee and beignets, quietly setting the tray on the table at his elbow and withdrawing without speaking. The aroma of the chicory-laced coffee and spicy beignets brought him out of his reverie.

He inhaled the spicy scent of the beignets and poured a cup of coffee, then set it aside to cool. He pulled himself to his feet, stretching out his stiff muscles.

Alphonse went to the window, reinforced with bulletproof glass. The skies were gray and overcast. Ominous dark clouds hung low and heavy overhead.

Christmas was a week away, and still he was alone.

His wife and his only son were dead. His beloved girlfriend was dead. Only one reason for him to live, and that was to recover Gabrielle.

He cursed again that Angelique had stolen Gabrielle from him, then went into his familiar reverie about how things would be when he finally found and retrieved her. He would raise her in this very mansion. She would be given the best education, study abroad as he had...and at his death, she would inherit everything he owned. His will had been recently updated to make sure his granddaughter would be his sole beneficiary.

She needed to be prepared to take over his empire.

Alphonse gazed out, unseeing, hands fisted, jaw tight.

Gabrielle Guillory was a remarkably good child. She sat quietly on her mother's lap, looking like the angel she truly was. This behavior only lasted a short time. Gabrielle got squiggly very quickly and ended up being passed around, from her mother to Big Jim, back to Angelique and then to

Derrick. She seemed to enjoy her throne, no matter whose lap she was reigning from. Her dark hair curled around her face, a contrast to her fair skin and incredible blue eyes.

Angelique was proud of her daughter, not only for her beauty but also for her sunny disposition. Gabrielle seemed to really like her new surroundings and the new people in her life, especially Big Jim and her aunt Leah and uncle Tyler.

Angelique had been raised Catholic, but she listened politely to this minister preach to his flock and prayed as a Catholic for the safety of herself and her daughter.

After the church services, Big Jim gathered all of his family and they invaded the small, home-style restaurant called Kelli's Deli. They shoved several tables together to make one long enough to seat the entire family, plus the sheriff.

"I really love this place," Leah announced. "It's almost as good as Gran's home cooking."

Fern Davis displayed a wide grin. "Why, thanks, sweetie. I do my best."

Leah leaned across the table to squeeze Fern's hand. "Your best is the very best, Gran."

Angelique opened the menu, scanning the pages. Everything sounded good, and the place smelled like delicious stuff to eat. "What's good here?"

"Everything!" several responded almost in unison.

"Well, that helps a lot." Angelique waited until others had ordered and then went for the chicken-fried steak with cream gravy and french fries. She listened to the family chatter, easing into the comfort of the Garrett clan as much as she could when some of the family had accepted her and some had not.

Derrick was a good friend of all three brothers. He sat beside her, chatting casually with Tyler and Beau, and also Colt. The only one remaining silent was Misty, Colt's bride.

On one hand, Angelique was offended, but on the other she was afraid. It wasn't a popularity contest. Not everyone would like her, but at least they should admit she was Big Jim Garrett's daughter. His illegitimate daughter, but his blood relation.

She hoped that at least the nonbelievers wouldn't go prying into her background and stir up the roiling miasma of her past.

"How about the mac and cheese with a hot dog for Gabrielle?" Leah suggested.

Angelique snapped out of her dream state. "Oh, yeah. She loves mac and cheese, don't you, Gabi?" She addressed her daughter, ensconced in a high chair between her and Big Jim.

Gabrielle nodded enthusiastically. "I wanna hot dog."

Angelique was regretting that the new outfit Gabrielle wore would have cheese all over it in no time, but the owner, Kelli, passed out plastic bibs for the little ones.

"Y'all feel free to wear anything on my menu, or I can fit y'all out with a grown-up-size bib." Kelli grinned at the table full of Garretts.

Big Jim looked around. "I think we're all pretty much wash and wear, but thanks anyway, Kelli."

They ate their meals with general enthusiasm. Kelli returned again to refill drinks and supply conversation.

When they were finished, Kelli brought the check and Big Jim held out his hand.

Derrick reached for his wallet and offered to chip in.

"Derrick, you may not be a Garrett, but you got your arm around my beloved daughter, Angelique, and that's good enough for me." Big Jim gave Kelli his Visa card, and that settled the matter.

Angelique felt relieved. Apparently her father was not a man to be feared. So she only had one scary grandfather to deal with.

Although Big Jim had offered to drive Angelique back to the Garrett ranch, Derrick informed him that they were going to hang out a while longer.

That may have irked Big Jim, but he made a show of laughing it off. "You kids have a good time."

Tyler fixed Gabrielle's car safety seat in the back seat of Derrick's truck. "You thinking of something serious with Angelique?"

"I don't know how to answer that," Derrick said. "I'm crazy about Angelique, but it's early days yet."

"But you do care about her, don't you?" Tyler gazed at him earnestly.

"More than I have ever cared about any woman… except my mom." Derrick grinned.

"Oh, yeah." Tyler grinned in return. "Sorry. I didn't mean to pry into your relationship. It's… Well, Angelique is my sister."

"Yes, she is." Derrick took a step away and closed the truck door. "I wish you could have a talk with your big brother. I can't imagine why Colt is being such an ass."

"No way! I'm staying out of that mess." Tyler shook his head vehemently. "Even Misty is acting all huffed up. She's backing Colt all the way."

Derrick shrugged. “I don’t blame you for staying neutral. Misty is just being loyal to her husband.”

“I guess, but I don’t want to get between Colt and Dad. Dad has made his decision, and he accepts Angelique without question. Dad knows that he had a, uh, relationship with Angelique’s mom, and he’s done the math. Besides, she’s got Garrett blue eyes and so does Gabrielle. Pop says Angelique is like a perfect combination of Sofie’s and his best genes.”

Derrick chortled. “You don’t have to convince me. I’m Angelique’s biggest fan.”

“Okay, here’s my last uncomfortable question.” Tyler leaned against the truck and crossed his arms over his chest.

“Shoot.”

Tyler cleared his throat. “How do you feel about Angelique having a child?”

Derrick stepped back and fisted his hands at his waist. “What the hell kind of question is that?”

Tyler held his hands up in a submissive gesture. “Hold on! I’m serious. My sister has a child. A beautiful child. Apparently, you’re dating her, whatever the hell that means.”

“I am…dating your sister, who has a beautiful little girl. They are a package deal.” Derrick huffed out a sigh. “I don’t know what you’re after. You’ve known me all your life.”

Tyler offered a little smile. “Exactly, and I’ve never known you to go out with a woman who had a child.”

“So?”

“So, maybe you don’t understand the obligations involved.”

Derrick glanced back at the restaurant. Leah and Angelique were standing inside chatting, each holding her own child. "Obligations? I can't believe you're giving me a hard time. Leah had Gracie when you two met."

"I want you to understand the complications. It's not just you and Angelique. It's the three of you. Gabrielle will become attached to you. If you're not serious about Angelique, I can't let you hurt them."

Derrick felt as though one of his best friends had slugged him. "I have no intention of hurting either of them. I-I love Angelique." He removed his Stetson and slapped it against his thigh. "The truth is, I don't think she's on board. I'm willing to give her some time, hoping she will—" He stopped abruptly, his face reddening. "I'm hoping Angelique will come to love me too." He couldn't believe he had made this admission to his friend. "Promise you won't mention this to Leah. I'm taking it slow, hoping things work out."

Tyler slapped him on the shoulder. "I won't say a word. Glad to know you're taking it slow and easy…and glad to know that you love her."

"Just keep it to yourself, will you?" Derrick said. "It's all up to Angelique."

Derrick and Tyler went back into the restaurant. Tyler gathered his wife, daughter, baby son, and Fern Davis and escorted them to his truck.

Derrick stood gazing at Angelique and Gabrielle. His chest filled with warmth when Angelique smiled as if she were fond of him. "Ready?" His voice became husky.

"I am. Let's get home."

Gabrielle was walking in a tight circle around her mother, her head down as she paced.

Derrick felt his brow furrow. "You want me to take you to Big Jim's?" He had hoped to have more time with her.

Angelique laughed. "No, silly. I want you to take me to your home."

Colt was livid. He had a death grip on the steering wheel and had tuned out his wife's chatter. Hopefully, she would get the message that he didn't want to talk.

He didn't want to talk about Angelique Guillory. He didn't want to talk about Derrick, his best friend growing up, looking all gaga about her. And most of all he didn't want to talk about his dad, the formidable Big Jim Garrett, absolutely wallowing in the bullshit that little scam artist was shoveling.

He turned in at the main entrance to the Garrett ranch, passing under the horseshoe-shaped arch emblazoned with the Garrett name overhead and bumping over the cattle guard. Ah, yes. *Home sweet home*. Only there was an outsider nestled in the bosom of the Garrett family… or at least huddled under Big Jim's protective wing.

Colton passed by his father's ranch house, still dark, as apparently Big Jim had not yet arrived home.

Misty was in the passenger seat, pouting.

Colt knew he deserved it, but he was not in the mood for discourse. He didn't want to be coddled or affirmed. He wanted to be wrapped in silence with his own dark thoughts.

He passed the turnoff to his middle brother's home.

Tyler had built a very handsome house for his wife and children and for Fern Davis, Leah's grandmother. Of the three brothers, Tyler seemed to have it all together. He had a music career and also maintained his status as a rancher.

Only the youngest brother, Beau, maintained a separate residence from the Garrett compound. His wife, Dixie, had inherited her childhood home and ranch property, and they chose to live apart from the others. Of course, Big Jim had bestowed additional acres on them to equal what he had given the older two.

Colt's back teeth gritted together. He wondered what his dad would be presenting to the woman he accepted as his daughter.

By the time Colt pulled into the drive of his own home on the ranch, he was a mass of simmering dark matter.

He turned off the motor and headlights and sat glowering into the darkness.

"Well, I've had about enough of this." Misty didn't wait for Colt to do the gentlemanly thing and come around to open her door. She opened it herself and slid down to the mushy ground. She slammed the door extra hard and stomped into the house.

Colton drew a deep breath and blew it out forcefully. "Guh-rate!" He pulled the keys out of the ignition and pocketed them, before climbing out and following his ticked-off wife into their house. He would be doing a lot of making it up to Misty for a while. He figured he should do a little more online shopping. Wrapped presents under the tree should be evidence of his true remorse.

Chapter 13

Big Jim turned on the lights on his front porch. He had gotten a call from Tyler that he was bringing his grandmother-in-law over to spend a couple of days. Leah's "Gran" wanted to do some serious baking, and using Big Jim's monstrous kitchen would make it easier for her to carry out her plans.

Big Jim was always happy to see the delightful little woman. In truth, he had not been looking forward to rattling around his house all alone. And the fact that she wanted to cook was even better.

When Tyler pulled up in front of the house, Big Jim threw open the door and stepped down off the porch to bring Leah's grandmother safely through the slushy snow and up the stairs. He waved at Tyler when they had reached the porch.

"Miz Fern, I'm so happy to have you here."

Tyler climbed out of his truck and retrieved a small suitcase and two bags of groceries, and heaved them onto the porch. "Just a little baggage, Dad."

Big Jim took the bags inside as Tyler's truck roared away from the house. "Miz Fern, you want to settle into your usual room, and I'll take these groceries to the kitchen?"

"That's mighty nice of you, Big Jim. I shore do like to do some cookin' in that nice, big kitchen."

"It wouldn't be Christmas without your pumpkin pie, Miz Fern."

Her eyes lit up as a wide grin spread across her face. "Don't you worry none at all, Big Jim. I'll be making my pumpkin and my pecan pie for our Christmas dinner. But it's the cookies and other goodies I need to make ahead." She gave him a big wink. "So that's what I'll be workin' on most all day tomorrow." She peered at him over the top of her wire-rim glasses. "You don't mind if I stay a couple of days, do ya?"

Big Jim beamed at her. "Not if my kitchen smells like cookies." He was grateful for the company. "And I hope you're gonna make us some of your cornbread dressing for Christmas dinner."

She tipped her head to one side and placed her index finger against one cheek. She made a face as though she was considering his request. "Oh, I suppose I could make some since you asked so nice."

"I'm asking nice because I plan to smoke a big ol' turkey, and a pan of your special dressing would make the perfect accompaniment."

She nodded, looking at him intently. "An' yew gotta have some of my smashed potatoes. If I make gravy, it will taste so good on tha dressin' an' potatoes. T'wouldn't be Christmas dinner without 'em."

Big Jim made appreciative sounds. "That sure does sound good, but don't forget, Miz Fern…all the kids will be here and everyone will be bringing something. You don't have to make everything."

"I suppose, but are you makin' a list?"

"Yes'm, and I'm checking it twice." Big Jim roared with laughter.

Fern blinked and then joined him in laughing.

"Y'know, I had a feelin' you was feelin' a mite lonely, an' I thought I'd come ta see you an' cook up a storm in your big ol' kitchen."

"You know, I'm really glad you're here," Big Jim said.

"Doggy!" Gabrielle squealed and made a run at Smokey.

Derrick quickly stepped between the two. He scooped up Gabrielle and lifted her high over his head. "Here you go!"

She giggled but kept pointing at Smokey. "I wanna pet the doggy!"

Derrick sighed. "Yeah, that's a doggy." He hoped that Smokey would be cool with a small, excited child. But knowing the dog was used to living with an elderly couple, he was hesitant to let the two interact.

Derrick tucked Gabrielle under his arm and carried her, football style, to his recliner. She was laughing and waving her arms wildly. He sat down and arranged the young girl on his lap, then whistled Smokey over. The dog came, wagging his tail. "Good boy," Derrick mumbled.

Smokey sat down by Derrick's boots, looking hopeful.

Derrick leaned down to scruffle the dog's ears, and Gabrielle reached to do the same.

"Good doggy." She delivered brisk swats on Smokey's head, but he seemed to like it and jumped up to put his paws on Derrick's thigh.

"What's all this?" Angelique came into the room and stopped, taking in the scene with raised brows.

"Um, well, your daughter is making friends with Smokey. I'm dog-sitting him for an elderly couple who had to go to the hospital in Amarillo."

Angelique smiled. "That's good. We never had a pet, so I'm glad she's learning about animals."

Derrick chuckled. "Just wait until tomorrow. I'll introduce her to Freddie, my longhorn bull."

"A longhorn bull? Is that different from any other bull?"

"A whole different breed. I have a small herd of longhorns that are really pets."

Angelique shook her head. "Pet bulls? Texas sure is a different place than I'm used to."

"Well, I only have a small herd. Your dad has huge herds of several different breeds. He couldn't possibly get to know his cattle the way I know mine." He shrugged. "My longhorns are not for sale."

"I think that's the way Big Jim feels about his horses." She sat on the sofa next to the recliner and reached to pet Smokey. "Nice doggy."

Gabrielle slipped off Derrick's lap to squat down by Smokey. She put her arms around his neck and leaned her forehead against the dog's head, crooning a little song to her new furry friend.

Derrick took a moment to soak up the scene. He was still irked at Tyler for questioning his feelings for Angelique, and even more so for his inferences that he might not be seriously interested in her because of Gabrielle. Spending the afternoon and evening with Angelique and her daughter was turning out to be most enjoyable.

Angelique had prepared their evening meal, and when he offered to help, she had shooed him away, but allowed him to entertain her daughter. It was as though they were auditioning each other. How would he feel if things heated up between them? Would they be able to form a viable unit…a family?

He took a deep breath and stood up, bringing Gabrielle with him to take a seat beside Angelique on the sofa. Gabrielle immediately got down and returned to give Smokey her full attention.

He put an arm around Angelique's shoulders. Brushing the hair away from the side of her face, he pressed a kiss against the side of her neck. He noticed her earrings. They probably weren't real, but they looked like a faceted oval diamond surrounded by a circle of smaller diamonds.

Derrick touched an earring. "Pretty."

She smiled. "They were my mother's. She passed away not too long ago." Angelique swallowed hard, signaling that the emotion was still raw. "She gave me her jewelry and some other things just before she—she died. And she told me who my father was and how I could find him."

He pulled her closer. "I'm sure glad you found him." He kissed her temple. "I'm sure glad I found you."

Angelique heaved a sigh and snuggled against his shoulder.

Man with his arm around his woman and dog lolling against his leg receiving attention from small child. Yeah, this was feeling good.

Fern Davis was up early. She had mixed up a batch of her oatmeal pecan cookies while the coffee was brewing, and now two sheet pans of cookies were in Big Jim's refrigerator to chill. Fern took off her apron and hung it over a ladder-back chair. She poured herself a cup of coffee and took it to gaze out the back door that led to the covered porch. There were glass panes inset, but she could see very little. It was still dark, but she had not been able to stay in bed any longer. She planned to have plenty of cookies and sweet treats for everyone in the Garrett family, which she considered to be her family now. Fortunately, her only granddaughter, Leah, had married Tyler, the one she considered to be the pick of the Garrett litter.

Fern would always adore the man. Tyler could do no wrong in her book.

Somehow, making cookies didn't seem nearly enough.

"That coffee sure does smell good." Big Jim reached for a cup and helped himself.

"Hope I didn't wake you," Fern said, turning from her reverie. "I was tryin' to be real quiet."

"Oh, no, Miz Fern. This is my usual get-up time." Big Jim took a sip of the hot liquid. "I got horses expecting me to feed 'em and scoop up their poop."

Fern laughed. "Sounds like chilrens."

"Might as well be." He saluted her with his cup. "Good coffee."

"I seen some bananas on the counter. You got plans for 'em?"

Big Jim shook his head. "They're all yours."

"Great. I'm a-gonna make us some banana bread that'll make yore toes turn up."

"Anything you want to use, just go on ahead, Miz

Fern. If you need anything else, I'll be happy to take you into Langston for shopping."

Fern's face crinkled up in a grin. "Aww, thanks, Big Jim. I'm purty shore I got all the makin's I need. But if I think o' anythin' I'll letcha know."

Big Jim drained his cup and set it in the sink. "I'll be back in a while. The kitchen is all yours."

Fern was still grinning long after he had gone. She took a few of the bananas and put them in the middle of the counter. Sure enough, Big Jim had brown sugar and regular sugar and flour. She had brought her own special concoction of spices, just in case, but Big Jim's kitchen seemed to be pretty well stocked.

She glanced out the back again, and the sky seemed to be lightening up a bit. Humming a few bars of one of her favorite hymns, she tied her apron back around her waist and removed a glass loaf pan from under the counter.

In no time at all, she had mashed up some bananas and had a loaf of her spicy banana bread in the oven. By the time Big Jim returned from his adventures in the stable, the aroma of freshly baked banana bread greeted him.

"Hot damn! I'm gonna take me a quick shower and come back for a slice of that delicious-smelling stuff."

"Take yore time, big fella. It cuts better when it cools off a little." She had already cleaned up after herself and was checking out another recipe.

Alphonse Benoit lay awake in his king-size bed. The sky was just beginning to lighten in the east. His bed coverings were heavy but warm.

For days, the sky had been gray and leaden, like a bulging underbelly ready to burst open, but the rain wouldn't come. Even the air felt heavy. Cold blasts of air coming off the water caused the windows to rattle.

His household was still abed. Only the live-in couple who worked for him were allowed to stay in his realm. The man cooked and shopped for the master and his guests, while the woman kept the place clean. Both were full-time jobs, considering the size of the estate. There were assorted groundskeepers who mowed and trimmed the lush yard, but they came and went on schedule.

Alphonse finally threw back his covers and searched for his house shoes with his bare feet. When he stood, he scratched himself and ambled to the bathroom where he relieved himself. The noise was amplified by all the hard surfaces in his bathroom. Highly polished marble walls, floors, and fixtures rebounded sounds and bounced them around. He sighed, shook it off, and lumbered over to the vanity to wash his hands in one of the sinks. No, he didn't flush. The maid would do that. He glanced at his face, dark with stubble. He would have to shave, but maybe not today. He didn't want to see anyone.

He wanted Remy back. He missed his rebellious only son who had refused to be involved in any of his father's businesses.

He wanted Sofie back. He ached for his beautiful lover. The woman who dared to boss him around…to refuse him…to amuse him.

And he wanted his only granddaughter back. No matter how much he wanted the other two, Gabrielle was alive and had been stolen from him. He would have her back.

He threw the hand towel on the floor and stomped back to the bedroom.

How could it be that Angelique Guillory had so completely disappeared? She was certainly not all that smart. Beautiful, yes. She looked so much like his beloved Sofie, except for those strange, almost turquoise-blue eyes, a trait shared by his Gabrielle.

Now, Alphonse was depressed and frustrated. His men, who were usually quite competent to carry out his wishes, had utterly failed.

For some reason, they couldn't get a handle on where Angelique might have gone. It was as though she had evaporated.

New Orleans had many ways to escape. There were highways and byways. There was an airport. There was the Gulf of Mexico leading out to the open Atlantic Ocean. There were many ports to the south. Could his son's slut have taken Gabrielle to live in Mexico or South America or on any of the islands in between?

No! She didn't have the wherewithal to travel extensively or to live elsewhere. She had to have holed up somewhere nearby. Perhaps with a friend.

Alphonse heaved a deep sigh. *Idiots!* He would have to come up with a new strategy of his own. He had wanted to have Gabrielle in his home by Christmastime. He wanted to spoil her like any grandfather. He wanted to shower her with presents and love.

Angelique awoke to the sound of her heart thudding in her ears. Her eyes opened, and she realized she was naked and held snugly against the warm sleeping body of the man she loved.

Derrick was breathing rhythmically, his well-muscled chest rising and falling as it should. He was slumbering while she was wrenched from the comfort of sleep by something that terrified her. But what? She swallowed, listening to the silence that pressed in on her from all directions.

Was it a dream?

Suddenly the image of Alphonse Benoit's face, almost purple with anger, reappeared in her brain. She trembled and must have made a sound, because Derrick stirred and gathered her closer. The warmth of his flesh stilled her trembling, and yet she could still hear the threat in Alphonse's voice. "If you take my Gabrielle, you will die. She will be an orphan with only her generous grandfather to care for her." He had made a clucking sound. "Such a sad story…but Gabrielle is a very lucky girl." And then he'd laughed.

Angelique had no idea of the time, but it was still dark outside. Try as she might, she was unable to return to sleep, mostly because she was on edge, but also because she was afraid she might again find Alphonse Benoit in her dreams.

She had to remember the reason she was here. She had to protect her daughter. That Gabrielle was now nestled in the bosom of the Garrett family was the most important issue. She figured that Big Jim would protect his granddaughter with all his considerable resources—but would that be enough to protect her from a New Orleans mob boss?

Angelique shivered again, her cheek against Derrick's

shoulder. Was it fair to expose the Garretts to the dangerous Alphonse Benoit's heinous power?

Derrick kissed her hair. "Are you okay, baby?"

She nodded, her hair making a scrunching sound against his chest. "Just going to go to the bathroom." She slipped out from under the covers and tiptoed from the room. She lingered in the bathroom because she had told Derrick that was where she was going, and she didn't want to lie to him. Sins of omission were a different matter. She gazed at her face in the mirror, noting her even-paler-than-usual pallor. Her eyes looked haunted. "No! Get out of my head, you evil bastard," she whispered.

Angelique splashed cold water on her face and mopped it off with one of Derrick's big bath towels. She slipped into Derrick's bathrobe and turned off the light before she crept to the other bedroom, where her daughter was bedded down. Gabrielle lay on her back, spread eagle, breathing in and out. Her dark lashes fanned out against her cheeks. *Beautiful child. My child.* Angelique sucked in a deep breath and blew it out forcefully. "And you can't touch her, Alphonse."

The temperature was dropping, and the sky was the color of gunmetal. Big Jim had saddled one of his favorite horses, Onyx, a black stallion that had sired several very handsome foals. Onyx had been obviously stir-crazy, stamping his hooves and tossing his magnificent head.

Big Jim felt a rush of pride knowing his horses were not only beautiful to look at but bred to perform. The blanket of snow covering the ground wasn't melting, but the threat of new snow hung heavy in the air. Big Jim felt certain that this was a brief window for Onyx to have a chance to run off his pent-up energy.

Big Jim kept to a path he knew, since the snow could hide a hazard that might cause his beautiful horse to injure himself. Yes, he took care of everything that belonged to him. His land. His cattle. His horses. His family…

And that included Angelique and Gabrielle. He felt a muscle in his jaw twitch.

He realized that when his sons had stayed out all night, he had merely chuckled, but that his daughter was partaking of sins of the flesh irked the hell out of him.

And that attitude also irked the hell out of him. Talk about your double standard!

Big Jim exhaled, his breath making a stream of white mist around his face.

Angelique was a grown woman with needs of her own. She'd had a young daughter without benefit of marriage, so she wasn't exactly a blushing virgin. But why couldn't Big Jim give her the courtesy of the same treatment he had given his sons…all three of them?

"Okay, Onyx. Let's shake it up, boy. I feel like a little run." He slapped his boots against the horse's sleek sides and enjoyed a brisk ride that let him release his concerns about his daughter.

When they arrived back at the ranch house, he saw Derrick Shelton's truck pulled up close to the house. Big Jim stifled the irritation gathering in his chest. Derrick was a good man. He was the sheriff now, a tried and true friend. He had grown up with Big Jim's own sons.

Onyx knew the way to the stable, so it would be fair

to say the horse took his rider home. Big Jim removed the saddle and rubbed Onyx down before tossing a wool blanket over his back and offering him water and the special high-quality grain he bought for his equine children.

When he trudged toward the house, Derrick and Angelique were emerging from inside. They kissed. A nice, light kiss. Not bespeaking passion; it looked like real caring between two people.

"Oh, hey, Big Jim." Derrick raised a hand as he stepped off the porch.

"Hey, yourself. You kids doin' okay?"

"Yes, sir. I've gotta get to work, or I would hang around and chat." He opened the door to his truck. "Miz Fern's cooking up a storm in your kitchen. Smells awesome." He shut the door and revved the motor before driving off.

Big Jim raised a hand in farewell and headed for the house. When he had stepped onto the porch, Angelique was still there, waiting for him.

"Hi, Dad. I hope you weren't worried about us."

Big Jim pulled off his leather gloves and reached for the door handle. He held it open for her to precede him. "Worried? Me? Of course not. You've got yourself a really good man there."

Angelique dimpled. "You're right about that. He's the best."

They went back to the kitchen, which did smell like a bake shop. "Mmmm… What smells so good, Miz Fern?"

"Must be these brownies I jus' whupped up."

"Yum," Angelique said. "Can't wait to try one."

Fern grinned at both of them. “Well, why don’t both o’ yew set yerselves right down an’ I’ll bring ya some.”

“I can’t pass that up,” Big Jim said. What he really couldn’t pass up was the chance to have a casual chat with Angelique without playing the dad card. “Where’s Gabrielle? I haven’t gotten my hug yet today.”

“She’s right there, Dad.” Angelique pointed to where Fern Davis was carefully removing freshly cut brownies from the pan with a spatula. Holding onto the leg of Fern’s sweatpants, Gabrielle grinned at him.

“Gran make me some cookies.” She waved the evidence at him.

“Well, looky at that, big girl!” Big Jim’s face split into a wide smile. “Come on over here, Gabi.” He held out his arms to her.

Gabrielle let out a squeal and raced across the room to be caught up in Big Jim’s arms.

He felt a surge of joy as he lifted her high overhead and then snuggled her close for a hug. “Hello, darlin’. You’re my girl, y’know that?”

“Hi, Gwampa!” She gazed at him, her blue eyes shining.

“You know what Grampa needs? He needs a big kiss right here.” He pointed to a spot on his cheek, and the little girl obliged him with a loud and very wet smack.

As he tousled Gabrielle’s softly curling hair, he glanced at Angelique. She was looking on with great amusement. “You got a great little girl here.”

“Yes, we do.”

Fern brought the plate with brownies and a couple of oatmeal cookies for Gabrielle. “Yew folks wan’ some milk?”

"Oh, that would be great. I can get it." Angelique started to jump up, but Fern waved her back to her seat.

"Yew jus' stay a-sittin' right there. I got this." Fern winked as she turned to the refrigerator.

"This is real tasty, Miz Fern." Big Jim munched his way through the first warm brownie.

Fern returned to the table with two glasses and a sippy cup for Gabrielle, while Big Jim lifted her into her high chair and scooted it up to the table. "Cookies and milk. Just what this big girl needed," he said.

"An' how 'bout yerself? How do yew like my brownies?"

"This is fabulous, Miz Fern," Angelique offered. "I love chocolate."

"I agree," Big Jim said. "Tasty as tasty can be. Maybe you ought to open a bakery, Miz Fern. We don't got one anything like that around here. I can be your silent partner and set you up with a nice place in town."

Fern waved him off. "Not me. I jus' wanna bake good stuff for tha people I care about. That's what makes me happy."

Angelique stared at Big Jim, her mouth open. She couldn't believe he was suggesting that this elderly woman open a bake shop. She wanted to scream at him that she and her lover had run a restaurant down in the French Quarter. But then again, she felt tongue-tied.

Big Jim seemed to have pigeonholed his daughter as some helpless little dimwit. It had been hard enough for her to get through the little drama with Derrick. At least Big Jim was acting as though he approved of Derrick.

Whether he truly felt this way would probably come out eventually. But in the meantime, at least, Angelique had no problem spending time with the one man who accepted her completely… Well, almost completely.

She heaved a sigh, opting at least to broach the subject. "You know, Dad…"

He turned back to her and patted her hand. This was much the same as when he had tousled Gabrielle's hair. "What's that, baby?"

"Dad, if you're in the mood to open a restaurant, I'm your partner. My boyfriend and I had a small restaurant in New Orleans. It was quite successful."

"That's nice, but you got a sweet little girl to take care of. You don't need to work outside the home. She is your full-time job." He looked at her as though this was a good thing.

She realized it was a good thing. He was willing to support her so she could take care of her daughter as he was taking care of her. They were safe. "Um, thanks, Dad."

"Now, you gotta tell me what you want for Christmas. If there's anything special you want, just let me know." He tilted his head to one side. "'Cause otherwise you might get a gift card, and that's no fun to unwrap."

Angelique shrugged. "Aw, I don't need anything. You've done so much for us already."

"No, really. I want to give you something you really want. This is my first Christmas with my daughter, and I want to spoil her. Maybe something you've always wanted." He nodded at her encouragingly. "Some little bauble? A nice piece of jewelry?"

She tried to smile, but couldn't quite carry it off.

"No. Not a thing. My mom gave me all her jewelry, and she had some really nice pieces." She touched the gold chain hanging around her neck. "We've got everything we need. You have taken us in and given us a safe place to live. You're providing us with everything we could possibly want."

"I hope so, honey. But if there is something you think of, you will let me know, won't you?"

Angelique tried to swallow, but her throat felt dry as the desert. "Sure."

"I think I gotta have one more of these chocolate things before I call it quits." Big Jim reached for the biggest brownie on the plate.

Chapter 14

Derrick drove into town and parked in front of his office. There were other trucks belonging to deputies with the official county emblem on the doors.

He climbed down out of the truck and gazed up at the sky. It looked as if a dark-gray blanket had been stretched overhead. The temperature was dropping, and there was an icy forecast.

Derrick went into the office, stamping the slush off his boots outside the door.

"Hey, Sheriff!" Duane, one of the longtime deputies, greeted him. "Gonna be a cold one."

"Yeah, and we know what that means." Derrick headed for his office, dreading the upcoming events of the day. There would be icy sleet. People would drive off the road and crash into each other. Power would go out and people would be shivering in their homes.

All of the county-owned vehicles were equipped with all-weather tires, which kept them from sliding around on an ice-covered highway. But he felt responsible for all the deputies, and their well-being was of prime importance to him. He had known most of them all his life. Known their parents and the girls they married.

"Hey, Derrick." Duane poked his head in the office door. "I'm gonna run out and check on the Mendez family. The old man has that breathing problem, and I thought I would make sure they're okay. He was wheezing pretty bad in church last Sunday."

"Sure, go on." Derrick waved a hand. "And you might also check on Miss Sarah. She lives out that way too. She's getting on in years and lives all by herself."

Duane gave a two-fingered salute and grinned. "I'll check them both out."

Other deputies were making rounds, too, so Derrick found himself alone in the office. He checked his email and the incoming statewide alerts. He printed them and took the stack of papers to his office. Two men had robbed a convenience store in the next county over, and a parolee had skipped bail and was on the lam from his latest arrest.

Derrick shook his head and tossed the papers on his desk, but one slid onto the floor. He bent down to pick it up and froze. There was the image of Angelique Guillory on a Wanted poster. He could hardly draw a breath. He felt as if he were being strangled. "Angelique!" He sat down heavily in his old wooden desk chair. The words on the page seemed to dance before his eyes.

Angelique Guillory was wanted in New Orleans for theft of jewelry valued at over $100,000.

Derrick sat staring at the paper for some time. He couldn't imagine any circumstances in which the sweet and sensitive Angelique Guillory he knew would be driven to steal a loaf of bread, much less expensive jewelry.

There had to be a mistake, but no. This was an alert from the New Orleans Police Department, and Angelique had arrived in Langston straight from that very city. He gazed at the beautiful face on the poster. The face of the woman he loved.

He swallowed hard, then folded the page and tucked it in his pocket. On the computer, he deleted one alert, and only one. He would have to have a serious talk with Angelique.

Derrick recalled how beautiful she'd looked, sleeping in his arms.

So trusting…

So innocent…

He hoped.

Gabrielle was fast asleep, but Angelique continued to rock her. Big Jim had relocated the big, cushy rocking chair to the room Angelique shared with her daughter.

It would have been easy to put Gabrielle in her bed, but for some reason it was as comforting to Angelique as it was to her daughter to hold the sweet little human and rock them both gently as she hummed a wordless tune.

She had been antsy all day, realizing that her life would be spent in this sort of comfortable void. Truly, she felt safe, a condition she had not enjoyed for some time. Since Remy's death.

She knew Big Jim would protect her and Gabrielle. The safest thing to do was to sit down and shut up. All of their needs were taken care of. They had a great place to live, plenty of food, and mostly kind people surrounding them.

As Angelique let her head drop back onto the headrest, an image of Colton and Misty sprang to mind. The expressions on their faces told the whole story. They didn't believe that Angelique was Big Jim's daughter, illegitimate or otherwise. She didn't think she quite rated complete hatred and loathing, but some serious dislike was emanating from both her oldest half-brother and his wife.

She pressed her lips against Gabrielle's soft curls. How could anyone dislike an innocent child and her not-so-innocent mother?

Okay, time to stop being a leech. Angelique stirred herself into action and put Gabrielle in the bed. Gabi was dressed in a warm pajama set so Angelique did not cover the child, but tiptoed from the room, leaving the door ajar so she could hear.

Big Jim had gone out to do his morning chores, mostly involving taking care of his animals and making certain his property was as he had left it the night before.

Angelique slipped into the kitchen, not at all surprised to find Fern had gotten there first.

"Good mornin'. How are ya, purty lady?"

Angelique swallowed hard. "Who? Me?" She raked her fingers through her hair. "I'm not exactly pretty."

Fern did an elaborate double take. "Why, whoever tol' yew that? Ye're about tha purtiest female I ever seen…other than my Leah, o' course." She gave Angelique a wink.

Angelique felt herself blushing. "Thank you, Miz Fern. I've never thought of myself as being pretty." She swallowed. "I guess it's because my mom was so very beautiful. Everyone said so."

Fern crossed her arms over her small bosom. "Well, I kin believe that, 'cause ye're a real beauty too."

"You're too kind."

"Kin I pour ya a cuppa coffee?"

"Yes, please." She accepted the cup Fern offered and

inhaled the fragrance. “This is really nice, but it’s not what I’m used to. In New Orleans, we add chicory to our coffee.”

Fern’s wisp of an eyebrow rose on her forehead. “Why, whatever for?”

“It’s a tradition. Cafe du Monde bows to the tradition and makes their coffee with chicory. It’s so lovely to go there in the morning and have a beignet and a cup of coffee.”

“Jus’ what is this chicory? Some kinda grain?”

Angelique smiled, remembering fondly the times she had shared a plate of beignets with Remy on an early morning, inhaling the fragrance of the chicory-laden coffee. “It’s actually the root of a plant that has a pretty blue flower. The root has been roasted, ground, and added to coffee for hundreds of years.”

“Hmpf!” Fern snorted. “Ain’t yew tha coffee expert.”

Angelique had to giggle at Fern’s skeptical expression. “Not really. But I was curious about it, and my mom always went the extra mile to make sure I was given all the information. She was amazing.”

“Sounds like she was a special lady.”

Angelique nodded, trying not to show the emotions crowding her chest. “She was,” she whispered, while reaching to touch the pendant she wore on a chain around her neck. A present from Sofie, her loving mother. She wore it under her clothing, just to feel as though her mother was close at hand.

Big Jim surveyed his domain from the saddle of one of his favorite horses. It was the big Appaloosa that had borne his weight for the past eight years. *Good horse.* Mainly Big Jim was watching his eldest son.

Colton was hauling bales of hay out to the herd of Black Angus that had gathered near the pasture fence. There was still snow on the ground. Although it hadn't snowed in a couple of days, the frigid temperatures hadn't allowed any snow to melt. Colt was industriously hauling a bale down off the back of the truck, clipping the baling wire, and heaving the bale over the fence.

For their part, the cattle were happy that their servants had brought food. Big Jim was angry with Colt and wanted to confront him, but on the other hand he didn't. He was glad to have Colt pitching in and helping out around the ranch. He knew that his son was trying to atone for his ill treatment of Angelique Guillory, but somehow Big Jim doubted the sincerity. He suspected that Colt had put a cap on his apparent mistrust of his half-sister, not wanting to face off against his father.

Big Jim blew out a deep breath, creating a stream of white vapor. He glanced up at the cloudless blue sky. There would be a deep freeze come dark. When it was very cold or snowing heavily, giving animals extra forage and supplement helped to keep their body temperature up to get through winter storms. "Good job, Colt."

Colt grinned and raised a hand in acknowledgment of his father's praise. "Remember when we planted that windbreak, Dad?" He gestured to the row of densely spaced cedar they had planted when he was in middle school. "They sure did grow in nice and tight."

"Sure did," Big Jim said. "North wind usually comes down hard. Good to have them on that side of the pasture." He remembered how he had rented an auger to drill holes and how his oldest son had helped him with the actual planting, holding up the spindly trees while Big Jim shoveled dirt around the roots. He heaved another big sigh. Colt was a good boy…a good man. But he had to come around and accept that Angelique was his half-sister and stop treating her like dirt.

"Let me help you with that, Son." Big Jim started to dismount.

"No, Dad. I've got it." Colt cut the baling wire around the last few bales of hay and picked one up to carry it to the fence. He hefted it over and returned to get the next.

"Thanks, Son." *Hard to stay mad at him…but then there's Angelique…and Gabrielle.* "Hustle up, and we can get back to the house. Fern Davis is there, and she's been bakin' up a storm making Christmas goodies. Maybe we can warm up with coffee and something tasty."

Colt's mouth tightened for a moment, but then he huffed out a breath and nodded tersely. "Sure, Dad."

Big Jim figured Colt was not anxious to come into contact with Angelique, but he refused to back off from his stance that Colt must accept her as his father's daughter, even if he refused to accept her as his own sister.

"I'm gonna head back. You come on right away." Big Jim picked up the reins and goaded his horse to turn around and head back to the ranch house, leaving Colt to follow in the truck.

He urged the big Appaloosa forward, enjoying the short sprint to the house. He pulled up to the stable and dismounted, leading his horse inside. He removed the saddle and gave the horse extra grain after he was back in his stall. "Good ride," Big Jim said, giving the horse a few pats on the neck.

By the time he had trudged back to the house, he found Colt sitting in his truck with the motor idling. Before Angelique's arrival, Colt would have barged right into the house he grew up in. Now he was waiting for an escort.

Colt turned off the motor and fell into step beside his dad.

Big Jim wanted to give him the proverbial smack upside his head, but controlled himself long enough to get into the house.

Sure enough, he found Angelique and Gabrielle in the kitchen. "Where's Miz Fern?" he asked.

Angelique smiled sweetly at him; then, glancing at Colton, her smile faded. "Hi, Dad. Um, Leah came to pick her grandma up. She wanted to take her to a doctor's appointment."

Big Jim frowned. "I didn't know she was feeling poorly."

Angelique shrugged. "She wasn't. Leah wanted to be sure she got a pneumonia shot. Miz Fern wasn't exactly enthusiastic about getting one, but Leah said she was protecting her and insisted she go with her."

Colt remained conspicuously silent.

"Got any coffee left?" Big Jim asked.

"Just made some." Angelique picked up the coffeepot. "How about you, Colt? Would you like a cup?"

Colt swallowed hard. "Yes, that would be nice." He removed his Stetson and tossed it on the back of a chair. "I better wash up a bit." He turned and went to the half bath near the kitchen.

Angelique pressed her lips together, but carried two mugs over to the table.

Big Jim washed his hands at the kitchen sink and dried them on a dishtowel. "I appreciate you, honey." He took a seat at the table and patted the chair beside him. "You can sit down and join us, can't you?"

"Um, I wouldn't want to interrupt your talk." She poured coffee into both cups but hurried back behind the counter. "I'm making lunch."

Big Jim could tell how uncomfortable she was. "What are you making?"

She shrugged. "Just some gumbo. I made some for Derrick the other day, and he really liked it."

Big Jim smiled at her. "I have a feeling Derrick would like anything you made for him."

A little smile, but she kept her eyes down.

"Where's my little Gabi?"

She smiled wider. "Right down here on the floor. She's playing with the pots and pans. She doesn't have much in the way of toys here."

Big Jim nodded. "Maybe Santy Claus will have something for little Miss Gabrielle to play with in his bag."

"That would be nice, Dad."

Colt returned then, turning to gaze at Angelique when she said the word *dad*. He looked away quickly and seated himself beside Big Jim at the table. He wrapped his hands around the mug of coffee. "Thanks," he mumbled.

Colt seemed to be as ill at ease as Angelique was.

Big Jim sipped his coffee, watching his children ignore each other. "That gumbo smells great, honey."

"I hope you like it. It's almost ready."

"Gwampa?" Gabrielle climbed to her feet, abandoning the pots and pans she had been playing with. She peeked around the side of the counter and let out a squeal when she spotted Big Jim.

"Yes, your grandpa is over there," Angelique said.

Gabrielle took off at a fast pace, running toward him with her arms raised and a wide grin on her face.

Big Jim gathered her in his arms and sat her on his lap. "I swear, Colt. Have you ever seen a prettier little girl?"

"Um, no. She's very pretty." Colt gazed at Gabrielle, his expression guarded.

"Here, you can hold her. She's about the cuddliest little one I ever saw. C'mon, Colt." He lifted her toward his oldest son.

"Uh, okay, Dad." He allowed Big Jim to pass Gabrielle to him but he held her stiffly, staring at her.

"Oh, you can do better than that. Let her sit on your knee." Big Jim gestured to him. "C'mon. She's adorable."

Gabrielle looked at Big Jim uncertainly. Her lower lip jutted out and trembled.

"Aw. See? Now you're upsetting her." Big Jim gave Colt a glare.

Colt eased Gabrielle to a sitting position on his knee and patted her back. "Um, hey, little girl."

"That's better." Big Jim leaned back. "I knew you could do it. I'm sure you and Misty want to have kids someday. Kids are wonderful…especially this little one." Big Jim leaned over to give her cheek a pat. "This big fella is your uncle. Can you say hello to Uncle Colt?" He pointed to his son.

"Hello, Unca Colt," Gabrielle responded, gazing at him uncertainly.

Big Jim glanced at Angelique, but she looked worried. He hadn't intended to cause her any distress, but this was her brother, dammit! There had to be some kind of relationship here. "Angelique, look at your brother here. Colton is getting the hang of being an uncle."

She gave a half-hearted smile, but her brows were still knitted.

Colt remained stiff, but when Gabrielle looked as though she might cry, he pulled her against his chest. "It's okay, Gabrielle. I'm trying here." He patted her back, and when she dropped her head onto his shoulder, his pats became soft rubs. She was examining him most carefully. Obviously she hadn't made her mind up about him yet.

Big Jim was relieved to hear Colt talking to Gabrielle in a soft voice. He wasn't about to congratulate himself yet, but it was a start. "Come join us, Angelique."

Angelique sucked in a deep breath and went to the table. She started to sit on the other side of Big Jim, but he pulled out the chair between himself and Colton. She hesitated but then slipped onto the chair.

When she saw her mother, Gabrielle turned and held out her arms. Angelique reached for her daughter, and Colton eagerly passed her. Big Jim could not tell which of his children was the most relieved.

Gabrielle's arms were wrapped tight around Angelique's neck.

A timer on the stove dinged and Angelique jumped up. "Gumbo's ready." She handed Gabrielle off to Big Jim and hurried to the simmering pot.

"Smells great, honey," Big Jim called. "I'll take a bowl."

She looked up at him, delivering a dimpled grin that caused a squeezing sensation around his heart. "Sure, Dad." She straightened her shoulders and gazed steadily at Colton. "How about you, Colt? Are you up for the gumbo experience?"

Colt managed a smile in return. "Just a cup. I still gotta get home and have dinner with my wife."

"Gotcha!" Angelique busied herself dishing up the gumbo. She brought a big bowl to Big Jim and a mug of the aromatic gumbo to Colton. Then she dished up a bowl for herself and came back to the table. She had a saucer with some pieces of chicken she had fished out of the pot for Gabrielle.

"Isn't this a little spicy for Gabrielle?" Big Jim asked, shoveling a spoonful in his mouth.

"Puh-leeze! My Gabi is a NOLA girl. She likes it spicy."

As if to underline the point, Gabrielle picked up a piece of the chicken that Angelique had cut up in small bites and shoved it in her mouth, her perfect little teeth chomping away.

Colt made short work of his small serving. "That's really good."

"Want to take some home?" Angelique offered.

Colt let out a sigh. "Better not. My bride is none too confident about her cooking skills, and I don't want to discourage her." He stood and took his cup to the sink. "Bye, Dad. See you tomorrow. Goodbye, Angelique." He gave a wave and left.

In the silence that followed, only the rhythmic sound of spoons scooping gumbo could be heard.

When he was done, Big Jim set his spoon down. "Glad you're getting to know your half-brother."

Angelique gave him a skeptical look, then rolled her eyes. "Is that what that was?"

Colton drove home…that was, he drove from the ranch house where he had been raised as a boy, where his mother had listened to his prayers and tucked him in, where his dad had taught him everything he needed to know to be a man and become a rancher…to the house he shared with his wife on the same Garrett property.

He parked in front of the house, happy that it was finally built. Inside, his wife and her younger brother waited for him.

But he turned off the ignition and sat in his truck, staring ahead without seeing.

Apparently, his father, the formidable Big Jim Garrett, had completely accepted that this Angelique Guillory was his daughter, the result of a college affair. And yet this girlfriend who Big Jim remembered so fondly had not bothered to tell him that she was carrying his child when she left school. Nor had she contacted him when the child was born. And this woman supposedly never told the girl who her father was until she was dying. He shook his head. And to what purpose?

He was awakened from his reverie by a sharp rap on the driver's side window. He jerked to attention and saw his wife standing outside, a concerned expression on her face.

Colt opened the door and climbed out of his truck. He leaned down to kiss the lips she offered. "Hi, Misty."

"Hi, Colt. I was worried about you." She tilted her head to one side as though that would allow her to have better insight. "I mean, you were sitting out here all by yourself… Is there something wrong?"

Colt shook his head, not sure how to tell his wife that his father had forced him to interact with the woman he suspected of taking advantage of him. That he had held her child and eaten her food. "No, babe. I'm a little tired. Thinking about a hot shower before doing anything else."

Misty gazed at him steadily, her large dark eyes peeling through his facade, layer by layer. "Is that all?"

"Um, no… Not really." He took a deep breath and blew it out forcefully. "But I'm not sure I want to open this can of worms right now." He kissed her again. "Give me a little time."

She frowned, but accepted his hand and they walked to the house together.

"Wipe your feet," she said, her voice a little hard-edged.

"Yes, ma'am." Colt made an elaborate show of wiping the slush from his boots.

Once inside, he shrugged out of his jacket and tossed it in a chair near the door.

Mark was sitting at the kitchen table working on his laptop. School was out for the Christmas holiday, so Colt wondered what had him working so intently.

"Hey, bud. What are you working on?" Colt went to stand beside Mark and look over his shoulder.

"Aw, nothin'." Mark made an ineffective effort to block Colt's vision. "I'm just messing around."

Colt backed away. "Sorry. Didn't mean to invade your space."

Mark shook his head. “No, I didn’t mean…”

“Don’t worry about it.” Colt walked to the bedroom he shared with Misty. He unbuttoned his flannel shirt and stripped the belt from his Wranglers. Next, he removed the thermal undershirt. It was important to dress in layers to maintain body heat.

“Mmm. Look at that hunky cowboy.” Misty stood in the doorway, smiling.

He turned to see her regarding him. She appeared to be more friendly than she first had.

Colt managed a grim smile. “Hey, I’m sorry I’m in such a crappy mood. Just had a hard day is all. I don’t mean to take it out on you.”

“I figured you would tell me about it if I shut up for a while.” She quirked an impish grin at him.

Colt heaved a deep sigh. “I really need to get my head straight. I’ve been working with my dad, which was okay, but it’s hard to keep my mouth shut when he’s rubbing his supposed daughter in my face all the time.”

Misty spread her arms and moved toward him. “Oh, Colt. I’m so sorry. I—”

He cut her off suddenly by raising one arm to ward her off. “Just give me a little time. I need a shower. I promise I’ll be human when I come out.”

She dropped her arms, her face looking as if he had slapped her. “Sure. You go ahead. I-I’ll be in the kitchen with Mark.” She turned so abruptly he knew he’d hurt her, but he so desperately needed to be alone to sort out his own emotions.

He watched her leave, torn between sadness and a deep-seated anger. He was angry with Big Jim, and he was angry with the way his father was shoving his supposed illegitimate daughter down his own son's throat. He was angry that he was so affected by her arrival and that his father completely accepted her without regard for his oldest son's feelings. He was angry that Big Jim hadn't asked for a DNA test but just bought her story outright.

Colt realized he was standing in his own bedroom with his jaw clenched as tight as his fist. He quickly stripped off the rest of his clothing and stepped into the bathroom. He turned on the water, not waiting for it to heat up. The shock of icy water against his flesh jerked him out of his snit. He heaved out a gasp of air and reached for the bar of soap, quickly lathering up his outsides to match the lather inside his head.

Chapter 15

That night Derrick called the landline of the Garrett ranch and asked to speak to Angelique. She was the only person he knew who didn't have a cell phone, which he now realized was odd in itself. After seeing her picture on a Wanted poster, he was questioning everything about her. He wanted it to all be a mistake. She could not be the person who had stolen over one hundred thousand dollars' worth of jewelry. She was such an innocent. Surely she had been wrongly accused. The woman was not the type to lust after riches. She was totally down to earth and honorable. Heck! She was the most adorable woman he had ever known.

"Hello, Derrick."

The sound of her sweet voice knocked him out of his confused state. "Hey, Angelique. I wanted to hear your voice."

"How sweet," she said. "I was missing you too."

"I-I think we should have dinner tomorrow night. I thought I could take you to the steak house. It's quiet and we can talk."

"That sounds nice, Derrick…but if you want, I can cook something at your place."

"No… No, that's all right. I don't want you to think I'm a cheapskate." He belted out a hearty laugh that sounded completely phony to his own ears.

"Oh, I would never think that." She made a scoffing sound. "I don't expect you to spend your hard-earned money on me. I'm not a gold-digger."

"I never said you were," he hastened to say. "I thought you might like to go out with me. Maybe I want to show off my beautiful girlfriend."

"Aww…how sweet. But you know I really enjoy cooking, and I made a gumbo today. Big Jim seems to enjoy cooking for me most, though."

"Honey, I'm sure it pleases him to take care of his daughter."

Angelique giggled. "That's what I think too. He's such a dear man. I wish I had known him when I was growing up."

He heard the note of sadness in her voice. Derrick had grown up with both parents in attendance, but he'd taken it for granted. Everyone had a family. Except Angelique Guillory. "Yeah, I wish you had too… I'm sure he's enjoying having his daughter and granddaughter living with him. He's just showing his love."

"I wish he would let me cook more often. I really enjoy it. Even Leah's grandmother comes over here to cook."

"Maybe it's that huge kitchen with all the professional equipment. Raising three sons there were a lot of big appetites to feed…and a lot of friends got to partake too."

"Lucky you."

"I was hoping we could talk about some things tomorrow night," Derrick said. "I'll pick you up at six. Is that okay?"

"Sure. I'll let my dad know he's got Gabrielle all to himself."

Derrick hung up, not sure what his motives truly were. He always enjoyed Angelique's company, but he hoped to pry a little information from her about her past life in New Orleans. Did she have access to anyone with expensive jewels?

~

With her husband taking a very long shower, Misty Garrett felt like pacing…or screaming…or throwing things. However, she refused to act the shrew so she sat at the table in the kitchen, across from her younger brother. "What are you working on, Mark?"

"Aw, it's nothing really." He shrugged, but he had been working on it for some time.

"Looks like something to me." She smiled encouragingly.

He heaved out a huge sigh. "It's an assignment our teacher posted for extra credit. She said since Christmas is the time when families get together, we could write a two-page essay about our family." He shrugged. "Ours is kinda messed up."

She nodded her head. "Big-time." The brother and sister were the only living members of the Dalton family. When she had been growing up, it was different. Her mother and father were living their dream on their own ranch. Misty was the middle child with an older brother and Mark was the youngest. She had enjoyed a relatively happy childhood…but then her mother died suddenly. Her father had dissolved in front of her eyes. The once-strong head of the family crawled into the bottle and drank himself into foreclosure of the ranch. Her older brother had fallen in with some less-than-savory friends who had eventually murdered him.

Dalton was not a name to wear with pride, and yet she and Mark were the survivors.

Misty made a face at her little brother. "Yeah, we're a pair, aren't we?"

"It's not funny. I'll have to read this in front of the whole class after the holidays."

"Aww. I'm sorry. You said this was extra credit?"

"Yeah, but I need it. I can raise my grade if I write a good essay." Mark rested his face on his fists. "This is just not fair."

"You've got time. Why don't you knock it off for tonight. We'll work on it tomorrow. I'll help."

Mark heaved a sigh and closed his laptop. "Thanks a lot."

"Let's eat." Misty decided not to wait any longer for Colt to decide he was ready to talk to his wife. She and her brother were hungry, and she was going to put food on the table. If Colt decided to join them, that was his choice.

Angelique insisted on cleaning up the kitchen after another of Big Jim's signature dinners. There was a loaded baked potato and what he considered a "small" bacon-wrapped filet. It was delicious, of course, but before he could clear the table she ordered him to stay put, have another beer, and she jumped up to clear it herself. "You take your granddaughter to the recliner and turn on the television. Chill out and let me at least get the dishes in the dishwasher,"

Surprisingly, he obeyed, taking Gabrielle off her booster seat and inviting her to join him in his throne, the big leather recliner in front of the huge wall-mounted television. "Come join us when you get done in there," he called. He ambled to the den, walking slow so Gabrielle could keep up.

"Sure will." It gave her some measure of satisfaction that she could at least accomplish this small task for him...that she could perform this tiny act, even if he wouldn't let her do much in the way of cooking.

As she wiped down all the countertops, she considered her date with Derrick the following evening. Twice, he had mentioned that they needed to talk. She wondered if there was a problem. Was he planning to break up with her? Was he going to tell her that he wasn't interested in any further entanglements with a woman who had a child?

She rinsed the dishcloth and wrung it out. No, surely he wouldn't take her to dinner if he wanted to break up. He would simply not make any more dates.

And he hadn't seemed to be upset about anything. In fact he had claimed he was going to be showing off his girlfriend. *I'm his girlfriend.*

She straightened her shoulders, not willing to allow her anxiety to eat away at her tenuous grip on confidence.

"Are you about finished in there?" Big Jim called to her. "Come on in and relax in front of the television. There are some good shows fixin' to come on."

She hung the dishcloth on a rack under the sink. "I'll be right there."

The next evening, Derrick drove into the Garrett family compound. It seemed to be all about living on the land, raising cattle and crops, and being in love.

Not a bad deal at all.

The drive to the house was lined with pecan trees, now dusted with snow. Derrick recalled being tasked, along with Big Jim's sons, with gathering those pecans. And later they would shell what seemed like tons of pecans. He would always be given a large bag to take home to his mother, who would transform them into pies and other treats.

Good times.

He pulled up close to the house and turned off the ignition and headlights.

Angelique was inside. And he had to find a way to question her without destroying their relationship. If he could get her to talking about her past life in New Orleans. It should be easy for a man to ask his girlfriend to share her past. Just conversation. *I can do this. By the way, honey…did you score a big jewel heist?*

Derrick climbed out of the truck and approached the house. The outside light was on. It was motion-activated, so it had automatically turned on when he first drove up, but after he sat inside the truck for a few minutes, it had switched off. As he stepped out, it blasted into brilliance again.

He stepped up onto the porch and rang the doorbell, the chime sounding hollow inside the residence. It was cold but the wind had stopped blowing. Nevertheless, he waited long enough for the cold to penetrate his clothing.

Then the door opened and Angelique's smile warmed him to his core.

"Well, let the man in, Angelique," Big Jim's voice boomed from another room.

She reached out an arm to draw Derrick inside. "You have to come in and say hi to my dad."

Derrick swallowed hard, suddenly insecure. "Sure." He stepped inside and managed to give her a quick kiss before following her to the kitchen area, where Big Jim Garrett sat at the table spooning applesauce into a bowl for Gabrielle. She was supervising, pointing with her spoon where he was supposed to dish out more.

"You sure do like this applesauce."

"I sure do like this applesauce," she echoed and then laughed when he looked at her and shook his head.

"Dad, you are spoiling my daughter." Angelique gave him a look of mock exasperation.

"Aw, she ate most everything else. I just cleaned her up, and I'm giving her a little help with this applesauce. It's messy, y'know?"

Angelique chuckled at that. "Yes, Dad. I do know. Now say hello to Derrick so he can take me to dinner."

Big Jim waved the spoon at Derrick. "Hello, son. You be sure and drive carefully and get my beautiful daughter home safe. Y'hear?"

"Um, yes sir." Derrick wondered why he felt as though he was in junior high school again.

Angelique tugged Derrick's arm. "We gotta go. I'm starving." She blew a kiss to Big Jim. "Take good care of your granddaughter."

He raised a big paw in farewell.

At the door, Derrick helped Angelique don her jacket, and she wrapped a scarf around her neck. It was a soft wool and was about the same color as her eyes.

"That's new, isn't it?" He touched the scarf.

"Yes. Isn't it pretty? Leah crocheted it for me. She

said she and her grandma and Misty get together to make things with yarn…mostly some kind of charity blankets for newborns of drug-dependent mothers at the hospital in Amarillo. Doctor Ryan got them interested."

"Good project." Derrick was familiar with the program where the infants, born addicted to various drugs, had to be detoxed and it was very hard on their tiny systems. Thank goodness there were kind people who volunteered to hold those infants and give them some attention. His own mother and her church friends had driven over to cuddle and rock the little ones.

He escorted Angelique to his truck and helped her climb up onto the seat. When he was behind the steering wheel, he realized she was chilled and turned on the heater. The drive to Langston was quite companionable. He wanted her to be in a comfortable and conversational mood.

"So, you never had snow in New Orleans?"

"Oh, no. It finally gets cold late in the season, and the fact that we're on the water makes it quite brisk."

"I'll bet," he said. "How about when you were a kid. Did you ever get to build a snowman?"

Angelique laughed at that. "Don't be silly. I couldn't build a snowman when we had no snow."

"Did you and your mom have any special Christmas traditions?" He glanced at her profile. *So beautiful.* She looked pensive.

"Well, my mother loved to cook, so we always made cookies together. When I was very young, we didn't have much money, so the goodies would wind up in the Christmas stocking." She gave him a pert little grin. "And pralines. My mom would always make pralines and give them as gifts. Everyone loved her pralines."

"Sounds great."

"And bread pudding," she said. "My mom always made a delicious bread pudding." She blinked rapidly. "Oh, I miss her so much." She seemed to have shrunk in her seat, her hands clasped on her lap.

They were approaching the city limits of Langston, a cluster of lights on the horizon delineating the boundaries. The Christmas lights gave them a cheery welcome to town. When Derrick pulled in at the steak house, Angelique's mood seemed to have plummeted. He reached over to place his hand on top of hers. It was as though he could feel the tension in her much-smaller hands gripped so tightly together. "It's okay, Angelique. I didn't mean to bring you down."

She nodded, her lips pressed together. "It's not you. I miss her so much. She was such a fine person."

"If she was anything like you, she was amazing." He lifted her hands to his lips and kissed them gently. "Let's go inside and get some dinner. That should perk you right up."

"Sure. I'm hungry." She reached for the door handle, but Derrick asked her to wait for him. He got out and opened her door, holding out his hand to help her down. "Thanks, Derrick. You always make me feel as though you really care about me. Like I'm a lady."

He pulled her close, wrapping his arms around her. "You are a lady…in every way."

Angelique gazed up into Derrick's eyes, knowing he spoke from his heart. "Thank you."

He tucked her hand in the crook of his arm and

walked with her up the steps of the steak house. He held the door open, and she was more than a little dismayed when it seemed that every one of the diners turned to stare at her. Derrick stood behind her, his hands on her shoulders as though he had just apprehended a felon.

A holiday tune was playing on the music system. "Have a Holly Jolly Christmas" was the message, and the tempo was most definitely upbeat.

The hostess approached with a wide smile. "Hello, Sheriff. Two for dinner?"

"Yes, ma'am." He gave Angelique's shoulders a squeeze. "Some place quiet."

The hostess led the way to a table in a back corner, but all along the way, people spoke to Derrick and stopped him to shake hands.

He pulled out a chair for Angelique, and the hostess placed menus on the table.

People were still staring. Angelique quickly picked up a menu and held it in front of her face.

Derrick frowned. "Is something wrong?"

Angelique felt a blush crawling up her cheeks. "Um, no. I-I wondered why everyone was staring. Is there something wrong with the way I look? Is it my outfit?" She patted the locket under her clothes.

"Aw, honey. How could you even think that way? You're always gorgeous." He looked around, waving at a few people. "I suspect they're checking you out. I'm a hometown boy, so everyone has to figure out who is this hot babe with the local guy."

She glanced at him, uncertain that this was the reason. Maybe they were speculating on Big Jim Garrett's illegitimate daughter. Maybe they were wondering why she was in the company of the handsome sheriff. Whatever the reason, their unabashed curiosity was disconcerting to say the least. "I don't understand why they have to stare. It's so rude."

He reached for her hand and brought it to his lips. A sweet kiss was enough to bring on another blush, but when she looked up, people were smiling. It was clear the hometown boy was making a public declaration of love.

Angelique's chest felt tight with emotion. She had found a wonderful man to fall in love with. Well, a second wonderful man.

He leaned close to whisper in her ear. "Tell me, Angelique… Do you ever miss New Orleans?"

"Sometimes. Since my mom passed, I don't have anything or anyone in New Orleans. There's nothing left for me."

He gave her an encouraging grin. "Well, if we were to go there together, what would you show me?"

Angelique's face must have shown her dismay. She couldn't imagine ever returning to the city where she had been raised. "What do you mean?"

He shrugged. "I've seen pictures of New Orleans, but mostly they're about Mardi Gras. What else is there?"

She swallowed hard. "It's a beautiful city with a long history. When I was a child, it seemed I was around people…my mother's friends, who were always laughing and giving me food. So I guess I miss the food."

The waitress came with ice water and to take their order, but they hadn't even opened the menus.

Angelique opened the plastic-wrapped menu, scanning the offerings, but Derrick knew what he wanted and the waitress noted his selections. They both turned to her. "I'll have the small filet with a side of green beans and a small salad."

When they were once again alone at the table, Angelique was relieved that the others in the restaurant seemed to have gotten over their interest in her. She released her pent-up breath, feeling the tight band around her chest loosen a bit.

"You were telling me about your mother's friends. Were they wealthy?"

She was puzzled by this question. "Wealthy? Well, maybe some of them were. I really don't know. They were people who were brought together by their love of music and good food…and they loved my mother, Sofie." Angelique was flooded with images of her mother interacting with her friends, laughing and singing and, most of all, loving her daughter every moment of the day and night. "She was amazing." Angelique touched her locket again. Just wearing it made her feel less alone.

"What's that around your neck?" Derrick asked. "I notice you touch it sometimes."

"Oh." Angelique drew the locket up through the neckline of her shirt. "It was something my mother gave to me. I hardly ever take it off." He leaned closer to examine it so she slipped it off over her head.

"This is beautiful," he said. "Really fine craftsmanship. Are those diamonds?"

Angelique shrugged. "Probably. My mom loved pretty jewelry."

He turned it over and studied the inscription on the back. "What does this mean?"

"It's French. *Mon seul et unique amour...* It means 'My one and only love.' That's what my mom used to call me." There was a catch in her throat. "I miss her terribly. I always thought she would be around to help me raise Gabrielle. I need her wisdom now."

Derrick handed her the locket. "Better keep that tucked away. It's too valuable to wear every day."

Angelique shook her head. "I will never take it off. See what she left me..." She clicked the tiny catch open and displayed two small black-and-white photographs. One was of a beautiful dark-haired woman who looked a great deal like Angelique, holding a little girl with equally dark hair and dimples. The resemblance was striking. On the other side was the image of a slightly younger Angelique, grinning in the arms of a young man.

Derrick's voice was raspy as he asked, "Who's the guy?"

"That was Remy. He was Gabrielle's father. We were so happy then." She could tell her words had affected Derrick. "We grew up together. From playmates as pre-schoolers to falling in love. Remy is dead."

"Oh... Sorry." Derrick frowned. "He looks quite healthy. Was there an accident?"

Angelique's jaw tightened. "It was ruled an accident, but his father killed him."

Derrick sat up straighter. "What? Killed him! You mean he accidentally killed him?"

She blew out a breath. "I really don't want to talk about it. It's still quite painful to me. I hope you can understand."

Derrick nodded and took a sip of his ice water before

he spoke. "Yes, I understand...but, sometime, when you feel up to it, I wish you would tell me more." He cleared his throat, but his gaze was steady and reassuring. "I love you, and I'm sure this Remy guy loved you. So I'm having a little anxiety now."

"What part of 'He's dead' did you not understand?" Angelique felt a flash of anger, but shook it off when the waitress brought their tea. She realized Derrick was honestly expressing his feelings. She had not known men who could talk about their feelings. "I'm sorry," she whispered when the waitress had gone. "I love you too."

He reached for her hand and placed a kiss on it, but continued to hold on to it, gazing at her silently until their food arrived.

"Hope you folks enjoy your dinner." The waitress had a high voice with a strong nasal quality.

"Thanks," Angelique said. "Everything looks great."

The waitress smiled and left them alone in the room full of other diners.

Derrick cut a slice of steak off and put it into his mouth. True, he was hungry, but he was also in need of something to do that didn't require talking. He had set out to learn more about Angelique's past, but he had found out more than he'd intended.

He tried to reconcile his feelings. Of course he'd known he wasn't her first love, but it had hit him like a semi truck to actually come face-to-face with a photograph of the woman he loved looking so happy in the arms of another man. *The father of her child.*

He watched as Angelique delicately cut into her meat and took a small bite. She smiled and made an appreciative noise.

Derrick took a moment to go over their conversation. She talked about her mother and her childhood, which had apparently been spent in the company of her mother, her mother's friends, and the New Orleans world of music and food.

When he had checked out the locket she always wore, he had seen the circlet of small diamonds arranged around the edge. The artistry and craftsmanship told him it was a one-of-a-kind piece. Her mother had liked jewelry. Maybe that characteristic had carried over to the daughter. She also wore diamond studs, but they were mostly covered by her long, thick hair.

Most of all, he didn't want the information on the alert to be true. He couldn't arrest the woman he loved and charge her with theft of jewelry.

He would have to investigate further…find out who the jewelry in New Orleans had been stolen from. Surely it would turn out to be a mistake. He would stake his badge on it.

Chapter 16

Big Jim had rocked Gabrielle to sleep. He couldn't resist holding her for a while, rocking gently. It reminded him of the way he had rocked his sons when they were young. Of course, he had merely been the dad...and his kids had been blessed to have been born to his lovely Elizabeth, so his role was more of a helper with the kids.

Elizabeth had made all the decisions about their day-to-day care, the food they ate, the time they were laid down for naps and bedtime, the clothes they wore.

Big Jim's role was to be the cowboy. He was the one who arose before daylight, grabbed some coffee, and headed out to take care of the stock. When he returned to the house, he would find his wife and sons doing well. The kids were clean, had been fed, and were excited to see their daddy. Then when his beloved Elizabeth had been so cruelly taken from him, he'd had to step up his game and manage to perform all of his usual tasks as well as figure out how to stand in for the best mother on the planet.

Thankfully, he had established the habit of gathering his sons in the big rocking chair for stories and the comfort of the soothing motion. Yes, there was something almost magical about a rocking chair.

Big Jim forced himself to abandon the sanctuary

of the chair. He stood with Gabrielle in his arms and walked slowly to the room she shared with her mother. He stepped into the darkened room and eased the sleeping child onto her bed. The nightlight cast a dim glow in the room, allowing him to see and admire his granddaughter.

Her dark hair was tousled and curled around her face, a counterpoint for her very fair skin. Her dark lashes lay as a thick fringe on her cheeks.

As quietly as possible, he backed out of the room, leaving the door open. He presumed Angelique would be home when she was ready to return, so he was trying to come to terms with this. He accepted that he felt differently about having his daughter stay out all night than he had as a father of sons.

Double standard? You betcha. He smiled in the darkness. He could guarantee that he would be there to defend both his daughter and his granddaughter if need be. He was their fierce protector, above all.

Derrick had seemed to be somewhat distracted during their dinner, but when they left the restaurant, he pulled her into a passionate embrace on the parking lot. Although the temperature was falling, his kisses lit a fire to keep her warm.

"Wow! What brought that on?" she asked.

He tried to laugh it off, but it was clear he was feeling something deeper. "Can't a man just plant a kiss on the woman he loves?"

She tried to match his mood. "Sure, Derrick. Plant one on me anytime."

He helped her into the truck and ran around to climb in on the driver side. "Brrr. It's going to be a cold one tonight." He stuck the key in the ignition and started the motor, revving it a few times. "Let's let it warm up a little." He reached over to stroke her cheek. "How about it? Do you want to go see a movie at the cinema?"

Angelique's breath came out in a white cloud in front of her. She shook her head. "I better get back to Gabrielle. I left her with my dad, and she's probably asleep by now."

"Want to stop by my house on the way to your home?"

She knew what he was asking. "Yes, that would be nice."

He reached for her hand and placed it on his very muscular thigh. He caressed her hand and then turned on the heater. The windows immediately fogged up, but he switched to defrost and returned his hand to hers as they watched the windshield clear.

Derrick drove to his ranch, jubilant that she had wanted to be with him. That she loved him and maybe she entertained the idea that they could have a future together…but first he had to clear her name.

When they arrived at his house, he left the motor running to keep Angelique warm while he ran up on the porch to unlock the house. There was no wind, but he felt as though he had just stepped inside a freezer. He crunched through the snow to turn off the ignition and then scooped Angelique off the passenger seat and carried her into the house. It was his plan to warm her inside and out, but he thought it might be easier to start with a warm girlfriend.

She was grinning when he nudged the front door open and carried her inside. He made sure to give her a kiss before he set her on her feet.

Just as he was securing the front door, the landline rang. It was an old-fashioned phone, a soft creamy yellow, mounted on the wall of the kitchen and with a snarled-up curly cord. Derrick blew out a deep breath. "Will you join me in the kitchen?" He held out his hand and walked quickly to the back of the house.

He gestured for Angelique to have a seat on one of the stools situated at the breakfast bar, then picked up the receiver. "Hello, Mom."

Angelique tilted her head to one side, her brows raised in question, but she began to shed her outer layers—the scarf, the gloves, the coat.

"Hello, Derrick." His mother's voice sounded way too cheerful. "How did you know it was me?"

He winked at Angelique. "Well, Mom, it was a fifty-fifty guess. It had to be either you or Dad because you're the only ones who still call me on the landline."

His mother made a scoffing noise. "Don't be silly, Derrick. We don't want to bother you at work. You might be arresting someone, and if your phone rings, you might let them get away."

"I see. What can I do for you tonight, Mom?" Derrick reached to take Angelique's hand.

"Well, of course your father and I want to know if you're coming home for Christmas."

There was a long silence.

Derrick cleared his throat. "Mom, this is my home. You and Dad are the ones who moved to San Antonio. You abandoned me here. Remember?"

"Of course I do, smarty pants." She made a snorting noise. "You know we moved here because of the milder winters, and your father has so many old Army buddies here. He gets to go play golf with them a couple of times a week."

"That sounds nice, Mom. I'm glad you're happy there."

"So, are you going to join us for Christmas here in our new home?"

Derrick heaved a sigh and shrugged, although she couldn't appreciate the gesture. "You see…I kind of wanted to spend Christmas with my beautiful girlfriend, Angelique." He kissed her fingertips.

"Oh, Derrick! You have a girlfriend?"

"Yes, I do, and she's right here with me. Do you want to meet her?"

His mother made a sort of squealing sound. "Of course I do. Put that young lady on the phone right now."

Derrick pressed the receiver against his chest. "Angelique, my mom wants to talk to you. You don't have to if you don't want to, but…"

Angelique had a big grin on her face. Her electric-blue eyes were dancing. "Oh, yes. I want to talk to your mother." She reached for the receiver, but Derrick let it dangle for a few seconds, uncurling some of the twisted cord, before handing it to her.

"Hello, Mrs. Shelton?"

"Oh, you sound so sweet," Mrs. Shelton cooed. "Your name is Angelique?"

"Yes, ma'am. It's Angelique Guillory."

"That's a lovely name. Are you from the Langston area? I don't recall any Guillory families."

"No, ma'am. I'm from New Orleans."

There was a loud silence that followed.

"Oh…I've always wanted to visit New Orleans." She held the phone away from her mouth, yelling. "It's Derrick's girlfriend. She's from New Orleans."

Derrick leaned over to kiss Angelique's temple. "You can give me the phone anytime, you know?"

"That would be so rude," she whispered.

It appeared that Mrs. Shelton had handed the phone off to her husband.

"Hello? Is this Derrick's girlfriend?" It was an excited-sounding male voice.

"Um, this is Angelique."

"Hot damn! Are you comin' with Derrick for Christmas?"

"Uh, well, I don't know. We really haven't, uh… finalized our plans."

"Aww. We sure are countin' on havin' you an' the boy come to San Antonio for Christmas."

Derrick leaned close to Angelique and spoke into the receiver. "Dad, Angelique wants to spend Christmas with her family, and I want to spend Christmas with her."

"Her family?" It was Derrick's mother who asked. "You're going to New Orleans?"

"Her family lives here," Derrick said. "The Garretts. You know the Garrett family."

"Of course we do. Elizabeth was one of my dear friends. So sad."

Angelique's lips pressed together. She looked as though she had been slapped in the face.

"Angelique and I will not be going to San Antonio for Christmas. Maybe another time."

There was a little more dithering on the other end of the line, but Derrick was finally able to hang up. He sat beside Angelique, his arms around her, and gazed into her eyes. "I had hoped to introduce you to my family in a more traditional way."

A little smile played around her lips. "You planned to introduce me to your family?"

He brushed a loopy curl away from her face. "Of course I did. I wanted to make sure you couldn't run away when I sprang them on you."

Angelique burst into a fit of giggles. "Seriously? Your parents sound really nice. I hope I get to meet them in person someday."

"You will." He gazed at her intently. "I know your family will have lots of plans for Christmas. They're wonderful and you will be all caught up in their plans, but I hope that our first Christmas together can include a little time for just the three of us."

"Oh, Derrick. That's so sweet." She blinked several times, but a single tear rolled down her cheek. "I guess I needed to hear you say that."

"That I have plans for us?" He couldn't keep from smiling. "Oh, I have plans, all right." He pulled her against him and kissed her lips, and then her neck. His hands swept over her backside, catching a handful of her firm rear.

She was wearing a pullover sweater, so he wasn't sure how to go about removing it, but his hand crept under it to caress the smooth flesh on her back. She pulled away, gazing up at him with her beautiful eyes. In one move, she slipped the sweater off over her head and then tilted her head to one side. "Is this what you were going for?"

He regarded the beautiful woman wearing a lacy purple bra and swallowed hard. "Um, yeah. I was getting there."

She gave him a sassy grin. "Well, I thought I would help you out." She slid her arms around his neck and delivered a kiss that jolted him like a lightning strike.

He pulled her closer, embedding her presence into his as their kisses deepened. "Oh, Angelique. I love you so much," he whispered against her hair. He fingered the lacy fabric of her bra, enticing her nipples to appreciate his attention.

"I love you, too, but I'm getting a little chilly. I think you need to warm me up."

"Yes, ma'am. I can do that." Derrick scooped her up and headed for his bedroom. "I actually changed my sheets just for you."

"I'm honored. What if I hadn't come home with you?" she whispered in his ear and then playfully nipped his earlobe.

"I would have tossed and turned all night thinking about doing this." He eased her onto the bed and managed to unhook her bra at the same time. He kissed and teased her nipples, enjoying her little gasps of pleasure.

She reached up to grasp his shirt and ripped the snaps open. The popping sound caused both of them to laugh. But when she pulled him down on top of her, her warm flesh set his insides on fire.

He unzipped her jeans and pulled them off, taking her panties with them. He flung them on the floor and tossed his shirt on top of them.

She was so beautiful, slim yet curvy and sexy as hell. She watched him wrestle his boots off and slide out of his Wranglers. There was a moment before they coupled that he realized he wanted her more than he had ever wanted anything…not only for this moment, but forever.

Her dimples twinkled as she held out her arms to him. "Come and get me."

"Yes, ma'am."

Colt lay awake in the dark. He had gone straight to bed without ever venturing out to where his wife and young brother-in-law were having dinner. He wasn't up for talking to her about Angelique Guillory.

When Misty came into their room, she did not speak to him, but quietly undressed in the dark and slipped under the covers to cuddle gently beside him. She lay her head on his shoulder and placed one hand on his chest. The message was clear, but Colt wasn't really open to anything. After a few moments she turned her back and embraced her pillow instead.

Colton was angry. Angry with himself. Angry with his father. Angry with Angelique Guillory, whoever she was.

He still wasn't convinced that she was a blood relative…but he had to accept that Big Jim believed she was his daughter. Apparently his relationship with someone named Sofie Guillory aligned with the arrival of her daughter, Angelique. But was this Angelique even related to Sofie?

The doubts were roiling around in his brain again. The smart thing would be to accept his father's mindset. If Big Jim Garrett believed Angelique was his daughter, then she must truly be his daughter…conceived before he married Colt's mother.

Colt inhaled and exhaled as quietly as possible. If he was feigning sleep, then he couldn't be huffing out sighs.

Okay, Angelique was his sister and Gabrielle was his niece. Apparently it was going to be this way from now on, so he might as well get used to it. Tyler and Leah had bought the entire story from the very start. He had no idea what Beau and his wife, Dixie, thought about the situation. They were playing their cards very close to the chest. Whatever their thoughts, they were polite to Angelique when they encountered her, mostly on Sundays…which must have given Big Jim the idea that they accepted her as his daughter and as a true Garrett, but without actually saying so.

He should have done what Beau did. Just shut the hell up. But no, he had to make a big deal out of it, telling anyone who would listen that Angelique Guillory was a scam artist…which caused Big Jim to want to protect his so-called daughter and granddaughter, no matter what.

And now, this very evening, he had been put in a position where he was forced to hold her child and be pleasant to the woman. His own father had manipulated him into interacting with Angelique.

But now it was done. He couldn't walk it back. Big Jim had bridged the gap between his two oldest children. She had appeared to be shy but followed through, complying with what Big Jim wanted. Maybe her presence was fulfilling some kind of need his father had.

Everyone knew how much Big Jim enjoyed being a grandfather. He adored Beau's daughter, Ava, and had embraced Leah's daughter, Gracie, even before Tyler adopted her, and now Tyler and Leah had presented him with a baby boy named after both his father and grandfather. Big Jim would walk past adults to get to his beloved grandchildren, and now he had Gabrielle living there with him, close at hand every day.

Colt had to accept it. Live with it. He turned over, facing away from Misty.

It might, he reasoned, be a good thing. Having someone living in the Garrett ranch house would probably be good for Big Jim. He wouldn't be lonely. He would make sure to eat three actual meals a day if he had someone to eat with. Big Jim was known for sucking down cup after cup of coffee or, alternately, uncapping a beer.

Okay, he would try to adopt Beau's attitude. He would be overtly accepting of Angelique and Gabrielle Guillory. But if it turned out that she was truly a scam artist, he would be on hand to expose her and protect his father.

Now all he had to do was figure out how to make it up to his wife. She was supportive and loyal. Misty was not one for subterfuge. She had espoused his idea that Angelique was not related and had not been subtle about it. There seemed to be a breach between Misty and Leah, who had once been the best of friends. Now, Leah appeared to be close to Angelique. Maybe because they were both outsiders, having been born and raised in other states. Whatever the reason, Leah and Angelique were thick as thieves and Misty was the odd woman out.

Colt would have to find a way to heal all these wounds. He had no idea how he could bring this about, but he had to. It was almost Christmas, and families were supposed to be together after all.

He turned over again and gathered Misty in his arms.

Tomorrow he would have to set about mending some fences. He would have to eat a big serving of crow, and he would have to find a way to make it up to his wife for being such a jackass.

"Listen, to me, Cormier." The veins in Alphonse Benoit's forehead were standing out and his complexion was a dark, murderous red. Not a good way to start the day. "You are police chief only because I say you are police chief. I did not put you in place to sit on your ass all day. By now, you should have found her. By now, this whole miserable business should be over."

"Um, yeah, I understand, Mr. Benoit." Cormier's voice was thin and quaky. "My men done been scouring the countryside for this here Angelique Guillory, an' I'm tellin' you she cannot be found." He coughed and cleared his throat. "I sent out an alert with her picture on it, saying she done stole some jewels. That's what you accused her of, wasn't it?"

Benoit's jaw couldn't get any tighter. With effort, he took a breath and blew it out. "That's what I told you. She stole all the pretty trinkets I gave her mama... and some other things that were very valuable. She's a thief!"

"Well, I ain't got even one nibble from any police department in any state in these United States," Cormier said.

"You idiot! She's hiding somewhere. Somewhere an idiot like you can't find her. Why can't you perform the simplest act?" He made a disgusted sound. "I'm sorry I put you in office."

Cormier blathered on for a moment. "Sir, I'm tryin' my very best, but there's only so much a man can do, especially if this woman got herself hunkered down somewhere."

Benoit's voice dropped an entire octave and came out as an oily caress. "But, trust me, my friend. You may not make it to the next election."

Silence.

"Do you understand what I'm telling you, Cormier?"

"Uh, yes, sir. I do understand an'..." His voice was just a squeak now.

"It would be so sad if a man such as yourself were to be killed in the line of duty. So sad, indeed."

"No—no, sir. Don' you even think about that. I-I be doin' my very best, but there ain't been no sightin' of this woman, or a woman travelin' with a young child, by any means of public transportation. Everyone who has ever known Miss Guillory has been contacted and interviewed... Interviewed quite thoroughly, I assure you. None of her contacts had any idea that she was gone, an' no idea where she would go. It's like she evaporated."

Silence.

"Evaporated... Now that's an interesting choice of word, my friend." Benoit chuckled. "I mean, when a man evaporates, it leaves so many questions unanswered... Like the family. Will they just go on forever wondering if the old man took off, or lies rotting in some gator's belly?" He smiled, thinking of how his threat must be affecting Cormier. "They would have to appoint someone else to take his job, and his pretty little wife would eventually find someone else." Benoit guffawed. "An' his kids wouldn't even remember him. What you think about that?"

"I unnerstan' what you saying, Mr. Benoit, but—"

"Friday. I give you until Friday. Don't you let me down, y'hear?"

Benoit disconnected without giving Cormier a chance to respond.

He heaved out a gigantic sigh. Why couldn't he have competent people? Why did he have to put up with these fools?

Speaking of fools, he thought he should check in with the other idiots, Breaux and Fontenot. He presumed they would not be sober enough to respond coherently this early in the day. From what he could tell, they spent their nights crawling around various New Orleans night spots, asking about Angelique, but according to them, no one had seen the missing wench who had stolen away his Gabrielle.

What was left to do? Put her picture on milk cartons?

"You're up an' crackin," Fern said. "Is there somethin' happenin' I'm supposed ta know about?" She had entered the kitchen planning to make coffee and start breakfast, but Leah was already in place.

"Morning, Gran." Leah consulted a recipe from the old index card file she had collected over time. "I wanted to get some goodies made. You know, for Christmas. It's always nice to have some treats ready to take to a social occasion or just to have on hand. I'll bet I gain five pounds without even trying." She let out a little giggle.

Fern nodded. "That's a fact. We both will." She poured herself a cup of coffee and took a seat at the kitchen table. "What do you got in mind?"

"Well, after breakfast I was thinking I should go on a cookie-making binge…and get Gracie to help. She likes to bake, and I want her to grow up loving to cook."

"Yup. Not like yer poor sister-in-law. That Dixie girl sure is a purty 'un, but it's a wonder Beau an' that lil' redheaded girl don't pass out from starvation."

Leah shook her head, but smiled. "Aw, Gran. She's coming along. Don't forget she has a business to run in town. I wouldn't know the first thing about managing a feed store. She's got her hands full."

"I guess ye're right. An' yore papa-in-law lays on a big spread every Sunday, either at a restaurant in town or he bobbycues up a storm." Fern sipped her coffee, looking quite thoughtful.

"He does, bless his great big old heart. Big Jim loves it when his family gets together." Leah was setting ingredients out on the counter, along with measuring spoons and cups, bowls, and a whisk. She looked so serious, Fern had to smile. *Such a good girl.*

"An' how 'bout that other sister-in-law o' yorn? Misty. I ain't seen her around here in a while."

Leah raised her head, pressing her lips together for a moment. "I'm staying out of that one. Misty has been giving me the deep freeze since Angelique and Gabrielle arrived. She sure has made it clear she isn't going to offer Angelique her friendship anytime soon."

"Aww, she jus' got a stick up her butt because her husbin Colt got one up his."

Leah was lining ingredients up on the countertop now. The dry ingredients, plus eggs and butter. "I suppose you're right, but I'm hoping it just blows over. I mean, it's almost Christmas and I'm sure not going to let their bad attitudes ruin Christmas for the people I love. It's the time of year for families to get together and show that they really care about each other."

"That's my sweet girl." Fern beamed with pride at the young woman she had helped raise.

"I'm so glad Angelique is here and that she has Gabrielle. I know Big Jim is thrilled to have them with him. It's really sad that she grew up without him." She shrugged. "But if it hadn't worked out exactly as it did, I wouldn't have my spectacular Tyler and he wouldn't have grown up the middle Garrett boy with the mother he adored. I'm just happy that Angelique found her father after all this time."

"You always look on the bright side."

"Yep. Mom's always got her sunny side up." Gracie came into the kitchen wearing her pajamas, robe, and huge fuzzy slippers. "Can I help you make breakfast?"

Leah paused in what she was doing to give Gracie a welcoming smile. She opened her arms, and Gracie went to be enfolded in a loving hug. "Of course you can help me. We're going to make some awesome cookies in a bit, and maybe brownies. But first we have to feed this house full of hungry critters, so how about if you heat up the oven and open the tube of store-bought biscuits. I swear they make 'em so light and flaky now it hardly pays to make them from scratch."

Gracie read the side of the tube of biscuits. "Preheat oven to 400 degrees. Okay…" She set about accomplishing this first step and then looked for a baking pan.

Leah watched her and then turned to Fern with a wink.

"Where are your menfolk?" Fern asked.

"I left JT lying beside his daddy. Tyler stayed up late last night working on a new song he's writing. So I'm letting him sleep in, as long as he's cuddled up with his son."

"Mom, what kind of cookies are we making?" Gracie whirled around, her face registering concern.

Leah chuckled. "What kind are you wanting to make?"

Gracie let out a long moan. "Oh, so many… Can we make those that look like little pecan pies? And the ones with the candies on top? Please…pretty please?" Gracie clasped her hands together to indicate begging.

"Sounds good to me."

"And I want to make a special batch for Grampa just from me."

"Of course. He's going to love them."

Fern helped herself to another cup of coffee, watching contentedly as two of her most favorite people in the whole wide world started preparing breakfast and got ready to crank out a lot of cookies.

Good day.

Chapter 17

"So, big fella, did you sleep well?" Misty poured a mug of coffee for her husband and slid it across the top of the breakfast bar. He looked haggard, but she was not going to comment on his appearance.

"Yeah. Slept like a baby."

"Liar," she breathed, giving him the full effect of her big brown eyes. She put the coffeepot back on the hot pad and turned to find him with one side of his mouth lifted in a sort of sappy smile.

"Well, I finally fell asleep for a little while." He raked his fingers through his thick, dark hair that he hadn't bothered to comb.

"I suppose you're going to finally tell me what has you so upset. I swear, you came home looking like a thunderstorm about to burst." She leaned her forearms on the counter, gazing up at him. "I wish you could be more open with me."

He set the mug on the counter. "Aww, honey. I had some things I needed to work out on my own. I'm sorry, but I felt it was better if I held off a bit."

She nodded solemnly. "I'll remember that. I can play that card too." She turned around, but he reached across to stop her.

"Okay, I promise not to be such a jerk in the future. Don't you go getting all feisty on me now."

She arched one of her fine dark brows. “Feisty?”

“You know what I mean.”

“I do, and I suggest we take our coffee outside and sit on the porch where we won’t be overheard by my little brother. He has some issues of his own to deal with.”

“Misty, it’s cold out there.”

She chortled. “Well, I suggest you cut the bullshit and get right down to it.”

Colt gave her a quizzical look, but picked up his mug and followed her outside. He was wearing Wranglers and a flannel shirt, but his fleece-lined jacket was hanging by the front door. “Brrr…”

“Yeah… Brisk.” She exhaled, blowing out a cloud of white. Going outside was probably not a good idea, but she had hoped that he would spill his guts and not keep circling the problem. She had pulled her long hair back into a ponytail earlier, and now her exposed ears were feeling the bite of chill air. She brushed the snow off one of the wooden deck chairs and settled as though she found this a normal activity. Gesturing to the chair opposite, she watched a frowning Colt do the same. He sat cupping his warm mug in his giant hands.

“I, uh, I worked with Dad yesterday.”

“I know that. What put the burr under your saddle?”

“When we were done, he insisted I go into the house with him…and…”

“And?”

He blew out a breath of his own, sending a stream of white to circle his face. “And of course, Angelique was there with her little girl.”

“Of course.” Misty had to clamp her jaw tight to keep her teeth from chattering.

"Well, Dad made me sit down at the table, and he handed the little girl to me. It was like he wanted to force me to interact with them."

"And did you?"

Colt shrugged and took a swig of his coffee that must be tepid at best. "I guess so. We exchanged a few words..." He swallowed hard. "I ate a cup of her gumbo. It's like this. Dad is so convinced that Angelique is his daughter, and I don't want to upset him at Christmas." He paused again as though confused. "I suppose she could be a blood relative. Her eyes are the same color as Dad's...and mine. Her little girl, Gabrielle... she has the same color eyes and the dark hair..." He heaved another heavy sigh. "I'm willing to admit the possibility that Angelique Guillory is Big Jim's daughter...and my half-sister."

"Is that all?" Misty wanted to run back inside, certain that her buttocks had frozen to the chair.

"What do you mean, is that all? It was a hard thing for me to get through. I had to sit there with Dad watching me and hold the little girl and talk to Angelique. It was like chewing on a tire iron."

Misty tilted her head to one side, evaluating what he had said. "Aw, poor baby. Did ums have to act all son-like for Papa Bear?"

"Yes, smart-ass. He's my father."

"So why was that so hard to say?" *Okay, I might be shivering a little.*

The Garrett blue eyes crackled like a Taser. "It wasn't so bad...this morning, but I hadn't come to terms with it myself last night. Why is that so hard to understand?"

"Just what is it you want me to do about it? After

all your complaining, now I'm supposed to go over and trade makeup tips with the woman from the Big Easy?"

"I don't know." He looked distinctly uncomfortable. "No, but be pleasant when we have to be in the same room."

"Like church?" *Yes, my glutes are iced over now.* "Or like when we go to your dad's house for a meal? Or when he takes us to dinner out somewhere?" She stood up, certain she had frostbite on her butt. "Or how about when we're exchanging presents on Christmas Day?" She turned and took a few furious steps toward the house. "Except I didn't get her anything. What do you think of that?"

Misty stomped into the house, which felt like stepping into an oven in comparison to the freezer outside, leaving a frowning Colt to follow.

She set her mug of cold coffee in the microwave and nuked it for a minute.

Colt came up behind her and kissed the side of her neck. He put his hands on her shoulders, pulling her back to lean against his muscular chest. "Are you really this mad at me for thinking we should accept Angelique?"

"I'm not mad at you for accepting Angelique. I'm mad that you twisted me inside out over it, and now you've figured out how you feel…but I'm really confused. There's no way for me to do an about-face and pretend that everything is hunky-dory."

"Aw, honey. I'm sorry I put you through this. I'm a jerk."

The microwave timer dinged.

"Yes, you are," she said, removing her cup with a

mitt Leah had crocheted for her. "And you're going to have to go shop for your own sister's present."

Big Jim had two horses saddled, and he walked them up to the house. Angelique was getting herself and Gabrielle dressed for the weather. He had chosen Onyx for himself and a sweet little mare named Fancy for Angelique.

She said she had never been on a horse.

He smiled. His daughter was a city girl.

But she was willing to give it a try.

Leah had shared her wardrobe, so Angelique was properly clad. He had to hand it to that girl. Leah had a heart of pure gold, and she would give anyone a hand up. He was very grateful that she had embraced Angelique as her sister-in-law without any question. She had taken one look at Angelique, noting the strong family characteristics, and taken her to her heart.

He hoped that someday Misty would feel the same way.

He wasn't entirely sure about his other daughter-in-law, Dixie, but with her work schedule, she had a good reason to be less available to Angelique. Dixie knew how vital it was to the Langston community that she keep the feed store open. She had inherited it from her father, as well as the ranch where she and Beau were raising Ava.

Beau managed the ranch and traded off childcare tasks with Dixie. Most days Beau got up early to tend to the stock, while Dixie spent quality time with Ava. Then they traded off, Dixie driving into town to take over for her manager, Pete Miller, who had worked for her father before her. She had changed up the hours so neither of them had to stay late to close, and the store was only open a half day on Saturdays. She had said that it was more important to her to be home with Beau and Ava than to accommodate the latecomers. And she had been right. When she changed the store hours, the community adapted.

Big Jim couldn't blame Dixie for not spending more time with Angelique. She was doing the best she could, and both she and Beau were cordial enough when they were with Angelique and Gabrielle.

Big Jim looped the reins over the porch railing. He started to go inside, but the front door opened and a wide-eyed Angelique came out holding Gabrielle by the hand. Gabrielle was wearing what Elizabeth had called a snowsuit, but he had no idea what they were called today. At least she would stay warm in that outfit.

Gabrielle's eyes were as wide as Angelique's. She pointed to the horses. "Gwampa. What dat?"

Both Big Jim and Angelique broke out in laughter.

"These are some big horseys, aren't they, sweetheart?" Big Jim reached for her, always thrilled when she reached back. Gabrielle grabbed him around the neck, almost dislodging his Stetson. He settled her in his arms. *Now to get Angelique up on the mare.*

She looked the part, wearing a pair of Leah's boots and denims...and a warm thermal jacket. She had been given a beautiful scarf, and she had it wrapped around her head and neck so she was set.

"Okay, young lady, see this here horse? She's a girl so let's call her a mare."

Angelique edged closer and reached out a tentative hand to touch Fancy's neck. "She's so big."

Big Jim chuckled. "Nah. Fancy is one of the smaller horses on the ranch. She's very gentle so I picked her out just for you."

Angelique nodded and swallowed hard. "Okay, what do you want me to do?"

Big Jim held onto the bridle and instructed her where to place her foot in the stirrup and how to hoist herself up into the saddle. Fortunately, she was agile and strong, although quite slim. Now she was astride Fancy and sitting somewhat precariously in the saddle, gripping the saddle horn. She looked terrified.

"Okay, honey. Now make sure and slip your right foot in the other stirrup. Be sure your boots are nice and snug in those stirrups." He checked to make sure she was well seated before handing her the reins.

"Is this the ignition? Where are the turn signals?"

He figured she was making jokes to hide her anxiety. "These are the brakes, so be careful how you use them. These straps pull directly on the horse's face. Her mouth, in particular. Now I know you wouldn't like anyone jerking on your mouth, and neither does Fancy…but she's a gentle little mare and she wants to go for a ride."

Angelique nodded her head rapidly. "Okay."

Big Jim knew she was scared, but he had to start somewhere. "We're going to take a little walk around the yard…maybe make a circle of the barn and outbuildings. Are you comfortable with that?"

She nodded again.

"I'm going to climb up on Onyx here, and we can do a little traipse around." With that he put his foot in the stirrup and hefted himself up by grabbing the saddle horn while holding Gabrielle firmly with his other arm. He congratulated himself on accomplishing this maneuver as he slipped his other boot in its stirrup. "You don't need to do anything, Angelique. Fancy will follow Onyx. Just hold on."

He settled Gabrielle in the saddle in front of him and placed her little hands on the saddle horn.

"My horsey," she insisted. She looked over her shoulder at him. "Is dis my horsey?"

"This is my big horsey." Smiling, he urged his horse forward, and they rode at a leisurely pace around the area in front of the house. "Feelin' all right?"

"Uh, yes."

He doubted that, but was convinced that introducing her to the joys of riding a horse would enrich her life and ensure that Gabrielle would be raised in the saddle, so to speak. "We better check out behind the barn...and around the grain bin."

"Sure." Angelique's jaw was set, and she was keeping an eye on Gabrielle, rather than paying attention to the fine points of riding a horse.

They continued the slow pace, with Big Jim making most of the conversation. "That's the henhouse. I have some exotic breeds in there, but my little Gracie is raising a couple to show in 4-H. That girl has the makings of a first-class rancher."

Angelique laughed at that. "A chicken ranch?"

Big Jim refrained from making any reference to the infamous whorehouse known throughout Texas history as the "Chicken Ranch." "It shows her interest in animals and caring for them. I'm goin' to let her pick out a calf in the spring. She can raise it and show it too. She'll probably be running the whole place before long." When he glanced at Angelique, she was still smiling. *She's getting there.*

Gabrielle was giggling and shrieking with glee, happy that her "horsey" was giving her a ride, but her nose was getting red, so Big Jim headed for the house.

When they had reached their starting point, Big Jim cautioned Angelique not to try to get down by herself. "Don't want you to get tangled up in the stirrups."

He swung down from the saddle and gave Gabrielle a hug. "Good girl. You're gonna be a fine little cowgirl. It's important to keep her from having fear of the horses."

"I a cowgirl." Gabrielle announced proudly.

Angelique raised her brows "Well, I think it's too late for me. I'm afraid of the horses. They're so big."

Big Jim went to her side. "Aw, honey. You can be a first-class rider. Just give it a little time." He instructed her to take her right foot out of the stirrup and talked her through the fine art of the dismount. "Good girl!"

Angelique chuckled. "Dad, you're talking to me as though I'm Gabrielle's age. Don't worry. I'm going to do this until I can jump a horse over a fence, or whatever it is you do."

Big Jim set Gabrielle on her feet and gave her little hand to her mother. "You're talkin' about a whole 'nother kind of horse riding. I just want you to be able to keep your butt in the saddle."

Angelique took Gabrielle into the house while Big Jim took the horses back to the stable. At first the house seemed very hot, but it was just the contrast to the chilled air outside.

She hung her jacket near the door and unwound the scarf from around her head and neck. It had done a good job of keeping her warm. Now she had to unwrap Gabrielle from the layers of fleece and insulated fabric between her and the cold, cruel world.

"My horsey!" she squealed.

"Yes, you and Grampa took a ride…on a horse…a horsey."

Gabrielle's wide blue eyes gazed up at her mother in delight. "Horsey. I go on horsey."

"Yes, you did." Angelique released a deep breath. "I think your grampa is going to make you into one fine little cowgirl." She gave Gabrielle a hug, thinking how different their lives would have been had she stayed in New Orleans…especially if Remy had not been killed.

Derrick hadn't heard from the Lawsons since the elderly couple had been taken to the hospital, but in the meantime, he had grown quite attached to Smokey. The dog had quickly adapted to Derrick's morning and evening routines. Smokey joined Meow, the cat, in accompanying him on his tour of his own property, checking on the stock, making sure feed was available, and spending a little extra time with Freddie.

When Derrick was done with chores and ready to leave for work, he realized Smokey was asking to go with him. He was standing beside the door, tail wagging and a doggy grin on his face. He would look at the door and back at Derrick while bouncing a little on his front feet. *Yes, he wants to go.*

"Okay, boy. But you gotta stay in the truck if anything heats up out there."

He locked up the house and opened the door to the truck. Smokey didn't hesitate to jump up and situate himself on the passenger seat.

Derrick climbed up and started the vehicle. It was cold, but he put it in gear and let it idle for a few minutes while he stroked Smokey's head. "It's gonna be lonely around here when the Lawsons come back." Smokey licked the back of Derrick's hand as if he agreed. Even Meow had gotten used to the dog.

The first stop for Derrick was to check on the Lawsons' place. It appeared to be locked up tight with nothing changed. He and the dog circled the house to make sure nothing had been disturbed and then returned to the truck. He knew some neighbors were taking care of their stock. *Good to live in a small town.*

Next, he drove to check on Miz Atkins, who was raising her granddaughters while her daughter was incarcerated. The girls were school age and had caught the bus that morning, but Miz Atkins was suffering from some sort of respiratory ailment and Doctor Ryan had ordered an antibiotic, which Derrick delivered.

"Ain't you the sweetest thing?" Miz Atkins declared when she opened the door. The house was warm and stuffy, and Miz Atkins was wearing flannel pajamas under a fleece bathrobe. She stepped back, opening the door wide for him to enter.

While he wasn't especially thrilled to be in such close proximity to someone who needed an antibiotic, he did step inside to keep from cooling off her house. "Here you go, ma'am. Doc says to take it until it's all gone and to call her if you're not feeling better in a couple of days."

"I sure do appreciate you for comin' all the way out here. Can I give you a cup of coffee to warm you up?" She was pale and her eyes were puffy, but she gazed at him hopefully.

"Thank you, ma'am, but no. I have to get to the office." He turned back to the door. "You get well, now. Y'hear?" He stepped outside and hurried to rejoin Smokey in the truck. "Good boy. Let's head to the office."

Derrick had been deeply concerned about the fact that someone in New Orleans was accusing the woman he loved of grand theft. While he had no doubt that Angelique was innocent, he wanted to get to the bottom of the accusation. Who had it out for her?

When he pulled up in front of the sheriff's office and opened the driver's side door, Smokey was ready to join him. His whole body was wagging in anticipation of adventures to come. "Let's go, buddy."

The dog followed him into the office and received a lot of attention from the two deputies inside.

Shep Collier and Randy Miller squatted down to pay homage to the dog, patting him and scruffling his ears.

"Are you keeping this dog?" Shep asked.

"No, I'm dog-sitting until the Lawsons are able to get home. I know they must be missing him."

"Aww, he's a good dog." Randy stood up and went to the front desk. "Got some calls for you, Sheriff." He gathered a few notes from the desktop and handed them off to Derrick.

He took the messages and went back to his office, with Smokey close on his heels. Settling behind the desk, he returned the calls and then sat, tapping the end of his pen against the wooden desktop.

He pulled out the alert and gazed at the image of Angelique. It was a casual photo, maybe taken by Angelique's mother or this Remy guy. She was smiling.

He punched in the number for the New Orleans Police Department. When the call was answered, he asked to speak to someone who could tell him about the case against Angelique Guillory. He was put on hold, where a mechanical voice advised him that, if it were an emergency, he should hang up and call 911 immediately.

He was about to hang up when the line was answered.

"Hello! This is Cormier. You got somethin' 'bout this Guillory woman?"

Derrick was put off by the man's gruff manner. "No, but I'm in law enforcement, and I wanted to make sure I had the details right if I'm going to distribute this to my men."

There was a long silence.

"Do you always check out each alert that crosses you desk?" The voice sounded skeptical.

"Not always, but this girl is really cute. If she makes it to Texas, I want to personally arrest her. You know… pat her down to make sure she's not armed and dangerous." He gave out a mirthless chuckle.

"Yeah, she's a hottie, all right." Cormier chortled along with him.

"Did she work in a jewelry store? How did she get her hands on all those trinkets, anyway?"

"No, she stole trinkets from one man… A family frien', as I understand it."

Derrick considered this. "What were they doing? Playing dress-up with a hundred thou worth of jewels?"

"Hah! No, this is an old Nawlins family we talkin' 'bout. The old man was friends with this girl's mama. If you happen to see this young lady, gimme a shout. I would jus' love ta get this one wrapped up real quick."

"Lots of pressure, huh?"

Cormier made a scoffing sound. "That's an understatement. That ol' guy wanna cut my heart out if I don't get on it."

"That sounds crazy. Who is this old coot?"

"Aw, he be one scary sumbitch. They say Benoit done kilt a lotta men…men who jus' evaporated…an' I don' wanna do that."

"Um, no. I'm sure not. Well, thanks for the information. I'll give you a call if anyone around here spots her."

"Yeah, you do that." Cormier disconnected.

Derrick sat staring at the phone for a long time. He turned to the computer and typed in the name Benoit and New Orleans. Immediately he got images of an overweight older man with a thick mane of dark hair that had gone white at the temples. There were newspaper articles showing him attending a lot of social events. There was a wife, but she had passed away. He had apparently been investigated for a number of crimes, mostly violent, but had been exonerated across the board, usually because witnesses did not come forward or disappeared.

"Evaporated…" Derrick whispered aloud.

Chapter 18

"Just what is it you expect me to do?" Misty crossed her arms over her chest. "I will do whatever you want. You're my husband, and it's your family we have to keep the peace with."

"Aw, honey." Yes, Colt sounded like a very tall and muscular child. "I don't know. Just play it by ear." He sank down into a cushy chair, pulling her into his lap as he went.

Misty rolled her eyes. "Christmas is coming on fast. I do not want to ruin Christmas. My little brother Mark has had enough bad holidays. We both have."

"What can I get you for Christmas? Money is no object." He placed a kiss on her cheek.

"You can't buy your way out of this one, Colt. Thanks to you, I have platinum cards in my purse. I might go on a spending spree that will make you cry like a little baby."

"I don't believe you. You're way too frugal to go on a spree." He gave her another kiss. "But I go to work with my dad most days. I'm depending on you to pick out gifts for Angelique and her little girl. I don't have the time or the inclination to go shopping."

Misty looked at him, deliberately cool. "You do know I have a job, don't you? I have to open the office for Breck. I have to be there in thirty minutes."

She slid off his lap, shrugged into her jacket, and wrapped a wool scarf around her neck. She pulled her leather gloves out of her pocket and put them on. “Well, I’m sure this mess will still be here when I get home. I’ll see you later.” She leaned in for a kiss.

“Aw, Misty. I’m going to see what Dad needs done, and then I’ll be back here. We’ll figure it out together.”

She rolled her eyes again and headed for the door. “C’mon, Mark. Don’t make me late.”

“I’m coming.” Mark came running down the hallway, struggling to get his jacket on and clutching his laptop.

“I’ll see you both later,” Colt said. He wrapped his arms around Misty and gave her another kiss and tousled Mark’s hair. “You all stay safe out there.”

“We will. Put your cap on, Mark.”

Mark pulled on a knit cap, and the two of them went out the door, across the covered porch, and into her truck.

She looked up to see Colt on the porch. He raised a paw in farewell. She smiled and waved back. *My hubby.*

She knew he would have mended some more fences with his dad by the time she got home…and might have an idea of how to mend fences with the woman he was now willing to admit might be his half-sister.

Mark’s sad mood seemed to have lifted somewhat. She planned to situate him at the long work table where she often put together legal documents or sorted forms. She wanted to help him with his essay, but thought it would be better to let him solve the problem for himself. It was her goal to make sure Mark had the support to become a strong and independent man.

He hadn't had good male role models until she married into the Garrett family. Now they were all there for him. But it was up to her to help him deal with their past.

Gracie couldn't possibly smile any wider. "Look at what Gran and I made."

"Whatever it is smells fantastic." Leah pulled her daughter into her arms for a mega hug. "I'm so proud of you for being such a great helper." She kissed the top of Gracie's head. "And thank you for being such a great big sister."

"Aw, Mommy. You always say that."

"And I always tell the truth." Leah picked up her baby son and nodded toward the kitchen. "Show me what you made."

Gracie almost bounced all the way to the kitchen, where Gran was washing a pan.

"There you are. I figured you would want to try one o' Gracie's pecan tassies." She put the pan in the draining rack and dried her hands on a dishtowel.

"See, Mommy." Gracie gestured to the kitchen table, where several items were arranged on cooling racks.

"Wow! This looks like a spread from *Southern Living* or *Better Homes and Gardens*." She put JT down, and he immediately started crawling toward Gracie.

"Ain't it purty?" Fern Davis stood to one side, with her hands on her hips and a big grin on her face. "She done a darned good job."

"Gran mixed it up, and I poked the dough into the mini muffin pans."

Leah was so impressed to see the miniature pecan

pies created when the dough was pressed onto the edges of the mini-muffin tins, the filling was added, and crushed pecans were sprinkled on top. "I remember you making these with me, Gran. I'm so glad you're carrying on the tradition with our best girl here."

JT was pulling himself up.

Gran's face crinkled up in delight. "I remember too. We made them every year."

"Good memories, Gran." Leah was grateful to have spent so much time with her beloved grandmother.

"I'll bet your grampa is going to love these." Gran untied her apron and hung it on a peg in the pantry.

"And we're going to make another kind this afternoon," Gracie said. "This is going to be the best Christmas ever."

Leah nodded. "You know what? I think you're right."

Angelique and Gabrielle were parked outside of Leah's house. It was so lovely that Angelique sat staring at it. It looked like Leah. Very pretty and well kept. She could see the love that had gone into creating this dwelling.

She sat gripping the wheel, wondering what her life would have been like if Remy were alive. If his father hadn't been a criminal. If he had been born to a normal family, they could have been married. Maybe they would have an adorable house to raise their daughter in. She leaned over, resting her forehead against the steering wheel.

It did no good to look back. What was done was done.

She couldn't go back even if she wanted to. New Orleans had nothing to offer her now. Her precious mother was dead. Her beloved Remy was dead.

Remy had rejected everything his father stood for. He refused to be inducted into his father's criminal network. When he had taken his inheritance from his mother and opened a restaurant, Alphonse had been furious. That Remy and Angelique were working alongside each other to make it successful was another source of irritation. Angelique and Remy would open the restaurant early and begin cooking up the special dishes that had brought them a loyal following. She would make crepes, light and airy, and filled to order. And beignets. The little pillows of spicy sweetness would melt on one's tongue.

There was a knock on the driver's side window, jerking Angelique out of her reverie. Leah was standing outside, wrapped in a blanket of some sort, and gazing at her with concern.

"Are you all right?"

Angelique arranged a smile on her face. "Oh, just daydreaming." She opened the door and stepped out to give Leah a hug. "Good morning, although it's a little late to say that."

"Not at all. Come on inside and sample some treats my grandmother and Gracie have been working on."

Angelique released Gabrielle from her safety seat and kicked the passenger door shut before following Leah into the cheery kitchen. "Oh, what smells so good?"

"Tassies!" Gracie announced gleefully. "Gran and I made them."

"Hello, Angelique," Fern called out. "We're a-bakin' up another batch o' cookies now. Gonna have some goodies to give out."

Angelique inhaled the aroma, trying to name the spices tickling her senses and reminding her of long hours in the kitchen. "I should make something to add to the goodies. I can make my mom's pecan pralines. Those are pretty good." She squatted down to help Gabrielle out of her insulated jacket before she sweated through her clothes.

Once released, Gabrielle looked around and then raced to Gracie's open arms. "Gwacie…I pway with you now."

"Come play with me, Gabi." Gracie gave her a big hug. "Let's entertain JT."

Gabrielle squatted down beside Gracie and peered at JT.

That girl is amazing. Leah's baby son was in a small mesh playpen by Gracie, and she had been playing with him. Now she was keeping both young ones busy.

Leah slipped off the little blanket-like thing she had slung around her shoulders and folded it neatly.

"That's really pretty." Angelique reached out a hand to touch the soft yarn.

"Oh, it's a throw. We make them for various charities. We want to help."

Angelique smiled. "I'm sure the caregivers appreciate that."

"The little blankets we make for the neonatal ICU go home with the babies, so they have something from us to take with them." Leah motioned for Angelique to sit at the table. "Want some coffee or hot cocoa?"

"Yum. I'd love to have some of your cocoa." She slipped off her jacket and spread it over the back of the chair before sitting down.

Leah brought two cups and seated herself at the table. "Sounded like a good idea to me."

Fern hustled over with a small plate featuring several kinds of cookies. "You girls oughta try some cookies with that there cocoa."

Angelique's eyes widened. "These look wonderful, Miz Fern. Like they came from some high-end bakery."

Gracie brought Gabrielle close to the table and pointed to the cookies with a chocolate kiss in the center of each. "I mostly made those. I hope you like them."

Leah raised her hand. "Wait! No peanut allergies?"

"None."

Leah breathed out a deep breath. "I'm a worrywart. People can be allergic to so much stuff."

Angelique selected one and took a big bite. "So good." She broke off part of the soft cookie and gave it to Gabrielle. "You're going to love this. It's yummy-nummy."

"Nummy," Gabrielle repeated, stuffing it in her mouth.

"You know, if you wanted to join us in baking some special goodies, you could do it over here to surprise Big Jim. You must have some special dishes to contribute to the Christmas dinner at your dad's place."

Angelique sat up straighter. "Really? I'd love to make some pralines. Dad has tons of shelled pecans on hand."

Fern rolled her eyes. "Whoo-ee! I'd sure love to have some real pecan pralines. I ain't had any in forever."

"That's a great idea, Angelique. Bring your pecans over, and I bet we have all the other ingredients." Leah made a sweeping gesture. "Our kitchen is your kitchen."

Angelique grinned her appreciation. She broke off more cookie to share with Gabrielle, reflecting that her dark mood had been lifted somewhat. She was able to set aside the dark and disturbing images of Remy and Alphonse, at least for the moment.

She realized that, other than her mother and Remy, and her mother's friends, she had never really enjoyed a close friendship with anyone, let alone someone closer to her age with children, food, and other interests in common.

She wondered if Leah would be so kind if she knew what Angelique was running from…if she knew that Gabrielle's father was the son of the scariest man on the planet.

She cast about to find some topic of conversation. "Um, did I tell you that Big Jim got me on a horse yesterday?"

Leah stared at her, wide-eyed.

"It was hilarious. I was so scared."

"Not a horse person?"

"Oh, it was scary, but Dad is so sure he can make me into a horsewoman. I don't want to disappoint him."

Leah smiled. "Your dad would be proud of you, no matter what."

Angelique wondered if that were true. What would happen if her past caught up with her? Would Big Jim be able to forgive her for her sins of omission if Alphonse Benoit found her here?

Misty got off early and thought she might do some reconnoitering at Rancho Garrett. With Mark in the car, she thought she had a good excuse to drop by Leah and Tyler's house to chat about the Garrett family and Mark's project.

"My Family Christmas" by Mark Dalton.

That was the title.

She thought Leah and Tyler could help out and maybe pave the way for a more united holiday without the war zone her husband had inadvertently created.

When she pulled up in front of Tyler and Leah's house, she saw that Angelique's vehicle was parked out front. It seemed Angelique was here too.

The two besties.

Time to rain on the party. "Come on, Mark. Let's visit our family."

When she and Mark had trooped up on the porch, the sound of their footsteps on the wooden deck must have alerted those inside of their arrival.

Gracie threw the door open. "Mom! It's Mark and Misty." She gestured for them to enter. "Everybody's in the kitchen."

Mark romped ahead behind Gracie, leaving Misty to bring up the rear. Mark squatted down beside Gracie to play with the two youngest of the family.

"Hi, everyone," Misty said, a smile plastered on her face. Leah greeted her warmly as did her grandmother, but Angelique sat at the table as if frozen.

Misty imagined she was in Breck's office, dealing with a client reluctant to talk. "Hey, Angelique. How are you doing?" She chose the chair next to Angelique to seat herself.

"Um, I guess I'm okay. How are you?" Angelique edged slightly away.

Oh, boy. I must have really been a bitch. "Pretty good. Just got off work."

Angelique swallowed visibly. "Oh, where do you work?"

"I am the office manager for the only lawyer in Langston. He's a great guy, but he's also a rancher, and he has to go to the county seat quite often, so I'm in the office by myself a lot."

"That doesn't sound bad."

"It's a great job… Uh, what kind of job did you have in New Orleans?"

"I worked in—in food service." Angelique's lips tightened. "Excuse me." She got up from the table and went to where Gabrielle was playing with JT and motioned for her to get up. "We better be going. Big Jim will be expecting me."

"I wish you could stick around a little while longer." Leah opened a cabinet and selected a reusable plastic container. "Let me send some goodies home with you to share with Big Jim." She filled the container with cookies and tassies while Angelique was zipping Gabrielle in her insulated jacket and pulling up the hood. Leah pulled on her jacket when Angelique was shrugging into hers. Leah shot a dark glance at Misty. "Let me walk you out, Angelique." She grabbed the container of cookies and ushered her out the door.

Well! Misty felt as though she had been smacked in the face. At least Angelique had raised a hand to wave at her before she ducked out the door. She could see Leah and Angelique embrace after her kid was secured in the back seat. Just seeing them hugging was worrisome. Somehow, Misty had slipped in her sister-in-law's esteem.

When Leah came inside, she looked upset.

Misty tried to keep it light. "I was hoping Angelique could stay."

"Gracie, why don't you take JT to the den?" The always sweet Leah had an edge to her voice.

"Yes, Mama." Gracie picked JT up and left the room, but glanced back with a worried expression on her face. Mark stood up, but stayed leaning against the wall as though afraid to get in the middle of the female confrontation.

Fern Davis stood by the range, but seemed to have frozen in place.

Leah gazed at Misty solemnly. "I don't know what's going on, but you need to stop using Angelique to play out your game. You and Colton have been mean to her since she first arrived." She shook her head.

"Why, I was perfectly nice to her," Misty said. "I don't know what caused her to leave."

"Oh, yes you do. It was your complete turnaround. One day you're dripping venom, and the next you're all sugar. The poor woman has a right to be suspicious."

Misty swallowed hard. *Time to give it up*. "You're right. Colt was trying to protect Big Jim. He thought Angelique was a fake. I'm sorry."

Leah made a face. "It's not me you owe an apology to. First of all, you weren't exactly subtle with your dislike, so if you truly want to make amends, it's going to have to be more than sweeping it under the rug."

Misty was shocked that the sweet and usually positive Leah was glowering at her. "I-I don't have any idea what you mean."

Leah rolled her eyes. "C'mon, Misty. I was there. I saw how much you hurt Angelique with your mean-spirited actions."

"I guess I didn't realize I was doing anything to hurt

her." Misty's mouth felt suddenly dry as the Sahara. "Colt was convinced she was out to scam Big Jim. I-I was angry with her."

Leah crossed her arms over her chest, raising a brow. "And why did you show up here today with all this goodness, sweetness, and light? What's the punch line? What else are you trying to do to her?"

"N-nothing, I swear." Misty spread her hands. "Colt said Big Jim is convinced she's his real daughter, and Colt doesn't want to ruin Christmas for everyone. He said he is going to accept Angelique's claim unless something comes up to prove it false."

Now Fern Davis was glaring at her. "So you jus' kinda pretendin' to believe her, but y'all kin take it back any ol' time you want." She made a scoffing sound. "That's not family."

"Um, I think we should be going now." Misty stood and slipped her jacket on. "I don't know what I can say to make things right." She strode rapidly to the door with Mark looking confused but following behind her.

"We're not the people you should be talking to," Leah said. "I love you, Misty, but you and Colton need to fix this...quickly."

"Yeah," Fern called. "Before you an' Colt ruin Christmas for all o' us."

Chapter 19

"Hey, Sheriff." One of Derrick's deputies appeared in the doorway to his office. "I just got a call from the Lawsons' son. He's taking them to live with him in Lubbock, and he asked if you could find a home for the dog and keep an eye on the little farm until he can sell it."

Derrick heaved a sigh and looked down at the dog, curled up close to his feet. "Well, I'm pretty sure Smokey already has a home, don't you, boy?" He reached down to pet the dog. "You're mine now."

"Aw, that's nice," the deputy said.

Derrick had been mulling over his conversation with the New Orleans police chief. He tried to piece it together with what he knew about Angelique.

Derrick had to wonder if Cormier was joking about the old "sumbitch" who killed a lot of men. He'd said this man was friends with Angelique's mother, so that sounded plausible. But would her mother hang out with someone who sounded extremely dangerous?

He was dreading it, but he would have to have a talk with Angelique about it.

When he called to ask her to dinner, she begged off, saying she'd had a bad day and wasn't feeling well—headache, she said. But she had agreed to let him pick her up for dinner the next night.

"I promise to be better company tomorrow night."

"Aw, Angelique." Derrick hated to think of her feeling bad. "You don't even know how to be bad company. I'll pick you up about six. How about Mexican food?"

"Yes, that sounds great." But her voice didn't quite sound as if she thought it was great. He hoped she wasn't planning on dumping him. Frowning, he didn't think that was the case, but he could tell she was upset about something.

He rolled his chair back from his desk, causing Smokey to uncurl himself and look alert. "Let's go home, boy."

He had been counting on having dinner out and had no desire to go home to his empty house and open a can of chili. But since he had Smokey with him, he couldn't go into any of the three local restaurants.

"Looks like it's the DQ drive-through for us, boy."

Derrick left the sheriff's office in the hands of two of his deputies who would soon be relieved by a new shift. He whistled and Smokey fell in beside him.

At the Dairy Queen, he ordered a fully loaded cheeseburger and an extra beef patty for Smokey.

He ruffled the fur around Smokey's neck, wondering how Angelique was doing. He hoped her headache had abated and that she would feel well the next day.

Gabrielle was fast asleep in her bed.

Big Jim had closed up the house and headed for his own bedroom.

Angelique lay awake, staring at the ceiling. She had replayed Misty's strange behavior over and over in her head and still couldn't figure out what she was up to. Definitely not acting in Angelique's best interests. Probably hoping to get close enough to dig up some dirt. It made Angelique sad to think someone could dislike her so much.

She tried to relax, flexing the tense muscles that were holding her prisoner.

It was a bright, moonlit night, even more so due to the snowy reflection. She had drawn the drapes, but the room was still quite bright.

She yearned for darkness, for sleep so deep that she might be able to forget the unplanned encounter with Colton's wife, Misty.

Colton…the biggest of the Garrett brothers. The firstborn, after her. The one who seemed to have a chip on his shoulder and who was openly hostile—as was his spouse, although her animosity had been displayed as a distant haughty pout.

But today she had almost cuddled up in her quest to pretend friendship. What could she be up to?

Angelique took a deep breath, filling her lungs and easing it out in the dark. She felt lonely. She should have gone out with Derrick. He was such a sweet man, and she acknowledged that she loved him…but she also felt guilty for loving him.

It felt as though she was being unfaithful to Remy, the only other man she had ever loved. Really the only other man she had ever known.

She and Remy had grown up together, due to her mother's on-again, off-again relationship with Alphonse Benoit. Angelique hadn't known what kind of man he was when she was a child. He was just Remy's father.

But as she grew up, she became aware of the fact that Remy was always operating under a level of fear of the man.

Her gut twisted at the memory. This line of thought was doing nothing to bring about the sleep she so desperately wanted. She tried taking slow, deep breaths. She tried imagining the ranch without the layer of snow. She tried thinking of the bread pudding she hoped to make for the Garrett family Christmas dinner. She wanted to contribute something that was typical of her upbringing in Louisiana.

But nothing seemed to work. Her brain kept the image of Remy's handsome face right under the surface of whatever she was attempting to erase him with. When she was most vulnerable, a memory would pop up to torment her.

Remy laughing and teasing her. Remy dancing with her. Remy working alongside her at their restaurant. Remy making love to her.

She surprised herself by letting out a little cry of pain. Surprised that she could still feel that much pain when she had tried so hard to get beyond it.

Remy was dead. He died in the fire.

Gasping for breath, Angelique sat up, hugging her knees. No, she couldn't think about the fire. She couldn't let the anger and the fear take over.

She had a new life here. She and Gabrielle were safe from the threats from Alphonse Benoit. All she had to do was keep her head down and become invisible as a member of Big Jim Garrett's family. "He is my father," she whispered.

Such a different relationship than Remy had with his

father. It seemed Alphonse had always inspired fear in his son. Remy's mother had died when he was a boy, and Alphonse tried to raise Remy in his own heartless image, but Remy was kind and creative.

When Angelique became pregnant, Remy wanted to marry her, but Sofie had been horrified. "No, baby. You do not want to be a Benoit. Promise me you won't consider it as long as Alphonse is alive."

Even Remy could understand Sofie's reluctance. He apologized time after time for his father's evil reign and promised he would never be a part of it. So Angelique had been content to remain his "fiancée" complete with a mammoth diamond ring.

Sofie had been involved with Alphonse for some time and apparently knew a lot about his criminal enterprise. While she didn't claim to be in love with him, she did enjoy his financial support and the way he lavished her with generous funds for shopping trips, fine jewels, and the rent for her apartment in the Quarter. She seemed to have no fear of him but tried to ignore his enterprise and concentrate on her daughter, her singing career, and supporting the two young people. She had taken great pleasure in their success, and when her granddaughter appeared, spent most days hanging out and providing care for Gabrielle.

Silent tears rolled down Angelique's cheeks. Tears of sorrow and loss. Tears for Sofie. Tears for Remy. Tears for abandoned dreams, and tears of anger.

She heaved a sigh of regret. *No going back.* She needed to stay here in the heart of Texas ranch country and become invisible. This was not a place Alphonse would search for her.

Sofie knew how to keep a secret. If she would not reveal the name of her father until she was dying of cancer, Angelique knew she would not have told Alphonse.

Angelique was stunned when her mother had gone to a hospice for her final days. "Why didn't you seek treatment?" she had asked, but Sofie laughed.

"Have you seen those women? Bald as a doorknob." She had stroked her lustrous dark hair. "We all make our own choices. How to live...and some of us choose how to die."

Sofie had given her daughter all of her worldly possessions. Her car...her jewelry...her bank account. "Just be happy, my precious."

Alphonse had been truly devastated by Sofie's death. He couldn't comprehend why she would keep her illness a secret from him. He was both enraged and sorrowful, mourning Sofie and desperate to hold on to what little family he had left.

Gabrielle and his memories of Remy.

Alphonse became aware of the passing of time and of his own age. He had intended to force Remy into becoming a part of his criminal organization. After all, he had built this empire for his son to take over. He was furious that his own son was more interested in baking and frying for the public than working with his father. His feelings toward Angelique were complex. He loved her as his beloved Sofie's daughter and also for being the mother of Gabrielle, his only remaining blood relative. But he also hated her, blaming her for Remy's kind and loving nature, for turning him against his own father.

Now he was willing to kill her to get his hands on his granddaughter.

Angelique couldn't stop shivering. She got out of bed and groped for her flannel robe. She slid it on and tied the belt before crossing the room to check on Gabrielle and then peek behind the drapes to gaze at the countryside. She was relieved by the total stillness. No sound. No movement. No murderous goons closing in on her.

She let the drapes fall back into place and sank onto the upholstered rocking chair Big Jim had moved into the room for her convenience. A lot of children had been raised in this house. That was a comfort.

After all, a man who would kill his own son would not hesitate to murder the woman who stood between him and his grandchild.

Colt tried to relax and go back to sleep. He had to find a way to apologize to Angelique and to his dad.

He snuggled Misty closer, inhaling the fragrance of her hair conditioner. Something sweet and floral. Something that was always a part of her.

Today he would climb out of bed, like any other day, and see what he could do to help his father around the ranch. He had no doubt that Big Jim had a list of tasks for the two of them to take on.

Misty would go into Langston to open Breckenridge T. Ryan's office and keep him and his clients in order. Mark was working on some project, or he might be able to loll around and watch television like most kids.

But Colt would find a way to let Big Jim know he regretted his actions and was ready to accept Angelique as his sister. He could not be responsible for bringing about an uncomfortable situation during the Christmas season. It had always been a special time of year. He remembered all the preparations his mother had once made leading up to Christmas. The baking and decorations had been spectacular.

And then, after she died, his father had taken over, trying to make sure his sons had a wonderful holiday. It was as though he wanted to make certain they didn't suffer any deprivation because Elizabeth was no longer with them.

Now their oldest son had ruined Christmas for everyone. Colt felt the pain of regret. *Merry Christmas, douchebag!*

The next morning, Big Jim noted that Angelique looked a little tired, and she was definitely on edge.

"Sleep well?"

She nodded.

"Where's my beautiful granddaughter?"

Angelique smiled. "She's sleeping in. It's still dark outside. I thought I would get up before you and see if we had what I need to make bread pudding." She had laid out some spices on the countertop. "It appears we have everything except French bread and bourbon."

He regarded her with a smile. "Trust me, we always have bourbon."

She smiled in return. "Good to know."

"And we can go into town to get some French bread. I think there should be some in the store in Langston."

"Good. The bread ought to be a couple of days old for the best results."

Big Jim tilted his head to one side. "Old bread? That don't sound too good."

"Trust me, Dad. This is a very old recipe from my mom's side of the family, and you are going to beg me to make it for you." She shrugged. "I'll check the 'sell by' dates and grab whatever has been on the shelf the longest."

"I'll make sure to take you into Langston this afternoon." He touched two fingers to his brow in a salute. "I'm gonna pour me some of that coffee and then see to the stock. It's supposed to snow again overnight, so I want to make sure they have extra grain and silage."

She turned with a surprised expression. "I have never heard that word before. What in the world is silage?"

He displayed a wide grin, raising his cup to her. "That's my future rancher daughter talking. I'm so glad you're interested."

"Of course I'm interested. It's like being dropped into a foreign country." She wiped her hands on a dishcloth and then leaned against the counter. "Enlighten me."

Big Jim took a seat at the dining-room side of the counter. He hooked the heels of his boots onto the rungs of the stool and set his coffee mug down. "Silage, my dear daughter, is the grass or other green fodder that we harvest without drying it. We store it in that little round metal building called a silo."

"That makes sense." She leaned both cheeks on her fists.

"Silage is winter feed for the animals. It's compacted, fermented, and stored in the silo so we can feed our cattle when snow is covering the pastures."

She smiled, looking so sweet it made his chest warm. "Is this rotten grass anything special?"

"We make it out of any grass crop, including maize,

sorghum, and other cereal grains. We use the entire green plant and not only the grain." He chortled. "You remember this, 'cause it's gonna be on the test."

"I will remember. My dad feeds his cows rotten grass."

Hearing a truck pull up, he looked out the window. "Looks like Colt is here, so I will see you in a while. I'll drive you into town later, and we'll get some of that French bread so you can make bread pudding."

"You'll be glad you did."

Big Jim pulled on his jacket and gloves, set his Stetson on his head, and strode out the front door. Colton and Mark were climbing out of the truck.

Mark spotted him and made a run at him, calling out his name. "Big Jim!"

Big Jim caught him with both arms, enveloping him in a hug. "How are you, son?"

"I'm good. I finished my essay for school. It's about family at Christmastime."

Big Jim gave him an extra squeeze. "Well, you can bet your new boots that the Garrett family is gonna have the best Christmas that ever was."

Mark gazed up at Big Jim in delight. "I can't wait. Leah has been telling me all about how the Garretts celebrate Christmas—" He stopped and gazed up at Big Jim. "I hope it's okay, but I wrote about the way you have Christmas and not about how bad our life was before...before..."

"Boy, I'm so proud to have you in this family. Just write about this Christmas, because it's the way all of your Christmas celebrations are going to be from now on." He gave Mark a big hug. "Now let's get on out to the stables, boy. Let's clean up after our horses and maybe we can take a little ride."

Mark let out a whoop and raced toward the stable.

Big Jim saw that Colt was leaning against the grill of his truck, his arms crossed over his broad chest. "Hi, Dad."

"Hello, Son. Something on your mind? You look serious."

Without a word, Colt pushed away from the vehicle and approached his father, arms extended for an embrace.

Puzzled, Big Jim wrapped his oldest son in his arms, surprised by the usually macho Colton's apparent vulnerability. "What's going on, Son?"

"I thought I would be able to have a chance to really talk to you today, but Mark wanted to be here, and I didn't want to disappoint him."

Big Jim patted him on the shoulder. "We can always talk, Colt. Anytime you like."

"Aw, Dad. I just made a mess of everything." Colt raked his fingers through his hair. "I came to apologize for being such a prick to Angelique. I honestly didn't believe she was your daughter."

Big Jim heaved a sigh. "Well, that was pretty easy to tell. I'm sorry you felt that way. Are you telling me you changed your mind?"

"Yes and I need to make it up to you and to her."

"Well, you don't need to do a thing for me, but Angelique is in the house. Why don't you go on inside and have a true heart-to-heart with her. She's a sweetie. I'm sure she's going to welcome your apology."

Colt sucked in a breath and blew it out. "I hope so."

"You go on inside, Son. I'll be in the stables with Mark." He watched Colt stride up onto the porch and into the house. He hoped that Angelique could find forgiveness in her heart that day.

Angelique was sitting at the table in the kitchen.

Gabrielle was in the booster seat happily eating scrambled egg and biscuit and drinking milk from her sippy cup.

Angelique was making a list of items she needed from the grocery store when Big Jim was to take her to town. Big Jim's larder was very well stocked, but she wanted to make something that would share her New Orleans heritage with the Garrett family. Maybe she could find some frozen shrimp?

She was startled when she looked up to find Colton Garrett staring at her. "Oh, uh… Your father is outside." She felt quite threatened by the intensity of his stare as well as his size.

"I know. Dad sent me in here to talk to you." He pointed to the table as though asking permission to sit.

This struck her as odd since he had grown up in this house, and sitting at this table should have been his right. She nodded, gathering her notes and pen. "What can I do for you, Colton?"

He sat down on the other side of Gabrielle, placing both of his big hands on the table. He seemed to be extremely ill at ease.

Angelique wished Big Jim was in the house. She couldn't imagine why the brother she had dubbed Mr. Grumpy Face was acting so jumpy.

He swallowed and spread his hands. "I wanted to apologize to you for not accepting you into the family. I found it hard to believe that my dad had fathered a child he didn't know about." His face had reddened, and he was having trouble meeting her gaze. "I'm so sorry."

"Oh, I don't know what to say." She was alarmed by his about-face. Was this some kind of trick?

"Let me say that my wife, Misty, is not to blame. She was following my idiotic lead." He shook his head. "I thought I was protecting my father from a scam artist."

This made her smile. "Me? You give me too much credit. I would have no idea how to carry that off."

"I'm sorry," he said again.

"I wanted to find my father. Can you understand that?"

He shook his head sadly. "No, I can't. I was fortunate enough to be born to two parents who loved me and were always there for me…until my mother was killed in an accident."

"I'm so sorry." She felt truly sorry for him, this man who had been so forbidding.

"Thanks. Dad really stepped up and made sure we were cared for." He spread his hands again. "I'm sorry we didn't know you." He seemed to be sincere.

"Me too."

Gabrielle had finished her breakfast and drained the last of the milk in her sippy cup. "I go potty," she announced.

Angelique busied herself getting Gabrielle down from the booster seat. "We'll be back shortly."

Gabrielle walked beside her, holding her hand, but Angelique glanced back at the man left sitting at the table. He seemed to be deeply depressed. She felt a pang of pity for the man who had been, if nothing else, openly hostile.

When Gabrielle had done her business, Angelique helped her wash her hands and then swiped at her face with a washcloth. She looked too cute in her warm fleecy pajamas, but Angelique changed her to a tot-sized red sweat suit with a Christmas tree on the front of the top.

Gabrielle was clasping her tiny sneakers when she raced back into the kitchen. Angelique followed behind her, surprised when Gabrielle ran straight to Colton and slammed into him.

He managed to snap to, and when he saw her coming, he held out his arms. She responded with giggles. "Whoa, little lady."

She seemed to find that hilarious and squealed her delight. She held out her shoes. "My chooz!"

"I see," Colt said. "Want me to help you?"

At her vigorous nod, he lifted her into his lap and slipped each shoe on, fastening each with the Velcro strap.

Angelique was encouraged by his gentleness with her daughter. Perhaps he had truly had a change of heart.

Gabrielle wriggled off his lap and ran back to Angelique, proudly showing her shoes.

"Thank you for being so nice to my daughter."

Colt offered a smile. "She's my niece too."

Angelique was filled with a sense of relief. "Yes, she is. Would you like some coffee?"

"Yes. Yes, I would."

This was a normal thing for a normal brother and sister to share. *Coffee*.

Chapter 20

"So, how does this extra-credit thing work?" Big Jim asked.

Mark was earnestly mucking out one of the stalls. "The teacher said we could earn extra credit in English if we complete a two-page essay telling about our family Christmas traditions. Only—only we really didn't have any…so I wrote about the Garrett family Christmas traditions that Tyler told me about."

Big Jim felt a rush of pity for all the things this young man had been denied by virtue of having been born into such sad circumstances. Big Jim realized he had the best of the Dalton family in Misty and her younger brother folded into the Garrett clan.

Now, it seemed that Big Jim would need to make sure Mark's Christmas was special enough to make up for all that he had missed out on in the past.

He wondered what present this fine young man would like to receive. He reviewed all of the things he knew about Mark, but other than horses, Big Jim couldn't recall anything he had mentioned that he liked. He would have to ask Misty if there was anything in particular Mark would like to find under the tree on Christmas day.

In a while, Colt joined them in the stables. Without a word, he picked up a shovel and began mucking out one of the stalls.

He seemed to be in a much better mood, so Big Jim figured he had worked things out with Angelique. At least he hoped so. He would have to take her pulse to make sure their encounter had been a pleasant one.

After the stables had been cleaned and fresh hay spread on the floor of each stall, the three saddled up their favorite mounts and took a short ride.

Big Jim had considered seeing if Angelique wanted to accompany them on this outing, although he knew in his heart that riding a horse was not her favorite activity. He didn't want her to feel left out.

After Colton and Mark had departed, Big Jim went into the house to clean up. When he emerged, he found Angelique and Gabrielle waiting for him, dressed in outdoor wear. "You girls ready to go?"

Gabrielle nodded. "I weady, Gwampa."

He loved that she reached for him, confident he would be there for her. "Grampa's here, darlin'."

"I have a list. Not much, but definitely essentials." Angelique followed him as he carried Gabrielle to his truck. "Don't you want to lock the door, Dad?"

"I'm sure everything will be okay. We don't get many unannounced visitors way out here."

She giggled. "Like me?"

He turned to her. "You're my family. Not a visitor."

Tears sprang to her big blue Garrett eyes.

Big Jim shifted Gabrielle and reached for Angelique with his other arm, drawing her into an embrace. "Aw, honey. I didn't mean to make you cry."

She nodded and sniffled against his chest.

He kissed the top of her hair, sensing there was something else behind the tears.

She pulled back, gazing at him, her face tearstained. "Actually, I think that was about the nicest thing anyone has said to me in a long time."

~

Gabrielle sat in the car seat Big Jim had installed in his truck. She proudly surveyed the passing countryside, calling out everything they passed. "Cows!"

"Yes, little darlin'. Those are your grampa's cows. Those are Angus, as a matter of fact."

"Angus cows!" she called out, her face alight.

Angelique was so glad her father was educating her daughter, as though he planned for her to be a part of his life for a long time to come. Although Gabrielle did not understand that Angus was the name of the breed, it would probably imprint on her over time. At least she could recognize that it was a cow.

They bumped over the cattle guard and made a turn onto the highway in the direction of Langston.

Big Jim cleared his throat. "So, you and Colt get things straight?"

Very subtle, Dad. "Yes, as a matter of fact, we did. He—he apologized for being…distant." She couldn't help but smile. "He said he thought I was some kind of a scam artist."

"You? It never entered my mind. I knew you were mine the moment you and Gabrielle entered my life… My girls."

"Don't get me started crying again. I just mopped up the tears." She swallowed hard. "Let me just say that I am so happy to be here with you…and I'm feeling very lucky to be a part of this wonderful family."

Big Jim looked at her and smiled. "I'm glad you made the effort to find your way here." He slowed as they entered Langston and drove the few blocks to the small grocery store. He turned off the motor and climbed out to release Gabrielle from her car seat. "Come to Grampa, little darlin'."

Angelique climbed down on her own, while Big Jim chided her.

"I would have come around to help you down."

Together they entered the store and Big Jim chose to carry Gabrielle around like a trophy he'd won. People stopped him to comment on his beautiful granddaughter. "We'll see you in church on Sunday."

Angelique made quick work of selecting several loaves of French bread that were close to the "sell by" date. Several cloves of garlic found their way into her cart, and she was glad to find shrimp in the freezer section.

"Mmm. Love me some shrimp. We can throw them on the barbecue."

"In that case, we better get more," she said. "Because these little shrimpies are headed for a pot of gumbo."

Big Jim tossed another bag of frozen shrimp into the cart. When they were done, they went through the checkout line.

"Which one of your sons does this little beauty belong to?" An older man dressed in cowboy garb was in line in front of them. His wife turned to stare too.

"Why, she's the spitting image of you, Big Jim. Look at those eyes." The woman reached out to touch Gabrielle, who clasped Big Jim's neck tighter.

"This little beauty is my daughter Angelique's girl."

He gestured toward Angelique. "This is Mr. and Mrs. Potter, Angelique."

Angelique felt her cheeks flame, but she smiled and greeted the couple. Big Jim must know he was stirring up the gossip in this small town, but he seemed to have no shame over having fathered a child out of wedlock.

When they were loaded back in the truck, he drove to the far side of town, although the Garrett ranch was back the way they had come. "Just a little stop to make."

Once again he wrestled Gabrielle out of the back seat and made it around to open Angelique's door. "What is this place?" She looked at the large building with a faded sign overhead. Feed and Seed?

Big Jim escorted her inside, waving to a man behind the counter. "Hi, Pete. How's it going?"

The man's eyes lit up when he recognized Big Jim. "Good to see you, Mr. Garrett. What can I do for you today?" He came out from behind the cash register.

"I thought we could look around. I've got grandkids who are all about animals."

"Right this way, sir." Pete gestured toward another room.

There were shelves of food for small animals as well as dog beds and crates of various sizes, and along one wall were some cages.

"In a few months we'll have some baby ducklings, chicks, and Easter rabbits," Pete said.

There was a cage with two rabbits in it. They appeared to be very different, although Angelique had never realized that rabbits came in different breeds.

Big Jim set Gabrielle down in front of the cages, her eyes wide. Angelique reached for her hand and squatted down beside her. "Bunnies."

"Did I hear my father-in-law out here?" Beau's red-headed wife came around the corner. She grinned when she saw them. "I thought that was you, Big Jim. Hi, Angelique. What brings you folks out in the cold?"

"Just looking around," Big Jim said. "Trying to find something special for Mark for Christmas. Any ideas?"

Dixie scoffed. "Well, of course I have ideas. How about taking a look at some of the hand-tooled saddles or other tack?"

"That might work," Big Jim said.

Dixie tucked her hand in the crook of his arm and led him away. "I might just let you have the family discount."

Pete slouched against the wall, grinning at Angelique. "I don't think I seen you around here afore."

Angelique took a big breath and blew it out. *On my own here*. "I'm Big Jim's daughter. You can call me Angelique."

"Well, Miss Garrett, I'm plum tickled to meet you. An' this'n must be your little girl. She looks just like you."

Angelique didn't know if she should correct him or not, but the fewer people around here who had ever heard the name Guillory, the better. "Nice to meet you, Pete. Tell me about these rabbits. They look so different."

He pushed off the wall and squatted down beside her. "There are over three hundred breeds. That there little brown one is a Holland Lop. Her ears hang down instead of standing up."

"She's really pretty," Angelique said. "What about the white one? It's so fluffy."

Gabrielle was straining to reach them.

"Ain't she a beauty? She's an Angora. Her fur is extra long." He opened the cage and brought the rabbit out so Gabrielle could pet her.

Gabrielle made a sighing sound as her fingers sank into the long, thick fur.

"Be gentle with the bunny." Angelique demonstrated softly stroking the down-like fur.

"Yeah, these are our leftovers. They were more expensive than the common breeds so they weren't grabbed up." He shrugged. "Now they're sorta like pets."

Angelique frowned. "'Leftovers' sounds so mean." The rabbit was snuggling in her arms, and Gabrielle was stroking its fur and cooing to it.

Big Jim came up behind her. "Looks like somebody done fell in love."

"My bunny!" Gabrielle asserted.

"Yes, I see." Big Jim nodded.

"Looks like someone found her present." Dixie was grinning. "Old Luke Hammons wanted to buy them for rabbit stew, but I said no."

Angelique let out a little yelp of protest. "What an awful idea."

Gabrielle was now petting the Holland Lop. "My bunny."

Dixie was grinning from ear to ear now. "These girls are best friends, and I can make you a good deal on the pair."

Big Jim let out a guffaw that ended in a belly laugh. "Quite the sales pitch, Dixie."

"They're so sweet. I've been hoping the perfect home would present itself…and here you are." Her eyes were almost as pleading as Gabrielle's. "C'mon, Big Jim. You can find room on that big old ranch for a couple of cute little bunnies."

Big Jim's ferocious brows drew together. "Wait a minute! I seem to recall that little Miss Ava has her own bunnies. Couldn't you take these two home and let them live in the little hutch we built in the backyard?"

Dixie huffed out a little snort. "It's too cold, and Bertram and Anastasia are now house bunnies. They have the run of the place."

Angelique gaped. "In the house? Don't they… I mean… Where do they…?"

"They are all trained to a litter box. These two are very polite little girls." Dixie crossed her arms over her chest. "I can give you a great deal on a crate."

Big Jim was chuckling and staring at Gabrielle. "I guess we'll have some house bunnies. You don't think I could say no to that." He pointed to Gabrielle who had her face pressed against the brown bunny.

Angelique thought her heart was going to burst. She kept her gaze on her daughter, wondering what her life would have been like if she'd had a daddy around to spoil her.

So the crate was loaded into the bed of Big Jim's truck, and the bunnies rode inside in a carrying case. Lots of bunny food and a bag of litter rounded out the purchase. The saddle was left to be personalized with Mark's name.

The drive back to the ranch was punctuated with sounds from the back seat as Gabrielle crooned and sang to her bunnies.

In the front seat it was hard to tell whose smile was widest.

When they arrived back at the ranch, Angelique took the groceries to the kitchen, storing the shrimp in the freezer but laying out the other items on the countertop.

Big Jim was busy finding the perfect place for "house bunnies" to be situated for the winter. He decided the den area close to the back door would be a place for bunnies to live. He tried to house them in their new crate, but Gabrielle insisted she had to hold her bunnies. Soon Big Jim, gentleman rancher, was reduced to herding rabbits.

He looked at Angelique from the other end of the dining room, the white Angora rabbit in his arms. "What are you makin' there, Angelique? Something sure smells good."

"I know Leah and her grandmother are making a ton of cookies, and I didn't want to compete with them, but"—she turned to grin at him—"I thought I would make something sweet from my own background. My contribution...and I couldn't resist using some of those beautiful pecans from your trees."

"Well, help yourself, Angelique." He looked at what she was making with great interest, but Gabrielle wanted to see the rabbit in his arms.

"This is a recipe my mother taught me. I thought it would be something I could wrap and include in presents. You know, to make it more personal."

"You know, I think I should taste one, just to make sure they're up to par." Big Jim looked at her hopefully.

"Sure. They're not quite set, but let me put one on a saucer. I hope you like them." She used a spatula to scoop one onto a small plate and handed it to him.

Big Jim picked the slightly soft confection up with his fingers and took a bite. "Delicious. Everyone's going to love them."

"I hope so." She shrugged and winked at him. "If nobody wants to try them, I guess I'll have to eat them myself."

"You got off easy, y'know?" Misty Garrett pulled off her leather gloves and stuffed them in the pocket of her warm, fleece-lined jacket. She stuffed the hand-crocheted cap Leah had made for her in the other pocket.

Colt huffed out a sigh. "You wouldn't say that if you were there. I felt like a real jackass." He surveyed his wife, her cheeks rosy from the cold. He helped her remove her jacket and hung it on a peg by the back door. Then he enfolded her in an embrace. "Welcome home, sweetheart."

She rose on tiptoe to offer up her lips for a kiss.

He smiled, gazing down at the beautiful woman in his arms, then took advantage of her offer. A kiss that started sweet but turned hot in seconds. "Whoa! That was the best kiss I've had in a few days. Does that mean I'm out of the doghouse?"

Misty reached up to stroke his hair. "Good boy."

"Brat!" He gave her a playful swat on her rear.

"What is that wonderful smell? Did you make chili?" Her eyes were wide with interest.

"Maybe I did...and maybe I made a pan of corn

bread to go with it." He released her and gestured to the kitchen.

"Oh, I'm starving. It was so cold I didn't go out for lunch."

"It's going to snow again tonight. Let me dish up a bowl of chili. Mark and I have been eating all afternoon."

"Oh, I better catch up while you tell me all about your encounter with your sister, Angelique." She went to the kitchen, washed her hands, and seated herself at the table.

Colt regarded her with amusement. "Coming right up." He ladled the thick and savory chili into a bowl and placed it on a plate beside a slab of corn bread. He brought it to the table with a soup spoon and knife along with the butter dish. "And what would her highness like to drink?"

"I'm good. Just sit down and tell me how it went with Angelique." She picked up the spoon and scooped a bite into her mouth and then made a moan of appreciation.

"You're welcome." Colton turned the chair around and straddled it backwards. "It was not as bad as I thought. Angelique was very nice, considering how I treated her."

Misty raised her brows in a question, but didn't stop eating.

"I told her that you weren't to blame." He spread his hands. "And she laughed when I confessed that I thought she might have been a scammer."

"Is that all?"

"We talked for a while about how we were raised. So different. I think she turned out pretty well, considering."

Misty spread a pat of butter on her corn bread. "So all is well in the Garrett family?"

"Yeah, I guess. Her little girl is adorable." He swallowed hard. "My niece."

She put the spoon down. "Are you thinking it's about time we do our part to carry on the Garrett name? You know…make beautiful little blue-eyed babies?"

Her expression was so hopeful, he had to smile. "We're getting closer."

She huffed out a sigh and picked up her spoon. "I'm ready, whether you are or not."

"I'm getting there. We finished the house. We both work. We're raising your brother." He shrugged. "I'm getting there."

She sent him a glowering pout. "Well, I'm already there. Both my sisters-in-law have children. Your half-sister has a child. What's the problem? Don't you think I'll be a good mother?"

He had to acknowledge that she had a reason to be ticked off. He wanted children but also wanted everything to be perfect before they began a family. "No, baby. I'm sure you're going to be a great mother. It's just—"

"Just what?" she snapped.

"What about your job? Are you prepared to walk away from it? Can you leave Breckenridge Ryan's law practice?"

She opened her mouth and then closed it abruptly.

"That's your answer," he said. "When you're ready to walk away, I'll be ready."

When Alphonse Benoit contacted Chief Cormier, he made it clear that the police chief should be using all the resources of the department to track down his missing granddaughter.

His blood pressure was through the roof, but Alphonse spoke in a calm, icy voice. "You know, I thought you would be able to perform a simple task for me. After all, you owe me your whole career." He made a scoffing sound. "Nobody would have chosen you for the important position of chief of police, but I got some people—some very important people—who owed me a favor. I am the reason you got to be where you are today, and don't you forget it."

"No suh. I can't never forget none of it." Cormier sighed. "I ain't heard nothin' 'bout your runaway. An' let me tell you, nobody here who knew her believes she stole anythin' from you nor nobody else."

"Dammit! I don't want to hear that, you lazy cretin. You have to find her."

"Well, I would if I could, jus' to get you off my back. I ain't heard nuthin' from nobody." He paused. "Well, some hick sheriff up in north Texas called because he thought she was a hottie." Cormier chuckled.

Alphonse groaned. "Shut up, stupid. I want to hear that you found Angelique and Gabrielle."

"You not gonna kill that purty girl, are you?"

Silence.

"I would advise you to keep your nose out of things that don't concern you."

"But…"

"Friday. You find her by Friday, or you'll be at the bottom of the Mississippi—feeding the catfish." Benoit disconnected.

Chapter 21

Derrick picked up Angelique just before six. It was already getting dark, and they were expecting a snowfall overnight.

He helped her to don her jacket and wrapped her scarf around her neck. "Bundle up, baby. We're in for a cold night."

She gazed up at him, her beautiful blue eyes wide with questions. "That sounds bad. Should we be going out?"

"We'll be fine. I have snow tires, and the heater is running in the truck." He gave her a kiss. "Don't worry. We're used to this kind of weather."

She shook her head. "Well, I'm not. It's never this cold in New Orleans."

He brushed a strand of hair away from her face. "You don't have winter in New Orleans?"

"Not much. I mean, it gets cold with all the humidity and the wind coming off the Gulf of Mexico. Really cold." She shook her head helplessly. "I can't imagine how miserable it will be to get even colder here in north Texas."

"Don't worry. It's pretty dry here, so even though the thermometer may drop lower, it doesn't feel that cold. We'll be fine."

"We will?" She still looked doubtful.

"Just a man and his girlfriend, out on the town." He grinned, hoping to allay her fears.

"I take it I'm the girlfriend."

"You're the woman I love."

"That will do. Let's go." She tucked her hand in the crook of his arm. "I hear tamales and enchiladas calling my name."

Derrick escorted her to his truck and handed her up into the passenger seat. "Buckle up, Angelique." He rounded the truck and climbed behind the wheel. "I hope you're hungry."

"As a matter of fact, I am. I spent some time making Christmas goodies. If you play your cards right, you might just be lucky enough to find some in your Christmas stocking."

He leaned over to give her a kiss. "I'll try to be an extra-good boy." He drove her into town and hustled her into Tio's Mexican Restaurant. The temperature was indeed dropping, and he hoped the snowfall would hold off until he had her safely back home.

Milita Rios greeted them warmly. "So glad you're settling in here, Angelique."

Angelique smiled, shrugging out of her jacket. "It's a lovely place with lovely people."

Derrick gave her a salute. "That's me she's talking about. I'm a lovely people."

Milita gave each of them a menu and walked away chuckling.

"Aw, you are a lovely man, Derrick." Angelique reached over to pat his forearm. A sweet gesture.

Their food arrived, and they enjoyed the meal and each other's company. Now he had to get serious about learning what, in her history, had caused the claim that she was a thief, and that perhaps, if Cormier was to be believed, a monster was searching for her.

He had her relatively alone. But how would she react when he asked her about the jewel theft?

"Um, Angelique, I have to ask you about something that came across my desk."

Her face took on a shrouded look. She blinked and glanced down at her hands. "Uh, well…whatever you have to do."

He reached out to cover her hands with his own. "Honey, I would never do anything to upset you, but something came up and I have to know the truth." He recognized the pain and fear in her eyes.

"Is that why you invited me out tonight?" The beautiful blue eyes fastened on him, feeling like a laser burning a hole in his soul.

"No, Angelique. I wanted to be with you…but something troubling came across my desk and I can't ignore it."

Angelique moistened her lips. "Ask me what you want to ask me."

"I'll show you this. It has been sent out to all law-enforcement agencies." He fumbled with his shirt pocket and brought forth the alert with Angelique's photograph. He unfolded it and set it on the table between them, smoothing out the wrinkles.

"What—what is this?" She picked up the paper and quickly read through the information. "This is ridiculous! My mother gave me her jewelry and the keys to her car. She wanted me to have all her possessions. I-I left most of our things behind, but I took her jewelry because it was portable and it was something she enjoyed. She loved to dress up and wear her jewelry. I-I didn't steal it."

He picked up her hands and kissed them. "I never thought you did. But there was something else. I talked to the New Orleans police. The chief, in fact."

She jerked her hands away, looking stricken. "Oh, no! You didn't!"

"Who is this guy Benoit? He's the one who accused you. He claims the jewelry is his."

Angelique was shaking her head side to side, tears running down her cheeks. "No!" It came out as a whisper. "He gave my mother some of her jewelry, but she had inherited most of it from her mother. So it was only right that she passed it down to me, and to Gabrielle as well. Don't you see?"

"I do. Trust me, I do." Derrick was at a loss as to how to comfort her. "We can contact this police chief and let him know you didn't steal it."

"Oh, please no." She gasped for breath. "The police chief is in Benoit's pocket. He owns him."

Derrick swallowed hard. "I can't believe that. He really raked this Benoit over the coals…said he had murdered people."

"He has… Alphonse Benoit is a vicious criminal."

Derrick stared at her in dismay. "How do you know him?"

She emitted a little mewling sound. "His son, Remy, was Gabrielle's father."

Derrick felt a sharp pain as though someone had stabbed him in the chest. There it was. The name of the man who had impregnated the woman he loved, and his father was a criminal who murdered people…and he was after Angelique.

"Was?" he asked.

She reached for a paper napkin and mopped at her eyes, then gave her nose a hearty blow. "Remy's dead. His father killed him." She reached for her jacket and shrugged it on. "I've got to get out of here. I'm ready to scream, and I can't do it in here." She stood up and walked to the door.

Derrick scrambled after her and tossed some cash at the register before following after Angelique. "Hey, wait for me."

The temperature had dropped considerably. Angelique had her arms clasped around herself in a solo embrace. She was shivering.

He came up behind her and embraced her. "I'm sorry I had to ask you about this. I don't want to make you unhappy." He shepherded her to the truck and helped her inside. When he climbed in on the driver's side, he started the motor, but the interior was like a walk-in freezer. His breath created a cloud around his face as he leaned closer to her.

"I'm so scared. I can't let him find me." She focused on Derrick. "You have to take me right home. I need to get Gabrielle and leave."

Angelique held Gabrielle as she slept, rocking her gently in the rocking chair in her bedroom. She was crushed. How could Derrick have gotten in touch with the one man who could lead Alphonse Benoit straight to her! She was terrified for herself and for her daughter. There was no way she would surrender Gabrielle to a murderous criminal.

Anger and fear were duking it out in her gut. She was furious at Derrick. Yes, she still loved him, but he was the last person she would have guessed would betray her.

She tried to breathe through the fury roiling her gut.

In truth, it wasn't his fault, because she had not confided in him. She had hoped her past would just disappear, with no reason to dredge it up.

Admitting that her beloved Remy's father was a monster, she had no choice but to do whatever it took to protect her daughter from him. Unfortunately, it meant that she would have to run away from a place where she had felt safe for the first time in a long time. She would have to leave the father she had never known, the man who had accepted her and given her a place in his family.

And she would have to leave Derrick, the man who loved her, and who she loved in return.

Angelique would give her life to protect her daughter. Her choices were to stay and hope for the best or to run away.

She swallowed hard, knowing she had to make a decision quickly and act on it. She should be putting her few belongings in the car and be ready to head out at first light.

A tear rolled down her cheek as she reflected on how different her relationship with Derrick had been. He was an honorable man, and all of the community seemed to hold him in high regard. And he was proud to have his community know he cared for her, openly holding her hand and giving her a kiss in public. It was a small town, where everybody knew everything about everybody else. They had to know that Big Jim Garrett's illegitimate daughter had tracked him down, bringing her illegitimate daughter with her. They accepted her, not because they feared Big Jim, but because they respected him.

She knew if she left now, she would never find another place so secure, so loving. Her heart sank as she thought about how Big Jim would feel if she disappeared.

Then there was Derrick. She would hurt him if she left. And she would never find a man like him again. She realized her mother had the best man she had ever known and that he would have married her if she had returned to him…but no, she had ended up as girlfriend to a monster.

She struggled to rise from the chair without waking Gabrielle and placed her in her bed.

Angelique looked around the room. It was so cozy. She had settled in like a bird on its nest.

She had enjoyed spending time at Derrick's ranch house where she had free rein in the kitchen, loving that Derrick had appreciated her cooking, a task she loved.

Oh, Derrick. I love you so much. How can I leave you? A shiver coiled around her spine.

Angelique decided to take some of their possessions to the car. It wouldn't hurt to be prepared to go on the lam. She took her mother's jewel case and a small bag with some of her clothing and tiptoed out of the room. She hadn't taken the time to put on her jacket, reasoning that she was only going to run out to her car and back into the house. Somehow, having something ready to go gave her a little confidence. She opened the door and crossed the porch, sucking in a breath when she realized how frigid it was. Big Jim had said the temperature would be going down that night, but she had never experienced anything that cold. Resolutely, she stepped down off the porch, gasping when the snow surrounded her ankle. *Must go on.* She plodded to her car and stowed the items on the floorboard behind the driver's seat.

She glanced up at the moon, bright white against a black and starry sky. She had never seen skies like this. Living in the city, with lights shining all night long, she could see the moon, but very few stars. This was a whole different sky, maybe a whole different planet.

A few more loads and then all she would have to do would be to secure Gabrielle in her safety seat and she could leave at a moment's notice.

She closed the door and turned, running smack into a solid wall of something with arms that grabbed her.

"Angelique, be careful."

She found herself in Derrick Shelton's strong arms. "What are you doing here?"

"I'm here to protect you, and I hope I can talk you out of leaving me."

She let out a little whimper. "Oh, Derrick. I'm so scared. I don't want to go, but I think I have to."

"No, you don't." He lifted her in his arms and carried her back up onto the porch and into the house before setting her on her very cold feet. The warmth that greeted her was like an embrace.

She took his hand and pulled him toward the kitchen area, as far away from the bedrooms as possible. "I know you can't possibly understand…"

"I'll tell you what I can't understand." He gazed down at her. "I can't understand how you can leave me when you know how much I love you. We can fix this."

She shook her head. "No, we can't. You have no idea how evil this man is…or how powerful. He wants my daughter because she is his only living blood relative."

"But she's your daughter. He has no right to her."

Angelique let out a snort. "He doesn't care. He takes what he wants and kills anyone who gets in his way." She gazed up into Derrick's kind eyes. "You have no idea how cruel this man is, and he's after me. I thought I could disappear and be a part of this wonderful family… a part of this sweet town…and…" She swallowed hard. "I had hoped that you and I could…"

"We can. I want to marry you, Angelique. I want to spend my life with you and Gabrielle. Maybe a few more kids along the way."

"Oh, Derrick. What a time to propose."

"Well, I could have picked a more romantic place, but you haven't given me much choice."

They glared at each other for a moment, and then she was in his arms kissing him and trying not to cry.

A bubble of joy rose in her chest, and…could it be hope?

"I do not intend to let you get away from me. I will protect you from this man who is after you."

She had both arms wrapped around his neck, and her feet were dangling off the floor. He felt so big and powerful to her now, but she knew how much power true evil could wield. "Please don't try to save me. If Benoit would kill his own son, think what he would do to you."

Derrick loosened her arms and stepped far enough

away to frown at her. "Angelique, I'm not that easy to kill. I'm the sheriff for this county, and I've faced off with some pretty tough felons." He laid a sweet kiss on her lips. "Trust me, this Benoit fellow will have to go through me to get to you."

"And me." This was the deep voice of Big Jim Garrett, leaning in the doorway to the kitchen. "Angelique, honey, if you think I'm going to wave goodbye while you disappear, you've got another think coming." He came into the room and took a seat at the counter. "You and Gabrielle are a part of this family, now and forever. Don't you forget that." He raked his fingers through his silvery mane. "I just found you and I'm not about to lose you, y'hear?"

Angelique swallowed the taste of her tears. "Yes, Dad."

"So, honey… Did you say yes to this yahoo's proposal?"

She sucked in a breath and heaved it out again. "Why don't we see if I live through this before we make any long-range plans?"

Big Jim's fierce brows drew together. "Dammit, Angelique. We're gonna get through this, as a family. This here's the sheriff, and you ain't goin' nowhere."

Beau Garrett cleared the breakfast dishes and rinsed them off before he lined them up in the dishwasher. It was the least he could do to… Well, he also walked his wife out to her vehicle and kissed her goodbye before he passed her the lunch he had made for her. "Stay warm, baby."

"I will." She made a kissy face and closed the car door.

He waved as she drove away, then made it back onto the porch to stamp the snow off his boots.

"Can I have some more cocoa, Daddy?" Ava still sat at the table.

"Sure, Ava. Let me heat up some milk." He opened a mason jar of the homemade cocoa mix his sister-in-law made. He stepped over Bertram, the large rabbit that now lived inside the house with his mate, Anastasia. He hoped that in the spring they would like to go outside to the hutch he and his dad had built for them.

These large rabbits were bigger than the average house cat, but Bertram was black and very shiny, and sometimes it was difficult to see him before he darted out in front of you…and then came to a dead stop.

Beau sighed and poured the hot milk over the cocoa mix in a deep mug and then tossed in some mini marshmallows. It was probably not a good idea to start the day with a sugar high, but he couldn't resist his daughter's grin when he plunked the mug down in front of her.

"I wonder what Santa Claus is going to bring my favorite girl?" He sat across from her at the table.

"Me, or Mommy?" she asked.

Beau nodded his head wisely. "Good question. You're my favorite daughter and your mommy is my favorite wife."

Big blue eyes regarded him. "Oh, Daddy. You're so silly."

"Hey, you're getting to be such a big girl… I hope Santa knows what you would really like to find under the tree. Did you send him a letter?"

"No, but I told Gramma. She said she would tell him."

Beau was not a fan of Dixie's mother, the woman who had lied her butt off to keep them apart. Now, they operated on a cold war basis. She lived in Dallas and as a family they visited her a few times each year. She drove up for visits, but Christmas was always a Garrett thing.

She could have other holidays, but Christmas had to take place on the ranch, at the church, and with the Garretts.

Now Beau had to wonder what secrets she had divined from his daughter. He exhaled, letting all his negative feelings go. Or that was what Dixie would tell him he was doing. In his heart, he wanted to give his daughter the best gift, but he had to reason that was ridiculous. He should be glad that someone was showering Ava with presents. If his own dad were to give Ava her heart's desire, he would not feel this sense of being put upon. Her grandmother had as much right to dote on her as her grandfather.

Beau sucked in another deep breath and let it out slowly. *Inhale…exhale…*

Chapter 22

"Um, Mistah Benoit! I wasn't expectin' you." Cormier's usual pallor had gone ashy. He had intended to be on his way back to his office after a long lunch with a lady friend, but he hadn't expected to find Alphonse Benoit waiting in his official police vehicle.

"Surprise," Benoit said. "It's Friday."

"Um—what is it I can do for you, Mistah Benoit?"

"It's interesting that you are far more polite when we meet in person." Benoit was looking smug, as though he knew something he wasn't sharing.

"I'm so very sorry if I ain't been polite in our phone talks." Cormier placed his hand over his heart.

"Well, it depends on what you have to tell me."

"What I got to tell you? Well, uh..." Cormier cast about for something plausible to share with this monster. "Um, y'know I told you 'bout that sheriff up in north Texas? He called this mornin' to let me know he got her in his jail... jus' waitin' for me to go git her an' bring her to justice."

Benoit's brows drew together. "And where is this place in north Texas? Do you have a precise location?"

"Why, o' course I do. I wouldn' never let you down."

Benoit glared at him, causing a shiver to coil around his spine.

"Well, it's a lil' town called Langston. Jus' a bunch o' hicks up there."

Benoit heaved a loud sigh. "And can you tell me why a New Orleans woman with no ties would uproot her child and end up in some hick town in Texas, of all places? She's a city girl. Always has been and always will be."

Cormier shrugged, trying to appear nonchalant. "Maybe you don' know everythin' about this Angelique Guillory woman. Maybe she got friends you don' know nothin' about." He hoped he carried it off. "Maybe she done met some man in one of them chat rooms. You know, a love hookup."

Benoit's face went from red to a deep burgundy. "That's impossible. She and my son were…" He broke off and reached for the door handle. "If you're lying to me, you will live to regret it…for a short time. You understand me?"

"Oh, yessir, Mistah Benoit. I got the big picture."

Benoit got out of the car and slammed the door, leaving Cormier shaken. He vowed that he would be prepared at all times, and the next time he laid eyes on Benoit, he would get rid of the man responsible for so much that was wrong in the Big Easy.

When Big Jim went out to tend to his horses, he was pleased that Colt was already there. The horses were prancing around in the corral, tossing their heads and circling the enclosure.

Colt had shoveled out the stalls and was in the process of sweeping them out with a large push broom.

"Hi, Son. You got an early start today."

"I did. Misty had to go into the office to meet

Breckenridge Ryan to sign off on some things. And then he was leaving for a court date in Amarillo, so I got up and out with her."

"And where is that rascal Mark?" Big Jim began to mete out the feed in the different stalls.

"He went with Misty."

Big Jim decided it was only fair to share Angelique's situation with his oldest son. He related everything he knew about the danger posed to both his daughter and granddaughter. "I can't let someone get to the girls."

Colt's brow was knit almost as tight as Big Jim's own. "So, what's the plan, Dad?"

"Well, Derrick is going to be here as much as he can. And we gotta keep our eyes open and be ready to protect her."

"This is some kind of crime boss from New Orleans? I can't believe he would track her down all the way here."

Big Jim shook his head. "Apparently this man is sorta nuts. She said he killed his own son, who was Gabrielle's father. What kind of man would do that?"

Colt's expression was grim. "Be sure to tell Tyler. We need to make certain our own families are safe."

"I was thinking we could close up the gate. I can't recall the last time I closed it. Make sure everyone has the code."

"Good idea, Dad. This place is pretty much off the beaten track." Colt shrugged. "We can't take any chances."

Big Jim's jaw twitched. "Looks like I'm gonna be armed and dangerous until this is settled."

Colt gave his dad a hard gaze. "Me too."

Leah and her grandmother heard the news that Tyler shared with them. "I can't believe that she has gone through all that. Poor woman."

"That's what Dad told me. Apparently this crazy old guy killed his own son, and now he's after Angelique. He wants to take her daughter."

Leah sucked in a sharp breath. "We can't let that happen. Losing Gabrielle would kill Angelique. We have to protect her."

Tyler folded her in his arms. "Of course we do. Derrick has holed up at Dad's, so he's on guard. Dad and Colt are on alert too."

Leah nodded, her hair making a scrunching noise against his starched shirt. "Just let us get past this. I was hoping we could have a really good Christmas. You know, make it special for Angelique. I don't think she's had a lot of happy holidays."

Fern cast a doubtful glance at them. "That lil' Angelique…she been through enough bad times ta last a lifetime."

"She has, but now she's here with us." Leah stopped, not sure what more to say. "How can I help?"

"Angelique and Gabrielle are going to stay inside at Big Jim's until this maniac is brought down." Tyler spread his hands and made a circle around their kitchen. "We're all very well stocked. We can hole up here and not be running around like human targets. In addition to Angelique and Gabrielle, we have our own children to think of. We have to protect everyone in our family."

"I know you're right. I can work on decorating for

Christmas and cooking with Gran and Gracie." Leah managed a little smile. "We can stay busy and keep our attitudes positive. We will get through this."

"Together," Fern said.

"Together," Tyler echoed.

Alphonse drove all the way to Texas. He didn't trust any of his henchmen to do the job. He figured he could be less noticeable than any of his employees.

Besides, he would not trust any of those idiots with his precious Gabrielle.

The drive was long and boring. He had thought about flying to Dallas and renting a car, but that would leave a trail that might be tracked back to him. Better to slip out of New Orleans in the middle of the night and drive straight through.

It was bitter cold and there was snow on both sides of the roadway, but the roads had been cleared and it was dry, a far cry from the humidity of his hometown.

It was midmorning when he rolled into the small town of Langston. He drove from one end to the other, but couldn't see anything that would cause a girl like Angelique Guillory to want to settle in. There was no industry. No malls. No fancy restaurants.

How would she make a living? Maybe she had some savings.

He drove past a couple of restaurants, and there was one lawyer's office with a closed sign in the window. No reason for a lawyer to be hanging around his office on a Saturday in this one-horse town.

Finally Alphonse located the sheriff's office on a

side street and drove past it a couple of times before parking across the street and down about a half block. He didn't especially want to advertise his Louisiana license plates.

There was no one coming or going into the sheriff's office. Finally, he stepped out and walked briskly across the street to see if he could find out if this sheriff did indeed have Angelique Guillory locked up.

If so, maybe she would be glad to see him…

Ha!

As if she would ever welcome his presence. He was Remy's father, damn it. Gabrielle's grandfather. He deserved some respect.

But he knew she would never allow him to have access to his granddaughter. He had to take matters into his own hands.

Resolutely, he opened the door to the sheriff's office and stepped inside. He was greeted by a blast of heat from a gas heater in the middle of the room. There were two uniformed men seated at two desks. One was working on his computer, while the other was poking at his phone.

He approached the one on the computer. "Pardon me, young man."

The deputy pushed away from the desk. "Yes, sir. How can I help you?"

"I understand you have a young woman being held here in your jail. I want to make her bail."

The deputy cocked his head to one side. "No, sir. You are mistaken. We don't have anyone in our jail at this time." He regarded Benoit stonily.

Alphonse Benoit felt his face flush. He could hardly

breathe. He was definitely going to kill Cormier. That bastard had sent him on a wild-goose chase.

He stepped back from the desk, his fists clenched.

"Sorry you were misinformed, sir." The deputy looked as though he was anxious to get back to work.

"I don't suppose you've seen this girl?" He displayed a photo on his phone of Angelique with Remy, taken at a time before Gabrielle was born.

The young man glanced up at it and then looked back at the computer screen. "Um, no, sir. I don't think I've ever seen her."

"Sorry to have bothered you." Alphonse turned to the other deputy but he was gone. Alphonse left the building, rage building in his chest. He would definitely make sure Cormier suffered for his lies. He would beg for death.

Now Alphonse was far from home and had no reason to stay here in this cruddy little excuse for a town. Snow and slush everywhere. He was tired and cold, but didn't want to stay over to rest.

He had not seen any hotels or motels anyway. Probably no one ever came here without good reason. He stepped off into the slushy street, intending to return to his car, but he spied the other deputy. Apparently he had stepped outside to smoke and had taken refuge on the far side of the building, away from the wind.

The deputy had ruddy cheeks from the cold, and he was breathing through his mouth.

"Say, young man. Can you take a look at this for me?" He produced the image of Angelique and Remy again.

The deputy took the phone out of his hand and tilted it away from the glare. "Why, sure. I don't know this girl but I've seen her. She's the sheriff's girlfriend." The deputy returned the phone and shoved his hands in his jacket pockets.

Alphonse swallowed hard. It felt as though a tight band had wrapped around his chest, keeping him from drawing a full breath. "I don't suppose you know where she might be?" He managed a benevolent smile. "She's my…uh…my niece."

"Oh, well…I believe she's staying with the Garretts. I saw them all together in church last Sunday." He nodded and went back inside the office.

A coldness gathered in Alphonse's chest. So she had taken up with another man now. Some yokel had already taken Remy's place in her affections. He felt rage that she would thrust aside her supposedly loving relationship so soon after Remy's death.

Well, in truth she had waited over a year. It was probably when Sofie died that she thought she might lose Gabrielle to him…

Stupid girl! She couldn't understand the advantages he could give the child. Now it had come to this. He must find Gabrielle and return her to New Orleans where she would grow up as a princess.

In fact, if Remy had never gotten involved with Angelique, he would still be alive. He would have followed in his father's footsteps instead of trying to be a chef. What a sissy occupation for a man!

Alphonse returned to his car. *So, she's here in Hicksville.*

All he needed to do was find her and make her give him Gabrielle. If she turned the girl over, he might let Angelique live.

Derrick and the Garretts had a plan. Angelique and Gabrielle would remain embedded with the Garrett family until this Alphonse Benoit was apprehended. Derrick wasn't sure what he could charge him with, but at least he could get him held for stalking and threats. Derrick had looked up his record, and there were a lot of near-misses. But Benoit was out of his element here. He didn't own anyone in Langston, and Derrick didn't think anyone would go against Big Jim Garrett.

Derrick had taken a few days' worth of clothes and Smokey and Meow over to the Garrett compound. He would stay in the bedroom that had belonged to Tyler, the first son to move out.

Smokey was interested in the house bunnies, but was on his best behavior. Meow had to be sequestered until she could be seen to be trusted with the bunnies.

Now that the front gate was secured, there was less chance that someone would be able to invade the homestead. Of course, a band of goons could wrench the gate open or drive a heavy vehicle through it, but that would instigate an all-out siege.

The Garretts had plenty of arms and ammo. They were hunters and enjoyed target shooting as well. But Derrick hoped he would be able to apprehend this Benoit without bloodshed.

The Garrett family had made the decision to go to church. It was Sunday, and they always attended church together.

Derrick would have preferred that they all stay under wraps, but understood their reasoning. Surely with him and the four big Garrett men to protect her, Angelique could go to church the Sunday before Christmas.

He left his truck at the Garrett ranch and rode with Big Jim, the two men in the front with Angelique and Gabrielle in the back seat. Big Jim's truck had a double gun rack in the back window, and Derrick knew the rifle and shotgun were loaded.

He himself was armed, which was not the way he had ever considered going to church. His .45 automatic was tucked in a holster at the back of his waist and his jacket covered it. No reason to alarm the churchgoers. Just the sheriff and the Garretts attending church services as usual.

When they arrived at the church, Big Jim parked right in front, with Colt, Tyler, and Beau pulling in to flank his truck on both sides. Together, they got out and assisted their wives and children to the sidewalk.

Derrick was looking around, checking out the street in both directions.

The church was decorated with garlands and lights, which were turned on at night.

Other families were arriving. People got out and greeted them, just the way it usually happened. Derrick carried Gabrielle and shepherded Angelique with his arm around her. Big Jim was close on the other side. They entered the church as a tight unit.

Once inside the very lavishly decorated interior, Derrick felt a little more secure. Tyler and Leah entered behind them with their brood, and Beau behind them with Dixie and Ava. They moved into the central part of the church, going to the pew they usually commandeered every Sunday. Right side, third row from the front was officially Garrett property.

Beau led the way with his family, and Big Jim was next. Derrick ushered Angelique in next to her father and followed her, feeling that she would be safe ensconced between the two of them. Leah and her grandmother were next with Gracie in between her and Tyler. Then Misty, Mark, and Colt flanked the outside of the pew.

Derrick kept glancing around. No problems he could detect. Just the regular local congregation. People he had known all his life.

"I wanna go to Sunday school," Ava said.

"Yeah, me too, Mom." Gracie stood up. "I can take Ava."

Leah glanced at Tyler. "I don't think JT will make it through the entire service. I better take him to the nursery. His nursery school teacher is so sweet."

Tyler turned to Derrick. "What do you think?"

Derrick shrugged. "Let me check it out." He stood, and when he did. Angelique stood to follow him. He carried Gabrielle, intending to check the exits at the back of the church.

The strange procession made their way to the rooms at the rear of the building, to the Sunday school and nursery. Everything was clean and bright. Other parents were delivering children to Sunday school classes. People were talking and calling to each other. Children were laughing. It was a good noise, allaying some of the fear in Derrick's gut.

Normal Sunday. Just another normal Sunday.

"I think it will be okay to let Gabrielle play, don't you?" Angelique gazed at him with her beautiful eyes.

Gabrielle was squirming in his arms. "I go play now." She pointed to the door.

Derrick wasn't sure this was the best course of action, preferring that they all stay together. But Gabrielle wanted to go to the nursery school, and who was he to keep her from playing with other kids her age? "I guess so." He passed her to Angelique and went to check the exits while she took her daughter.

He checked the two fire exits and both were locked, but a wide brass bar could be used to push outside in case of a fire. He tested to make sure the exits were both secured, and then returned to Gabrielle and Angelique, happy to see Angelique and the teacher peeling the little girl out of her warm insulated jacket and knit cap.

There were other children in the room and two nursery-school teachers.

"Be a good girl for Mommy." Angelique kissed Gabrielle on the cheek and joined Derrick at the doorway.

They stood watching her as she approached another child, her face aglow.

"Let's go back to the family," he said. "Big Jim is probably chewing nails."

There were more people coming down the hallway toward them, so they threaded their way through to the main part of the church and into the Garrett pew.

Angelique held hands with Big Jim. She looked okay to Derrick, as though she wasn't afraid. The church filled with congregants and, in time, the organist took a seat at her instrument and the choir assembled, climbing onto the dais where their chairs were aligned in two rows on one side.

The minister entered from the back and took his place at the podium. Derrick checked out the leaflet and reached for the hymnal to look up the first song. It was an old favorite for the Christmas season, "What Child Is This?" Derrick settled back in the seat and slid his arm around Angelique's shoulders.

The service went on as expected. Derrick was on alert, although everything seemed to be secure. More Christmas hymns and prayers for the congregation, for those who were ill, for special needs, for those serving the military…and finally the service ended with the congregation greeting each other. Hands were shaken. Hugs were shared. People began gathering their things and moving to the aisles.

Derrick and Angelique headed for the nursery, moving against the current of individuals hoping to get home quickly. He was aware that Leah and Tyler were following them and maybe some more Garretts.

When they turned down the hall with the nursery, they heard a scream, and a large, burly man exited one of the rooms.

Angelique screamed. "No! It's Benoit. He's got my daughter."

To his horror, Derrick realized the man was carrying Gabrielle, and he had a handgun. He pushed Angelique against the wall. "Stay here!"

The man gazed at Angelique and raised his weapon, but Colton Garrett stepped in front of her just as Benoit fired his gun. Colt was thrown backward but remained on his feet, his big form shielding Angelique.

Tyler called Colt's name and reached to support him, as Derrick charged at Benoit.

Benoit ran toward the exit, bashing through the fire door with his shoulder, while Gabrielle screamed, "Mommy! Mommy!"

Derrick did not draw his firearm, not wanting to take the chance of harming Gabrielle, but he pushed through the fire door in pursuit of the man attempting to kidnap her.

Benoit fired again, hitting the doorframe close to Derrick's head. He jerked back, but immediately ran at Benoit who held Gabrielle in front of him as a shield.

"Alphonse, please don't hurt her." It was Angelique, who had followed Derrick out the door.

As Benoit aimed his gun at Angelique again, Derrick rushed him, grabbing his gun hand and taking him to the ground. As he hit the hard-packed earth, Benoit expelled a loud breath and released Gabrielle. She rolled away, and Angelique ran to scoop up her howling child.

Derrick knocked the gun away and flipped Benoit on his stomach. He didn't have his cuffs with him, but he had brought plastic zip ties, thinking they might be less distracting during church services.

"Get off of me, you oaf!" Benoit was red-faced and yelling. "I'll kill you, hillbilly."

Derrick planted his knee in the middle of Benoit's back and informed him of his Miranda rights while tightening the ties. "No, you are under arrest and won't be killing anyone."

"You don't know who I am. I'll kill you."

Derrick called for a couple of deputies to pick up the prisoner and an ambulance for Colt. The deputy arrived almost immediately and hauled Benoit to the county jail in Amarillo.

Angelique held Gabrielle clasped to her chest as the little girl bawled. Derrick shepherded them inside, out of the wind. Colt was sitting on the floor against the wall with Doctor Camryn Ryan squatting beside him. She held a towel to his shoulder, and he looked remarkably pale for a big, robust man.

Colt raised his hand when he saw Angelique and Gabrielle. "Thank God!"

Angelique knelt down beside him. "Colt, I can't believe you stepped in front of me."

Cami Ryan made a scoffing sound. "Well, if he hadn't, you would probably be dead. The height of the wound would have been about the same level as your head. That man was shooting to kill you."

Angelique emitted a soft moan. "He meant to kill me and take Gabrielle. Thank you so much for saving me, Colton."

Colt gave her a one-sided grin. "Aw, I couldn't lose my only sister, could I?"

Derrick reached down to give Colt a handclasp. "Good job, man."

"I'm going to send you to the hospital in Amarillo by helicopter. The bullet missed all vital organs. It went through this nice meaty shoulder and embedded in the wall behind you, but you're going to need some of my fancy needlework."

Misty knelt beside Colt with Mark huddled nearby. "Can I go with him?"

"You can ride with me," Cami said. "I'll be driving right to the hospital."

Misty nodded. "Thanks. Big Jim, will you take Mark back to the ranch?"

"Misty, we're all going to the hospital in Amarillo." Tyler stood by Big Jim, leaning against the opposite wall.

"That's right," Big Jim said. "I can't just sit at home when my boy has been injured by a bullet in his shoulder."

Derrick raised both hands. "Why don't I take Mark back to the ranch with Angelique and Gabrielle? Leah, how about you and your kids?"

"Tyler is dropping us at our house on his way to Amarillo." She stood, clutching JT to her chest, with her grandmother and Gracie beside her. "So it will be all the Garrett men in Amarillo tonight."

Cami looked around the group assembled in the hallway. "Colton is not dying. The bullet sliced a groove in his shoulder. It needs to be tended. No vital organs involved. He's going to have a nice scar to brag about, but he's going to bounce back in no time."

"Will I be home for Christmas?" Colt inquired.

Cami grinned at him. "I guarantee it, if you mind your doctor."

Chapter 23

Angelique opened the ranch-house front door with Mark and Derrick right behind her. "Brrr… Come in and get warmed up."

Derrick carried Gabrielle, bundled up in her quilted jacket. After her day of fright and screaming, she was worn out. They all trooped to the kitchen, where they peeled her out of her outer garments and Derrick carried her to her bed, with Angelique at his side.

She arranged her daughter and stood beside the bed, feeling drained.

"She's a beautiful little girl," Derrick said. He put his hand on Angelique's shoulder.

This simple gesture gave Angelique the invitation to embrace him with both arms. She was shaking. "I feel so bad about Colton getting shot. He was the one who didn't accept me when I first arrived, and now he laid down his life to save me."

"Trust me. You couldn't have a better champion. You're a Garrett, and the Garretts stand together. They've been through some tough times."

"I can't believe that I lived through this horrible day. Thank you for getting Alphonse before he killed me."

"Honey, I would never have let him get to you, but I thought we were safe in church. Benoit is going away for a long time."

Angelique pulled away, looking up at him with tears in her eyes. "You don't know him. He has connections all over. I can't relax until he's been convicted."

He cupped her cheek with one hand. "Shooting a Garrett around here is a pretty big deal. No juror is going to let him walk."

"We'll see." But his words gave her comfort. Could this be the time Alphonse Benoit actually received the justice he deserved? No telling how many of the bodies of his enemies would never be found.

When they returned to the kitchen, Angelique prepared a simple meal. It always gave her pleasure to cook for others and to see them take pleasure in her efforts.

Derrick was always easy to please. She decided to start preparations for her bread pudding, which she hoped would be a part of the Garrett feast on Christmas Eve.

Mark was typing away on his laptop, completely absorbed.

Derrick moved to a stool at the counter so he could "supervise" Angelique's cooking.

Angelique assembled the ingredients needed and began putting them together. When she covered the bowl of bread chunks soaking in the egg mixture and put it in the refrigerator, Derrick looked surprised.

"I thought I was going to get a taste tonight."

"It's better if the bread soaks up all the custardy mixture overnight, or at least for a few hours. This way it will be ready to go when others are cooking. I'm hoping everything will go well for Colt and he can come home. It would be a shame if he were to miss being home for Christmas Eve with his family."

Derrick reached for her hands. "Don't you worry about Colt. He's a tough guy, and this won't set him back much. I don't think the hospital can hold him if he's ready to go home."

Indeed, Colton Garrett had refused to be admitted to the hospital in Amarillo. In fact, after Dr. Camryn Ryan had thoroughly examined his shoulder, made certain the wound was clean, and stitched him up, he had insisted on returning to his home with his wife.

"Big Jim will take us back to the ranch," he said. "All I want to do is be home with my family."

Cami had raised an eyebrow and admonished him about the possibility of infection or popping his stitches.

Misty had assured the doctor that she would not allow him to lift a finger. "We want to be with our family for Christmas."

So Cami had relented and extracted a promise for him to appear in her office the day after Christmas or call if he experienced any fever or extreme pain.

Now he lay in the dark, in bed with his arm in a device to keep him from moving it. Misty was curled up beside him, but not touching him. She usually melded with him when they slept. But due to his injury, she was curled up with her pillow instead.

The painkiller he had been given at the hospital had worn off, and although he had been issued a small number of those same pills, he was reluctant to ingest anything.

He was a man, and as a man he should be able to stand up to a little pain. But somehow his shoulder pain was throbbing in time to his heartbeat. He tried to find a more comfortable position, but he really had to stay on his back. He wished he could adjust his pillow, but that was also difficult without the use of both arms.

Mostly, he didn't want to disturb Misty. She had been through a lot in the last twenty-four hours. She had lost people she loved in the past, and that was still raw. The thought that she might lose her husband had really stressed her out.

No, baby. You're not getting rid of me that easily.

Colt inhaled… That hurt. He twisted to his uninjured side… That hurt. He raised his head and quietly swung his legs off the bed… That hurt a lot.

Sitting on the side of the bed wasn't helping, so he stood as quietly as possible and took a few steps toward the door.

"If you're looking for your pain meds, I put them on your bedside table with a glass of water." Misty spoke quietly without rising.

"Oh, thanks." Now he felt like an idiot for trying to fool her. He sat back down on the bed and reached for the container, shaking one of the tiny pills out into his palm. He hated that he was not strong enough to rise above his pain…but he needed to sleep. And he wanted to celebrate Christmas Eve with his family without howling in pain in the middle of the festivities.

The Garrett family tradition, since the three sons had grown up and branched out with their own families, was to spend Christmas Eve with one's wife and children and then to go to Big Jim's house on Christmas Day for a feast and to exchange presents.

He had an idea that this year, with Misty and Mark,

would be special. After his brush with death the previous day, he was especially grateful for the life he had, and for those who enriched it on a daily basis.

He closed his eyes, glad that the pain was abating. *Good drugs.*

~

Derrick had left the Garrett compound early on Christmas Eve so he could check on his own property and take care of his stock.

Somehow, after he departed, Angelique felt the loss.

She was still finding it hard to believe that Alphonse Benoit had been taken into custody and that he might actually serve time for shooting Colt and attempting to kidnap Gabrielle. But she knew he was a very powerful man and had a long reach, so she was feeling anything but secure.

When she was up and dressed, and had awakened her very fussy daughter, she took her to the kitchen to see if a little breakfast would improve her mood.

"Well, there's my girls." Big Jim greeted them by hefting his coffee mug in their direction.

"You're always the early bird, Dad."

"Gotta get up early to make sure things are set for the day. This time of year is easy. All I gotta do is tend to the stock."

Angelique bounced up and down a little, but Gabrielle's lower lip was jutting out and she laid her head back down on Angelique's shoulder. "Sounds like work to me."

Big Jim set his coffee on the countertop and gestured for Angelique to hand Gabrielle over to him. "There's my girl. Looks like she's been sheddin' a few tears. What's the matter, honey?"

Gabrielle sort of melted onto his shoulder.

"She didn't sleep well, Dad." Angelique shook her head. "Neither did I. I kept seeing Alphonse Benoit's angry face." She couldn't repress a shudder.

Big Jim was bouncing now, and patting Gabrielle's back. "That is one bad man. But I don't think we'll have to worry about him anymore. At his age, going to prison for attempted murder and kidnapping will probably finish him off."

Angelique heaved a sigh. How to tell him that Benoit was the devil incarnate? "Um, I don't think you understand what a bad person he is. He has many henchmen working for him who would do whatever he wants...like kill people. One phone call and someone can disappear forever with no trace."

Big Jim's brows almost met in the middle. "You don't say? That's worrisome."

Worrisome? He obviously didn't grasp the enormity of Benoit's web of evil. "In New Orleans he's like the godfather of crime. Connected to all kinds of criminal activity."

"Well, this ain't New Orleans. You gotta have faith that the judge and jury will be able to put him away forever."

Angelique gripped her hands together. "That won't put him out of business. He can manage his empire from inside a jail cell."

"And you said this bad man's son was our little Gabrielle's daddy?"

She nodded. "Remy was a totally different person.

He was sweet and kind and very creative. We were making a good life together, and Alphonse couldn't stand that we were not dependent on him or involved in his businesses. He had wanted to groom Remy to take over."

"Sounds like you had yourself a good man." Big Jim looked solemn.

"He was. We had opened a restaurant, and it was quite successful for such a small place. My mom would sing there some evenings. Remy and I prepared the daily menu and served the patrons." She shook her head. "Alphonse couldn't stand that, so he ordered his goons to burn the place down." Her throat tightened. "But Remy had gone in early to make some preparations for a big party we were catering..."

"You don't mean...?"

"Yes, my Remy perished in that fire... Alphonse killed his own son."

Angelique went to the refrigerator and took out a large bowl containing fresh eggs from Big Jim's own hens. She set it on the counter and sighed, glad that he had never known such evil. "Over easy okay?"

"Aw, that'd be swell, darlin'." Big Jim offered an encouraging smile. Gabrielle had fallen asleep on his shoulder. At least one of his "girls" was at peace.

Leah was surprised when Tyler turned on the Christmas tree lights earlier than usual. "What's up, Ty?"

He went down on one knee to rearrange the presents. It seemed that he was searching for something in particular. "Just thought I would take this opportunity to have a moment with my beautiful wife." He rose to his feet. "Where is everybody?"

"JT's in his crib, and Gran and Gracie are in the kitchen making biscuits."

"Good." He held out his hand, and when she placed hers in it, he drew her into an embrace, kissing her tenderly. "Have I ever told you how much I love you?"

She grinned up at him. "Yeah. All the time...and I love you right back."

"After what happened at the church yesterday, it made me even more aware of how fast things can change." He squeezed her tighter. "When Colt got shot, it was so sudden...blink of an eye."

"I know. It was terrifying. Misty thought she'd lost him." Leah shook her head. "There was a lot of blood. She was really upset. I understand how she felt, but Colt was incredibly brave."

"Yeah, he wasn't about to admit he was in pain. He's always been like that. The big brother couldn't be a wimp in front of his little bros."

Leah grinned and shook her head. "Men!"

But she noticed that Tyler was still grim-faced. "Seriously, Leah. I'm trying to tell you I would die if I lost you. I always took it for granted that we would grow old together, but my mom was killed on a church bus accident after a women's retreat." His mouth tightened. "It changed all our lives."

Leah stood on her tiptoes to offer her lips and was rewarded with a passion-loaded kiss. "Don't worry. You can't get rid of me, cowboy. We're going to be ancient old people sitting in our rocking chairs, holding hands."

He gave a little smile. "Well, I wanted this Christmas

to be special for us, and I wanted you to have something that you could look at and know how much I love you." He presented her with a small wrapped present.

Leah felt a tightness in her chest. She was so happy in her marriage, and so grateful to have connected with Tyler after the horror of her early adolescence.

"Open it!" he urged, a wide grin on his face.

She untied the bow, and the paper fell away to reveal a small box from a jewelry store. "Oh, Ty!" She swallowed hard and lifted the lid to reveal a pair of sapphire and diamond earrings. "They're beautiful."

"Your birthstone, right?"

"This is far too expensive." She felt tears sting her eyes. "I mean, I don't need anything so extravagant."

"Honey, I needed to give you something special. You can't deny me the pleasure of giving my beautiful wife a present."

"I love these earrings, and I love you."

"I love you more," he whispered.

Beau was having trouble keeping his happiness hidden from his beloved wife. She had just gotten off the phone with her mother, who had a bad head cold and didn't feel like driving up to spend Christmas with them.

Beau felt like whooping with joy. Mamie was not the nicest person on the planet, having lied about everything to keep him and Dixie apart. Not his favorite person.

"This one's for you, Ava." Dixie handed a present to their daughter. "It's from your grandmother." She leaned against Beau's shoulder as they watched Ava tear into the large package.

The package was filled with clothing, which was good since Ava was a young clotheshorse. She held up each item for her parents to appreciate. "I like this one best."

"Gorgeous," Dixie said.

"That will look great on you, baby." Beau leaned back on the sofa, his arm around Dixie. He kissed her on the temple. "What did I get you?"

Dixie roared with laughter, her eyes twinkling. "A Ferrari."

"I was feeling generous, wasn't I?" He leaned over to give her another kiss.

"Well, I'm pretty sure I'm worth it." She snuggled closer. "Seriously, what did you get me?"

"A suntan." He let his head loll back on the sofa, looking particularly smug.

"C'mon. I looked at all the presents under the tree, and I didn't see anything from you to me. Have I pissed you off?"

He chuckled. "All the time."

She punched him on the arm.

"Here. I got you this card." Beau shuffled some magazines around on the coffee table and unearthed a fat envelope.

"A card? You got me a card?" Her green eyes were scorching him. "I got you a new Stetson, a great western shirt, and a subscription to *Farm and Ranch* magazine."

"You are a great shopper, and I love everything you got me."

She glowered at him, but held out her hand for the square envelope. She opened it, and her eyes opened wide. "Wow!"

"What do you think? Is there enough sunscreen on the planet to keep my favorite redhead from getting burned in Aruba?"

"We're flying to Aruba?" Her eyebrows had almost reached her hairline.

"For a week. It's the honeymoon we didn't get to take."

"But what about Ava?"

"Dad will spoil her rotten…or she could stay with Mamie. That way I wouldn't have to spend much time with her."

Dixie heaved a big sigh. "You're never going to forgive her for lying to us, are you?"

"No!"

Angelique's first Christmas Eve as a part of Big Jim's family had been exciting. He'd told her that all of her half-brothers and their families would be descending on them Christmas Day, but generally, his sons spent Christmas Eve with their wives and children.

Big Jim loved the treats she had made for him.

He had told her that he had given each of his sons a section of land when they had married, but since she wasn't a rancher, he knew that wouldn't be something she could use. "I just want you to be happy, honey."

"I'm really very happy, Dad." She sucked in a deep breath. "I'm trying to believe that Alphonse will really serve time and not pose a threat to me or Gabrielle."

"That is one crazy old sumbitch." Big Jim shook his head. "But don't you worry. You got your whole family here to keep you two safe."

"Thanks, Dad, and thanks for the annuity you set up for Gabrielle. I appreciate that you're thinking about her future."

"She's a smartie. I want to be sure she can go to any college she decides on." Big Jim cleared his throat. "But I had a hard time figuring out what my only daughter might like on our first Christmas together."

She smiled and shook her head. "You don't need to give me anything. I have everything I need, thanks to you."

Big Jim's face morphed into a parody of surprise. "What? Now you tell me. And here I was thinkin' maybe you might want to open a little restaurant in Langston. Misty has been checking out available locations."

Angelique let out a scream that brought Gabrielle to her side. "Mommy's fine, sweetie. Your Grampa just made me very happy." She smushed both Big Jim and Gabrielle together into a giant hug. "I can't think of anything better. Oh, I'm so excited."

"I know how much you enjoy cookin', and I thought maybe you could bring a little variety to our town. Lord knows we all been eatin' at the same three places forever."

Angelique spent the rest of the afternoon making notes and contemplating menu items. She couldn't believe the joy bubbling up in her chest. She had operated for so long on fear and anger, but now she was filled with hope.

It was late afternoon when Derrick knocked on the door. When she opened it, he stepped right in and swept her into a passionate kiss.

"Wow! That's the way to say hello," she said.

"That was Merry Christmas and I love you, all rolled up into one." He gazed down at her intently.

Angelique felt a wave of warmth sweep through her body. "That is even better. I love you too."

"I was counting on that," he said. "And I've got a very important question to ask you." He dropped down on one knee right inside the doorway and pulled something out of his pocket. "I am hoping that you will marry me and spend the rest of your life being loved." He produced a diamond ring with an antique-looking setting.

"Oh, Derrick. Yes, I will marry you." Her throat felt tight, and she could hardly speak as Derrick slipped the ring on her finger. "This is so nice."

"It was my grandmother's ring. My parents brought it with them when they drove in last night. They can't wait to meet you and Gabrielle in person."

She swallowed hard, blinking away tears. "I-I hope they like me."

He picked her up and swung her around. "They're already in love with you."

"Dad!" Angelique let out a loud yell.

Big Jim came to the front door at a trot. "What's wrong, honey?" He eyed Derrick suspiciously. "Did this yahoo do something to you?" He gestured to Derrick.

"Yes, he did." She extended her left hand for him to admire.

Big Jim examined the ring. "So, are you gonna marry this guy?"

"I am," Angelique assured him.

Chapter 24

"Wake up, Angelique. Santy Claus musta come down the chimney last night, 'cause there's a whole bunch of presents under the tree."

Angelique had had trouble getting to sleep the previous night. She went to bed wearing her engagement ring and kept twirling it around. Somehow, she was afraid to take it off for fear it would disappear. It was all the more valuable in that Derrick's grandmother had worn it and that his parents had wanted him to place it on her finger.

But when she finally slept, it was a deep and restful sleep.

Now her father had to rouse her out of bed. "I'm coming, Dad."

Gabrielle was on her bed, but was wide awake.

"Oh, you big girl. I'm going to get you right up." Angelique slipped out of bed and put on her robe. When she lifted Gabrielle, her daughter wrapped her arms around Angelique's neck, giving her a fierce hug. "Good morning, precious girl."

Angelique was haunted by the thought that Alphonse Benoit had come so close to kidnapping Gabrielle. She wondered how safe they would be, now that he knew for sure where they were living. He could still reach out to his many goons. His money would buy him anything. There were so many people in New Orleans who were terrified of the man.

She hugged Gabrielle closer, and stepped out into the hallway, surprised to find Big Jim leaned up against the wall, his arms crossed over his broad chest. "Dad?"

"Good morning, ladies." He reached for Gabrielle. "How did you sleep?"

Angelique laughed. "Like a dead thing…" She swallowed hard. "Sorry. I know it's not a laughing matter, and I'm really sorry Colt got hurt."

"Me too, but he's a tough guy and he's on the mend. They'll be over a little later. We usually have a late breakfast together with the whole family. Miz Fern is bringing her biscuits."

He hung an arm around Angelique's shoulders and walked her down the hall to the living room where a large Christmas tree was brightly lit and seemed to be embedded in a sea of presents.

Big Jim squatted down with Gabrielle, allowing her to gaze at the glowing tree in delight. "I think Santy Claus brought a little somethin' for you, honey. Look at that big box with the red bow on it." He pointed to it and nodded when Gabrielle looked at him.

She ran over to drag the box away from the tree. "Gwampa, you help me."

"Sure thing, baby girl." Big Jim helped her wrestle the oversize bow off and ripped the paper to reveal a doll house. It was obviously scaled for very young girls and made of sturdy plastic, the better to withstand a small child climbing on it.

"What a nice present." Angelique clapped her hands together. "Perfect for a little girl."

"I happen to know that old Santy Claus got a little help from his sweet Leah." He reached for an envelope on the coffee table and offered it to Angelique. "This is for you. I wanted you to know you were a part of the family and this family is a part of the land."

"Yes, I know." She shrugged. "And now you have me. City girl from New Orleans who spent most of her time working in a restaurant. I promise to try really hard to learn to ride a horse."

"Aw, that would be nice." Big Jim leaned over and gave her a hug. "Riding is something me an' the boys do together, so I wanted to share it with you, too."

"I'll figure it out," she said. "If you're going to teach Gabrielle to ride, I better be able to keep up."

He gave her a kiss on her forehead. "That's my girl."

Those words warmed her heart more than anything he could have said.

"I wanted to give you a little something before the others get here. I'm giving you a really sweet little mare. Her name is Cinder, and she is a beautiful little Arab with lots of champions in her bloodline. Her papers are in this envelope."

The idea of owning a horse was sort of terrifying, but also thrilling. Angelique had seen her father's black Arabian horses, and they were amazing. "Thanks, Dad. I'll probably fall off her, but hopefully I'll bounce."

"You'll do fine. And Misty made arrangements for us to look at a couple of locations that might be perfect for your restaurant, if you're still interested."

Angelique swallowed hard. "Oh, yes. I'm still interested."

Big Jim gave her a wink. "Looks like it's going to be a really busy new year."

There was a commotion in the front of the house as

Tyler and his whole family tromped inside along with Derrick Shelton.

"Hey, Dad," Tyler called. "Breakfast ready?"

They all came to the living room, shedding outerwear. Coats and jackets were piled on the sofa along with scarves, caps, and gloves.

"Hey there," Big Jim greeted them. "Let's get this breakfast chaos party started before the rest of 'em get here."

Angelique locked eyes with Derrick. She waggled her left hand, showing him the ring he had placed there the previous night, causing him to grin. As the others cleared the room, he waited until they were alone to wrap his arms around her and lay a sizzling kiss on her. "Hello, my fiancée."

"Merry Christmas to my fiancé," she sighed.

"Merry Christmas to you too, baby. How are you feeling after your exciting night?"

"Feeling relieved that Alphonse is in jail, but not trusting that he won't be able to get to us. You don't know how powerful he is." She pressed her lips together.

He gazed at her intently. "You know that I will protect you. Benoit will go to prison. I'm sure he won't be released after shooting up a church, trying to kidnap a little girl, and shooting a Garrett. He's signed, sealed, and delivered."

"You don't know how he can get his goons to do his dirty work." She shook her head. "I'll always be looking over my shoulder."

Derrick's brows drew together. "I hope there will come a time when you can get over your fear."

Big Jim yelled at them from the kitchen, "Hey, you

lovebirds! Better come on in here and grab one of Fern's hot biscuits, or I may eat 'em all up."

Beau and his family came into the house and walked back to the kitchen with them. They sat around the big table and chatted. The only people missing were Colton and Misty.

Angelique hoped that he wasn't feeling worse. It would be terrible if they missed this family celebration because of his injury. She was afraid to ask about him, in case she was the only one who was unaware of his state. But everyone seemed to be waiting, and in a short time, Misty and Colt arrived.

"'Bout time," Big Jim said.

"Oh, you know Colt," Misty said. "He likes to make an entrance."

Colt grinned, but he was wearing a sling on his right arm. He made eye contact with Angelique and winked.

Angelique breathed a sigh of relief. All of her family was gathered in this room. Leah said grace and they began passing food items. Truly, Fern's biscuits were light and layered. Angelique received many compliments on her bread pudding.

Just as they were finishing up, Derrick received a phone call and rose from the table to take it. When he returned, his expression was hard to read.

"What's up, Derrick?" Big Jim asked. "You look like you ate something that didn't agree with you."

Derrick shook his head. "No, sir. I'm not sure it's a good topic of conversation at the table." He glanced around. "Especially with the children here."

This caused those sitting around the table to exchange glances and raise eyebrows. But when the table was being cleared and the children had gone into the den, Big Jim cleared his throat and looked pointedly at Derrick.

"Don't know if this is a good thing or a bad thing, but the man who tried to kidnap Gabrielle and who shot Colt has passed away. The call I got was to inform me that he had a massive heart attack in his cell last night. It was fatal."

Angelique heaved a huge sigh. "Oh, that's wonderful… I mean—"

"I know what you mean," Derrick said. "It's a relief that he won't be around to threaten you and Gabrielle anymore. But I kind of wanted to see him serve a long sentence."

Angelique felt as though her insides were soaring. "You have no idea what a relief this is. I have feared Alphonse all my life. He was evil incarnate." She shuddered. "You have no idea how much power he wielded…and he wanted his son to work with him…to be as evil as he was."

Big Jim's kind eyes regarded her. "But his son wasn't all that evil?"

Angelique had to smile at that. "He wasn't evil at all. Remy was kind and funny and creative. He didn't have an unkind molecule in his entire being."

"So, that was a problem?" Big Jim asked.

Angelique shrugged. "It was a problem between Remy and his father. Alphonse blamed me for what he called Remy's 'weakness.'"

Big Jim shook his head. "I can't imagine a father feeling that way about his son, but then, I can't imagine a man as cruel as that man." He walked into the den to be with his grandchildren.

Angelique gazed up at Derrick. “So it’s over. I don’t have to run anymore.”

Derrick wrapped his arms around her and pulled her close. “It’s time to stop running and build our life together.” He kissed the top of her head. “I hope you like my house, but you can make any changes you want. I’ll try to make sure you and Gabrielle will be comfortable there.”

“You have a lovely home, and I’m sure we’ll be comfy cozy…” A giggle bubbled up from her insides. “But where will my horse live?”

Derrick held her at arm’s length. “You have a horse?”

“I do now. Big Jim gave me Cinder, a beautiful black mare.”

“One of his champion black Arabs? That’s fantastic. Maybe he’ll let you breed her with one of his studs. We can raise some Arabians.” He appeared to be very excited.

“She was my Christmas present…and Dad is going to help me open a restaurant in Langston.”

“That should keep you out of trouble.” He picked her up and swung her around.

Angelique clung to him, releasing the fear she had carried inside her for most of her life. She embraced the joy blooming in her heart, happy to build a life for herself and her daughter with the man in her arms.

About the Author

June Faver loves Texas, from the Gulf Coast to the Panhandle, from the Mexican border to the Piney Woods. Her novels embrace the heart and soul of the state and the larger-than-life Texans who romp across her pages. A former teacher and healthcare professional, she lives and writes in the Texas Hill Country.

HONKY TONK CHRISTMAS

You're in for a rockin' country Christmas with *New York Times* bestselling author Carolyn Brown

Out-of-work journalist Sharlene Waverly is determined to finally write that mystery novel, until she's charmed by the Honky Tonk's stories of romance come true. She decides to write a romance so hot it'll melt the soles off a cowboy's best eel-skin boots, and she finds inspiration in the hot cowboy who's helping her get the Honky Tonk renovated in time for an unforgettable Christmas shindig. With his whiskey-dark eyes, Holt Jackson is the perfect present to find under the mistletoe...

"Makes you believe in Christmas miracles."

—*The Romance Studio*

BLUE SKY COWBOY CHRISTMAS

Joanne Kennedy's Blue Sky Cowboys series reminds us that there's really no place like home for the holidays

Weary from a long deployment, Griff Bailey has been dreaming of a quiet Christmas on his father's ranch. But all his hopes of peace are upended when he finds his one-time fling Riley James has moved in.

Riley swore off dark, dangerous men a long time ago, but there's something about Griff she still just can't resist. It'll take a miracle for these two stubborn former lovers to open themselves up again, but isn't that what Christmas is for?

"Full of heart and passion."

—Jodi Thomas, *New York Times* bestselling author, for *Cowboy Fever*